GENUFLECT

By Tracy R. Twyman

GENUFLECT

© Tracy R. Twyman
2016-2017
All Rights Reserved
ISBN # 978-1-962312-19-6

1st Edition
6/16/2017

Front Cover Artwork:
Jesse Peper
"Here Ends the Work of the Sun"

Jesse-Peper.org

No part of this publication may be reproduced in any form or by any means, electronic or mechanical, including photocopying, recording, or by any information storage or retrieval system, without permission in writing from the publisher.

Thanks to those who helped in various ways: Rich, Jesse Peper, Alexander Rivera, Philip Gonzalez, Leon Zhelev, the press office of Bloomberg London, and the staff of the British Museum.

And to those whose sagacious revelations preceded me, for good or for evil: Hermes Trismegistus, Gaius Valerius Catullus, St. John the Divine, Hippolytus, Wolfram von Eschenbach, Abraham the Jew, Johann Daniel Mylius, Athanasius Kircher, Michael Maier, Jacob Boehme, Johannes Valentinus Andreae, Goossen van Vreeswyk, John Dee, Sir Francis Bacon, William Blake, Marquis de Sade, Comte de Lautreamont, Franz Cumont, Jessie Weston, Joseph von Hammer-Purgstall, Thomas Wright, Eliphas Levi, Fulcanelli, Margaret Murray, H.P. Lovecraft, Carl Jung, Emma Jung, Iwan Bloch, J-K. Huysmans, Luis Buñuel, Salvador Dali, Man Ray, Marcel Duchamp, Aleister Crowley, Manly P. Hall, Robert Graves, Stanley Kubrick, Alejandro Jodorowsky, John Balance, Alan Moore, Matthew Barney, Joscelyn Godwin, and Nicholas de Vere.

Nota bene: While several of the characters in this story have certain aspects based on known, powerful figures in the modern world, I make no claim that these people are involved in any nefarious deeds such as those depicted here, nor is it my intention to malign them. These characteristics were borrowed for artistic purposes only.

About the Author

Tracy R. Twyman has been writing about the esoteric side of history and current events for over 23 years, dealing with topics like secret societies, ancient myths, demonology, ceremonial magic, divination, alchemy, mind control, mystical royal bloodlines, and the hidden history of money, to name just a few. Her major books include *Baphomet: The Temple Mystery Unveiled* (with Alexander Rivera), *Clock Shavings*, *Solomon's Treasure*, and *The Merovingian Mythos*. She has been a guest many times on numerous radio talk shows, including Coast to Coast AM and Ground Zero with Clyde Lewis. She has also been seen on several television shows, including National Geographic's "Is It Real?" and Jesse Ventura's "Conspiracy Theory." Learn more at TracyTwyman.com.

Other Books by Tracy R. Twyman

Baphomet: The Temple Mystery Unveiled (with Alexander Rivera)
Clock Shavings
Money Grows on the Tree of Knowledge
Solomon's Treasure: The Magic and Mystery of America's Money
The Merovingian Mythos and the Mystery of Rennes-le-Chateau
Mind-Controlled Sex Slaves and the CIA
The Arcadian Mystique: The Best of Dagobert's Revenge Magazine
Hocus Pocus: The Magical Power of St. Peter
The Judas Goat: The Substitution Theory of the Crucifixion
The Choice Vine: Mary Magdalene, the Sacred Whore, and the Benjamite Inheritance
The Cutting of the Orm: The Secret Calendar of the Priory of Sion
Dead But Dreaming: The Great Old Ones of Lovecraftian Legend Reinterpreted as Atlantean Kings

Read more from the author at:
TracyTwyman.com

Contents

Chapter 1: Autodidact de Occultis	1
Chapter 2: Opportunity Knocks	6
Chapter 3: Plane Problems	9
Chapter 4: Answers Lacking	12
Chapter 5: Terribilis est locus iste	20
Chapter 6: Eros and Anteros	24
Chapter 7: Regnum Defende	29
Chapter 8: Non Sequitur	36
Chapter 9: Oriental Club	42
Chapter 10: Scrying at Stratford Place	51
Chapter 11: Temple Tavern	59
Chapter 12: Easter Sunday April Fool	68
Chapter 13: Raven Conspiracy	78
Chapter 14: Rerouting…	90
Chapter 15: Empyrean and Beyond	95
Chapter 16: Tower House	109
Chapter 17: Saturn's Return	115
Chapter 18: Omnia Cum Deo	147
Chapter 19: Rose Mountain	165
Chapter 20: Equinox of the Gods	176
Chapter 21: Taurobolium	199
Chapter 22: Archons Uprooted	237
Chapter 23: Prison Coffin	274
Chapter 24: Opera of the Phantom	327
Chapter 25: Albion's Aeon	366

Should the whole frame of Nature round him break,
In ruin and confusion hurled,
He, unconcerned, would hear the mighty crack,
And stand secure amidst a falling world.

— Horace, *Odes*

Chapter 1: Autodidact de Occultis

> To know the secret or the formula of God is to be God.
>
> To know the secret or the formula of the Devil is to be the Devil.
>
> To wish to be at the same time God and Devil is to absorb in one's self the most absolute antinomy, the two most strained contrary forces; it is the wish to shut up in one's self an infinite antagonism. It is to drink a poison which would extinguish the suns and consume the worlds.
>
> — Eliphas Levi, *The Key to the Mysteries*

Hello there. Thank you for reading this book. I hope it will be of interest to you.

This is intended to be a record of the incredible things I experienced at the end of March and beginning of April 2018, leading to the historic events of this year that you no doubt already know about. I need to write this down before my memory fades completely. This is already starting to happen, so I must work quickly.

I got myself into this mess because I am good at what I do. But there is also very little market for what I do, so I have to take what I can get whenever it comes around.

My job is the sort of thing that only exists in horror movies. I investigate the occult. I study the anthropology of religions and cults, both old and new, from around the world. Then I apply the patterns I see there to the study of other things. And I always get interesting results.

Most of my work just involves reading books and websites: lots of rare books and extremely obscure documents. Many rare, out-of-print texts can be found online for free if you know where to look. Google Books, JSTOR, Bartleby, and Scribd are good resources for this sort of thing. Also, the interlibrary loan program is amazing. I can't believe that a library halfway around the world will loan me, a complete stranger, a book with only three copies known to exist, again, usually for free.

Only a fraction of my research material involves books about secret societies or magic spells. A lot of it includes chasing down details about historical events and personages, or comparing the motifs used in myths, folklore and fairy tales. But I don't pretend to be an "academic," per se. No university would fund my work, because none of it can be used to advance the political movements embraced by present-day college culture, or to prop up the pet theories of tenured professors.

In pursuit of the esoteric, I have at times accidentally revived doctrines and theses that have been long- abandoned by modern mainstream academia, often with no good reason for the rejection. My work tends to validate the worldviews of writers from previous eras whose entire approach to scholarship, and the assumptions it was based on, have been thrown out by today's universities along with the bathwater. I find that quite often these modern exemplars of learning end up just quoting other modern authors, who of course share their own biases about historical events and people, without checking the primary documents related to the subject in question.

This becomes an endless loop of reflection, as if in a hall of mirrors, until the author of a research paper ends up essentially quoting himself by quoting seven other writers he knows who are working within the same small milieu and whose ideas can be traced directly back to him. They are so busy patting each other on the back that nobody takes the time to track the evolution of the belief system that is being constructed between them, which may one day be taught to public schoolchildren like a catechism. If they were to do this, they would quite often find themselves having to reevaluate the work of classical writers that has been dismissed heretofore because the underlying approach to research used to construct it is no longer considered politically correct.

Strangely, what seems to be the hallmark of this older approach to history, anthropology, and comparative mythology is simply the assumption that once can find significance in the similarities between divergent traditions from different cultures. Also, it is apparently now controversial to suggest that symbolism is always symbolic *of* some kind of prototype with inherent meaning. Today's academics revel in depriving man's ancestral traditions of meaning because they can project whatever they want onto it. While undergrads majoring in Diversity Studies protest "cultural appropriation" on the other side of the campus, myth and anthropology students are bullied into ignoring how the religious beliefs and ritual practices of one group have influenced another.

So I knew that my bills would never be paid by a government grant or university donors. I have to compete in the marketplace with all the other nonfiction writers for reader who, for whatever reason, are interested in this type of subject matter. Of course, those people are usually weirdos.

In seeking further information beyond book-learning I have, at times in the past, actually socialized with some of these weirdos. In other words, I've joined cults and secret societies that I've been invited into, mainly to see how they worked. I had also practiced several forms of divination, both in these groups and on my own. I found this to be a useful way to find clues pertaining to the rest of my research.

All of that became too dangerous for me at a certain point, however. So for the last few years, until about two months ago, I had socialized with almost nobody. I abstained from both ceremonial magic and reading oracles. I contented myself with utilizing the knowledge I had amassed, the published information already available, and my own intuition. By now I had developed a knack for understanding how mystical traditions worked, and could often anticipate what I would find in my investigations.

This operated as a sort of sixth sense. I may have put the Ouija board away, but it was as if my mind was a divination tool of its own. It was like there was a radio receiver in my brain that I could never switch off. But I could usually tune it to specific wavelengths to pick up on information about whatever it was I was interested in learning about at the time.

For the most part, this has been independent research, and I have published my findings in print-on-demand books that I produced myself. I have also done radio interviews to promote the books and, when lucky, paid speeches, usually to small crowds. I've made a little niche for myself as the world's foremost expert on several very specific topics that I have pioneered on my own.

But the living has never been easy. When the March hare began to herald the approach of Spring, and everyone seemed to be rejoicing, I alone, it seemed, was downcast. I faced a slew of problems that could be solved only with money. I could barely even use my own phone because of the non-stop calls from bill collectors.

In particular, Barclays Bank called at least three times a day to discuss the licensing fees I owed to the British Museum. This was in regards to the photos of the "Mete coffer" (as I call it) that I had printed in my most recent book, *The Baphomet Papers*. It had been hailed as a masterpiece by fellow occult researchers, but ignored by the general public due to its size and the obscurity of its subject matter. Therefore, these fees from the Museum would cost me more than I had made on the project so far, and I could not afford to pay them.

Illustration from the lid of the Mete Coffer

Chapter 2: Opportunity Knocks

> The fish thinks about its hunger, not about the fisherman. It is the master who seeks the disciple.
>
> – Alejandro Jodorowsky *The Holy Mountain*

Therefore, I was very glad when Leopold Black, Baron of Alphamstone in England and a peer in the House of Lords, contacted me through my website on Tuesday, March 20, the spring equinox, saying he wanted to hire me to do a private lecture. He wished for me to give a talk about the Mete coffer. This is an item that had been forgotten in the back catalogue of the British Museum until I identified it as one of the alleged "Templar artifacts" written about a century earlier by Orientalist Joseph von Hammer-Purgstall. When I wrote back to the Baron and asked whom the lecture would be for, he said he belonged to a group called the Worshipful Society of Butchers, and that they met at the Oriental Club in London once monthly, usually around the full moon.

He sent me a link to his personal page on the Houses of Parliament's website. I then used Google and found the Butcher society's Wikipedia entry. Apparently, it was one of the few livery companies in the City of London that was still dedicated to its original trade: butchery. Most of the others had evolved into mere fraternal organizations with rituals and regalia, meeting for dinner and raising money for charity several times a year. The society's motto pertained directly to this practical matter:

> Omnia subiecisti sub pedibus, oves et boves.

This is a Latin quote from *Psalm* 8:6-7: "Thou hast put all things under man's feet, all sheep and oxen." Their company arms featured three winged bulls, and two severed bullheads, along with two axes. The group's concerns seemed primarily about beef production.

It was unclear to me why a trade organization such as this would be interested in hearing from me about esoteric archeology. I also didn't understand why they needed to meet at the Oriental Club, when from what I could tell it seemed that they had their own property, Butcher's Hall, 20 minutes away in a different part of town.

Nonetheless I acquiesced to a video Skype conversation with the Baron. I found him taking tea in a poshly-decorated room, sitting in a brown wooden armchair lined with black leather, with his feet upon a matching Ottoman. He was wearing a Navy-blue dinner jacket and trousers with a white shirt and an azure-colored velvet robe and light brown leather cap toe Oxford shoes. He seemed rather at home there, so I asked if this was his house. He shook his head sideways and said he was at "the Club House."

Nice, I thought. *At least the Club has money.* An unseen hand was holding up the camera—a smartphone, I presumed. He said it was his nephew, also a member of the club.

He promised a payment of $10,000 if did the lecture, $3000 of it up front. He also demanded secrecy, which I thought was a bit odd. But hey, $10,000 is more than I'd made in the last six months combined. I couldn't justify turning it down, so I agreed.

Over the next few days, as I tried to prepare my lecture, my sense of foreboding grew strong. But the Baron promptly purchased my plane tickets and hotel for the week in question, at a cost in excess of $7000. This was, in my mind, legal consideration for the verbal contract, and assured me that these people were serious, not just wasting my time. The reviews for the Regent Palace Hotel at Piccadilly Circus were a bit *meh*, but I felt I had no right to be a snob and demand better.

Still, walking into a room full of British aristocrats to deliver a message about a Satanic Templar artifact is very intimidating, especially to a group of people calling themselves "Worshipful Butchers." I wondered if they would accept my theory. The illustrations on the sides and lid of the coffer, I proposed, indicated that the Knights Templar, the Pope's own specially-chartered warriors of Christ throughout the medieval Crusades, were having ritual sex with boys, and sacrificing them, in an attempt to destroy the created universe.

The first part of this claim—the ritual murder and gay pedophilia—is just what the Templars had already been convicted of and burnt at the stake for by the King of France in the early fourteenth century. These rites were allegedly all part of their secret worship of a demonic entity named "Baphomet," which my book was named after. The last part, about destroying the universe, was my own unique contribution.

Two obvious objections to the very idea spring up immediately when you consider it. First, why would anyone want to destroy the universe? Maybe a miserable and depressed person would desire that, but why a whole organization of men from wealthy families involved in an incredibly successful material enterprise, as the Templars were?

Secondly, how could any "ritual" done by men destroy everything that exists? Many people today think it's possible that the behavior of mankind as a species could destroy life on Earth *as we know it*. But the destruction of the universe as a whole seems like a bit much, doesn't it?

Granted, the Templars lived in a world where the universe was thought to be much smaller, and of a different arrangement than what is generally accepted today. Still it seems quite an ambitious nihilistic anti-goal. Certainly, it is not immediately obvious how pederasty and human sacrifice would bring that about, even in the most twisted occult logic. But the most twisted occult logic is not immediately obvious, by definition, as I was soon reminded.

Chapter 3: Plane Problems

Hell from beneath is moved for thee to meet thee at thy coming....

—*Isaiah* 14:9

My first plane departed from PDX in Portland, Oregon on the afternoon of Tuesday, March 27. It immediately occurred to me, as soon as I squeezed my body into the seat, that I was going to die of deep-vein thrombosis long before reaching my destination the next day. I could not fathom how I was going to stay in that unpleasant position for the better part of twelve hours with just one layover in Houston. As if to punish me for my weak thoughts, the situation escalated from bad to worse.

When we got to Houston, we found that there was a storm over the area, and the plane couldn't land until it passed. We circled in the air for a couple of hours waiting for that to happen. Then the captain announced over the PA system that we would be diverted to a military base in Austin. There we would refuel and wait for things to clear up in Houston.

All this time I had waited without using the restroom on board, not wanting to force the people next to me to stand up so I could squeeze past. This proved to be an awful decision. By the time I realized how badly I needed the toilet, there were ten people standing in line, as I could see when I stood up from my window seat to look.

I decided to use the skills that had gotten me through grade school, where we were only allowed to use the bathroom during lunch. I sat down and tried my best at transcendental meditation, hoping to take my mind off my bursting bladder. But whenever I try to concentrate on anything in public, someone in the vicinity feels compelled to interrupt me. This time was no different.

"I'm dying for a cigarette," said the man next to me in a thick Arab accent.

With that, Harut Al-Hazrat dragged me into a conversation. He was a peculiar young man with long, unkempt hair forming Polish plait, dressed in black trousers with a black shirt and trench coat. His English was good, but he mumbled. I had to lean in close to hear him, which was an annoying strain. But the talk took my mind off my discomfort somewhat, and that helped pass the time.

When he found out I was going to England ultimately, he told me that his first name was "the Arabic equivalent of Arthur." Specifically, he claimed that the king of Camelot's name was "derived from Harut," and that this figure of Western mythology was based on a character from pre-Islamic Mesopotamia. I smirked at this.

I told him what kinds of books I wrote. This prompted him to talk about his years of study under a Sufi *murshid* in Washington, D.C. Then he bragged that he could use prayer to summon UFOs, to which I said, of course:

"You should summon a flying saucer to pick us up and take us to Houston!"

I laughed at myself. He didn't.

"Actually, storms help bring the UFOs," he said. "They open up holes in the sky, which are portals for the saucers. They also use the extra electricity in the air to fly and to make light."

"Oh," I said, shaking my head vigorously in the affirmative.

The old white lady next to him glared at us in disapproval. I don't think it was just that our conversation came off as stupid. I felt that maybe she didn't like Arabs, and thought that I was flirting with him, which perhaps she didn't think young white women should be doing. Maybe I was reading too much into her icy stare, but I am usually right about these things.

The plane sat on the tarmac for another three hours. During that time, the toilet began to overflow and the contents actually started to roll down the aisle. While the flight attendants attempted to deal with that, inadequately, an Asian woman two rows ahead of me stood up, crying hysterically, and shouted that her grandmother had passed out next to her. Paramedics soon boarded the plane and took her away. A party of four native Texans then demanded to be let off the aircraft also, stating that they could drive to Houston before the plane would ever get there.

Eventually, though, the plane did return to Houston airspace, and successfully landed. By that time, my conversation with Harut had died down, as we were both choking on the stench of the overflowed toilet and trying not to piss in our pants. I said goodbye to him as we exited the plane.

Then, after using the bathroom as quickly as possible, I hurried over to the first United Airlines booth I found that had an employee present. The airport was ominously empty except for my fellow displaced passengers, who were scattered around frantically trying to find someone to reschedule the connecting flights they had missed.

When I got to the United Airlines booth, attended by a middle-aged black woman, I found there was no need to hurry. There were no more flights to England departing that night. Instead, I would take a shuttle to the local Marriott, where they had arranged a room for me, and wait for a flight the following morning.

I then asked where I could find my luggage. The woman informed me that my suitcase was on its way to another destination somewhere else in the United States.

"You'll have to catch up with it *some other time*," she said flippantly, as though it didn't matter when or where I eventually found my suitcase. I couldn't believe it.

"You mean I have to do this lecture in England without even a change of clothes?" I whined, to utterly deaf, indifferent ears. "I don't even have my make-up or shampoo because I'm not allowed to take it in my carry-on!"

She started at me blankly, waiting for my tantrum to end, waiting for me to realize I wasn't special and that my problems didn't matter to her at all. When I looked down, I noticed that she was handing me a small black nylon bag with a zipper and the United Airlines logo on it. Inside was a collection of travel-sized toiletries.

I took the bag and my laptop case, the only possessions I had with me anymore, and slinked away dejectedly, muttering "thank you" with total insincerity. As I walked over to the departure zone to meet my shuttle, I passed a statue of George W. Bush, for whom Houston's airport is named. I took it as an omen that my mission would fail.

Chapter 4: Answers Lacking

> If any part of your uncertainty is a struggle between your heart and your mind, follow your mind.
>
> — Ayn Rand, *Atlas Shrugged*

At the hotel, I had tried calling Leopold with a long - distance calling card, using the phone number he had given me. It rang and rang with that odd, nervous ring they use in the British telephone system. But nobody picked up. There was no voicemail or anything. I had never called the number before, as I had no reason to. All of our correspondence had been through email except for that one Skype conversation.

I checked the number in my email archives twice using my laptop and the hotel's Wi-Fi. I was certain I was dialing correctly. I even used Google to make sure I was punching the city and country codes right. I was. I slept for a few hours, and then tried again at dawn, which was 11 AM in England. But there was still no answer.

So I had no choice but to give up on that. I logged into my email again, and was surprised to find nothing from him there either. I wrote him a message telling him what had happened, and asked him to make sure my greeting party was aware of my new arrival time. I then hurried down to have breakfast in café at the hotel lobby, as I had not found anything to eat since the previous morning.

While I ate my raisin bran, I used my laptop to check the news. A toolbar at the top of my browser that points out significant anniversaries for each date reminded me that it was "Spy Wednesday," a name for the Wednesday before Easter. Finding this interesting, I clicked on the link provided, which lead to a Wikipedia article.

As I suspected, the definition of the word "spy" being used in this instance is the verb form meaning "to ambush or ensnare," because this is the day on which, they say, Judas Iscariot betrayed Jesus. The Catholics observe this day with the *Tenebrae* ("Darkness") liturgy, in which they gradually extinguish all the candles on the altar. When the last one is out, and the church is completely dark, the *Strepitus* is performed. This is a loud crashing sound, often made by the priest abruptly shutting a large Bible, that is made to mimic the earthquake traditionally said to have occurred at the moment of Christ's death. Tenebrae was originally written to be performed on Good Friday, the anniversary of that death, and is still in some places, while in others it is performed the day before, on Maundy Thursday.

This reminded me of an image I'd seen in Joseph von Hammer-Purgstall's 1818 treatise *Mysterium Baphometis Revelatum*, which I'd had translated from the Latin and published last year along with my own "Baphomet" book. It was from a ceremonial stone bowl, one of the many "Templar artifacts" he'd discovered in churches in Europe located on their former properties. It showed a naked woman kneeling on the ground between two images of a figure identified on several of the artifacts as "Mete," a hermaphrodite entity. The woman was pouring water out of a vase onto the candles of a candelabrum called a "seven- branch" (what the Jews call a *menorah*).

According to Church Fathers Clement and Philo, both of Alexandria, the flames on the seven-branch represent the seven classical planets recognized in antiquity. The symbolism of this ceremony seems a bit like what Mohammed did by reducing the number of idols in the Islamic Kaaba from 360 to just one, a stone representing the monotheistic God. In the *Tenebrae*, all but one of the "heavenly lights" once worshiped by pagan man were put out except for one (representing the Sun, with the Sun re-baptized as Jesus Christ).

Hammer -Purgstall thought that the Templars were secret devotees of Ophite Gnosticism, a Greco-Roman mystery cult that viewed creation as a prison controlled by the power of illusion. The goal of their rituals was to dethrone the "Archons" above so that they could break out of the jail. The Archons were the rulers of fate, seen as being identical with the visible "planets" of the ancients, among which the Sun and the Moon were

14 Chapter 4

included at the time (the others being Mercury, Mars, Venus, Jupiter and Saturn).

Each Archon was viewed to rule one of the "heavens" defined by what we now call its "orbit." These seven heavens were thought to be stacked above the earthly realm, as though in a layer cake, each another layer of confinement, keeping our souls locked away from the source of pure spirit, accessible somewhere beyond the sphere of Saturn.

Jehovah, the god of the Bible, was thought by Gnostics to merely be one of these Archons, identifiable with Jupiter, a.k.a. Jove, whom the Greeks called Zeus. His mother, the Gnostic wisdom goddess Sophia-Achamoth, was added to the seven to form the *Ogdoad*—the Eight. Hammer-Purgstall thought that Sophia-Achamoth was worshiped by the Knights Templar in the form of "Baphomet" or "Mete."

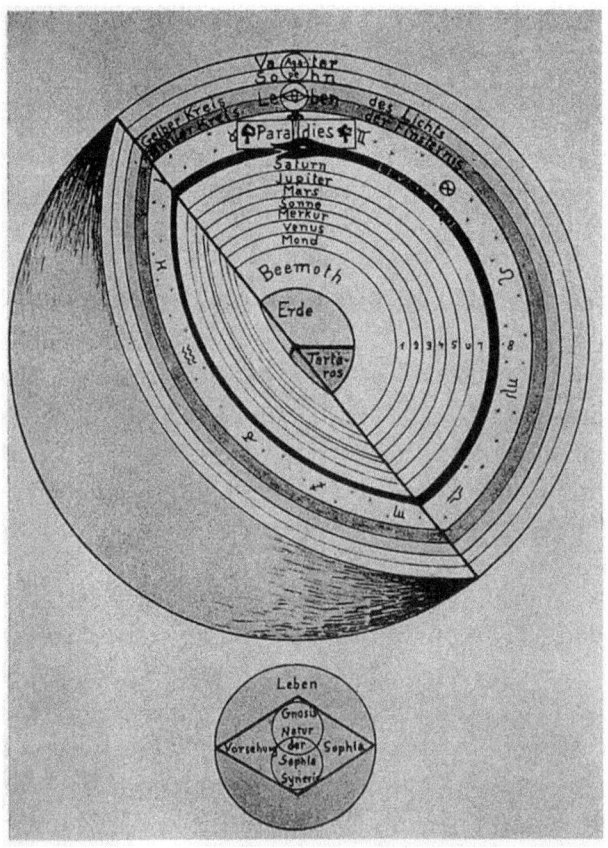

This latter name, he thought, could be traced back to the Greek figure of Metis, the first bride of Zeus. She played a very important role initiating and upholding his rule as king of the gods. Like "Sophia," her name translated directly to "wisdom," specifically "cunning," "prudence" and "wise counsel." To understand what happened to her, we have to go all the way back to the "Genesis" story of Greek mythology.

Zeus was the son of Chronos, who had to castrate his father Ouranos in order to escape the womb of his mother, Gaia. Ouranos had deliberately prevented his children from being born, cognizant that one of them was fated to overthrow him as the king of the gods. When Chronos later engendered his own children with his wife Rhea, he became aware of a similar fate that was to come from one of these progeny. So he devised his own way of dealing with it by swallowing them upon birth.

But just as Gaia had schemed against her husband to aid her son Chronos in fulfilling his destiny (by supplying his with the castration knife), Rhea came up with a plan to save her son Zeus from ending up in his father's stomach. In this case, she substituted the baby with a decoy in the form of a stone wrapped in swaddling clothes. Later, they say, Zeus found a way to poison his father, causing him to vomit up all the other children that had already been swallowed. Zeus and his siblings then fought their way to supremacy, overthrowing Chronos. The clever witch who conceived the poison plot was the goddess Metis, Hammer-Purgstall's "Mete," whom Zeus subsequently married.

As the story goes, Zeus, just like his predecessors, gained knowledge of a prophecy that if he bred with Metis, one of the children would overthrow him. Having already consummated the wedding and impregnated her, his solution was to swallow the mother before the birth even happened. He was able to do this, some say, by tricking her into turning herself into a fly, so that she was small enough to go inside his mouth. However, other depictions of the act show him eating her limb by limb at full size.

Whichever way it happened, as with the Olympian gods in the gullet of Chronos, Metis was immortal, so she remained alive inside Zeus. Eventually she gave birth to a daughter, the wise Athena. Metis worked from within Zeus' body to hammer out a coat of armor for her daughter to wear. The hammering caused Zeus discomfort, and so he had his head cleaved open to alleviate the pressure. This allowed Athena to escape.

She went on to become an important goddess to the Greeks, associated, like her mother, with wisdom. But for some reason Metis did not escape with her daughter, and remained inside Zeus. He reportedly utilized her as a source of wise council during his reign, and she was often depicted supporting his throne from underneath, propping it up, like a royal slave.

What a raw deal, I thought as I ponder these stories again. *I wonder what kept her from leaving with Athena. Was it the chains?*

On the Mete coffer, the goddess was shown holding a pair of chains. The Sun was shown attached to the top of one chain, and the Moon to the other, with the solar and lunar faces shown upside-down. These chains also appear to have been shackled to Mete's legs. The image seemed to me to be showing her in the midst of breaking the chains from her ankles while simultaneously dragging the heavenly bodies down from the sky.

Was the destruction of the Archontic order Mete's revenge for being imprisoned and enslaved by Zeus? I wondered. *The Gnostics saw Sophia-Achamoth as a heroine trying to help them escape the jail of illusory existence. Maybe the idea is that she's trapped inside here with the rest of us, so her escape is also our chance for escape.*

On the "Templar artifact" that featured the candelabra being extinguished, the figure of Mete on the right is holding the chains (without the heavenly bodies included), which the horned figure of Mete on the left is holding a banner displaying Arabic writing. Hammer-Purgstall's translation of this writing includes the phrases "Mete is exalted" and "one and seven were our race," referring, he thought, to the Gnostic belief that Sophia-Achamoth was the mother of the other seven Archons.

If Mete is exalted, I thought, *that means that she's somehow escaped from inside Zeus. But how? Maybe through the rectum?*

The reason I thought about this was not just because it's the only obvious way out if one's been swallowed. It also occurred to me because another phrase written in Arabic on Mete's banner next to the candelabra is: "He makes return easy through the rectum." Hammer-Purgstall hadn't really deciphered the meaning of this, except to identify it as being related to the rumored Templar rites of sodomic pederasty, now confirmed because of their confessions to the Pope, documented in the Chinon Parchment released by the Vatican in 2007. But now, as I pondered this, I wondered if that was why the Sun and Moon were shown upside-down.

Perhaps it is really Mete who is upside-down, I thought, *coming out through the rear exit. Maybe that's the meaning of the message he found on the back of the idol of Mete carrying a baby.*

I was thinking about yet another "Templar artifact" depicted in a line drawing in Hammer-Purgstall's work. It showed a figure of uncertain sex in a hooded robe holding an infant.

On the back of the idol, Hammer-Purgstall reported that there was a message written in code. It was in Greek, but with Arabic letters, and transposed out of order. When decoded, they spelled out this message:

> Omnipotent Mete sprouting, a debauched woman springs
> up for our race through *prokton*.

Prokton in the Greek word for anus.

Then another meaning of the inverted Sun and Moon (or, in the alternative interpretation, Mete shown hanging upside-down) also occurred to as I sat there thinking. I had written in *The Baphomet Papers* that what we call "Satanism" was largely influenced by Gnosticism and its spiritual war against the creator of this physical universe. This is where the Satanic principle of inverting Judeo- Christian symbols, prayers, and rituals came from. I argued that the Knights Templar may have themselves been the originators of this tradition, considering their secret initiation rite of urinating on the cross and denying Christ, again confirmed through recently-revealed non-coerced confessions of the knights. With this in mind, I thought of a new idea.

I combed through files on my computer until I found folder with the Hammer-Purgstall pictures, including the lid of the Mete coffer, the picture of the hooded idol holding the baby, and the image the naked lady pouring water on the candles in-between the two Metes. I looked at them both with contemplation. While the *Tenebrae* is a Christian ritual, the one illustrated on Hammer-Purgstall's "Templar artifact" was, according to him, a more Gnostic interpretation of it. He related it to the fact that Church Fathers (Justin Martyr in particular, for instance) had accused Gnostics of practicing a blasphemous rite called "the Upsetting of the Lamps." *If this is truly a depiction of a Templar rite*, I thought, *it was undoubtedly meant as a sacrilegious celebration of the destruction the Archons. They might have even done the whole* Tenebrae *as an overtly Satanic black mass, snuffing out the light of the Sun too, and thus killing Christ, according to the symbolism.*

As I finished my breakfast at the hotel restaurant, I decided to move on to the Drudge Report for the day's headlines. I found that the previous day there had been yet another precipitous fall in the value of the pound. You may recall that this had been happening ever since the government had decided to essentially nullify the meaning of Britain's plan to exit from the European Union. They had put it off indefinitely in a state of declared emergency that everyone assumed would never be lifted.

This was good for my exchange rate while visiting, but bad for the natives, I knew. What was worse, the government refused to acknowledge the obvious cause of the instability, blaming it instead on the recent string of homegrown terrorist attacks in the name of ISIS, necessitating yet more police state expansion.

In the UK, from what I read, everyone was actually pining for a royal decree to overrule the elected government, which had so clearly been derelict in its duty to honor the will of the people. The newest Prime Minister was even more faithless than the last. But although the Queen hadn't been seen in over three months, she still occasionally signed documents, and appeared to be set to live forever. She was rumored to be bedridden on something akin to life support, albeit still conscious.

People such as me, persistent hounds of alternative news data, had kept up on the rumors. However, the topic was being censored in the mainstream news, and all major social media platforms had placed it on the ever-growing list of forbidden topics. If the rumors were true, I knew, then the Queen was unlikely to be leading any revolutions against the government on behalf of her beleaguered subjects. As I read the news, I compulsively reloaded my email, hoping to get word from Leopold, who by now should have noticed that I hadn't arrived on time. But it was in vain. He said nothing. Another phone call placed from my room again yielded no results. Eventually I boarded the shuttle, rode through a giant forest of floating roof tanks filled with petroleum products, and then boarded another plane. Although I stayed on the aircraft for another fifteen hours, with two stops along the way, the rest was a much smoother ride than the first leg. I had the entire row to myself, so I got to stretch out and rest. I used the bathroom whenever I wanted. They fed us a couple of meals and showed us a movie, the new remake of *Zardoz*. I hate remakes, so I didn't put the headphones on to listen. Instead, I laid on the seats and tried not to wonder if Leopold Black had gotten my message yet.

Chapter 5: Terribilis est locus iste

> Boasting a prime location and unbeatable prices, the Regent Palace is easily one of the best value lodgings in London. Within minutes of entertainment, fine dining and shopping venues, the hotel is attractive to both business and leisure guests seeking the ultimate bargain. Accommodations all consist of colour TV, direct dial telephone and wash basin and of the 888 rooms within the hotel, 385 have their own en-suite bathroom.
>
> —regentpalacehotel.co.uk, 2005

My fake -it-'til-you-make-it false bravado had kept me going through this inauspicious adventure so far. But that began to fade when I was finally able to take my phone out of Airplane Mode and into Sprint Global Roaming. I used the Gmail app to check my email. When I found that there was still no answer from Leopold Black, and my heart began to sink.

I was actually wondering if this had all been an elaborate and expensive joke, in which several thousand pounds had been spent just to waste my time. The fear must have been apparent on my ashen face because as I went through customs, the young white English lady who interrogated me about my business in the UK gave me special attention.

"Are you alright?" she said, looking me over with suspicion. She stared straight into my eyes to intimidate me, forcing me to stare back. "Your face looks very … pale."

Well, I am naturally quite pale, and I must have looked even more so as I stood there in front of her. But I got the feeling that she actually thought I might be wearing heavy make-up to hide a darker complexion. I could feel her trying to "unmask" me with her eyes. Then she just came right out and said it.

"Frankly you look a bit off."

Now I could feel myself getting angry. *Off what?* I thought. *Off my rocker?* I couldn't let it boil over, though, as this was a delicate situation. I knew she was just being vigilant because of the stabbings by ISIS agents that had happened at Gatwick, the other London airport, a week previous.

I thought of a way to express my annoyance that would surely shut her up and allow me to be on my way. "Ma'am," I said, "are you telling me that you find me suspicious because of the *color of my skin*?"

Her face curled up into the trademark regretful half-smile of white guilt. This look is usually only given to ethnic minorities who have just been subjected to special scrutiny because of their race, only to be found innocent. I returned it with the most genuine smile I could muster, and reached out to take back my passport from her after she finished stamping it.

As I made my way to the baggage claim area, I searched fruitlessly for the sight of a chauffeur holding a sign that said "Pamela Auger." But none was forthcoming. I watched all the luggage from my transcontinental flight circle around the conveyor belt 15 or 20 times. After determining that my suitcase was not on it, I filed a report with United Airlines staff and made my way out to the taxi stand, wondering what the Hell I was going to do next.

I got into a black taxi with a Pakistani driver. We drove for about forty minutes to get to my hotel. Thankfully he did not make any small talk. Instead he listened to endlessly looped reports about the currency crisis and the latest ISIS attacks in Europe on Sky News radio while he muttered under his breath about the traffic. London was in many ways just how I remembered it from previous trips there, but the vibe was a bit more intense. As we passed 10 Downing Street, I saw soldiers with machine guns.

Twice we went through tollbooths on the way. When we got to the first one, the driver asked me if I had any cash to pay it. I told him I didn't have any local currency yet, so he charged it to my card with the rest of my fare. I was glad I had insisted that Leopold pay three grand up front. If I had come there with only my own means to support me, I wouldn't have even been able to finish the cab ride. Piety had come to me as of late, and so I thanked God that I was OK so far, even though I wondered, as I always have, which god I was praying to.

I was even more grateful to this unknown deity when I found that my room was still reserved for me. As I checked into the Regent Palace, where plaques on the wall proudly boasted of the building's historical significance, I anticipated enjoying a shower, a nap and room service in what I thought would be opulence, judging from the elegant décor of the lobby. I was ready to flop down immediately, but found I had to walk up several flights of stairs. Someone was presently stuck in the elevator, and a half-dozen firemen were working to try to rescue them.

When I finally reached the seventh floor, room 729, I was breathless. I shoved the key in the hole (for they still used metal keys in this old building). When I stumbled in, I just about tripped over the narrow bed. It actually looked like a prison cot. And the room was barely big enough to hold it. In fact, the bed was the only thing in the room. There was no furniture, and no space for any. If I had brought my suitcase, I don't know where I would have put it.

"Oh my God," I said out loud to myself. "Are you kidding me?" I couldn't believe that the Baron of Alphamstone and his friends at the WSB were so cheap that they booked me for such a terrible place.

Despite my shock, I really needed to pee. So I located the bathroom, which was accessible through a narrow door that stood right next to the foot of the bed. There were two steps leading up to it because the floor of the bathroom was raised up about a foot higher than the main room.

It was about the size of an airplane restroom. There was a small toilet, and a little pedestal sink with a tiny basin that sort of hovered over the toilet seat. Next, to it was a diminutive shower with a tile floor and a plain blue plastic curtain. It reminded me of a shower I used at a campground in Ohio once.

After I had washed and relieved myself, I went back into the main room, put on my dirty clothes again, and opened the window. It only opened about an inch, and the only view was of the hotel's roof, along with the windows of other upper-floor rooms. The top floors of the building, which I was on, only had rooms around the perimeter. This created a trapezoid-shaped space between them when the building was looked at from an aerial view, as I discovered later from looking at the site on Google Earth. The window had been fixed to only open an inch so as to prevent people from walking out on the roof.

I suppose it should not have surprised me, considering the state of the other accommodations, when I realized that the hotel did not have any Wi-Fi available. When I couldn't find a signal, I used the gray 1950s-era rotary phone attached to the wall to call down to the lobby. When they told me there was no internet, I tried calling Leopold again, and again got no answer. Since I could clearly accomplish nothing from my hotel room, I packed up my laptop and headed out into the streets of London.

Chapter 6: Eros and Anteros

> Love is the law, love under will. Nor let the fools mistake love; for there are love and love. There is the dove, and there is the serpent. Choose ye well!
>
> — Aleister Crowley, *The Book of the Law*

I walked out of my hotel and into the throngs. It was still mid-morning, and there were people out everywhere. The lady at the front desk had told me there was a bank across the street where I could use the ATM. I looked, and my chest instinctively constricted with fear as I saw the familiar logo of Barclays, the company that called me three times a day regarding my 3000-pound debt to the British Museum. But I needed cash and I figured there was no real danger in using their ATM.

I walked over and used the machine to extract 100 pounds from my bank account. I then stepped into the corner shop next door and bought a bottle of Orangina to break one of the 20-pound notes. I had the Indian kid at the counter pour the resulting 20+ coins weighing approximately one metric fuckton into the outside pocket of my laptop case. My shoulder smarted under the weight, and my body leaned right to compensate.

"When are they going to make a one -pound note, for God's sake?," I muttered to myself.

I walked out of the store and immediately noticed a statue of Cupid standing on top of a fountain at Piccadilly Circus, which was directly in front of me. I decided to sit underneath it while I looked at a London Underground map that I had gotten from the front desk at Regent Palace. I was trying to figure out how to get to the Houses of Parliament on the tube.

The place where I sat happened to be next to a plaque that explained the statue. As it turned out, it was actually a figure of Anteros, the brother of Eros (the Greek version of Cupid). He was the god of "counter-love," and he bore butterfly wings instead of the cherubic wings of his brother. This, as Wikipedia explained to me on my phone for 20 cents a minute, was taken by most to mean that he was the god who punished unrequited love. In other words, if you were in love with somebody and they didn't love you back, you could call on him to get revenge.

My sixth sense for occult symbolism started to itch at the sight of this explanation. It just didn't seem *complete*. It felt to me like a cover story to hide the dirty truth, as I so often found whenever I dug beneath the surface of folklore and mythology.

The interpretation offered by the designer of the fountain was even more tame, calling Anteros the "god of selfless love." It was supposedly meant to be a monument to Lord Shaftesbury, a Peer of the Realm and philanthropist from the late nineteenth century. He had worked all his life to improve the lot of miners, children working in factories, and lunatics living in asylums. The statue was meant to represent his love for people who could not return his love.

This struck me as an odd, awkward and forced metaphor. Why conflate charitable and reformist work with something that is obviously an erotic symbol? In fact, at the time it had been installed, there had been many objections to its "pagan sensuality." Most people in modern times still assume that Shaftesbury Fountain is a statue of Eros when they see it.

As if to underscore this, there was even an adult theater called "Eros Cinema" that had once stood right in front of the statue. Indeed, the entire corner had been a haven for burlesque parlors, dirty movies, and prostitution. There was even a debunked rumor going around that "Piccadilly" was an old word for prostitution in some language.

The most significant aspect of the statue, as far as I was concerned, was the arrow he was aiming with him bow. Because Lord Shaftesbury made most of his reformist efforts through the House of Lords, the arrow in Anteros' bow had been designed to aim directly at Parliament, just where I was headed. I decided that was no coincidence, and that I had better be on about my business.

When I looked again at the tube map, however, I found that there was no train going directly there from the Piccadilly station. I would have to either walk to another station or take a series of trains. So I decided once again to rely on Google, and found that it was better for me to take bus number 159 by walking over to the corner of Haymarket and Orange Street.

I stood up and began to walk east down Coventry Street. Then I took a right to go south on Haymarket, and my eyes were instantly drawn to another interesting landmark. It was right in front of the doors of the Criterion Theater, underneath the balcony. Again it was a statue decorating a fountain, this one of four horses all reeling back on their hind legs. The inscription on the fountain identified them as the "Horses of Helios," the sun god.

I took a picture of it with my phone and walked on. But I kept looking behind me. It was as if I could feel their eyes on me—the horses, that is. After walking about two blocks, I saw the red double-decker I was looking for headed my way. One block ahead was my bus stop, marked with a sign, which I reached just in time. No one else was there, but the driver spotted me and pulled over. I asked her to announce my stop, and she said she would.

It wasn't very crowded, but I remained standing behind the driver so that I could watch for my stop. Seven minutes later I was at Westminster Station, on Parliament Street. I walked to the corner of Bridge Street and saw Big Ben up ahead on the left—or, more properly, Elizabeth Tower, as "Big Ben" is really the name of one of the bells inside.

I crossed the street to the corner that the clock tower was on, then followed the crowd to an opening in the fence where people were walking back and forth. Up ahead, I saw a man walking in through one of the doors in a corner of the building, right beneath the clock. So I followed him, walking past a hedged enclosure with an opening in the side. As I went past I saw a fountain featuring statues of an emaciated unicorn and several other macabre-looking heraldic creatures.

When I got to the door, I was rebuffed by a security guard, who told me that "strangers" had to enter through St. Stephen's Gate down the street. So I walked back past the hedges and turned left when I got to the sidewalk. I went on until I saw the statue of Oliver Cromwell on my left that the security guard had told me to look for.

There I turned left onto the walkway that led directly to the visitors' entrance. I walked down a ramp towards a vaulted doorway, in front of which there were two security guards wearing plastic gloves. They frisked me and searched my laptop case. Then they let me in.

I entered a giant, empty hall with stone floors and a huge vaulted ceiling made of carved wood. I then turned left to go up some stone steps and through an arched wooden doorway with a clock above it that led to "St. Stephen's Hall." This was a corridor where the walls were covered with beautiful full-color murals of scenes from British history, and stained-glass windows depicting more such scenes above that.

All along the walls were white stone statues of important Englishmen, including some inset into the walls in the corner, and stone benches covered with leather the color of Brunswick green. Brilliant chandeliers hung from the ceiling. At the end of this hall was another vaulted doorway underneath yet another clock, which led to the "Central Lobby."

I went through the door and emerged into an octagonal room situated underneath an amazing gold-covered mosaicked dome. There were more stained-glass windows beneath the dome, and many more statues set into the wall. Then I looked down to see a giant black eight-pointed star in the middle of the mosaic floor, composed of two squares at opposite angles. The points of one of the squares were aligned with each of four corridors that led elsewhere, including the one I had just come out of. The points of the other square were aligned with statues set between these, presumably of important British politicians from the past.

I strolled up to the secretary's desk in the corner to my left. Behind it stood a white man in a black suit with a white blouse and a black bowtie. He was talking on a black desk phone. I waited for him to finish his conversation. After a few seconds, he looked up at me, put his hand over the receiver, and asked what he could do for me. I told him that I was a friend of one of the lords, the Baron of Alphamstone.

"Can you buzz his office to see if he's there?" I said hopefully.

"Excuse me," the man replied, looking very confused. "The Baron of Alphamstone?"

"Yes, Leopold Black," I said. "Please see if he's in. If not, I'll leave a message."

When he heard the words "Leopold Black," he raised his eyebrows.

"Can I have your name please?" he said.

"Sure," I replied. "My name is Pamela Auger. He knows who I am."

"Would you have a seat on one of the benches please?" he then asked. He started talking into his phone again.

He had pointed to my left at a blue leather bench, one of several lining the walls. It was right behind a statue of some guy named William Ewart Gladstone, and underneath a smaller statue that was set into the wall. I sat down there, and turned around to check out the statue above me.

But then I heard footsteps approaching, so I turned to look in front of me. There were two men in their 30s approaching me. One had Persian features and dark hair in a Beatles cut. The other one was white and ginger, with curls and a mustache. They were both wearing gray suits of slightly different shades.

"Ms. Auger," said the Indian. "Would you come with us, please? We'd like to speak to you about the person calling himself 'the Baron of Alphamstone.'"

Chapter 7: Regnum Defende

Nobody was really sure if he was from the House of Lords.

—The Beatles, *A Day in the Life*

The food served to MPs and their guests at the Terrace Café in the House of Commons, where I was taken by my two new friends from the Security Services, seemed rather plebian, a bit like the lunches served to kids in public schools in the US. However, I was assured by Agent Paris and Agent Chesterfield that the ingredients were high quality, local, and completely free of GMOs. I picked out some lasagna, and both men ordered a sandwich, with coffees all around. Chesterfield, the redhead with the thin mustache, insisted on paying.

We sat outside on the terrace overlooking the River Thames, right next to the café, a sort of black-and-white- striped tented structure with glass walls. The two agents took seats across the table from me, with their backs to the river, so that I could enjoy the view. The giant Ferris wheel, the London Eye, was spinning in the distance off to my left.

I didn't know what to say, and I didn't know what they were going to say. But it seemed likely they were going to tell me there was something phony about Leopold after all. Therefore, I would likely never see the rest of the money he had promised me.

Whatever they were going to say, it was going to be a let-down. I was already embarrassed that I had let myself be fooled somehow. I braced myself for bad news and nervously picked at my lasagna. It was extremely bland, if it's possible for blandness to be extreme. Paris noticed the look on my face when I took my first bite.

"Is this your first time in England?" He looked me straight in the eye, penetratingly, and I knew that he knew what I was thinking.

They just don't use spices in this country for some reason. I don't know how I knew, but I just knew that he knew, and that he knew I knew. The words that I was thinking were being transmitted directly into his brain, and it was as though I could see them reflected in his eyes. This is a bad rapport to establish with a government agent who is about to interrogate you. I looked at the river to break the eye contact. A cruise ship drifted by, packed with tourists. "No," I said. "I've been here once before, as a teenager. Family holiday."

"So what's your business here now?" Chesterfield asked directly.

"Research," I answered. "I mainly want to have a look at some of the museums. I'm a writer."

"Oh yes, I've seen," said Chesterfield, grinning. "Dan Brown kinda stuff. Occult mysteries and such." He showed me his phone, a Samsung Galaxy, which was open to an amazon.com page with all of my books listed.

"Dan Brown writes fiction," I replied, cold. But I should have just let it go. *Don't offer them any information*, I reminded myself. *And don't let that Persian guy read your mind.*

"So what's your business with 'the Baron of

Alphamstone'?" Paris asked with a sneer, making finger quotes. Forced to look back in his direction, I concocted something on the spot, knowing he wouldn't believe me.

"I was supposed to interview him about his family history. They're supposedly related to the Merovingians. Dan Brown kinda stuff."

I returned my gaze to the redhead, whose stare was less invasive and yet somehow more charming, more seductive, perhaps because he seemed safer. But I knew I shouldn't let down my guard with him either. I drank some of my coffee. It was cold already, and watery, with a grimy sediment on the bottom. Chesterfield cleared his throat and prepared to lecture to me.

"Alphamstone, my dear, is a village in Essex with less than 100 residents. It is not associated with a barony. The man you are calling 'the Baron of Alphamstone' is actually Thomas Weir, a man whose been living on benefits for over 20 years because of 'psychological disabilities.'"

He made finger quotes too. I noticed his left middle finger was shorter than the others. I stared at it. The tip was missing.

"Wood shop accident," Paris said behind me, showing off that he was reading my thoughts again. "Frankly he's so clumsy I don't know why they ever let him on the service." He chuckled.

"Oh, puff off," said Chesterfield, waving his butchered hand at his colleague as if to dismiss him.

"I don't understand," I said. "There's a page about Leopold Black, Baron of Alphamstone on the official Parliament website."

"He's not a peer," Paris insisted. "He's not noble at all. He just pretends to be so he can sell fake fancy titles to credulous foreigners. Especially Americans. They're a gullible lot when it comes to this stuff. Even you, and you're an investigator."

He wagged his finger at me as if to chastise me. He was openly demonstrating the fact that he was fully aware of what kind of writer I was, unlike his partner, who played dumb.

"Well he never sold any titles to me," I said, ignoring his slight. "I never gave him any money. In fact ..."

I stopped. *Better not mention the lecture*, I thought, *or the Oriental Club, the Worshipful Society of Butchers, the money he'd sent me, nor the fact that he-or they-had paid for my trip. Better not even think it.*

"Was he paying you for something?" Paris asked. Of course. He had picked up on my thoughts.

"No," I replied, assuming that as a non-citizen I had no real obligation to tell them the truth about something that was surely none of their business. I opened my laptop, found the open Wi-Fi from the cafe, and tried to load the Baron's page on the Parliament website. To my surprise, I got a 404 not found!

"I don't understand!" I said. "It was there just a couple of days ago!"

"Let me see," said Chesterfield. He leaned over my right shoulder, and put his left hand on the back of my chair to steady himself. Then he pressed in closer and pointed at the domain name at the top of the page.

"That's not the official Parliament website. It's two letters off." He put his thumb on the touchpad and the backspace, then shortened the URL to what should have been the index page. It was 404 too. The entire website was gone.

"He hired someone to make a fake version of the Parliament website with an entry about him in it. The real one is parliament.uk, not co.uk."

I felt like a total dumbass. *Oh, how he fooled me!* I thought. *And I took money from him, in notable amounts! Where did he get it? From selling titles? Is that how he was able to rent out the Oriental Club so he could shoot that video conference with me? All this time he was just a jobless conman?*

My head was full of questions, but I certainly couldn't ask these two guys. In fact, I felt that I needed to lose them right away so that I could get to the bottom of things on my own.

"Well lads, thank you for revealing the truth to me," I said. "I feel pretty stupid. But I guess it's better I find out now rather than after I write a book or an article based on something he told me." I closed my laptop and started to pack it away, signaling that I was ready for them to let me go.

"I guess I'll just move on to my real reason for being here, which is the museums, as I said." I stood up to leave.

"Oh we can take you!" said Chesterfield. He actually grabbed my wrist to keep me from leaving. "Which one are you going to first?" He smiled at me, and then self- consciously softened his grip on me for a second before dropping it completely. Paris shot him a disapproving glance.

You dirty bastard.

I read the thoughts, as he intended me to.

"The British Museum, of course," I replied.

"Well let's go then," said Chesterfield, lightly brushing my lower spine with his left hand as he pushed my chair back in for me. "Can I carry your case?"

"No thank you," I said.

The contact between his hand and my back created some kind of electrical charge that radiated through the rest of my body and left me feeling flushed. I knew that he was trying to charm me, probably using sophisticated conversational hypnosis techniques, and it was working. Worst of all was the feeling that Agent Paris knew exactly what was happening and was laughing at me for it. I looked, and sure enough, he had a sneering grin on his face as he regarded me.

I waited with Chesterfield outside in the Old Palace Yard while Paris walked down Millbank to the "Q-Park" on the other side of the Abingdon Street Gardens to pick up their car. As we stood there, Chesterfield asked about my books. I gave him vague answers, not willing to make the effort to describe my work to a newbie.

He didn't seem to mind. He just kept smiling at me. He tried to get me to give him my email, purportedly so that he could buy some of my books directly from me. But when I put him off by telling him just to get them from Amazon, he changed his tactic.

"Look, the truth is that the Security Services have an ongoing investigation on this Weir fellow," he said, suddenly acting serious.

"Who?" I had forgotten the guy's "real" name. "The one you called the Baron of Alphamstone! You're a witness. We may have more questions for you. You'll have to give us your email, and your address, and your phone number too. There's some paperwork you'll have to fill out in the car before we let you go."

For a moment I found the thought of him calling me in to his office to detaining and interrogate appealing for some reason. I chalked it up to the mind control tactics he and his partner were both using.

Must be something they teach you in training, I thought. We heard a honk as a black Vauxhall Astra Elite, recent model, pulled up in front of us. The doors unlocked. Chesterfield opened the rear door and gestured gallantly for me to enter. Then he boorishly slid in right beside me instead of taking the passenger seat in the front as I would have expected him to.

He stared at me lasciviously, an evil gleam in his green eyes and his red eyebrows cocked at a devilish angle. I was sure he was going to grab my pussy right there, Trump-style. But instead he reached into a pocket on the back of the seat in front of me and pulled out a packet of carbon-copy forms for me to fill out.

"Put your contact info here, initial here, and sign here," he said. "You're just acknowledging that you voluntarily answered our questions, and that you weren't *forcibly detained*." He said that last part with far too much enjoyment.

It took 15 minutes to get to the museum. We had to cross the river twice, and pay a toll. We first crossed to the other side via the Lambeth Bridge, and as we turned on it, they both proudly pointed out to me their agency's headquarters, a building called Thames House located further on down Millbank.

"So did Weir actually make an appointment to meet with you in the House of Lords today?" Paris asked as he drove. It was the first real question either of them had asked me.

"No," I said. "He just told me to look him up there next time I was in town. I guess he never expected that I'd actually show up."

"When's the last time you spoke to him?" Paris queried.

"Probably a week ago," I said truthfully. My lies were getting sloppy.

"So you told him you were coming to London to do research?" Paris inquired.

"Well, yes," I said. I couldn't think of a way around it.

"But you didn't make a specific appointment to meet?" Paris pressed.

"No, just an informal agreement," I replied. "I just said I'd drop by sometime, that's all." I was hoping he wouldn't probe further.

"So did you talk to him on the phone?" Paris asked.

"No, just email," I told him. I didn't want to mention the Skype conversation, or the phone number he'd given me where nobody ever answered.

"Well, said Chesterfield, tenderly grabbing my hand and folding my fingers around a business card. "Here's my number, if you remember anything that might be useful to us. Especially if he contacts you again. Don't tell him that we spoke, or that you found out the truth about him. Try to make an appointment with him, and then let us know where you're going to meet."

I looked at the card. It had the *Regnum Defende* MI5 logo with a dragon-tailed lion surrounded by portcullises and pentagonal rose symbols. It was a good thing Her Majesty had these two fine men to defend her realm from the mischievous conmen trying to sell titles to fake baronies. I mentally laughed at the ridiculous situation I now found myself in.

"Sure thing!" I said. The car came to a stop in front of the south entrance of the museum, with its massive columned pediment in the style of ancient Greece. I managed to get out of the car somewhat smoothly without making further promises or giving away any more information. But not before Chesterfield kissed my hand ridiculously, causing his partner to shake his head in embarrassment.

The car sped off as soon as I shut the door. I walked quickly through the courtyard and up the large steps to the doorway, eager to get out of open view as quickly as possible.

Chapter 8: Non Sequitur

> The great secret of magic, the unique and incommunicable Arcana, has for its purpose the placing of supernatural power at the service of the human will in some way.
>
> To attain such an achievement it is necessary to KNOW what has to be done, to WILL what is required, to DARE what must be attempted and to KEEP SILENT with discernment.
>
> – Eliphas Levi, *The Great Secret*

Having finally shaken loose of my interrogators, I wandered through grand halls filled with the greatest treasures in the world in a blind daze, hardly noticing any of it. After paying my donation to get in, I entered a large open court with an egg-shaped reading room carving out a large chunk of space in the middle. The first room I saw to my left was full of Egyptian stuff. I sat on a blond wooden bench underneath a gigantic broken bust of Ramesses II and tried to collect my thoughts.

So Leopold is a fraud. Where is he now? Have the police and MI5 already questioned him? Presumably he hasn't been arrested yet. But perhaps they shut him down, or he shut himself down, realizing the game was over. But what was the game?

The agents' claims made no sense. Leopold hadn't tried to sell me any titles, which surely would have been the point of faking his membership in a wealthy British gentleman's club. It would have been an expensive ruse.

He had been seeking information from me, rather than trying to convince me of anything. He had spent a considerable amount of money on me, rather than trying to get me to buy anything. He'd lied to me about being a baron and a Peer of the Realm, but without mentioning anything about providing titles for others. So what was the point then?

I was too worked up about all of these questions to take in the museum properly. But that wasn't really why I was there. I wanted to see for myself the very items of interest which I had travelled all of this way to talk about, but had never actually laid eyes on.

I walked back out into the Great Court and up to the closest information desk. This was a large black circular object near the entrance. Several agents were working there, all wearing uniforms of black pants and blue shirts.

They all were busy with other customers except one on the end. She was an overweight Persian lady in her 20s, with her hair in a messy bun. Her name tag said "Parveen." I walked up to her.

"Hi," I said. "I was wondering if you could tell me how to find one of the items in your online catalogue."

"Certainly," she said. "What do you know about it?"

"It's a limestone coffer, item number 1866,1229.143 in the Duc de Blacas Collections," I said, reading off information from an email accessible on my phone. Parveen typed into her computer.

"Hmm," she said. "That item number is coming up as not found. Was it donated by Louis de Blacas, or Pierre?" "Louis, I believe," I said. She looked disappointed. "That's a large collection, unfortunately," she said. "What else can you tell me about it?"

"Well, it was labeled as having an image of Cybele on the top."

She typed into her computer some more, presumably using keywords. Then she shook her head sideways again. "Well, I'm not finding any limestone coffers at all, I'm afraid," she said. "Could it be in another collection?" "That's impossible," I said. "I knew it wasn't on display, but it should still be here."

"Who told you it was here?" she asked.

"The museum staff!" I answered, feeling frustrated. "Through email! They let me search through the digital catalog until I found it. Then I paid them to take some better photos of it, which they sent me."

I combed through my Gmail archives until I found an attachment containing the photos of the lid of the Mete coffer. Then I turned my phone around to show Parveen the image of a naked, crowned, and bearded Hermaphrodite gleefully pulling the Sun and the Moon, upside-down and out of the sky with a pair of chains attached to both the heavenly bodies and the ankles of the goddess.

"Cybele is a goddess, not a Hermaphrodite," Parveen smugly informed me.

"That's not what Catullus said," I snapped back, not having time to explain the numerous counter-traditions indicating that the "Magna Mater" or "Great Mother" worshiped by both the Persians and the Romans was originally described as a hermaphrodite that had been castrated and cast out of Olympus by the other gods. "Anyway it was your museum that labeled it Cybele," I said.

"And you said you got that photo from us?" she asked, sounding incredulous.

"Yes," I replied. "And I paid this institution to take good photographs, which I published in a book last year for the first time, even though this artifact has been mentioned in books about the Knights Templar with only line drawings available to print for over one hundred and fifty years. I am the one who brought this historical item, which your museum has been sitting on and ignoring, into the light of day. And now I'd like to finally see it."

Parveen wasn't looking at me or my phone anymore. She was typing into her computer again. When I stopped talking, she looked up.

"What did you say your name was?" she asked. "I didn't say," I told her. "But I'm Pamela Auger. I'm a writer." She hit the keys a few more times.

"Oh yes," she said. "I see that you still have an outstanding balance of 3000 pounds for photograph rights." She smiled a "gotcha" smile, and her eyes gleamed. "Yes, and the item in the photo that I owe money for the rights to is the one I'm asking you to locate for me right now," I smiled.

Surely she's just an information desk clerk, not a collection agent, I thought. *Her primary job is to help visitors find things they're looking for, not to catch people who owe money to the museum.*

"Well, I'll call in the Accounts Receivable department. Maybe they can help us figure out where this coffer is, and I'm sure they can work out some payment arrangements for you. Just a second." She picked up her phone again and smiled evilly.

Have I really pissed her off that much? I thought. *All this just because I mentioned that I had made history with an item they'd been ignoring?*

My honesty, and perhaps my arrogance as well, was about to screw me out of a chance to see the coffer, and instead drive me straight into the greedy hands of bill collectors. I suddenly wanted to flee.

I turned around with the intention of doing exactly that. But then I bumped into a body in light brown leather cap toe Oxford shoes and a light brown suit that was topped with a familiar old face. It was Leopold Black! At that moment, even though I knew he was a fraud, I was happy to see him. *But what's he doing here?* I wondered.

"I thought I might find you here," he said. "Looking for the coffer?"

"Yes," I said. "But they're having trouble finding it. They seem more interested in talking to me about the money I owe them. And that's not the strangest thing that's happened to me today. Why haven't you been answering the phone?"

I wasn't sure if I should tell him what I knew or play dumb and pump him for information, as Agent Chesterfield had encouraged me to do. But I desperately wanted to get away from that information desk before Accounts Receivable showed up.

"Well you won't find it here anymore," he said. "It's gone. It's been stolen."

"What?" I said, disbelieving him. Despite what Parveen had told me, I couldn't accept that anything could be stolen from the British Museum without it being a news story. Also, Leopold/Thomas was a known liar.

"Yes, it's gone, and we need to get gone too," he said. "Come with me."

"OK," I said. "I'd like to get a decent coffee. I also need to find a clothing store. They lost my luggage, and I've been wearing this outfit for three days."

We headed towards the entrance, but from behind I heard my name being called by a deep male voice.

"Ms. Auger!"

"Walk faster," said Leopold. "We can't let them catch us."

"You mean Accounts Receivable?" I said. "I'm just going to leave. They can't make me stay." Still, I did walk faster. The voice called me again.

"Ms. Auger, please come back here for a moment!"

Now I was almost running, panicking, wanting to avoid confrontation. Leopold kept pace. We sprinted down the steps and across the courtyard, with now two pursuers, whom I saw peripherally to be large men in dark suits, following behind at a steady pace but not running after us.

As we neared the curb of Great Russell Street, Leopold hailed a black car with tinted windows that looked like its arrival was perfectly timed. He opened the back door and basically shoved me in. Before the door closed, I heard that same familiar voice shouting at me from behind us:

"Ms. Auger, we need to talk. There's something you need to know!"

Leopold shut the door, and the doors locked automatically. That's when I realized that this was not a taxicab, as there were no meters and no official identification. It was a private car. The driver, a blond guy in his thirties with a dark suit and black bowler hat, took orders from Leopold.

"Take us to the Club, Miles" he said to the driver. Miles nodded and sped off, just as one of the men following us, who I saw to be black and husky, reached for the door handle, and missed. Now my survival instinct kicked in.

"Leopold, I agreed to go down the street for coffee with you, not to get in a private car. Where are you taking me?"

"To the Oriental Club, of course," he said. "You're going to make the presentation I hired you to do." A chill went through me.

Who is this man that I've foolishly gotten into a car with, I thought, *and what is he going to do to me?*

"Actually, I'd like to get out now," I said. I then addressed the driver. "Can you pull the car over please?"

He ignored me. My fear turned into a full freak-out.

"I demand that you let me out of this car right now!" I screamed. I picked up my phone, though I didn't know how to call the equivalent of 911 in this country. I didn't have time to think about who to call because Leopold snatched the phone out of my hand with a forcefulness that surprised me for a man his age.

"Pamela, do not panic, or I will give you a reason to panic," he said.

What a scary thing to say! I thought.

I unlocked my door and reached for the handle, ready to take my chances and jump out straight onto the pavement below, hoping I could aim for the sidewalk at least instead of being crushed immediately by the car behind us. But Leopold grabbed my hand and pressed something cold and hard against my chest. I looked down. It was a silver handgun. I sat back, terrified.

"What do you want from me?" I sobbed.

"Just your professional analysis," he answered. "Now cooperate."

Chapter 9: Oriental Club

Between South Molton Street & Stratford Place: Calvary's foot: Where the Victims were preparing for sacrifice their Cherubim… their inmost palaces Resounded with preparation of animals wild & tame.

—William Blake, *Milton*

At times like this, you find yourself wishing you'd attached a rider to your contract.

The client must provide his actual legal name. No involuntary transport of my person (kidnapping). No guns or threats of murder. Pick me up at the airport, for Christ's sake. Return phone calls and emails related to business in a timely manner. And never, ever book me at a hotel room that cannot fit both my body and my suitcase simultaneously. Also, of course, a cancellation clause in case the above requirements are violated.

But no recourse seemed available to me at that time. So I tried to calm myself down, wiping the tears from my puffy, reddened face that had not had the benefit of make-up in days. I concentrated on Leopold's hands, which I looked at close up for the first time. I noticed that they were both scarred all over and horribly contorted. It was almost as if each phalange had been separated from the others at some point, and then it had all been grafted back together again, badly.

I looked out the window to my left and saw a public park. A sign said "Hanover Square." I recalled that this was near where the Oriental Club actually did meet, at some place called Stratford House. But Leopold was holding my phone, so I couldn't use it to confirm this. I wondered what they were going to do with me, how much it would hurt, and if anyone would find my body. Finally, I turned again to my captor and inquired as to whether the projector and screen had been set up for my PowerPoint presentation.

"You'll have everything you need," I was told gruffly.

The car stopped abruptly and pulled up next to the park.

"We walk from here," Leopold announced. The doors unlocked and he leaned over to pull the handle on my door with his right hand while he grabbed my right wrist with his left hand, which was so gnarly that my skin tried to crawl away from my body as soon as he touched it. He then wrapped his entire arm around mine so that he had firm control of my whole upper body. He pushed me out along with himself, and we emerged stuck together. He then pulled me over to the corner, where we crossed the street after Miles drove off.

I guess we just looked like a typical May-December couple. People walking past us didn't seem to notice that he was pressing a gun against my side, or that I was under extreme duress. I couldn't believe that something like this could happen in a large city in broad daylight. But it was happening.

When we got to the other side of the street. Leopold stopped me for a moment and looked around. There was nobody else in our immediate vicinity. In front of us was a multi-purpose office building. I saw a sign for a Lloyd's TSB bank in the lobby, and next to that, Barclays, again. In my fear and paranoia I tried desperately to understand what was going on. I turned to look at Leopold.

"You don't work for Barclays do you?" He shook his head sideways and laughed. I realized that didn't make any sense, especially since he had paid me thousands of dollars and spent thousands more to bring me here.

That's a silly way to collect a debt, I thought. Just then I felt someone come from behind and grab my left arm. It was Miles. He must have already parked the car.

"This way please," he said politely as he and Leopold both dragged me off.

They marched me past another building and across Hanover Street, then down a few doors to the left. We paused in front of the glass door of an art gallery with no name, simply labeled with the address, "10 Hanover." In the middle of the day, it was closed and empty.

There was a touchpad for an alarm. Miles keyed in the code while Leopold held me firm, never loosening his grip on my arm or the pressure of the gun on my ribcage. The door opened and I was ushered inside.

The lights were off, but I could see the main room from the daylight coming through the glass door. I only saw two art pieces on display in the otherwise empty room. One was a giant Band-Aid, about a foot long, stuck to a canvas on the back wall, right next to a staircase leading down. The other was a large square canvas on the wall to my left, maybe 8 feet by 8 feet, painted black with three yellow discs arranged in a downward-pointing triangle formation. Leopold noticed me noticing it.

"What are you thinking?" he asked curiously.

"Oh I was just thinking that this reminds me of an image I saw in a movie once," I told him.

This whole experience is like being in a movie, I thought to myself.

"Which one?" he prodded.

"I think it was *Invocation of My Demon Brother*, by Kenneth Anger," I answered.

"Ah yes, the Aleister Crowley worshipper with the horrible amateur movies that everybody calls 'art,'" he said.

They shoved me to the left side of the room, around a bend, so that we were now out of sight from the front door. Leopold let me go and gave the gun to Miles, who now pressed it into my back underneath my left shoulder blade. Leopold lit a cigarette with a zippo. They were Chesterfields. I didn't even know they made Chesterfields anymore! That, of course, made me think fondly of my favorite MI5 agent, wishing he and his partner were there to save me.

"Actually," Leopold explained, "the yellow dots in the Kenneth Anger movie form a downward-pointing triangle. This," he said, jabbing his thumb at the painting behind him, "is based on the coat of arms for William Pitt. There's a statue of him in the park across the street."

He started to walk towards the stairs and then stopped again. He turned around and looked at me, wagging his gnarly index finger at me.

"But see, you were picking up on an Aleister Crowley vibe. That's why I hired you. There's more than just logic and knowledge at work in your brain, though there is that. You're using a sixth sense to do your research too. I've known it for some time. That's why you're the one we need."

He turned around and headed down the stairs. Miles and I followed.

"Why," I asked. "What's this got to do with Aleister Crowley?"

When we reached the bottom of the stairs we were in a dark unfinished basement. I couldn't even see the walls to tell how large it was. Leopold turned towards me and ignited his lighter to illuminate his face.

"Crowley's Astron Argon club had an office in that building down the street, at 10 Hanover Square," he said, pointing back up the stairs. "Or at least, in the building that used to be there."

"But aren't we in 10 Hanover now?" I said, confused. I remembered the address on the front door.

"We're in 10 Hanover *Street*. The Square is down there, he said, continuing to point. Miles winced.

"It's OK Miles," Leopold assured him. "She needs to know these things. Now, Crowley and his friends had access to the underground tunnel network beneath these streets, which leads to what was once the sub-basement of where the Oriental Club *used* to meet, at 18 Hanover Square."

"So not Stratford House?" I inquired.

"That's right," he answered. "They moved to Stratford House in the 60s. It's just a quarter-mile away from here. But before that, Oriental Club was just a few feet away from Astron Argon's office, right across Hanover Square. Now Crowley spent some time there, not as a dues-paying member, but as a guest. And the person who invited him in, whose name I shall withhold, also shared with him a secret which *should not* have been disclosed, about the tunnel network. Crowley and his friends then began making nefarious use of the tunnels. We know this because when we were exploring down here, we found one of his secret shrines."

"What tunnels?" I asked. "And who's 'we'?"

"The Worshipful Society of Butchers," Leopold replied. He walked over to a grimy tile-covered wall, which I could now see only because of the flame from his lighter, and unlatched a hook that had been keeping a thin wooden door closed. It swung open, revealing a toilet, a sink, and an overflowing trash can. Miles let go of me and gave the gun back to Leopold, who held it sticking out towards me. I now had nobody holding me, but I dare not try to run.

Miles pulled the trash can out of the bathroom and into the main room, to get it out of the way. Then he brushed aside the remaining pile of used paper towels, revealing a green wooden hatch door, which he raised. Underneath was a deep shaft, with at least two rungs of a metal ladder visible from the top.

This must be the entrance to the secret network of tunnels they were talking about, I thought.

Miles went down first. Then a few seconds later, Leopold insisted I follow. I put the strap of the laptop case around my neck and let it hang from my back as I climbed down. Leopold extinguished his flame, and waited for me to get to the bottom, still in pitch-darkness. There Miles grabbed me with both hands, and whistled to announce this. Then Leopold descended down the ladder himself.

When he got to the bottom, he flicked his lighter back on temporarily and pointed his gun at me again. Then Miles let go of me, and reached into his coat pocket to pull out a long silver cylinder. It was an LED flashlight, which he turned on, allowing Leopold to put out his lighter and return it to his pocket.

"I'm sorry that I have to point this gun at you," said Leopold. "But I know that I can't trust you to cooperate yet." He pulled something out of his inner coat pocket and snapped it to unfurl it. It was a cloth, like a scarf.

"Turn around," he said. I complied. He tied the cloth over my eyes. I was completely blind.

"Oh come on," I said, "I can barely see as it is."

"There are some details I just can't trust you with," he said. "Miles, take her bag please."

Miles relieved me of my burden, which actually was *quite* a relief, physically. But now I had to worry about how I was going to get it back. Leopold then grabbed me from behind by the left shoulder.

"Put your arms out to your side, please," he instructed. I complied, bewildered.

"Forward three paces, please, and through the archway," Leopold continued.

I walked ahead. After two steps, I felt a wall on either side of me. With a third step I walked through a passageway between them. I stepped into an open room of some sort. I could tell this because there was a change in air pressure, as well as in the acoustics of our footsteps, and a gentle breeze from above.

"Where are we going now?" I said.

"You tell us, my dear Virgil," he commanded.

"What do you mean?" I asked.

"Directly ahead of you are the entrances to three different corridors that you can go down," Leopold explained. "Three different avenues all leading to the light. Three different *Ways* through *Strength* and *Beauty*.

"But remember," he lectured, "these paths all intersect with each other at several points on the journey. So in the long run, there will be numerous opportunities to change the road you are on. Therefore, fear not the outcome. Simply make a choice, and move ahead. But to make sure that you are perfectly lost, and therefore your choice all the more arbitrary, we shall give you a few spins around, just like a game of pin the tail on the donkey."

Leopold took me by my left hand, and Miles took me by my right. Then they both began to spin me in a counter-clockwise direction.

Suddenly I understood, at least in part, their purpose for bringing me here. Leopold had surmised my clairvoyant powers when he realized that I was using intuition and divination tools in my occult research. He had figured out why I had been able to penetrate esoteric mysteries so deeply.

Perhaps he's also overestimated my powers, I thought, *and assumes I can control them. Maybe he doesn't realize that they work sporadically at best, and aren't always reliable. Either way, it's certainly was starting to look like he brought me here to serve as a soothsayer.*

"Are you guys trying to use me as a human dowsing rod?" I asked, as I was being turned by them like a corkscrew.

"In a way, yes," Leopold replied.

They spun me around seven times, at the end of which I was, as they intended, dizzy and completely disoriented. I stumbled forward a few feet. My hands caught the left side of another archway.

"Excellent choice," said Leopold. "Steady on."

I walked on through the archway, and into a narrow tunnel, with Leopold's hand on my shoulder once again. I reckoned that Miles was somewhere behind us.

"Don't you know where these tunnels lead? Or are you expecting *me* to tell you? Because *I* sure as Hell don't know."

"Yes, I know where they lead, dear. But I'm just not sure what station we need to be at next. So I am counting on you to intuit that for us. Don't worry, I have complete faith in you."

And so we walked on, for what felt like a quarter of a mile, until we hit a wall. I sensed that we had reached another crossroads. I scuttled to the left and found that there was indeed a passageway there, so I turned left. But then I hesitated after a few steps. It smelled wet and moldy, like dirty towels.

"Maybe we should go the other way," I said. "This might be leading into a sewer."

"It's not," said Leopold. "Go on."

"But there's a passageway going the opposite direction too, isn't there?" I asked. I got the sense that there was, and that I might have made the wrong choice.

"Don't second-guess yourself," said Leopold. "Keep going."

We trekked on for about another quarter of a mile. At one point I was sure that I heard a subway train passing over ahead, and Miles confirmed it. Then sometime after that I saw, in my mind's eye, an old wooden door, with a padlock on it. I stopped dead in my tracks.

"There's no point in going on," I said. "There's a locked door. We would need the key."

"She's good!" said Miles. I then heard a keyring jangling, and a key being inserted into the lock.

"Come on through," he said, guiding me through the door with his hand on my shoulders. "There's only one direction to go in from here."

I stepped forward. Leopold stepped through behind me. Then he told me to stop.

"Go ahead and take the hoodwink off, Miles," he ordered.

The blindfold was removed. Now I could see the brick walls and floors of the corridor we were in, illuminated by the LED flashlight. It seemed centuries old. Up ahead several hundred feet, there was an opening leading to a round room, also lined floor to ceiling with brick.

"You found it," said Leopold. "Congratulations."

"I thought you needed me to guide you," I said resentfully.

"We do," he replied. "That was just a test. A warm-up exercise."

Miles pushed me forward again. I walked on, but just then I smelled something familiar. It was an odor I couldn't forget because of the years my parents spent tending a small ranch in Sherwood, Oregon. It was cow shit, unmistakably.

"Are there any animals down here?" I asked. "It smells like cow patties." It seemed improbable, but my nose didn't lie. I sensed the beast's life force, and its fear. Then I heard it low mournfully.

"Yes, well…" Leopold's voice trailed off for a moment. Miles pushed me forward again. Then Leopold finished his sentence.

"Animals often crap themselves the moment they realize they're about to die."

I stumbled through the doorway into the room, terrified now, as a single fluorescent tube light hanging from the ceiling came on. This revealed the scene in front of me. A man in a black leather veil and a matching leather apron over a brown suit was standing in front of four-foot-high wooden table covered also in black leather, with a large axe held aloft.

Upon this table was pressed the neck of a bull, being held with a rope round its neck by another man, similarly dressed. The man with the axe brought it down on the neck of the bull, who bellowed loudly at the moment of first impact. The head came rolling off, and the blood began spurting outward in jets as I collapsed and fell down onto the brick floor, staring up at the beehive-shaped brick ceiling and the tube light beneath it, which got shot with a jet of blood just before I passed out.

Chapter 10: Scrying at Stratford Place

> The Duke of Wellington is said to have given the founders of the Oriental Club two pieces of characteristically succinct advice: 'Have a club of your own' and 'Buy the freehold.'
>
> — Anthony LeJeune, *The Gentlemen's Clubs of London*

I awoke with my face laying on my arms. I was seated in a straight-back wooden chair with no armrests. My arms and head were lying on a long rectangular dining table, where I was seated at the head. Sitting around the rest of the table were maybe a dozen men and women of various ages, mostly white but not exclusively. They were all dressed quite properly, as if for a night at the opera. All of them were staring directly at me. I saw in their faces, variously, curiosity, amusement, concern, and pity.

At the other end of the table was a projector screen arranged on a stand. The décor around me was Victorian, everything in a red-stained wood. Bookshelves filled with antique books lined the walls in front of me and to my left.

Against the wall to my right was a little wooden table with two chairs. Leopold sat on the right side of the table, with a black rectangular object in his hand. Another gentleman, considerably older than him, sat on the left. Both looked very stern.

I turned to look behind me. There was a portrait of the Duke of Wellington hanging over a white marble fireplace. I knew from the research I had done before the trip that I was in one of the dining rooms of Stratford House, where the Oriental Club held their meetings.

Finally, I looked down at my own person and took note of my condition. I felt terrible. I was tired and dehydrated, with a pounding headache and sore muscles all over. But one condition had improved.

I was no longer wearing the same soiled clothes I'd had on since I left Portland. Instead, I was sporting an elegant blue gown and matching pumps, with a lacy white shawl, white pearls around my neck, and a matching bracelet around my left arm. I reached up and ran my hands through my hair. It had been curled. I tried to rub my eyes, but the young lady next to me put her hand on my arm to stop me.

"Oh, don't ruin your make-up," she said. "I worked hard on it!"

So they had changed my clothes and made me up, I thought. *That means I was naked. What else did they do to me?*

"We had you fixed up a bit," said Leopold. "There's a dress code in this club."

I glared at him. *How did they do all that without waking me up?* I wondered.

I figured they must have given me a sedative after I passed out, which would explain why I still felt groggy.

They could have done anything to me, I thought.

"Don't worry, we had the women change your clothes and bathe you," Leopold said. "Your decency was kept intact the whole time."

That only made me feel slightly better, and since I knew he was a liar, I didn't fully believe him. Still, I was nice to have fresh underwear. But then I thought of the bull decapitation, and the blood spurting out. And the gun at my back. And all of the lies.

Not so nice, I thought. *Who are these people?*

"So is this the Worshipful Company of Butchers?" I asked.

"Society," Leopold corrected.

"You mean to tell me that *this* is how the livery companies of London conduct themselves?" I shouted.

"We are not a livery company," the ancient man next to Leopold insisted. "We are a different sort of entity."

"We conduct butchery only when necessary, and to a specific end," said a young man on the other end of the table on the left side. "We carry on the traditions of sacrifice, and spill the blood that is needed, but only to keep things in balance."

"To satisfy the divine commandments" said a woman across from him. "To preserve the sacred order."

"One for the Lord, and one for Azazel," said Leopold, undoubtedly knowing that this reference would have meaning for me, having read my Baphomet book where it was mentioned.

"We watch over the pillars that hold up the sky," said another man, immediately to my right, "and the portals that lead to the other realm. We make sure nobody *abuses* these things, no matter how powerful they might be on Earth. The mighty are always seeking means to even greater power. But some things must be kept inviolate, or else everything will be destroyed."

"What does all this mean?" I said to them pleadingly. "And what do you want with me?"

Just then a door on the far end of the wall to my right opened, and in stepped Miles. He switched off the light, and Leopold clicked a button on the object he was holding. The projector came on. A line drawing of the lid of the Mete coffer appeared on the screen in front of us. There was Mete pulling the Sun and Moon down with chains. The ancient man next to Leopold spoke again.

"Do you stand by your interpretation that the image on this coffer represents Mete pulling the gods of heaven down from the sky?"

"Yes," I answered. "I am convinced of my hypothesis and have no reason to think otherwise."

"You've really let the cat out of the bag," the man said contemptuously. "Knowledge like this is dangerous. It can give the wrong people the wrong ideas, and that is what you have done."

"What in the world do you mean?" I said. The man on the far end of the table on the left, who had spoken before, replied to me.

"There is now a very powerful and evil magician who is attempting to challenge the powers of the Archons, spurred on by the content of your book. And it has come down to us to put a stop to it."

"You mean he's trying to make the sky fall down with a child sacrifice ritual?" I asked, referring to my theory regarding what I believe was the Templars' most important secret ceremony. "So someone's trying to escape the material world? To penetrate the gates of the gods above and overcome them?"

"Yes, said Leopold. "The Baptism of Wisdom. Just as you described in your book."

Well, I didn't describe it in much detail, I thought. *Nobody knows the details. I just figured out what I could from looking at a few pictures.*

"I was really just theorizing," I said. "Based on what I saw, and my research. I'm not even sure if I was right, and I said so in the book. I certainly didn't think anybody in modern times would take the idea seriously. How can you destroy existence by doing a ritual?"

"If anybody ever does figure it out, well enough to explain the mechanics of it rationally, by then it will be too late," said the woman to my left—the one who had done my make-up.

"That's not what we need to know right now, Pamela," said Leopold. He clicked his clicker again, and the picture on the screen changed. "What we need to know from you now is what you see here."

I looked at the picture. It looked like a map. In fact, it looked quite familiar to me. I had been studying similar pictures for days before coming to London, planning my trip there, listing all the lovely historical monuments I would visit while I was in town for what I *thought* was legitimate business. But the map in front of me now was upside-down.

So is this another stupid test of my psychic abilities? I wondered. *Like how they forced me to divine my way to the slaughter room they had already set up for me in the tunnels?*

I felt like I had no choice. I had to play along, to stay on their good side long enough to figure a way out of Stratford House before those weirdos killed me. So I spoke my mind.

"Well, it's London of course," I said. "The City of London, the old town. But you need to turn it around. Anything else? We can play with a deck of cards. I can probably guess at least one out of ten."

"By Jove!" exclaimed Leopold, leaping to his feet. He walked over to the projector and turned the picture around. "She's right! Look, there's St.

Paul's." He pointed to a dark circle in the middle, the same feature I had identified as matching up to St. Paul's Cathedral.

"And there's the Gherkin," he continued, pointing at another spot to the right of it. "Remember Miles," he said to his valet. "The part that was sticking up like a thumb?"

So this is a modern map of the City of London, I thought, realizing that the Gherkin was that pickle-shaped skyscraper that dominated the skyline. I knew that the part of town officially known as "the City of London" (controlled by "the Corporation of London") is merely a borough of what is now "Greater London." I also knew that it still roughly comprised the same space as the original Roman square mile known as "Londinium."

Although it was often described incompletely as the "financial district" of Greater London, it was really a separate legal entity from the rest of the British empire. The Queen was traditionally supposed to ask permission from the Lord Mayor of the City of London to enter the square mile to conduct formal business. This is where the centers of corporate power, in counterbalance to regal and ecclesiastic power, were currently based. The Bank of England, the Stock Exchange, and the London Bullion Market Association were there, along with most of the corporate headquarters of Britain-based financial institutions. Even the "Temple" area where the Knights Templar had once kept a preceptory, was located in the City, and had always been the cornerstone of the British court system.

Why are they showing me this map, I thought. *And how did they not realize that it was a map? What did Leopold mean about "that part that was sticking up"?*

I didn't wonder for long. The man on the left at the opposite end of the table gave me the answer.

"This is a diagram we made just an hour ago, of the liver of the bull that we just sacrificed in the basement, which you were a witness to."

So I'm here to read entrails? I thought. *But I wasn't trained as a haruspex! I know nothing about divining from livers. Yet somehow I knew that this liver looked like the City of London. How on Earth is it even possible for the liver of a bull to look like a borough of London?*

"So what are you looking for?" I asked.

"Where's the cancer?" asked Leopold. "Tell us where you see the stronghold of the evil magician we described."

"Did you take any photos of the actual liver?" I asked.

"Yes!" Leopold smiled. "That was Miles idea. He took a photo with your phone."

Miles was smiling too, proud of himself. He walked over to me, pulled my phone out of his coat pocket, and handed it over. As soon as I turned it on, I saw the photo of the bloody liver and almost retched. It was mostly the memory of the kill that caused the reaction. I looked up at Miles again.

"Thank you Miles," I said. "Can I have my laptop case back also?"

"Oh yes," he replied. "It's sitting next to the projector."

I looked down at the photo again and tried to clear my mind, looking for "the cancer," whatever it was. The longer I remained useful to them, I figured, the longer I would remain alive. As I stared, I saw a ring of sickly green appear on the liver for a moment, right on the end of a triangle of whitish discoloration Then the circle vanished, but the white triangle remained. There was a similar triangle of lines formed on the diagram on the projector.

"I think I see something," I said. "Here, between St. Paul's and the Gherkin."

I got up and walked over to the projector, then pointed on the diagram to where I had seen the green circle appear on the photograph. "It's right on this triangle here. I saw it with my mind's eye."

"God damn it's that fucking Jew bugger!" said a man on the right side of the table. "The one who thinks he's more powerful than the Queen."

"Don't be so vulgar!" said a woman sitting next to him, looking at me nervously. "We're not against Jews or homosexuals. We aren't barbarians."

I looked away from her. *That's exactly what you are*, I thought.

"It doesn't matter. He'll do us all in if we let him," said another man, addressing the entire room. "That's why he bribed the City to let him buy the meth room. That's why he built that bulky, impenetrable mass in the center of the City. He wants to do it there, right there. To cut a hole in the sky and bring down the pillars it sits on. Doesn't that make sense now?"

No, it doesn't make sense. I thought. *Did you actually say 'meth room'?"*

I had no idea who they were talking about. I didn't care. While everyone was talking to one another, I took a moment to kneel down and pick up my laptop case. As I was down beneath the table I punched a few buttons on my phone, grateful that I had input Agent Chesterfield's phone number already while I was sitting in the Egyptian room at the British Museum.

I silenced the speakers but left the mic open. Then I rang his number and put the phone in the outside pocket of my case, which I left open. I returned to my seat at the end of the table.

"What specifically are you afraid is going to happen," I asked Leopold, locking eyes with him.

"Pamela, whether you understand or not, rationally, I know you get it intuitively. There really are pillars that hold up the sky. They keep the layers of existence from crashing in on each other. And there are those who are looking for power beyond this world. The man we are telling you about wants to make Atlas shrug for real—no metaphor. We sacrifice bulls to the Archons, to maintain the cosmic order. But he wants to kill the Celestial Bull, and tear down the columns that uphold creation, so that he can climb up, out of here, and rule the destroyed worlds from above. He believes he can make the gods themselves bow down to him. And in the process we may all be crushed or annihilated."

"You can't really believe that's possible," I said. "We can't take the chance that it might be," the old man next to him answered.

Just then, another door opened up, this time on my left side, and a man dressed like a butler came through.

"What's the meaning of this!" the old man shouted. "I told you to give us absolute privacy."

"I'm sorry sir. It's the police. I had to let them in," the butler replied.

Behind him, two metropolitan police in black uniforms came through, followed by Agent Paris and Agent Chesterfield. Paris pointed directly at Leopold. Then he grabbed the butler by the collar angrily.

"You told us he wasn't here."

"I didn't let him in," the butler insisted. "He must have sneaked in somehow." He looked around. "Well a *lot of you* didn't come through the front door. How's that?"

"All right, take him in," said Chesterfield. The police handcuffed Leopold as Chesterfield walked over and took me by the arm.

"You should take his valet in too," I told him loudly. "They both kidnapped me at gunpoint from the British Museum. Then they took me down to some dungeon and killed a bull in front of me."

Everyone in the room stopped dead. The room was silent. Everyone stared at me. The WSB members all had looks of complete horror on their faces.

"Will you *testify* to that?" Agent Paris asked me. Miles stared me down cold, and shook his head sideways.

"No," I answered. I grabbed on tightly to Chesterfield's arm.

"Then just take Mr. Weir," Paris told the policemen. "The rest of you, get out of here. Club's closed for the night."

They all began to file out. I tried not to look at anyone directly anymore, and stared at Chesterfield's shoes.

"Let's go," he said to me. I grabbed my laptop case, still looking down, and walked out, letting Chesterfield lead so that he could usher us through the exit line. I could feel Leopold's eyes on my back, and I wanted to get out of his line of sight as soon as possible.

Chapter 11: Temple Tavern

> O, plump head waiter of 'The Cock,'
> To which I most resort
> How goes the time? 'tis five o'clock?
> Go fetch a pint of port!
>
> — Alfred Lloyd Tennyson, *The Cock*

Chesterfield took me down the stairs and out the front of Stratford House to the sidewalk, at the end of the cul-de-sac called Stratford Place. I didn't see much of the opulent building because I was looking at my shoes the whole time. When we got outside into the early evening air, he suggested we duck into the bookshop in the building next door, covered by an immense glass rooftop garden, thus avoiding the rest of the Society of Butchers as they scurried away. It turned out that this building housed the local Kaballah Centre, and it was their book shop. We stopped in front of a display of commentaries on *The Zohar* so that we could speak for a moment. But when we noticed that everyone in the shop was looking at us, we quieted down to a whisper.

"So you overheard what was going on when I called you and you traced the call to find me?" I asked. "I was shocked at how quickly you arrived."

"Not exactly," he answered. "We had been tracking your movements with your mobile phone since we dropped you off at the museum. Then we lost you for a while. We thought you might be in trouble, so we hovered in the area where we had last tracked you. I actually combed through the Tape Nightclub looking for you, and through the Bond Street tube station. Then we picked your signal up again at Stratford Place. We were lurking outside this Kaballah Centre, thinking you were probably here, when I got your call and realized it was coming from the Oriental Club."

"They took me to an art gallery on Hanover Street," I said. "Then we went through an underground tunnel to a tiny room shaped like a beehive, where they beheaded a bull. Then I passed out and woke up in that room you found me in. Why were you tracking me in the first place?"

"Because I didn't feel good leaving you at the Museum with that creep Weir still afoot," he answered. "And I was right to be cautious."

Just then his cell phone rang, and he answered it. I could hear the other side of the conversation bleeding through. It was Agent Paris. He was suggesting that they take me into "the office" (at Thames House, presumably) for questioning, and let Weir sit in a cell all night waiting for interrogation tomorrow.

"Oh no," he said. "Let me take her out for a drink, and I'll talk to her there. She's had a rough day. I'm sure she could use a bite and a quaff." He winked at me.

"You old dog," I heard Paris say. "Just make sure you get some real intelligence from her this time before you let her go."

"Oh don't worry," said Chesterfield. "I won't let her get off easy this time." He chuckled. I didn't. He looked away from me.

"I'll show up tomorrow morning with a full report," he promised his partner.

"So do I have any choice about going out for a drink?" I asked.

"Not unless you'd rather be questioned at an MI5 office building," he replied. "So just let me know: where would you like to be interrogated, my dear?"

"Do you know any pubs in the Temple district?" I asked. "I'd like to see that old Knights Templar church again," I said.

"I know just the place," he replied.

Paris had the company car with him, so we walked out to Oxford Street, and across to Bond Street Station, where we took a ten-minute ride on the Central line to Chancery Lane Station. There, we exited on Holborn, went west to Chancery Lane itself, then followed that road south down to Fleet Street, where our destination was. On the way he pointed out the famous silver vaults, and the former address of Aleister Crowley's London residence (although the actual building he'd lived in was demolished in 2006). This was his way of flirting, as it was when he told me he had thought I was "cute before, wearing the stinky old jeans and a sweater with no make-up."

"But now you look positively radiant," he added.

"Thanks," I replied. "I guess I clean up well, at least when I have a personal stylist and I'm lying unconscious."

"You mean they changed your clothes while you were passed out?" he said. He looked horrified.

"I don't think they violated me," I said. "At least no more than what I've already told you about."

We arrived at Ye Olde Cock Tavern, a pub which had been around since 1549. Samuel Pepys, Charles Dickens, and Alfred Lloyd Tennyson all drank there. After we'd eaten and drunk our fill, Chesterfield said, we could take the back door out the pub and through the enclosed courtyard to see Temple Church just before it closed for the evening.

We ordered beer and "beef burgers," as they call them. Then we stuffed ourselves while I spilled my guts to him about everything that had happened since my adventure began. I told him all about the Mete coffer and Leopold, the alleged lecture I'd been hired to give, the flight delay, Leopold dropping out of contact, and being questioned by him and Paris at Parliament, where I found out the truth about Leopold's identity from him and Agent Paris.

Then I recounted my experience at the museum, where I learned that the coffer was gone, ran into Leopold for reasons unknown, and was chased outside by people I thought worked for Accounts Receivable. Finally, I described the kidnapping, the blindfolded march through the subterranean passage, the bull sacrifice, and the forced divination from the bull liver at Oriental Club. I even mentioned, in passing, their claim that they needed help locating an "evil magician" who intended to destroy existence as we knew it with a ritual to topple the "pillars of Heaven."

"Chicken Littles!" said Chesterfield, amused. "'The sky's falling!' What a bunch of nutters."

He couldn't believe it was that the real Butchers' livery company was involved, especially considering that Leopold had lied about his name, his so-called barony, and his phony seat in the House of Lords. So Agent Chesterfield got out his smartphone to investigate.

"What did you say it was called again?" he asked. "The Worship Society of Butchers? Or the Worshipful Company? Because 'Worshipful Company of Butchers' is the name of the actual livery company."

I dug through the email archives on my own phone.

"Leopold called it 'Society.' He said it several times." I pondered for a moment. "They did actually tell me specifically that they weren't a livery company but a 'different sort of entity.' So I guess I was looking at the Worshipful Company's website all along, thinking it was for Leopold's group. But it looks like the Butcher's Society is just as fake as his supposed peerage."

"Which would explain why they meet at Oriental Club instead of Butcher's Hall," he said. "Because anyone who can meet the dress code and afford the fees can book time there, even if they don't belong to the actual Oriental Club, which you say Weir never specifically told you he was a member of."

"But the butler acted like he hadn't let them through the front door," I said. "So maybe they sneaked in through an underground tunnel. Maybe there's a member of the club who knows a secret way in, and let them through. Something that connects with the tunnels I was inside of. And there must be a much wider entrance to the tunnels somewhere, or else how did they get the bull down there in the first place?"

Chesterfield asked me to bring out my laptop so that he could look at a larger image than his phone screen. After just a few seconds, he let out an "a ha!" and swiveled the screen around to show me something.

"Is this the room where they beheaded the bull?" he asked.

He showed me a report on a building survey from the City of Westminster from 2014. It was commissioned to make sure the new expansions of the Bond Street tube station at nearby Hanover Square didn't interfere with the Stratford House basement. This basement did, as the report showed, jut out significantly from the front of the building, so that it was essentially underneath the middle of Stratford Place, the street out front. Like the rest of the building, the basement dated back to 1774. A photograph included in the report showed that beehive ceiling, which I'll never forget.

"So if there is another intersecting tunnel that leads to 10 Hanover and all the other places you went, it must have been built without city permission sometime after 2014," said Chesterfield. "And somehow the people building the tube tunnels never ran into it either. Unless one of them is in on it. Which is possible."

"Really" I said. "You think there are people building new secret tunnels underneath London even today?"

"Oh, we know there are," he answered, hushing his tone again. "Look, the new boom in both residential and commercial real estate in London is underground. The wealthy are building basements three and four levels down, because square footage is so valuable here. Hundreds of applications are being approved every year. There have got to be some that get built without permission."

Chesterfield rolled his eyes up sucked in his lips, like he was debating whether or not he should tell me something. Then he continued.

"We at MI5 have found several. We've busted some, we're watching others. We think there are hundreds more that we haven't found yet. That is something I should not have told you. But maybe now you can trust me with something you wouldn't have otherwise told me." He looked at me deeply, expectantly.

"I've actually told you everything I know," I replied. "Everything I can think of that you might be interested in."

"Well let's go do something *you're* interested in," he said, standing up. "Let's go look at those dead Templars across the courtyard over there."

We went down the stairs from where we had been sitting and out the pub's backdoor. Then we walked through the enclosed courtyard, past the tomb of the Irish writer Oliver Goldsmith (which, we were warned by the bartender, was haunted), and through the backdoor of the medieval Temple Church, built by and for the Knights Templar.

I hadn't been there on my first visit to London. This was my first time seeing it. But I had seen many pictures of the old tombs of the Templars recessed in the floor there. Each tomb was decorated with a life-sized relief on top depicting the deceased in full armor, usually with a dog at his feet. I didn't have any revelations until Chesterfield spoke up. "It's funny how their legs are all crossed isn't it?" he said. I looked at the Templar effigies. Indeed, the crossed legs were very peculiar.

"And they all look like they're in pain. Almost like somebody just kicked them in the balls. Or chopped their dicks off with a sword. Ha ha!"

He spoke too loudly. The two people who were sitting there in the pews quietly praying looked up.

"Sorry!" he said nervously. But it got me thinking. "You know, the Roman cult of the goddess Cybele had a fully castrated priesthood. They called them the Galli. They would become possessed by the goddess during their festivals. Then they would go crazy and cut off their own genitals in a frenzy, in honor of Attis, Cybele's consort, who had done the same thing. And Attis was often depicted with his legs cross, just like these Templars."

"So the priests castrated themselves to be like him, because they thought that's what their goddess wanted?" Chesterfield said.

"Yep," I replied. "That was how they were initiated. A couple of days later, they would put the severed sex organs in a sacred coffer and parade them around in a celebratory procession. They actually had all these festivals in late March, around the Spring Equinox, right about now. The castration rite was called the Day of Blood. That was on March 24."

"Really," said Chesterfield. He was going pale. "Yeah, I said. Nobody ever points out that this was the day that men in the Heaven's Gate cult castrated themselves before they committed suicide. They believed that they were going to be taken up into a portal that they thought was riding past Earth with the Hale Bopp comet that night. They thought they needed to be castrated to get in. They wanted to be the "eunuchs of Heaven" that the Bible talks about. Some people think that comet was actually Nibiru, also called Planet X, which the Babylonians identified with the time of the Spring Equinox."

"My little joke brought all that to mind, did it?" said Chesterfield, in a very un-joking manner.

"Well I was thinking about the Mete coffer. The British Museum labeled the picture on the lid as being "Cybele." And Hammer-Purgstall said that it looked like her, except she's got a beard, and she was labeled Mete. He was sure that she was the same figure as the 'Baphomet' demon that the Templars supposedly worshiped in their secret ceremonies."

Chesterfield nodded. I continued.

"He also said that the Templars were covertly practicing Ophite Gnosticism. And the Ophites were said to have incorporated the Cybele cult into their syncretistic system. Now here we have the Templar knights, depicted on their tombstones with their legs crossed as though they've been injured in the genital region. It's just like the Fisher King in the Grail stories, which the Templars were associated with. It's all starting to add up. Look!"

I typed a few words into my phone, and brought up Eliphas Levi's depiction of the Templar demon Baphomet.

"Look," I said again. "This is Baphomet. This is the way the occultist Eliphas Levi depicted him. I'm just now realizing why he showed the demon with a caduceus coming out of his crotch instead of a penis, even though he said it was a hermaphrodite. Because it was actually a castrated hermaphrodite, just like Catullus said Cybele was originally."

I guess I didn't care if Chesterfield was able to follow my logic. I was mainly saying it out loud for my own benefit, to aid my thoughts. By this time, the two people trying to pray peacefully in this house of God had gotten up and left in disgust. Chesterfield looked at me directly with a pained expression and stood silently for a moment. At last he spoke.

"Pamela, I think there is something that you need to see. Let's go back to the tavern so we can use your laptop there. You'll need a drink after you see it."

Chapter 12: Easter Sunday April Fool

> April is the cruelest month.
>
> – T.S. Eliot, *The Wasteland*

We walked back into the pub and up the stairs to the third floor. We picked a table next to a window that gave us a view of the former location of the Bank of England, now moved to Threadneedle Street near Walbrook. This same building, on the western side of the corner of Chancery Lane and Fleet Street, had been, before that, home to the very pub we were standing in at one point. However, the original pub burned down in a fire, as we learned from an informative plaque mounted on the wall near our table.

I plugged my computer in and started it up while Chesterfield went and got us a couple of double-shot whiskeys with beer chasers. Then we both sat with our backs to the window and the computer screen on the table in front of us. That way, we figured, we could make sure nobody walked in on us and saw what was on the computer screen. We both downed about half of our whiskeys. Then Chesterfield took a small black thumb drive out of his pocket and held it up in front of me.

"This file was sent to MI5 through our anonymous tip page. It was encrypted into a video of a cat playing with a ball of yarn, and wrapped with a malignant virus which we were able to neutralize. Then we decrypted the video, which I'm about to show you. Don't tell anyone I showed you, or I will lose my job and go to prison."

I nodded. He plugged the drive into my computer. "Play it from the drive. Don't copy it," he insisted. *Obviously*, I thought to myself.

I opened the drive, and then the file, which was named "easter.sunday.april.fools.mov." Chesterfield grabbed my hand and clasped tightly as he looked at the screen in absolute dread.

The video—or rather, the video of the "film" (for it was, it appeared to me, shot on 35 mm black and white celluloid)—started with a sequence of three old-fashioned title pages of the type once used for dialogue on silent films. They said:

> In an effort to birth a grand new cultus, 'the synthesis of all persecuted beliefs'. . . .
>
> . . . the Grand Chaplain of the Temple Militia remarried Our Father to the Great Mother. . . .
>
> Together they engendered a child destined to upset the order of the Aeons.
>
> The son became the Sun, the Sun became Our Father. Then he married the Great Mother again.

The next scenes are hard to describe, because they are so awful. I shall do so matter-of-factly, because that's all I can do.

First, we saw a group of boys, ages spanning from ten to twelve. They were all wearing suits and ties and smoking cigarettes on some steps outside. The shot widened to show the now-familiar statue of Anteros at Piccadilly Circus, with the sign for the Eros Cinema visible in the background. Then there was another title page.

> Enticed by the promised revelation of love's mysteries, the Easter Fool stumbles down the rabbit hole into the lair of counter-love.

In the next shot, framed up on the boys again, an adult white male hand emerged from screen left holding a copy of *Playboy Magazine*. The cover featured the back of the head of a white rabbit who was watching a woman in a blue dress smiling in front of a film camera. When the kids saw the magazine, their faces lit up as they grabbed at it excitedly. The one on the left got his hands on it first. Then the adult hand holding it started moving over to the right, with the child following along. At that point, the film abruptly cut to the next title page, which said:

> The fish has been caught, and is dragged down to Hades.

This cut to a shot of a bust of the Roman god Serapis, a.k.a. Hades, Dispater or Pluto, with his traditional *modius* (a grain- measuring basket) on top of his head. This was set against a dark background. Next, there was a wider shot of the head, showing that it was sitting on top of a crumbling column. This was followed by a shot with an even broader frame, revealing that the column was part of the decayed foundation of an ancient rectangular building now in ruins.

There were never more than two or three stones stacked up in any one place, so no part of it was more than three feet high. But it looked like it was set up inside of larger, more modern windowless room, with a metal-plated light switch visible on the wall. Beneath the dilapidated stones one could see, in places, a tiled checkerboard floor.

Laying down on his back across a row of these ancient blocks was the same boy lured by the magazine in the previous scene. He was now naked, blindfolded, and screaming hysterically. Two figures in hooded black robes with black bird masks were holding him by the hands and feet as he flailed.

The camera then zoomed in to focus just on them. Next, a figure in a leather veil and apron, just like the two men I had seen in the basement of Stratford House, stepped into the scene. Meanwhile, a third figure, again wearing a black bird mask, held a stone bowl beneath the boy's crotch and used a white-gloved hand to hold the genitals up about a finger's width.

The butcher then brandished a pair of cleavers. The camera zoomed in to the child's sex organs, which were snipped off. Huge amounts of blood, as well as the parts themselves, were collected in the bowl before the camera finally cut away from the gaping wound and thrashing limbs to a black screen.

At this point, Chesterfield paused the video as I ran to the bathroom to vomit. I wretched and wretched until nothing but bile was coming up. Thankfully, nobody else was using the other stalls, and the facilities were quite tidy. There's nothing worse than puking in a dirty public toilet.

Once again, I thanked the Lord for small favors. Something about being on my knees in front of the "throne" made me want to pray. I noticed that I had a tendency to do this, and this only, as my expression of religion.

Why didn't I thank God when I survived the kidnapping and the bull sacrifice? I wondered. *And why didn't I pray for my own safety throughout the entire event, or before? Why don't I pray for God to get me out of this mess right now?*

And there it was. I stood there in front of the bathroom mirror wondering why I wasn't taking a particular course of action.

It hardly even amounts to action in the physical sense, I thought. *Unless you actually choose to kneel down while praying, or to speak your prayer out loud, which most people don't even do these days.*

Not only that, I thought. *A real religious person would have prayed for others too. Prayed for the boy in the film, and others who were victimized like him. Prayed that the perpetrators be brought to justice. Maybe they would even pray that the guilty ones come to realize their evil and ask for forgiveness before it was too late.*

But I just stood there staring at myself, trying to use my thumb to wipe away the eye liner that had smeared due to the perspiration that came with vomiting.

If you think about it though, I could have been more cowardly. Not once did I think about running away from this entire sordid affair. I was under no obligation to continue my involvement. I could have gone straight to the airport and insisted they move up my departure date, since I still had the tickets for the flight home. Instead, I returned to the table and sat back down next to Agent Chesterfield. I asked him if there was more on the video.

"Sadly, yes," he answered.

I asked him if I really needed to see it. He said it "might be helpful." So I agreed. I took a few more minutes to finish my whiskey and beer. Then we continued.

The next scene showed the bowl with the gore in it being placed by gloved hands with robed arms upon an altar that was shown sitting among the same ruins. There were two other bowls that were similar, but empty, sitting on top of the altar as well. The next shot showed the sides of the altar. One featured a tree from which hung two flutes and a *tympanum* — the ceremonial hand drum used in the rites of Cybele — was hung, along with two pipes.

The relief on the other side of the altar showed two of her *Galli* priests, wearing their traditional Phrygian hats. They were carrying a coffer on poles mounted on their shoulders, just like the Ark of the Covenant was depicted as being carried. On top of the box was the Hetoimasiac throne of the goddess, depicted in aniconic form with a *cista* — a ritual basket — placed as a stand-in for the invisible goddess.

I instantly recognized this as a genuine altar of Cybele that once belonged to a wealthy gentleman in London at the turn of the twentieth century, whereabouts now unknown. I had read about it recently in the JSTOR archives while doing research for an article I had published in an anthropology journal. I knew there was another side to it, not shown in the film, which depicted the goddess standing with a bowl in her hand while two *Galli* stood at either side of her. Both were shown crossing their legs uncomfortably, just like the Templar effigies on the graves at Temple Church.

Next, the film showed the gloved hands straining the organs out of the blood in the bowl with a slotted ladle. They were then placed in two other bowls: the penis in one, the testicles in the other. The hands then lifted each bowl, one at a time, while another pair of gloved hands appeared from off screen and placed a small, form-fitting basket beneath each one. Following this, the baskets, with the bowls still inside, were covered with a wicker lid so that each one now resembled the basketed *cista* that were depicted on top of the throne shown in relief on the side of the altar.

After that, the second set of hands gave the first pair an ancient-looking cylindrical metal casket, about four inches tall and two inches in circumference. It was decorated with dilapidated scenes of men fighting with various wild animals. It was carried by a metal chain that it hung from.

The first pair of hands took off the top of the casket, which remained hanging from the chain. They then removed a small ball made of metal wire, dripping wet, which hung on a chain of its own and contained a dark substance. I figured it was a strainer containing herbs of some sort. The hands poured liquid that looked like murky water from the casket into the bowl with the blood while the second set of hands held the basket lid up.

Then a more modern-looking metal bucket with a handle was given to the first pair of hands by the second pair. It contained a clear, thick, slimy substance that appeared to be fat, which was poured into the bowl with the blood. Then a large metal spoon came into the shot from screen right, and was used to stir the contents of the bowl.

Following this, the film cut to another shot. The camera was pointing down at the bowl in the basket, with the lid off and the spoon still in it, which now appeared to be sitting on one of the ruined walls. Then, three erect and circumcised adult white penises appeared from off screen. Three large white male hands, ungloved, were seen masturbating them. After almost a minute, all three penises had ejaculated into the bowl, one right after the other, with only a few seconds in-between each climax. The penises then left the screen. Gloved hands appeared again to stir the mixture with the spoon and place the basket lid back on.

The subsequent shot showed what was unmistakably the Mete coffer, sitting there on the antique stone bricks stacked next to the altar. The lid with the picture of Mete was removed by one set of gloved hands, and the three baskets were placed inside by another pair. The lid of the coffer was carefully replaced. Then came a title page which read:

> We process in the patterns [sic] of the Sun -runner.

In the next shot, four figures in dark robes with hoods and black bird masks were seen circumambulating an old building with a gurney mounted on their backs and the coffer riding on top. In front of them was another hooded figure, shorter than the others, with a white veil draped over his or her face, and held on by an attached headband. This person was holding a small metal aspergillum and was using it to spray lustrations onto the building as they walked around it. Then we were given a wide shot, and we could see the building they were walking around, topped with a large dome. I thought it was most likely St. Paul's Cathedral there in London. They walked around it seven times.

Then the scene changed, and we saw them walking along a street in London, next to a building with a tiny metal grate embedded in its corner. The camera focused on the grate as the people with the coffer walked past. The short veiled person stayed behind and shook the aspergillum at the grate, behind which we could see a small, roughly-hewn, somewhat square white stone, about half a foot wide and a few inches tall.

Then the shot changed to show the group marching along the Thames. They were walking next to a building positioned right on the shore of the river with two wooden ramps leading out of a large opening on the side facing the water. This led down to a couple of small boats that were docked right next to it. The shot was head-on as the entourage walked forward.

This cut quickly to a shot inside one of the boats. The coffer could be seen sitting in the foreground without the gurney or its holders. It was sitting on top of one end of a mid-tone-colored blanket folded in half. A gloved hand on a robed arm folded the other end of the blanket over the coffer.

Next, the camera raised up. All we could see above the sides of the boat was sky, but we could tell when the boat started moving from the change in the clouds. Then we saw it turn left and go underneath something. Suddenly everything went dark. Then there was another title page. It said:

Sacrifice to the guardians of the tower.

In the next shot, a metal cage with several black crow- like birds was shown. Another gloved hand reached for the lock and opened the cage. Then one of the basketed *cista* was shown sitting on grass in front of a park bench.

The shot widened, and we saw the birds standing in the surrounding grass, pecking at the inside of the basket. Then it was opened, and the contents—bloody bits of flesh (presumably the sacrificed testicles)—were emptied out onto the grass. All of the birds immediately converged upon them and began eating them.

As the birds walked away with the meat in their beaks, a gloved hand came onscreen holding a shovel with a handle about three feet long. It was pushed into the dirt beneath the grass. Then the shot widened to show a man (judging by the shoes) in a black robe with a sun face mask pressing down the shovel with his foot to insert it deeper.

Next we were shown a stone effigy of a tomb with the stone rolled out, standing empty. We could tell it was an effigy when the camera panned up quickly to show a cross mounted above. There was a dove winging its way down to the bottom of the cross, and two angels kneeling in prayer on either side of it.

Then the camera panned down and showed a close -up of the tombstone. On it were etched the words "Why seek ye the living among the dead?" Then the thumb of a wrinkled white male hand came forward from behind the camera and covered up the word "Why."

In the following shot, a young, barely -pubescent girl wearing an Easter dress and bonnet was shown holding hands with a finely-dressed man and woman whose faces were not shown. The first shot showed mostly just her.

In the second, we saw the group from behind. They appeared to be at a church, as pews and a statue of the Virgin could be seen in the background of the second shot.

The girl looked very sad. Quite inappropriately, she seemed to be wearing make-up on her face. She had eyeliner, eye shadow, and lipstick on. Her face was made pale with cake foundation. After this shot, another title page was shown, which said:

The Sacred Marriage of the Stone and the Bosse.

The next image was filmed looking through the front windshield of a car driving through a gateway underneath a medieval-looking archway. It was very tall, with one large arch in the middle, through which the car drove. Then there were two more narrow openings on either side, only wide enough for foot traffic, or perhaps a bicycle.

There was a structure on top almost as tall as the arch itself. It featured two statues, each set inside of a niche, and between them a stained-glass window. Extending outward on either side were tall hedges, and behind these, an even taller black metal fence. The two smaller archways were barred by metal gates of the same style, but the gate for the large one in the middle was set open.

It was raining, and the wipers were on as the car went under the arch. Beyond was a driveway lined with trees. We saw the car go down the driveway to a very large red-bricked manor house.

This cut to the interior of a decayed medieval-looking stone room with a small round window showing only darkness beyond. Two hooded people, this time wearing lion masks, stood on either side of the window holding torches, which appeared to be providing the light. The camera pointed down. There, the same girl from the scene before was now shown standing in a white robe, shivering and crying. Eyeliner streamed down her face while two people with robes and bird masks held her by the arms.

Another man then stepped into the picture, also wearing a dark robe, but with a sun mask. He was holding a staff that ended in the shape of a small erect phallus. The staff was dark, but the phallus was light-colored. The girl was forced by the people in the bird masks to bend down on one knee before the man in the sun mask, and to hold her hands in front of her in an attitude of prayer. The people in the bird masks demonstrated to her how she was to hold her hands. Then afterwards she sat there pleading and sobbing for a few seconds, another title page came up.

> See the Virgin genuflect to Our Father.

We then were shown a close-up of the girl's face as the sun-man put the phallus-wand directly up to her lips. She turned away in disgust. I noticed that it looked almost as though it were covered with actual human skin, and I wondered if it was.

Next, we saw the phallus-wand's tip submerged into one of the basketed *cista*, shown sitting on the floor. The wand was used to stir the mixture of blood, fat and herbs, which now looked quite congealed. The natural lubricant caused the dildo to glisten in the torchlight. Following that, there was a shot from the side of the girl lying on her stomach on a blanket on the ground with the top of her head butted up against a roughly-hewn, vaguely square-shaped stone.

The poor girl screamed and balled her hands up into tight fists as the man in the sun mask knelt behind her. He inserted the wand into her rectum, much to her extreme agony, pushing and pulling it several times. Her pain then seemed to increase immensely when he mounted her and replaced the wand with his own swollen member. As she screamed, we saw the girl's head repeatedly bang up against the stone which, I noticed, resembled the one seen earlier in the film sitting behind a grate in the corner of a building. Then came another title page:

> "The sacred womb is seeded with the ancient rite.
> Afterwards, an Easter egg is laid upon the chamber floor."

The last shot was horrifying and disgusting beyond measure. While I regret to have to disturb you further, dear reader, these things must be said. What we saw was a tight shot of a string of beads covered in dark slime being pulled by an off-screen gloved hand from a swollen, prolapsed and distended anus. The beads were white and carved from either stone, ivory, or some form of bone.

Between each set of ten round beads (yes, I counted), there was a bead carved into the shape of either a hand or a foot, for a total of four. At the end of the string there was one made to look like a Janus head, with the face of Jesus on one side, and the face of a skull on the other. After this came out, a large black mass which I presumed to be bloody stool began to emerge amid profuse bleeding. But before it took any discernible shape, the film mercifully ended.

When the final, awful shot at last faded to black, I was in shock. I was also flushed and sweating heavily as another wave of nausea overtook me. I went to the bathroom to empty my stomach again.

Chapter 13: Raven Conspiracy

> The weeping child could not be heard,
> The weeping parents wept in vain;
> They stripp'd him to his little shirt,
> And bound him in an iron chain;
>
> And burn'd him in a holy place,
> Where many had been burn'd before:
> The weeping parents wept in vain.
> Are such things done on Albion's shore?
>
> — William Blake, "A Little Boy Lost" from *Songs of Experience*

After a few minutes I returned to the table to join Chesterfield, who was sitting there looking sad and sick.

"So what have you figured out so far about it?" I asked

"Well, several things," he answered. He appeared to perk up at the thought of doing something practical to solve the problem. He took a fancy red ceramic pen and a small notepad with a black leather cover out of his jacket pocket. Then he opened the notebook and used the pen to enumerate items on a list he had made.

"First, we think it was shot in 1950s. That's what we presume from the 'Teddy boy' style of dress worn by the kids in the opening scene. The *Playboy Magazine* is from March 1956. That's also the last year that Easter fell on April first, which will happen again this year, in three days."

"So that's the meaning of the reference to Easter and the 'April fool?'"

"Yes," he said. "Unless you can add some occult wisdom about the significance too."

I thought about it. "The only thing I can think of to add right now is that the New Year used to be celebrated on March 25th in medieval Europe, around the Spring Equinox."

"Ah yes, the Feast of the Annunciation, when Mary was impregnated by God. Or 'Lady Day,' as we call it in the Church of England," said Chesterfield. I continued.

"Yes, and it was part of a week-long festival that would end on April first. So when the New Year began to be celebrated on the first of January, those who still clung to the old dates for the holiday were called 'April fools.'"

"Hmm. So April Fool's Day is part of a festival connected to the old New Year's Day, which just so happens to come one day after that "Day of Blood" for the goddess Cybele that you told me about, where they would castrate the priests."

"Yes," I said. "In imitation of what Cybele did to her own son Attis. She forced him to be her lover. Then when he predictably fell in love with a younger woman, she got mad and castrated him while he was tied to a tree, so that he bled out and died. But then she felt guilty afterwards and decided to resurrect him. That's why the resurrection of Attis was celebrated the next day, March 25, by the eunuch priests of the Cybele cult."

"On Lady Day?" he asked, incredulous.

"Indeed," I replied. "And this of course is all connected to the symbolism of Easter, obviously. Death and resurrection of the sun god. Attis often had a crown of sun rays, just like Christ has a sun halo."

Chesterfield raised his eyebrows, and then opened his notebook again.

"We've also figured out several of the locations shown in film. Now here's where it gets really disturbing."

"How could it be any more disturbing than it already is?" I asked.

"When you realize where these places are and who would have had access to them, you will see what I mean. First, there's that building they were walking around. That's St. Paul's Cathedral."

"I thought as much," I said. "I saw the dome."

"It's always been open to the public, yes," said Chesterfield. "But why did they feel so comfortable walking around dressed up in those bizarre costumes with a box containing the severed genitals of a kidnapped boy? It seemed like they were out early in the morning."

"Yeah, and the box they were carrying was the Mete coffer I was telling you about," I added. "The one that Leopold said had been stolen from the museum." At this, Chesterfield was very surprised.

"So you mean they borrowed it back in 1956, then put it back, and someone stole it again this year, right before the next April Fool's Easter?" he suggested.

"It appears that way," I said. "Also, I'm pretty sure the altar they used is a real ancient Roman Cybele altar. Someone wrote about it in this old antiquarian journal." I opened up the PDF that I had downloaded from JSTOR on my laptop, and showed him that the altar had once been owned by a Mr. G.A. Warren of Streatham Hill, London, in 1892, though nobody was sure where it came from or where it went to after that. The pictures of the item matched up perfectly with what we had seen in the film.

"So we're dealing with a network of ancient artifact collectors, thieves and borrowers that has been operating in London in continuity for at least 62 years, possibly much longer," he said. "And they've been using these artifacts in rituals where children are raped, tortured and mutilated. Good God." He shook his head. Then he continued.

"The archway that the car is seen driving through–that's Temple Bar itself."

I gasped. *The former entryway to the old City of London, right here in the Temple district!* I thought.

"Isn't that right in this neighborhood, next to Temple Church?" I asked.

"It used to be near here," said Chesterfield. "But in 1880 it was sold to Henry Meux, a brewer, who brought it out to his mansion in Hertfordshire, a place called Theobald Park."

He showed me a website with recent pictures of the interior of the building.

"That's where they raped the girl!" I exclaimed, shocked. It was clearly the same place, with the same little round window and peeling stone walls.

"Right," said Chesterfield. "He bought it on the advice of his wife, Valerie Meux, who was a famous socialite and antiquities collector. There's actually a little chamber within the upper part of the archway, and they say Lady Meux used to have dinner parties there with King Edward VII and Winston Churchill." He showed me the Wikipedia page, which confirmed these statements.

"Wow," I said. "She must have been really important."

"Strangely, yes," he answered. "When she died, widowed and childless, she left Theobald Park, and indeed her entire estate, to a young man in the Royal Navy whom she'd just met, named Hedworth Lambdon. He had to change his last name to Meux to satisfy the terms of the will. Later the property became a secondary school, which it would have still been at the time this film was shot. Now it's a De Vere hotel."

"So someone who worked at the school must have been involved," I said.

"It seems that way," he agreed.

"What about the ruins where the boy was castrated?" I asked.

"Don't know," he said. "We're still working on that."

"Then what about facial recognition of the kids in the film?" I said. He shook his head.

"They don't match up with any face of any child reported missing from that time period," he replied. "Nor do they match with any face of any child that has yet been uploaded to the internet anywhere in the world. So we have a team of people scanning the yearbooks from all the surrounding schools for the era in question, hoping to find a match. And if we had photos of adults to compare them to, our computers could tell us whether or not they are the same people, within an infinitesimally small margin of error. But we would need at least a clue as to where to look."

"So you think the kids might have survived after this?" I asked.

"I don't know, I hope," he replied. "But from what you told me, it sounds like at least the castration victim may be dead. Bled out like Attis, as you say. Plus that's how these kid sex crimes usually end."

"Yeah, but in her cult they survived to become her priests. And it was voluntary, or so they say."

"What about the stone behind the metal grate in the side of the building?" I asked. "The one that they were sprinkling with holy water?"

"That's the London Stone," said Chesterfield. "It's actually one of our most important historic relics, but it's been largely forgotten. It used to be the center-point from which everything else in the city was measured. Until recently, it was actually stored in the corner of a building on Cannon Street, just as you saw. Now it's in the Museum of London. Nobody ever talks about it. But some people think it's the stone that Arthur pulled the Excalibur sword from."

"Oh yes, I've heard of this," I said. "It *is* amazing how little it's talked about. But John Dee, the court astrologer for Queen Elizabeth I, believed that it had magical powers. He even moved to Cannon Street to be near it." Chesterfield laughed.

"I didn't know that. But I *did* know about Dee. He was much more than a court astrologer. He was the first 007. He did all sorts of shady special ops on Her Majesty's Secret Service. The folks at SIS consider him a godfather of sorts."

This was amazing to hear from a person in Chesterfield's position.

"I've heard that before," I said. "But I wasn't sure if I should take the claim seriously. Now I *have* to believe it."

I looked up the London Stone on Wikipedia to refresh my memory. I found a picture of it sitting behind the grating in the recess that used to house it.

Then I did a Google search, and landed on a poem in Middle English from 1521 called "The Marriage of London Stone and the Boss of Billingsgate." This was the same phrase used on one of the title pages in the horrible film!

"Uh, Chesterfield, look at this," I said.

"I know," he replied. "I've seen it. We found it when we analyzed the film. But I don't fully understand the significance of the poem, or why its title was used in the film. However, the building next to the River Thames with the boats docked next to it was Billingsgate, the fish market. *Old* Billingsgate, before they moved it to Canary Wharf on the Isle of Dogs."

I looked up "Bosse of Billingsgate" next, and landed on a sample on Google Play Books from a recent work called *The Secret Lore of London* by Iain Sinclair. There, it was explained that the "Bosse" was actually a phallus which in pre- Christian days had been venerated as a form of the "Great Mother" goddess Britomart, after whom Britain was named.

Another Great Mother, just like Cybele, I thought to myself. *And only a hermaphrodite goddess like Cybele could be represented with a phallus.*

I read on. I learned that until the seventeenth century the Bosse had stood there at the gate of Belin (now Billingsgate), believed to provide protection. It was named after Belinus, who, as I recalled, was an ancient king of the Britons, as well as a Celtic sun god, thought by many to equate with the Babylonian Baal. Orientalist L.A. Waddell had argued in his book *The British Edda* from 1930 that there was a single person behind the myths of all three figures.

Baal, in turn, was analogous to Attis. Like Attis, Baal was a victim who played essentially the same role with the goddess Inanna (a.k.a. Ishtar) that Attis did in the Cybele cult. The anniversary of her murder of her own son/ husband, for the exact same reason that Cybele killed Attis (erotic jealousy), was observed as a holiday of morning by her worshippers, as it was with Cybele's. Likewise, Baal's resurrection was celebrated joyously a few days afterwards. This took place during the Spring Equinox, which was also their New Year's Day, morphing eventually into the European holiday of Easter, which was named after Ishtar/ Inanna.

There in Mesopotamia, her priests were called the *Gallu*, almost the exact same word as the title of Cybele's priests, the *Galli*. It's derived from the Sumerian word "gal," meaning "cup" or "vagina." The *Gallu*, just like the *Galli*, were also castrated and dressed as women. In both cults, the priests were actually considered women from this point on, and addressed as such.

The Babylonian equinox rites also included the sacrifice of the Celestial Bull, Gugalanna, just like Cybele was honored with the *taurobolium*, a bull sacrifice in which her priests were completely drenched in the blood of the victim. This was performed in Cybele's specially-outfitted slaughterhouse temples, known as *metroons*, after her title "Magna Mater" ("Great Mother").

Could this 'metroon' be what that one guy at the Butchers meeting meant when I thought I heard him say the words 'Meth room'? I wondered.

Then I remembered that a couple of years ago, Oxford University had created a 2/3 scale copy of the arch from the Temple of Baal in Palmyra, Syria after ISIS had destroyed the original, and had the replica erected in Trafalgar Square in London during the Autumnal Equinox of 2016. I recalled that the original had been blown up right after the Spring Equinox of that same year, which I pointed out during an interview on a paranormal radio talk show, *Ground Zero with Clyde Lewis.*

At the time, Mr. Lewis and I had talked about the fact that the Islamic State's original name, which the Western media still insisted on using, was identical to that of Isis, the Egyptian word for the goddess same goddess as Inanna and Ishtar. Amazingly, while I was sitting there at the pub in England reading more about Isis, I stumbled upon information that the portion of the River Thames that flows through Oxford is actually called "the Isis." Thus one of the university's rowing teams has the same name as the Egyptian goddess, and the Islamic State.

This got me thinking about the origin of the name "Thames," so I looked that up too. There are theories circulating that it might have come from any of a number of words from various languages that all denote the concept of darkness. But nobody's certain.

As for the River Isis, some old maps have the entire river labeled with that name. A few historians have suggested that it was just a truncation of the Latin name for the river, "Tamesis." But then there were people saying that there was a temple of Isis in roman London located on the banks of the river near the present-day on ramp to London Bridge.

So then it makes sense for the river to be named after her, I thought.

Then I remembered Tammuz, another Semitic name (derived from the Sumerian "Dumuzid") for the figure of Baal, the sacrificed son of Inanna/Ishtar.

Is that the possible origin of 'Thames'? I wondered. *If the river from its source to Dorchester was once called 'Isis' after the Great Mother, maybe the river from there to its mouth was named after her castrated zombie son and consort.* It seemed like a reasonable thesis, and when I Googled it in the form of a question, I found the writings of many who agreed with me.

My head was reeling with all these connections. Then I read more about the Bosse of Billingsgate in the "Secret London" book. It said:

The local porters would insist on passers-by kissing the Bosse or else they picked them up and bumped them on the seat against the stone.

I figured this was a sanitized version.

In other words, anal rape with the sacred dildo would at least be simulated, I thought. *Or worse, not simulated.*

I showed my findings to Chesterfield. Now we understood, at least in part, the symbolism of the anal rape "marriage" ceremony we had witnessed.

"I think that the London Stone was used in the rape scene," I said. "It was the square rock that they kept knocking her head against."

"I know," said Chesterfield.

"So that means they somehow had access to it," I noted.

"Yes," he replied curtly. I suppose I was stating the obvious.

"Also, the goddess Cybele was symbolized by a stone," I added. "She was worshiped in the form of a black meteorite in Rome. I've even seen claims that the Kaaba stone in Mecca is actually the Cybele stone."

Chesterfield was silent. His arms were folded in front of him. He was angry and depressed. I reviewed the scenes in my mind, trying not to dwell on the suffering I had witnessed. Instead I focused only on the objects, the places, and the symbols involved. Then I remembered what became of the boy's testicles in the film.

"What about the birds in the cages?" I said. "The ones that were fed with the … meat?"

"Yes, that might be the most disturbing, really. Those are the famous ravens of the Tower of London."

"What are those?" I asked.

"You don't know?" he said. "Nine ravens are always kept at the Tower of London. It's been going on for hundreds of years. There's a legend that if there aren't at least six ravens on site at any given moment, the kingdom will fall. You haven't heard this before?"

"No," I answered.

"Well the thing is, those birds are guarded at all times. It's a matter of national defense. The only way anybody could get access to them would be if the Raven-Master allowed it."

I Googled this term and, sure enough, found a video of the current Raven-Master, dressed like the guy on the Beefeater vodka bottle. He was feeding nine birds with clipped wings in the very same park where we had watched their predecessors eating what might have been the raw testicles of a young boy.

"So it's looking like a rather large conspiracy then," I said.

"Is that a joke?" said Chesterfield. "I'm really not in the mood for jokes right now."

"It's just a term for a criminal collusion," I said. "By definition that's a conspiracy, even if it doesn't involve people in the government, which this clearly does." I was so sick of the way in which intelligence agencies use the term "conspiracy theory" (a phrase actually invented by the CIA for this very purpose). They made it a term of derision that could be used to belittle anyone who tries to figure out what they and their deep state accomplices are up to.

"Oh," said Chesterfield, still looking dour. "I thought you were referring to the fact that a group of ravens is called a 'conspiracy.' Like a 'murder of crows.'"

"They are?" I thought that was hilarious, yet I dared not laugh. "But aren't ravens the same as crows?"

"They're in the same family," he replied gloomily.

"So where's the estate where the Temple Bar was moved to?" I asked.

"It's a bit far out," he answered. "But anyway, it's not there anymore. It was moved back to the City of London a few years ago."

"Really?" I said. "Where is it now?"

"Oh, it's over in Paternoster Square now, in front of St. Paul's," said an older brunette woman standing in front of our table. She was wearing a white apron over a pink dress with a name tag that said "Mary." She worked for the pub.

Chesterfield and I both jumped in our seats. We hadn't realized that anyone was standing there.

"Sorry to startle you," she said. "I just wanted to let you know that we're closing the kitchen for the night. But we still have two hours 'til last call."

"That's alright," said Chesterfield. "I think we're done drinking here anyway, and I'm certain we won't be hungry for awhile." He started shutting down my computer.

"They just moved the Temple of Mithras too," Mary said. "It's going to be right down the street from St. Paul's. It's opening tomorrow."

"Excuse me, did you just say 'the Temple of Mithras'?'" I asked.

"Yep," she said. "It used to be out there at Temple Court, on Queen Victoria Street. But then someone bought it, dug it up, and moved it to the new plaza they're building on Walbrook, next to the Mansion House."

"You mean the Mansion House where the Lord Mayor lives?" asked Chesterfield.

"The very same," said the waitress.

Mary left and we began to pack up our things. I reminded Chesterfield that the word 'Meth room,' had been used in the divination meeting at Oriental Club.

"Maybe he was saying *mithraeum*, I suggested. "That's the Latin word for a temple of Mithras. I didn't even know London had a Mithras temple, or else I might have thought about that. But it's also strange that *mithraeum* is so similar to *metroon*, the name for a Cybele temple. I wonder if there's a connection."

Then as I turned around to pick up my coat, I noticed a person watching me in the window of the building directly across the street — *not* the former Bank of England building, but another one to the east of it on the opposite side of the corner of Chancery Lane and Fleet. As soon as I caught sight of the figure, it disappeared.

The room across the street was too dark for me to see any details. I wondered how long he or she had been watching us, as well as how clearly the details of my computer screen might have been from that view, since our table was well-lit. This remained on my mind as we exited the tavern and walked out into the brisk night air.

Chapter 14: Rerouting...

> Many roads Thou hast fashioned: all of them lead to the Light.
>
> – Rudyard Kipling, "The Song of Mithras" from *Puck of Pook's Hill*

I wasn't sure what Chesterfield had in mind for me next. But I intended to tell him that I was too physically exhausted to continue for the night. He seemed annoyed about something. I couldn't help worrying that it wasn't just the disturbing investigation, but actually me that was pissing him off. I was just about to open my mouth about this when a familiar black Vauxhall Astra Elite pulled up right in front of us. The tinted driver's side window rolled down.

"Car service!" Agent Paris called out to us.

"Where did he come from?" I asked Chesterfield. "He called while you were in the toilets," Chesterfield replied. "He offered to pick us up. But you're welcome to walk back to the tube station by yourself if you want. As for me, I'm freezing my arse off!" He rushed over to back car door and opened it, then stepped aside.

"Are you coming?" he asked. I got in. This time, he closed the door and then got into the front passenger seat instead of sitting next to me.

"Thanks for the ride, Parvin," he told his partner.

"Parvin? Is that your first name?" I asked Agent Paris. "I know a lady at the British Museum with almost the same name."

"It's a common Persian name for both men and women, with several variants," he answered. "It's Farsi for the Pleaides."

"Oh," I said. "That's interesting. Say, would you mind dropping me off at the Regent Palace?" Chesterfield turned around and stared at me incredulously.

"You seriously want to go back to the Regent Palace?" he said. "That place is a dump! And the Worshipful Butchers know your room number. It's not safe!"

"Well, I don't have anywhere else to sleep," I said. And I can't stay awake much longer." I would have gleefully laid down on just about any horizontal surface right then.

"Chesterfield and I were wondering if you'd like to have a slumber party at his place tonight," said Paris. The car fell absolutely silent. I was sure there was a punchline coming. After an awkward minute, I felt I had to say something.

"Well, I'm not normally in the habit of having slumber parties with groups of men that I've just met." I set it up and waited for the punchline. *Knock knock, who's there?* Finally, Chesterfield responded.

"And we *are normally* in the habit of having people we want to interrogate arrested, then held without formal charges for as long as legally possible. But we thought we'd get more cooperation from you if we approached it in a more friendly manner. Besides, aren't you curious? Don't you want to help with the investigation, to see where it leads? It's directly related to your Templar research, isn't it? And haven't we already figured out so many amazing things together?" He turned around to face the front, but Paris continued with the argument.

"We need your help solving this case, Pamela. There are sensitive details that we can't make public which are so bizarre and arcane that only an expert like you could us help analyze them. And really, there aren't any other experts like you — not in your particular subjects."

"Look, honestly, if you want my help, let me return home tomorrow, and we can correspond through email," I said. "I'm not doing this off the books anymore, and I'm certainly not going with you guys to Chesterfield's apartment."

"You're in this whether you like it or not," Chesterfield rebutted. "You are connected to the *fake* Baron of Alphamstone, to whose apartments in Chancery Lane we traced the transmission of the child porn and torture video you and I just watched at the Old Cock Tavern. And that video showed children being raped and mutilated. So now we think this might have been done by the same people who you say kidnapped you and forced you to watch the killing of an animal. Therefore, if you don't want to help us find the people that did these things, and bring them to justice, to stop them from hurting anyone else, I've got to assume it's because you haven't told me the truth, in which case you're not a victim, you're an accomplice."

"Wait a minute," I said. "You traced the origin of the video? So the anonymous tip page wasn't really anonymous?"

"Of course not, don't be stupid," said Chesterfield. Paris studied my reaction in the rearview mirror as he turned through a roundabout.

"And you traced it to Chancery Lane, that same street that we walked down to get to the pub at Temple?"

"Yes, and of course you know who lives there."

"I don't know anything about it," I answered. "You said Aleister Crowley used to live there. That's all I know."

"Oh, so Leopold Black never gave you the address to his apartment next to the silver vaults?" Chesterfield asked, not believing me. As he spoke I noted that we were coincidentally going right by the silver vaults on Chancery Lane once again before turning west on High Holborn.

"I assumed that he lived in Alphamstone in some grand estate!" I said. "I obviously didn't know anything about him that was actually true. I told you that!"

"And now we're telling you that he's involved in making these child torture films, in addition to everything else we've told you about him," said Agent Paris. "Doesn't that make you want to help us stop him?"

"Yes," I said. "But why do we have to do it at Chesterfield's house? Surely that's not MI5 procedure." "Well, MI5 may have been decapitated tonight, or else, it is thoroughly compromised," Paris answered. "And nobody outside the agency knows it yet, except you."

"What do you mean?" I said, thoroughly confused.

"Explain."

"For some reason, our Director, Mr. Pindar, made a special request to interview Thomas Weir personally in the basement of the Old Bailey, right after he was booked and about to be transferred to a holding cell. Then the two disappeared shortly thereafter."

"So Leopold is on the loose right now?" I said. "And he's kidnapped the Director?" For some reason I couldn't stop calling that man by his fake name.

"Either that or they're both in on it, which is what I suspect," answered Paris. "So do you understand why it isn't safe for you to go back to the hotel, or back home, or for us to have you interrogated through the normal channels? We have to figure out what's going on by ourselves, or else none of us are safe. And who knows what the bad guys are going to do next, or who else may be in danger."

"Isn't that an extreme accusation?" I said.

"We've had Russian agents directing both MI5 & MI6 before," said Chesterfield. "I don't see why these occult weirdos, whatever they are, couldn't worm their way into that den of vipers as well."

I assumed he was talking about the allegations from the best-selling 1980s book *Spycatcher*, claiming that Roger Hollis had been a Russian spy when he served as MI5 Director General in the 50s and 60s. The author believed that Hollis and many others were in league with the infamous Cambridge Five spy ring that had already been caught and defected. Of course, these allegations had in no way ever been proven, as Chesterfield had implied. But I wasn't going to argue with him. He was probably right anyway.

"So how did they disappear from the prison?" I asked. "How many others are in on it?"

"The number of accomplices is unknown, but it needn't have been very many. All that was required was a few dumb cops following orders without question. Turns out there's a trap door in the floor of the Old Bailey's basement that leads to the sewers, out of which they disappeared."

"So is anybody looking for them?" I asked.

"Yeah, we've got cops and other agents up to their necks in shit looking underneath the City for them, but so far nothing," said Paris. "They really could be anywhere by now. Our guys let an hour pass for this *interrogation* before anybody checked on them." He was obviously disgusted.

Just then, the cell phones of both agents rang at the same time. They had different ringtones. It was a jarring cacophony. They both answered, received some sort of shocking news, and then looked at each other in horror before hanging up. Paris abruptly turned his vehicle around and changed the destination on his GPS.

"Where are we going now? What's going on?" I demanded. Chesterfield turned around and looked at me solemnly.

"Director Pindar's head was just found spiked to the main arch of Temple Bar at Paternoster Square," he said.

Chapter 15: Empyrean and Beyond

O Satan, my youngest born,
art thou not Prince of the
Starry Hosts, lo And of the
Wheels of Heaven, to turn
the Mills day & night?

—William Blake, *Milton*

Before I had time to absorb the news, we were already there, pulling up on Warwick Lane, right next to the monument. The area was already cordoned off with a flurry of police presence. We all got out of the car simultaneously and began to walk briskly towards the action. A woman in a mustard-colored trench coat, who seemed to know both agents, hurried towards us. She briefed them on what she knew while I stood aside. Then Paris continued to talk to her about details while Chesterfield relayed the highlights to me while.

"The head was tacked to the front," he said, "and the body was stuffed inside the upper chamber."

"The same location as the rape scene in the video," I noted. Chesterfield nodded.

"They used to hang the heads of traitors on Temple Bar," he remarked.

"So Leopold considers the Director of MI5 a traitor?" I said, thinking aloud. "And he was able to kidnap and kill him after the man requested a private meeting with him? I thought you said he was a fake nobleman running a scam for money. How does he have the power to do this?"

"That's what I'm trying to figure out," he said. "In the meantime, Miss Beverly Equitone is the acting head of MI5 until a replacement is made. Now I have no idea what side she's on, or what the sides in this matter even are. But there's something else I want you to see."

He grabbed my hand and walked me over to the monument, then lifted the cordon to let me underneath. We walked to the little door in the back, sitting open and guarded by two Metropolitan police officers with bright reflective yellow jackets. Chesterfield flashed his badge and asked the cops to let us examine the crime scene, to which they both nodded in affirmation. Then we walked up the tiny stairway into the upper chamber which, Chesterfield informed me, had at one time served as a small prison.

There were three police officers in the room: a white man taking pictures, a white man dusting for fingerprints, and one white woman with green hair (the faded remnants of a punk-looking dye job), who appeared to be supervising them. There was blood splattered on the floor. Chesterfield asked them if the body had already been removed.

"No, just the head," said the lady cop. The body's up there."

She pointed up to the ceiling in the middle of the room. The body hung naked from the rafters, tied with black wire by the hands and feet so that it was curled into a circle with the stomach pointing down. In addition to the removal of the head, there was a puncture wound near the navel.

"So *that's* how the blood got splattered like that," said Chesterfield, apparently to himself.

"Yeah, all over the black magic symbols on the ground," said the photographer.

"What do you mean?" I asked. I didn't see any black magic symbols.

"You have to use blue light to see them," he said. "450 nanometers. And I had to use a special camera to photograph it." He flicked off the one light in the room at the switch. He handed me and Chesterfield each a pair of amber-colored goggles. Then he pointed his blue flashlight where the blood drops were. To my surprise, I did see symbols standing out, looking white in the light, written underneath the spatter.

An invisible ink had been used to create an arrangement of words, letters, and other symbols. At the top it said "To Empyrean and Beyond," with an odd sigil forming the exclamation point. It was a circle with a dot in the middle, topped with an arrow pointing upward, the astrological sign for Uranus.

Beneath this was one of the oldest magical devices used in the Western world, the Sator Square, a palindrome which goes:

        SATOR
        AREPO
        TENET
        OPERA
        ROTAS

The entire display took up an area of about a foot square.

"It's all written in semen," the photographer said.

"The invisible ink used by SIS!" said Chesterfield.

"What do you mean?" I said, waiting for an explanation. "Yeah, what *do* you mean?" the photographer asked. The other male cop, the fingerprint collector, came closer to listen.

"Well, see," Chesterfield continued, "it was really an inside joke. It was a reference to the fact during the First World War, when the spy service was new just then being formed, they used semen as an invisible ink for sending secret messages to each other. 'Every man his own stylo,' they used to say. Their director, Mansfield Cumming, came up with that himself.

"His last name was *actually* 'Cumming'?" I said. I couldn't help myself.

"This guy's first name was actually 'Côme,'" Chesterfield replied without humor, pointing to the body above us. He pronounced it like "comb."

"It's a French variant of the name 'Cosmo,'" said the photographer.

"I wonder if that's why this message was written in this medium," the fingerprint collector interjected. "It could have been a reference to Mansfield Cumming's invisible ink, something that would be understood only by people who work in national intelligence and security, or who are familiar with their history."

Chesterfield shrugged his shoulder. "Who knows at this point. We assume it's the killer's semen, right? I mean, it doesn't keep well, so he must have jerked off somewhere right here, don't you think?"

"Yes, before he strung up the body," said the fingerprint guy.

"So did you find a source pool of semen?" asked Chesterfield. "Or did he collect it in his hand, or a cup or something, before he started writing and drawing with it?"

"He collected it in the victim's eye socket," said the green-haired lady, who walked towards us now, looking deadpan. "The director was subjected to 'ocular penetration.' We found spermatic fluid around and within the left eye socket, but we haven't yet determined if the victim was still alive when it was deposited. And the eye is missing."

Chesterfield's eyes widened in horror.

Skullfucked, I thought. *I guess it really* does *happen. How awful.*

"Oh, I think he must have had a larger supply than just that one inkwell," said the fingerprint collector. "I think he brought a supply with him, kept fresh somehow. He would have needed more to do all this writing."

While the three cops discussed this, Chesterfield pulled me back a few steps, closer to the stairwell, so that we could speak to each other directly. He lowered his voice—not to a whisper, but just enough so that we wouldn't interrupt the others.

"What's this about?" Chesterfield asked me, pointing to the symbols.

"It's an ancient magic spell. The oldest one they ever found was in the ruins of Herculeaum near Vesuvius. It means 'The ploughman Arepo works the wheels.' But nobody knows who Arepo is, or what the whole thing means at all.

"What's it supposed to do?" he asked.

"I think it could be used for blessing or cursing, whichever you choose," I said.

I realized this was totally vague. But my mind was distracted by the other graffiti next to the magic square. On either side of it were the "Alpha" and "Omega" symbols. Beneath the Alpha on the left was an image of a crudely- drawn penis and testicles descending into a vase. Underneath the Omega symbol there was a picture of a baby's head emerging from an identical vase.

"So I suppose the other pictures represent what happened to the boy in the movie," Chesterfield theorized. "Also, the castration, and maybe the references in the film to laying 'an Easter egg.' It could be connected to this picture of the baby hatching out of the vase, right?"

"Yes," I said. "And Empyrean is the highest chamber in Heaven, although I don't know what that weird arrow is about."

"Oh," said Chesterfield. "I thought for sure it was a quote from Buzz Lightyear."

I ignored his joke, although I had noted the similarity to the phrase "To Infinity and Beyond" as well. I also thought about the final segment of the film *2001: A Space Odyssey*, entitled "Jupiter and Beyond the Infinite," although in Arthur C. Clarke's original plans for the story, the planet named was Saturn.

"There's more," I said. "I recognize these images. They came from the Templar artifacts in the Hammer-Purgstall book—the one I had translated and published along with my own book last year."

I shook my head in an effort to snap myself back into reality. Then I dug into my phone and Google-image- searched until I found a website where some asshole had illegally uploaded a PDF of my book about Baphomet. I skimmed through the document until I found the image I was looking for.

"Here it is," I announced. I showed him the picture of the human figure (let's assume it's male for the sake of grammar) sitting on an eagle. He had what looked like a dead goose or duck draped over his head, so that the bird's neck dangled over his face, its beak lining up with his chin. Behind him, the bird's wings were extended out, as if they were coming out of his own back.

Two identical stomach -shaped vases were depicted sitting next to the figure, one on either side. The one on the right had a baby emerging from its top, beneath an angry sun face (exactly where the Omega symbol had been substituted in the version in front of us). The vase on the left side had a crudely-drawn penis and balls descending into it beneath a crescent moon with a sad face, in the same spot where the killer had placed the Greek Alpha in his disgusting homage.

In the original line drawing in Hammer-Purgstall's book, the genitals had been omitted. They were only restored when the picture was reprinted a few decades later in Thomas Wright's scandalous book *Worship of the Generative Powers*, about the allegedly widespread penis-worshipping "cult of Priapus" in early Christian Europe. Wright had believed that all of the disembodied penis votives discovered throughout the continent and British Isles were part of a secret movement to worship a virile satyr with a giant schlong by venerating idols of the schlong itself. This supposed underground religion reportedly engaged in wild orgies, bacchanalias and witch sabbats where the Goat God of Lust was honored as the Devil.

All this purported veneration of male sexuality seemed to me so incongruent with the present use of this symbol by a cult that practiced emasculation, as seen on the film *Easter Sunday April Fool*. (I was assuming, of course, that there was some connection between whoever produced that film and whoever murdered Pindar.) But, as I noted to Chesterfield, if someone believes that there's magic in men's genitals, then it isn't farfetched to imagine them removing someone else's genitals in a ritual to be used for magical purposes.

"So far we've got a secret society that does rites involving the symbols of the Templars, Cybele, Priapus… What else? It seems like a hodgepodge of nonsense," said Chesterfield. The photographer flicked the light back on as he exited down the stairs behind us.

"Well, Eliphas Levi wrote that the aim of the Templars had been to create 'the synthesis of all persecuted beliefs,' meaning a combination of all heresies and pre-Christian religions," I said. "Pope Pius IX accused them of trying to start a new religion, inspired by cabbalism, Gnosticism, and heretical beliefs about John the Baptist. Hammer-Purgstall believed that the Templars were Ophite Gnostics, or Naassenes. And Hippolytus described the Naassenes as a cult of synthesis derived from the mystery religions of Rome, but mixed with Christian heresy, including blasphemous inversions of Christian symbols and myths. He said they practiced horrible sex rites. Let me find the quote."

I Googled on my phone until I found what I needed. But it said more than I had remembered. I read it out loud:

> On account of these and such like reasons, these constantly attend the mysteries called those of the Great Mother,

supposing especially that they behold by means of the ceremonies performed there the entire mystery.

The succinctness of his claim stunned me. I actually took a step back in awe.

"Oh my God," I said. "The Great Mother. That's Cybele. He said that the Naassenes secretly worshiped Cybele. That means Hammer-Purgstall believed that the Templars did as well. Which would explain why they might have depicted Mete or Baphomet on the coffer looking much like Cybele. It would also explain this picture of severed genitals going into a vase. And why the Templars were buried with their legs crossed. And why Eliphas Levi's Baphomet is missing his penis."

Suddenly Chesterfield piped up with an amazing contribution that I didn't expect.

"You know what else Hippolytus said? He said that St. Paul was a eunuch, because he thought that Jesus was too. That's what he said Paul thought the term 'eunuchs of heaven' meant. Just like the guy in the Heaven's Gate cult you told me about. And here we are now, right next to St. Paul's Cathedral, standing underneath the dead body of a man quite possibly murdered by a castration cult."

I was impressed with his commentary. I did not think that Chesterfield would know anything about Hippolytus!

"I studied for the seminary before I became a spook," he said, responding to my obvious bewilderment. "And by the way, that set of beads we saw at the end of the movie?"

"Yeah?" I said, encouraging him to go on.

"They're actually called 'paternosters.' It's a monk's rosary, for reciting the paternoster 150 times, the same as the number of chapters in *The Book of Psalms*. That's why there were 50 beads. You're supposed to go through the set three times a day."

"And don't forget the Mithras connection too," said a voice coming from the staircase below. Agent Paris was walking up to join us.

"How did you know about the Mithras connection?" I asked. "We just found out about it right before we left the tavern. Surely Chesterfield hasn't had a chance to tell you."

"Well, I was just thinking about the magic square on the floor," he answered. "The photographer came out and showed me a photo he took with a UV-sensitive camera. The Sator Square is associated with Mithras, right?"

"It is?" I said. I hadn't thought so.

If I'd read that before, I'd forgotten it. But Paris came over and showed me a website open on his phone addressing the theory that the talisman had originated with the Mithraic cult.

Apparently, the "Sator" (a Latin word meaning "ploughman," "planter" and, by extension, "begetter," "producer" or "father") was thought to refer in this instance to Saturn, the planet to which the highest grade of Mithraism was dedicated. The letters of the square could be rearranged to make the word "Paternoster" twice, Latin for "our Father." This was thought to be a reference to the title of this grade, "Pater." The two "Paternosters" could then be combined to form a cross, with four remaining letters — two letters A and two letters O — to stand for "Alpha" and "Omega" on each side of the cross. The resulting formation looked like this:

As I continued to read the website on Paris' phone, I learned that in the Mithraic *taurtoctony* (the tradition containing their famous bull-slaying fable), Mithras apparently allowed the beast's testicles to be severed by the pinchers of a scorpion. Then they were offered as a sacrifice to the moon goddess, who used the blood and sperm within the testicles to engender new forms of life on Earth. Mithras then began to harvest and cultivate these lifeforms, thus forming his association with agriculture.

I recalled that Chronos (a.k.a. the Roman Saturn) had been said by the Greeks centuries earlier to be the inventor of agriculture. This matched up with what I was now reading about Mithras, who was seen as a form of Saturn. I learned that images of Mithras reaping corn stalks emerging from the rectum of the sacrificial bull have been discovered in more than one *mithraeum*.

The website quoted another author claiming that in Mithraic rites, a bull would be sodomized by the priest and then killed as soon as the priest climaxed. Pointing out that the Mithraic temples forbade female members, the quote segment stated that the cult's misogyny was represented in their creation myth. Mithras had been born from a rock instead of a woman. Furthermore, it also said:

> To eliminate the female principle from their creation myth, Mithraists replaced the Mother of All Living in the primal garden of paradise (Pairdaeza) with the bull named Sole-Created. Instead of Eve, this bull was the partner of the first man. (It doesn't take much imagination to figure out what happened between Man and Bull. Man engaged in bestiality by raping Bull and then killed Bull out of repugnance, fear and guilt. And then sought out other Bulls so he could do it all over again....) [sp.]

I had to admit, I didn't really know enough about Mithraism, and this was a surprise to me. As my head spun with a thousand new theories, I gave my companions the Cliff Notes version of what I had just read, then handed Paris' phone back to him.

"Oh, why can't we be more like our ancient ancestors," said Chesterfield sarcastically to the ceiling. "They were so much more in touch with *nature*. Ugh!"

Paris had wrinkled his nosed in disgust. "Yeah, well that's not all. Turns out there's a magic square just like this in a church in England. And guess where."

He pressed the "back" button on his phone's internet browser, and brought up another page. It was an article from *The Telegraph* titled "Unique Sator-Rotas Square Discovered." It said the location was a sixteenth-century Anglican church dedicated to St. Barnabas in none other than Alphamstone, the location of Leopold Black's fake barony. There was a picture of a white female priest, older with short grey hair, wearing glasses, and standing next to an inscription of the magic square on a medieval-looking wall.

"Unbelievable," I said. "This is amazing."

I wondered to myself if the word "Alphamstone" contained a hidden reference to "Alpha" and "Omega," given the connection between the church and the Sator Square, as well as the fact that these two Greek letters were written next to the version now on the floor in front of us. I also recalled once seeing a terrible low-budget movie from the 1970s called *Curse of the Alpha Stone*. It was about a professor who discovered an alchemical substance that made men sexually violent, and even turned gay guys straight.

"So what was it about Mithras that you and my partner found out while you were at the Olde Cock Tavern?" Paris asked. I struggled to remember. We had been drinking, and so many shocking things had happened that night already.

"Her friends at the fake Butchers' Society said that some guy somewhere in London was doing something nefarious at a Temple of Mithras," answered Chesterfield. "Then our waitress told us that there was a Temple of Mithras in London that had just been moved back to its original location on Walbrook, a stone's throw from St. Paul's. She said that tomorrow they're opening the new building that it's in."

"Yeah, that's at Rosenberg Plaza right down there," said the punk-haired lady cop. I had already noticed that she'd been eavesdropping on me, Paris and Chesterfield as much as possible.

"They're having a ping -pong tournament there tomorrow as part of the festivities," she continued. "I'm on one of the teams that's playing."

"A ping-pong tournament?" I asked. "To celebrate a temple to Mithras opening?" I couldn't see the connection.

"Well it's not just the temple," she replied. "That's just part of it. There's the rest of the Plaza too. It's huge. Two buildings, one of them the most massive in London really. Not the tallest, but the biggest in bulk. And there are going to be several restaurants in the lobby, including a pizza parlor with ping pong tables, where I'll be playing on the same team as my son Dennis."

I looked at her with my mouth slightly ajar. I must have looked stupid. Both MI5 agents eyed me curiously. I pulled them both close to me and whispered, very faintly this time, since I knew the lady cop was trying to catch every word.

"Do you remember a scandal called Pizzagate? From right before the US Presidential election two years ago?"

"Um, no, that's an English football scandal" said Chesterfield. He was referring to something else that went by the same name.

"Yes, I remember, but I thought it was bullshit," whispered Paris. "Fake news? Russian propaganda?"

"Kids supposedly getting raped and dismembered by cultists," I said through barely-parted lips. "Just like you saw on the Easter film, right?"

Chesterfield stroked his chin and thought. Agent Paris' phone rang again and he went off to the corner to answer it. I asked the lady cop what time the opening ceremonies were at the *mithraeum*.

"I believe they begin at noon tomorrow," she said. "That's when they cut the ribbon with giant scissors. The rest happens shortly after that."

"Well that sounds like something too good to be missed," said Paris, who had ended his call quickly returned already. "Now I think we should leave this dreary scene in the capable hands the Met. As for us, we've got to be going. Come along friends."

He nodded at me and Chesterfield while beckoning towards the stairway with his right hand. We took the hint and followed him immediately, telling the lady cop, who introduced herself as "Drexella," that it had been pleasant meeting her. I told her my name was "Amanda Styles." I made it up on the spot.

"The only 'Drexella' I've ever known is the wife of an American TV preacher," I said to the other two as we descended the stairs.

"Quiet." whispered Paris. We remained mute until we got out of the Temple Bar and a few feet away from the police cordon. Paris walked us over to the pylon with the golden flame on top in the middle of the square. Then Chesterfield and I huddled next to him to hear what he couldn't say in front of the cops.

"So Miss Equitone's secretary just called. She wants me to meet with her and some people from Scotland Yard tomorrow. I tried to get her to push it 'til noon, saying it's been a long night. But the latest she would accept was 10 a.m. So we'd better get someplace where we can safely sleep and do our research as much as possible before then."

"What about me?" said Chesterfield. "Shouldn't she want to talk to me as well? I handled the Weir case with you."

"Yes, I thought that sounded odd too, perhaps ominous of an internal investigation of you. So we'd better get our shit together tonight and tomorrow morning. Who knows what's about to get dropped on us."

"Sure," said Chesterfield. "So do you know where this Temple of Mithras is going to open tomorrow? Drexella said it was close."

"Just over there," Paris said, pointing west. "Where Cannon Street and Queen Victoria meet.

"Isn't that about where the London Stone used to be displayed at the Cannon Tapps?" Chesterfield said to his partner. "Remember reading that last night?"

"Ah yes," Paris answered. "Well isn't that interesting."

As he spoke, I walked around the column looking for symbolism. I found a plaque stating that the pylon—called the "Flaming Orb Monument"—had been installed in 1996, which explained its modern, boring appearance. The plaque also said that the monument acted as a ventilation shaft for an underground service road.

Then I noticed a small metal door a few feet around to the right. It was slightly ajar. I reached for the handle and pulled it. Sure enough, it opened right up to a dark cavern inside, and a subterranean spiral metal stairway leading down into the unknown depths below.

"Do you suppose they could have gotten out of the sewers through here?" I said. Chesterfield and Paris were staring in stupefaction.

"Well, we'll find out," said Paris, grabbing my hand and removing it from the door handle. "I'm sure the CCTV footage is back by now. Let's go tell the cops what we found. Then let's get out of here."

We all walked briskly back to the police cordon area around Temple Bar and stopped at the edge of the tape line. Paris stepped over the tape and talked to an older white man in a black trench coat with salt and pepper hair. He must have told him about the stairway beneath the pylon, as they both pointed and looked at it. Then the man told Paris something that made him shout out.

"Christ on a crutch! What the bloody Hell?!" He was enraged. The man shrugged and shook his head sideways. Paris spat on the ground and then marched back over to us.

"Well guess what. The power on the whole block was blacked out for about ten minutes, inexplicably. None of the cameras recorded the action. Imagine that." This gave Chesterfield great fear. Clearly a deep-level plot was afoot.

"We need to go right now," he said. "Before somebody kills us."

Chapter 16: Tower House

> …Participants are free to use the information received, but neither the identity nor the affiliation of the speaker(s), nor that of any other participant, may be revealed.
>
> – Chatham House Rule, Royal Institute of International Affairs

We drove in somber silence to Chesterfield's cozy little one-bedroom flat in "Tower House." This was a gigantic 120- year-old former "Rowton house" (a type of worker's hostel) in Whitechapel. The first thing I noticed was a white marble bust of Pallas Athena, yet another wisdom goddess, placed above the inside of his front door.

"You must be a huge fan of Edgar Allan Poe," I said. "Nevermore!" said Chesterfield jokingly. "I was mostly into him in college, when I installed that thing, and I've actually lived in the same flat since then. Just a lonely bachelor. But I keep it there to remind me of my mother, whose name was Lenore. And that's also the name of my cat." He picked up the fat gray kitty, who had come to rub on his leg.

"Oh, has your mother passed?" I said. "I'm sorry." I sat in one of the two brown leather armchairs set in front of the fireplace and facing the large flat-screen television mounted on the wall. Paris took the other. The fireplace was gas-powered with ceramic logs. Chesterfield turned it on straight away. Up against another wall, perpendicular to the armchairs and television, was a blue and red plaid-patterned tweed-covered sofa, where he began piling our coats and bags on the right side.

"She and Dad both," he said. "Long ago."

He pointed to a lovely old framed black-and-white photograph of a young white couple standing with a baby before an Anglican priest.

"Here they are having me christened at St. Martin's, right next to St. Paul's. They're both Christopher Wren-designed churches. My parents named me Martin after the church. Care for a Laphroaig?"

He stepped into the adjoining kitchen and began pouring three scotches on ice without waiting for a reply. Then he carried them over to us without spilling a drop, just like a pro. After sitting down on the couch next to Agent Paris with his cat and a drink of his own, Chesterfield flipped on the telly.

It was already tuned to the Sky News channel, which was playing a commercial for Barclays Bank. Then it cut to a report about the murder of the MI5 Director at Paternoster Square. It looked like the news has just hit. Chesterfield turned up the sound.

The news report was slightly truthful and slightly misleading, as I suspected it would be. They said that the Director had been interviewing a "suspect in an espionage case" at the Central Criminal Court when both men had disappeared. A short while later, police issued a report to the media that Director Pindar's body had been found at Temple Bar in Paternoster Square.

No details were given about the condition of the body or the use of underground tunnels to escape. They didn't mention the name of the "suspect" or any of the real charges against him. They did state that Equitone was the current acting head.

The Prime Minister, who had been informed of the news, released a statement expressing condolences for Pindar's family. She also promised that there would be a press conference on the matter the following day. A panel of b- team reporters and intelligence experts began to speculate wildly based on what little information they had. Chesterfield turned the volume down again to a whisper.

"Now," he announced, pointing to the ceiling with his contorted right index finger, "since we are under the protection of the rose, let us use these last few moments of consciousness to speak freely with one another."

I looked up to where he was pointing. There was indeed a red and white Tudor rose painted on the ceiling, with green leaves poking out between the five petals and a golden bud emerging in the center. I knew that *sub rosa*, or "under the rose," was a code that meant "under the protection of mutual vows of secrecy." The paint was cracked, just like it was on the rest of the ceiling and walls. It looked like it could have been there for centuries, and most likely had been.

"Chatham House rules, right?" said Paris, winking at him. "Everybody says what they think and what they know. Afterwards we all forget who said what."

"Exactly," Chesterfield replied to his partner, smiling and nodding. I said nothing, and promised nothing, which is why I feel free to share this information with you now.

"So is this an all-out coup now or what?" Chesterfield asked Paris, getting things started. "Do you really think it's the Cybele-worshipping Templar dick-cutters, or is it the Russians?" The last part he said with an air of humor, which Paris picked up on.

"Naw, it's the Illuminati," said Paris, only half-joking. "Pindar's a Frenchy by birth. Never trust those frogs. Never forget how they chopped off all those Christian heads during the Revolution. Or how they helped the American colonies with their treason."

"Your name is Paris, for God's sake!" Chesterfield shouted, throwing a couch pillow at his partner playfully.

"But he was a Trojan Prince, Martin," said Paris. "Just like Brutus, who founded London as New Troy. I'm no frog-lover, my friend. They've always conspired against the governments of Europe. Them and the Jews, just like my mum said."

Paris drained his glass and then got up to refill it, taking Chesterfield's with him also. I was still nursing mine. In fact, I was starting to nod off. I caught myself leaning forward, and straightened up. Chesterfield responded to Parvin's playful pretense at racist paranoia.

"You Asians always think the Jews did everything. What about the Jesuits? They burned down London in 1666. And they've been diddling all the altar boys for at least as long. They hanged that guy at Blackfriars Bridge in the 1980s. This job tonight was a lot like that, you know."

I too had thought the same about Roberto Calvi's murder in 1982, allegedly done at the behest of a bizarre Masonic group called "P2" or *Propaganda Due*. Despite the papal ban on Catholics joining masonry, P2 had become a power within the Vatican itself, as well as in Italy and Latin America. Calvi, a member of P2, had worked for the Banco Ambrosiano, an

Italian bank which had been doing business with the order, which included laundering illegal money for the Vatican.

After the money-laundering scheme was discovered by Italian authorities, and prosecutions began, Calvi was found hanging from a bridge over the Thames. He had fled the country after his initial arrest, presumably running from prosecution but also, according to his family, because of threats from the P2 goons. The newspapers speculated that the manner of his death was a Masonic retribution ritual for traitors to the brotherhood. The bridge they had chosen, Blackfriars, was thought to have been used as a reference to the *frati neri*, or "black brothers," a nickname that P2 members had chosen for themselves.

"You know what my dad told me?" said Paris. "When he worked for SIS he found out that those P2 guys killed Paulo Pasolini too. Right while he was editing *120 Days of Sodom*. All that crap about him raping the prostitute boy with a stick was a lie, and they set that kid up."

Chesterfield arched his eyebrows in surprise. I too was intrigued that the conversation had turned down this avenue. I would not have imagined that MI5 agents, and even agents of MI6 (a.k.a. "SIS," whom Paris' father had apparently worked for) would be investigating the murder of an underground filmmaker because of his adaptation of an obscure unfinished porno-horror novel from the eighteenth century. The possibility of a P2 connection to this was completely foreign to me. Paris leaned forward and continued in a lower voice.

"The truth is the Jesuit Masons got him. There were several rolls of film that were supposed to be in the movie which got stolen. In those rolls, Pasolini had told the truth about what the Satanists in the Vatican are all up to. And it's just like that Pizzagate stuff you were talking about, Pamela." He pointed at me.

I was struggling to stay awake, but I was very interested in what he was saying. I recalled as best I could the facts I knew about Pier Paulo Pasolini, the film director. He was murdered in 1975 by a male teenage prostitute, who ran over him with his own car at a beach in Ostia, Italy. Supposedly, the director had hired the kid for sex, but then tried to sodomize him with a large stick, against his will, leading to his own violent end.

The only reason why I knew about it was because as a teenager I had been a fan of a band called Coil, who wrote a song about the murder. I had also seen Pasolini's last film, *Salo, or the 120 Days of Sodom*, which he had been editing when he died. It did indeed depict the brutal rape and murder of young teenagers, both male and female. In the story, they were kidnapped on the orders of a group of aristocrats and powerful clerics. The men in this group then imprisoned them in an isolated mansion where they all eventually died in the most awful ways. It was based on a Marquis de Sade novel, with the location changed from revolutionary France to fascist-era Italy.

"Well now I've heard everything," I said, conscious that I might be slurring a bit. "I'd heard that the Papists burned down London. I've heard Father Malachi Martin say that there were Satanists running the Vatican now. But I didn't know that P2 killed Pasolini."

"Yeah, well they got Malachi Martin too," said Chesterfield. "They cursed him with a demon that finally overcame him. Don't think that was an accident."

The dead Irish cleric he spoke of had been an accomplished exorcist, and everyone knew he was the guy that the priest in the *Exorcist* movie was based on. Father Martin died of a cerebral hemorrhage after a fall in his Manhattan apartment, which he told friends had been caused by a demonic attack. Purportedly, he was also a close confidant of Jean Paul II, and was privy to many Vatican secrets, which he wrote about in several books.

These included the fact that—he claimed—Satanists had infiltrated its highest ranks. He said that the widespread molestation of children in the Church was being organized by the Satanists for ritual purposes. Father Martin also alleged that the Pope had told him the third secret of Fatima, given by the Virgin Mary to three children in Portugal in 1917, which the Church has never openly revealed. According to him, it was a prophecy that the Final Pope would be "under the control of Satan."

"So why are people in the spy business more paranoid than everyone else?" I asked.

"Because we don't just think we know, we know we know," said Chesterfield. He aimed the remote control at the TV and tuned it in to one of the other channels. It showed a lady dressed up kind of like Napoleon, waving a British flag from the point of a scabbard while singing in a high-pitched operatic voice.

"Oh yes!" said Chesterfield excitedly. "This is from 2009!" He cranked up the sound.

Just then the singer got to the chorus. The whole audience, and the two men in the room with me, joined in the singing. Then I realized that I vaguely recognized the song from hearing it before somewhere.

> Rule Britannia! Britannia rule the waves!
> Britons never, never, never shall be slaves!

They both resounded gleefully and drunkenly through the rest of the performance. It ended with a strange encore that came after the initial round of applause from the audience, and even after a summation from an off-screen presenter stating that it was recorded at Royal Albert Hall. When it was over, my friends informed me that this was a sample from the "Last Night of the Proms," which was some kind of traditional annual patriotic opera show.

I had finished my whiskey, so Chesterfield got up to get us both another. Paris declined a refill, and instead chose to stretch out on the couch when his partner stood up. As for me, this seems to be the last thing I remember from that night.

Chapter 17: Saturn's Return

> O Rose thou art sick.
> The invisible worm,
> That flies in the night
> In the howling storm:
> Has found out thy bed
> Of crimson joy:
> And his dark secret love
> Does thy life destroy.
>
> —William Blake, *The Sick Rose*

When you wake up from a dream, do you sometimes find that you can't remember what order things actually happened in? Do you ever wonder if your mind has really just organized things the way you remember in an effort to create the illusion of causality—that one thing led to another? Is it possible that the order of events has been imposed *ex post facto* by your own conscious mind upon waking? Do you ever wonder if perhaps your mind has even inserted certain story elements after the fact to give form to an otherwise incoherent chaotic cacophony of sounds and images from the abyss of the unconscious? Does this explain why humans allegedly see everything while dreaming in black and white, like colorblind dogs, but remember it otherwise?

I am pretty sure the part that I remember being "first" in that night's dream was actually inserted at the end, as I began to wake up. I walked into a room like a dark cave, with an orb of light shining from the top, and reflecting on a mirror that covered the wall in front of me. There was a man a dark suit standing there in front of me looking at the mirror. But I could not see his face. I *could not* look at it for some reason.

I tried to look at the mirror to see his reflection. But suddenly in front of his head, where I should have been able to see the left side of his face, a black-and-white photograph had been superimposed, showing a squinting old balding white man with a mustache who I didn't recognize. The sight of him frightened me. Then he spoke. I found his voice harsh and menacing.

"I want to scare you so that you'll remember when you wake up."

At that moment, I recall being utterly terrified. I was dreaming. Not only that, but someone else in the dream knew that I was scared, and he had the power to cloak himself. That meant anything could happen. I thought in lucid dreams you were supposed to be able to realize your power in the situation and take control of the narrative. But here this person seemed to be exercising control over my dream life. And of course, like the worst of my nightmares, I was frozen, unable to scream or move.

"I'll put the important part here at the end so that you won't forget it." He laughed. His voice was masculine but he had the wicked laugh of a mean old lady.

Somehow, the scene shifted to that of two giant, slimy worms having disgusting sex. They were glued to each other on both ends, like they were doing the old "69" position. It seemed like they were both fighting and fucking, trying to simultaneously eat and rape one another.

Then I remembered how it happened. I was going backwards in time it seems, upon reflection. I had been sleeping, and then something woke me up. Somebody was on top of me. I had thought I was alone, but someone was on top of me. I woke up and realized I was fucking someone. Or rather, perhaps, that someone was fucking me.

I couldn't be sure. I couldn't tell if it was a man or a woman, or even what kind of thing I was.

Am I a worm? I remember wondering. *A blind worm?*

I couldn't see anything. All was dark. I tried to push him off.

Him?

I reached out and grabbed something: a knife.

I stabbed at the attacker blindly, but immediately my thigh was filled with shooting pain.

Then finally, I could scream. Finally he got off of me. Finally I could see, as the light came through the window. Chesterfield opened the blinds, hollering obscenities.

I was awake now. He was in his boxer shorts and wife-beater with an open white terry cloth bathrobe, looking at me like I was a maniac.

"What the fuck is going on!" he shouted.

"You were raping me!" I answered, shielding my eyes from the light. My vision was still blurry. My head was pounding. A hangover.

"No, I was merely *sleeping* next to you!" he responded. "*You* rolled over on top of *me*. Then you started stabbing yourself with my nose-trimmers."

"Eww!" I recoiled. I found that I was on the floor between his bed and his radiator, kneeling down in front of him. I looked down at the wound in my leg, still bleeding and throbbing. I pressed down on it with my hand as I realized I was in my underwear and wearing a man's white undershirt, just like the one Chesterfield was wearing.

"You took my clothes off while I was sleeping?!" I shouted in outrage. "That's the second time that's happened to me in the last 24 hours! What the fuck!"

Chesterfield shrugged as he took his bathrobe off and draped it over my shoulders.

"No," he said, "I went into the kitchen to get us some cheese and crackers. When I got back to the living room you were gone. I found you lying in my bed dressed as you are now, wearing *my* undershirt. It was clean, you know."

"Good," I thought. I was already grossed out about having it on. He walked out of the room for a moment and came back with a wet washcloth for me to put on my injured thigh.

"I guess I really tied one on then," I said. I was embarrassed that I had gotten drunk enough to black out like that. I was also very sick to my stomach.

"Yeah well file your sexual harassment complaint up your arse," he sneered, not looking at me directly.

"I'm sorry!" I said.

He seemed to accept this, but I could tell his feelings were still hurt. To get away from the awkwardness, I asked to use the bathroom.

I was in there for a while. It was spacious compared to the one in the Regent Hotel, although it too lacked a bathtub. However, like the rest of the apartment, it was surprisingly clean for a bachelor pad, and I enjoyed a nice hot shower.

As the fresh steamy water pounded down on my face, I thought about by dream, especially the worms. I made me think about the story of Chronos again. You'll recall that he swallowed his babies as soon as they were born, afraid that one of his children would usurp his position as king of the gods.

I envisioned Chronos with his mouth constantly on the mother's vagina as soon as the mating had finished, to make sure nothing escaped. I imagined that he probably also had to be quite careful that none of his semen spilled out anywhere else, because the sperm of all immortals is described in the myths as being super-fertile, capable of generating progeny on anything it touches. As per example: Aphrodite, who was born from the semen that clung to the sides of the bloody penis of Ouranos as it fell into the seas below. This was, of course, after his son Chronos cut it off.

The Greeks said that Ouranos was the Sky and his wife Gaia was the Earth. They were the first parents in the universe. They produced Chronos and the rest of the Titans, a nasty brood of dragons, giants and monsters.

At one point, it was said, Ouranos and Gaia were one being, presumably locked in endless sexual embrace, if you consider the fact that they were engendering children together, along with the rest of the known details. The myths didn't spell it out, but one can deduce that the castration took place inside the mother's vagina, the exit being deliberately blocked for the offspring by their father's penis. This brings the obvious question: where did the weapon (said to be a ceremonial scythe called a *harpe*) come from?

Some said he did this because of a "prophecy" that Ouranos would be killed and have his role taken over by one of his children. It is uncertain whether the prophecy arose within his own mind, or if his wife told him that, or perhaps some unnamed third party. Some versions say he feared his children's births because he somehow knew that they were simply too ugly to be looked at. I figured this meant that they represent the chaos the preceded creation, what the alchemists call the *prima materia* of the universe, which had not yet taken any definite form.

Chronos did in fact take over as the leader of the gods. He and Rhea, his wife, ruled over a time recalled as the "Golden Age." It was described as a time when everyone was free and nobody was called into the service of another. At this point, "everybody" presumably consisted of just Chronos, Rhea, and their Titan siblings.

But it wasn't until after Chronos was usurped by Zeus, and the Titans vanquished, that one of their number, Atlas, was conscripted with the arduous task of holding up the sky on his shoulders. This was done to prevent the sky, Ouranos, from "resuming his embrace" with Gaia the Earth. If this were to happen, they said, everything that exists would be snuffed out. It is only because Atlas does his job that we have a "stage" upon which to act (as Shakespeare would describe the worldly plane).

So how and where, then, I wondered, *did events of the Golden Age occur, when nobody was there to keep the Earth and Sky apart, since no person was slave to another?*

I also recalled that the same story was told in the Kabbalistic *Zohar* about the serpent-demons Lilith ("night") and Samael ("the blind one"), who had once been two halves of the only creature in existence. God had split them apart deliberately, castrating the male, but they still longed for one another. It was said that if they were ever able to mate again, it would destroy creation. These demons were associated by nineteenth-century occultist Stanislas de Guaita with the hermaphrodite Baphomet in the sigils he created, one of which was later adopted by the Church of Satan as its official logo.

Satan, it seems, wants to see what is separate become whole again, in order to undo God's creation, I thought to myself, and not for the first time.

When I came out of the shower, I found that Chesterfield had gone to the Alder Gate Cash & Carry, which was apparently nearby. There he had bought me a pair of dark gray jeans, just my size, and a red sweater that fit perfectly, from. He had also brought us all coffee and a bag full of scones from Starbucks. Paris, who was just coming awake, took his coffee and scones into the bathroom without looking up.

Maybe he's mad at me too, I thought. *Chesterfield probably told him what had happened between us in his bedroom.*

Chesterfield was also being gruff, not talking much other than to say "you're welcome" blandly when I thanked him for the clothes and coffee. We both sat down at the little white Formica table in the kitchen's breakfast nook and starred at our laptops for a while.

It was 8 a.m. now, and I thought I should probably check the news first. Yet I couldn't shake the image of the mating worms in my dream. I knew that Leviathan, that dreaded sea serpent in the Bible, was often depicted just like the Ouroboros, swallowing its own tail, and encompassing the entire cosmos within its coil.

Like the monstrous Titans, Ouroboros was a representation of the chaos that was thought to preexist the creation of matter. But sometimes it was depicted as two serpents shown swallowing each other, much like the mutually fucking and devouring hermaphrodite worms in my dream.

I looked it up, and sure enough, earthworms are hermaphrodites, so this is how they mate. I remembered that the words for "worm" and "serpent" were the same in ancient Sumer: *orm*. I decided to look to see if there were any etymological links between *orm*, "Ouroboros," and "Ouranos." What I found was something better.

As it turned out, "Ouranos" and "Ouroboros" are definitely connected. I used "Google Translate" and found that the word which Wikipedia had rendered as "sky" actually means "rain-maker," or, more specifically, "urinater." Rain was thus likened to urine from the sky. And Ouroboros didn't mean "tail-swallower," as the same source had claimed. That was clearly a euphemism. I discovered a more literal rendering: "urine-drinker."

The Ouroboros is the uncreated one, I thought. *He needs nothing. He produces what he needs. And because he is eternal, because there is no future where he is, that is sufficient.*

But like Gaia and Ouranos, I mused, *this Eternal Serpent was cut up. Isn't that in Egyptian myth somewhere? Worms can regenerate if you slice them in half, and that's what this one did. It became two. Then they started fucking and sucking on each other. It meant the same thing because their mouths and their wombs were the same thing. And the "children" in their wombs were the source of their nourishment. Their wombs were also their stomachs.*

This seemed to me like a logical deduction to make from the known details of the story. I felt a flash of pride that I had figured it out. It was an ancient riddle that probably very few had even realized *was* a riddle, much less pondered about, in the intervening millennia.

But where did the knife come from to cut the worm? I continued to wonder. Its necessary existence represented some kind of perverse blasphemy that I hadn't divined yet.

"Have you figured out anything relevant to our case yet?" Chesterfield said, at last breaking the silence that must have been bothering him. I jumped a bit, startled.

"I don't think so. Not so far," I said.

"What are you doing, looking at cats?" he chastised. "We're running out of time here!"

I looked down at my computer dutifully. After a minute of staring blankly, I asked a stupid question.

"What exactly am I supposed to be looking for?"

"Well, let's go over the case again, shall we?" He got up and began to pace around the kitchen. "It started last Saturday, March 24, five days before I met you. Now you say that's the Day of Blood, when the cult of Cybele used to do their castration rituals. That's the day on which MI5 received the anonymous upload of *Easter Sunday April Fool*."

"Which you admit was not really anonymous," I interjected.

"Right," he acknowledged. "That film depicts—I would say, 'documents'—a boy being kidnapped from Piccadilly Circus right before Easter 1956. And this event took place at the exact same intersection where you chose to stay in a hotel room yesterday, just before Easter, which falls on the same day this year that it did in 1956."

"No, Leopold's people booked the hotel," I insisted. "I had nothing to do with it."

"OK, fine," he said, dismissing my objection with a wave of his hand. "So anyway, the film shows the boy being castrated among ancient ruins somewhere in a ritual you say is similar to the initiation rites of the cult of Cybele. The boy is then possibly killed and fed to the ravens at the Tower of London."

I shrugged my shoulders. I knew that the story, true though it was, sounded insane.

"Then in the same film, a little girl is sodomized next to the London Stone in the upper chamber of Temple Bar, which was then sitting on property attached to a boarding school. The girl is first raped with a dildo on a stick, which, as it turns out, is connected to the symbolism of the ancient monument of Billingsgate in London. It's also similar to the way in which medieval witchcraft cults used to introduce intoxicating substances into the orifices of the initiates at Sabbaths."

I nodded.

"Then, at the same time that I am, illegally and against my employer's protocol, allowing you to see this film, my ultimate boss, the Director of MI5, is kidnapped by your fake baron friend and then killed in that very same chamber of Temple Bar, which has now been moved to Paternoster Square. But…"

He pivoted on his foot and then turned to face me, pointing at me accusingly.

"Temple Bar originally sat right next to the Olde Cock Tavern in Temple, where you ask me to take you while all of this stuff is coincidentally happening. The Director's head is mounted to the front of the bar like he's a traitor, and the murder scene includes a Mithraic magic square, which also shows up at this Alphamstone place that your fake baron friend pretended to be from. It also includes alleged Templar symbols of severed male genitals in a vase that just so happen to be showcased in your latest book. And this brings me to the subject of you, Pamela."

He sat down next to me and put his face within an inch of my own, looking at me sternly. I could almost feel his red mustache tickling my cheek. He continued.

"You claim that this same person kidnapped you yesterday and forced you to witness a bull sacrifice in a secret underground tunnel. But you also refuse to testify to this fact, which is why we don't have his co-conspirators in the fake butcher company arrested, and why he is then able to escape."

There was a lot of anger in his voice, and his words indicated that he might not really believe what I told him about what happened to me the day before. Or, at least, he wanted me to think so. It was supposed to make me feel bad, and it worked, even though I knew I was in no way to blame for anything. I decided to ignore his manipulation tactics.

"Yes," I acknowledged. "And bull sacrifices are associated with both the cult of Cybele and the mysteries of Mithras. Also, a bull sacrifice was depicted on the side of the allegedly Templar-originated Mete coffer that disappeared from the museum. So maybe I should research that angle to connect the Templars, Mithras and Cybele. Because I still don't know how these things all go together."

I looked back down at my computer and began to type into Google. Chesterfield sat back down at his laptop and resumed his own research.

I started off by looking for connections between Mithras and Cybele. I found quickly that a debate had been raging among scholars on the subject for the last 250 years. They couldn't agree on whether or not these two cults, both of Eastern origin and active concurrently in the late Roman Empire, were related at all. It was mostly modern scholars who were claiming that they were not.

Cybele had been adopted into Hellenistic Greece from their western Anatolian colonies as early as the sixth century BC. The Greeks compounded her with Rhea, the wife of Chronos and mother of Zeus. The aspect of her relationship with Attis, some historians said, was really only fully adopted by the Western version of the cult after the Romans absorbed it into their official religion in the second century BC.

But as I had mentioned to Chesterfield before, the *Gallu* of the temples of the Great Mother Goddess Inanna in Sumer also practiced the same rite, and had a myth about the son of the goddess which was identical in many ways to that of Attis.

Mithraism, however, had been imported from Persia much later, starting in the first century after Christ. There were many obvious differences. Mithraism was an all-male cult that, at first blush, seems to promote masculine attributes and shun everything feminine. It was popular in the military, particularly among the foreign legions, and indeed, that's where it had originally begun its spread throughout the empire.

It took a couple of centuries for it to be anything more than a barely tolerated subterranean mystery school (operating literally underground, in caves on the frontiers, and in the basements of other buildings in cities). But eventually, some of the emperors were converted, and the cult, which had originally forbidden its members to join any other religious groups, began to allow amalgamation with the followers of "Sol Invictus" ("Invincible Sun"), a.k.a. Helios. This new and improved Mithraism became the dominant religious force at the end of the empire, until its rival, Christianity, with which it shared mutual influence, eclipsed it altogether.

Early in the twentieth century, two authors—Franz Cumont and Jessie Weston—separately published important works arguing that Mithraists had also made formal pacts with Cybele worshippers. Cumont had stated it as though it were established fact in his 1903 book *The Mysteries of Mithra*. There he had argued that:

> ...in conciliating the priests of Magna Mater, the sectaries of Mithra obtained the support of a powerful and officially recognized clergy, and so shared in some measure in the protection afforded it by the State.

He also pointed out that the temples of both cults (*mithraeums* and *metroons*) were often very close to one another. In Ostia in Italy, where the oldest known *mithraeum* has been found (along with dozens of others scattered throughout the same town), the two temples were actually attached contiguously. Cumont suggested that they may have shared ritual materials, and perhaps even conducted joint rituals.

Now, wasn't Ostia the place where that Pasolini guy was murdered? I thought to myself.

If the two cults did work together, it would actually put to rest one of the points of argument between historians on the subject. Cumont had claimed that both the Cybelists and the Mithraists practiced the rite of *taurobolium*. This was the ceremony wherein the priest would rip open the guts of the victim on a platform with a metal grate over it so that the blood would pour down onto an initiate positioned below. It was a form of sanguinary baptism, after which the recipient was said to be *renatus in aeternum* "reborn for eternity").

Modern scholars, criticizing Cumont, argue that, although the central myth of the cult is about Mithras hunting and killing a bull, a true *taurobolium* would have been impossible to conduct inside of a tiny underground *mithraeum*. But they ignore the fact that Cumont had already addressed this issue. He said the evidence suggested that Mithraists performed few if any of their own sacrifices of.

Instead, he thought that they most likely contracted this work out to a professional *victimarius* (sacrificial butcher), which was a common practice at the time. Any *metroon* would have been equipped for this, and the Cybelists may have been the ones to fulfill this purpose. Cumont also noted that *mithraeums* were usually built directly upon a source of running water. He proposed that the relatively sophisticated plumbing systems they usually sported might have been useful to the Cybelists, and that access to these things might have been traded to them by the Mithraists in exchange for help with butchery.

It occurred to me that Cybele's anti-male transvestite priesthood and the Mithraists' aversion to femininity may have made them an odd yet complimentary pair: they both were against traditional sexuality. Furthermore the mythologies of both cult figures complemented each other in the same way. I told you before that according to some sources, Cybele wasn't always just a woman. Prudentius, a Roman Christian poet, writing in the fourth century, said in *Peristephanon*: 10.1071-3:

> Both sexes are displeasing to Cybele's
> holiness, so he keeps a middle gender
> between the two.

As I mentioned, initiates of Cybele's priesthood went through an orgiastic public ritual in which they were expected to go mad on drugs and wine. They would then become possessed by the goddess, just like Attis, so that they would be inspired to castrate themselves just like he did. These priests were thereafter referred to as women, just like the *Gallu* priests of Sumer before them, and just like a post-op transgender person would be in modern times. Like the *Gallu*, they dressed in women's clothes, spoke in affected effeminate voices, and sang in an effeminate manner that was supposed to be pleasing to the goddess.

Earlier, in the first century BC, another Roman poet, Gaius Valerius Catullus, had written in *Carmina*, Poem 63 about how Attis castrated himself and thus became a priestess of Cybele. From that point on, she was thereby immediately referred to as feminine:

> Over the vast main borne by swift-sailing ship, Attis, as with hasty hurried foot he reached the Phrygian wood and gained the tree-girt gloomy sanctuary of the Goddess, there roused by rabid rage and mind astray, with sharp-edged flint downwards dashed his burden of virility. Then as he felt his limbs were left without their manhood, and the fresh spilt blood staining the soil, with bloodless hand she hastily took a tambour light to hold, your tambourine, Cybele, your initiate rite, and with feeble fingers beating the hollowed bullock's back, she rose up quivering...

Later, when her reason returned to her, she lamented the loss of her penis and the fact that she was now a "slave" to the mother goddess:

> Then when from quiet rest torn, her delirium over, Attis at once recalled to mind her deed, and with lucid thought saw what she had lost, and where she stood, with heaving heart she backwards traced her steps to the landing-place. There, gazing over the vast main with tear-filled eyes, with saddened voice in tristful soliloquy thus did she lament...

This all appears to be an echo of the earliest versions of the Cybele myth, influenced more closely by the Phrygian version. In these, she was called "Agditis," and was said to have originated in the realm of the gods. She had been formed when some of Zeus' semen fell upon a rock called "Agdo." But the other gods found Agditis to be a freak, and so they had her castrated, and cast her down to Earth. This, then, would explain why Cybele was sometimes represented by a rock, particularly a meteorite—a "stone that fell from heaven."

As the story continues, according to a Greek travelogue from Pausanias in the second century AD, the goddess then became pregnant with a boy, whom she abandoned at birth and left for dead. The boy was born so beautiful that he was rescued by a she-goat that felt pity for him. Eventually, when she found him again, his own mother fell in love with him.

He was later engaged to a princess. But during the wedding, Agditis/Cybele possessed his mind and inspired him to castrate himself, resulting in his death. Afterwards, in regret, she "persuaded Zeus to grant the body of Attis should neither rot at all nor decay" (according to a travelogue of Phrygia written in the second century AD by the Greek geographer Pausanias). This is the skeletal story, upon which a variety of flourishes about the boy's death, resurrection, and alleged "love" for his mother were added.

Some obvious parallels between this and the story of Mithras jump out right away. Just as they say Agditis was born from a *petra genetrix* ("fecund rock"), so too was Mithras. Votive depictions of the god's birth show him emerging as a fully-grown young man, with a torch in one hand and a knife in the other, which he used to find his way and tear himself out.

On either side of the rock they always depicted the two *Chiaramonti* ("Torchbearers"), two male youths who wore Phrygian hats just like Mithras, and just Attis Cybele's *Galli* priests. The *Chiaramonti* were also often shown in that same peculiar cross-legged attitude; just like how Attis and the *Galli* were often shown, whether standing or laying; just like the effigies of the cross-legged knights on the graves at Temple church. The names of the two *Chiaramonti* were Cautes and Cautophanes. Each held a torch, with one pointing it upwards, and the other pointing it downwards, respectively. Seeing this reminded me again of Eliphas Levi's depiction of the Templar demon Baphomet, with one hand pointing up, and the other pointing down, along with a torch burning between his goat horns.

The ultimate provenance of Mithras is a mystery. It was a true parthenogenesis, "fertilized by the heavenly father's phallic lightning," as Barbara Walker wrote. He was truly the self-born," like the nameless figure identified by Jesus in the apocryphal *Gospel of Thomas*, where he said:

> When you see him who was *not born of woman,* fall down
> upon your faces and worship him; that *one* is your Father.

Thus during the initiations, according to the one - surviving Mithras Liturgy, inductees took an oath to the god which included the words:

> I... who was born from the mortal womb of (his mother's name) and from the fluid of semen, and who, since he has been born again from you today... resolves to worship you.

In the myth of Mithras, when the time came to have progeny of his own, he chose to mate with a rock because he detested females. A writer known as "Pseudo-Plutarch" wrote in *De Fluviis* 23.4 about a certain mountain in Armenia called "Diorphos." This was named after "Diorphos the Earth-born (or the Titan)," about whom it was said:

> Mithras, who wanted to have a son but hated the race of women, ejaculated onto a stone. The stone became pregnant and — after the appropriate time — produced a boy called Diorphos.

The name of this figure brought to mind the myth of the "Orphic Egg" from the Orphic Mystery Schools, which went back to Greece in the fifth century. They taught that the primordial being was a figure named "Phanes," whom they also called "Eros." The creator of this egg was "Nyx," whose name meant "Night," just like what the name of the Kabbalistic demoness Lilith translates to. I felt that Phanes might also relate to Ophion, a serpent who, with his Titan bride Eurynome, was said to have ruled the Earth for a spell after being "cast down" by Chronos and Rhea. This again indicates an identification with Diorphos, the son of Mithras, identified with Chronos/Saturn.

Depictions of Phanes with his body surrounded by a serpent, strongly resemble the images of the *leontocephaline* (lion-headed) version of Mithras as Saturn (also shown wrapped in a snake) that were found in many *mithraeums*, as were Orphic depictions of the cosmic egg. Other related symbols include the one-snaked rod of Asclepius and the double-snaked rod of Hermes, the caduceus. This last object was shown by Eliphas Levi sitting between the legs of Baphomet instead of a penis.

Like Baphomet, the Persians had originally seen their *Mitra* as an intermediary power, helping connect creatures on our plane with both the celestial powers above and the infernal powers below. In the Roman mystery school version, he became identified with Saturn, the furthest from Earth of the planets then known about, seen in classical astrology as the highest of the heavens. But he was also identified, especially in the latter years of the Roman Empire, with Sol, the Sun. In the old geocentric systems, Sol occupied the middle sphere of the heavens, with other spheres, including those of Jupiter and Saturn, on top of that.

The worshippers of Sol Invictus, like the Egyptians, saw the Sun as the ultimate symbol of an omnipotent god. But in the Mithraic Mysteries, which attempted to incorporate this cult in its later years, the initiate made a symbolic journey through each of the heavens, in imitation of this enhanced story of the adventures of Mithras. This did not merely involve him passing through the various gates of Heaven with special passwords. This (taught by Gnostic and Hermetic schools as necessary for the soul to ascend to the highest realm after death). Rather, in this case, it seems that Mithras actually conquered the intelligences that ruled over these spheres, subduing them to his will.

After slaying the bull from which the material world was made, he ascended this stairway to heaven, the "ladder of lights" we know as the seven classical planets, until he got to Sol's kingdom. There, after the sun was overthrown, the luminary was forced to bow down on one knee to his new master, Mithras. The two then shook hands as friends, and then feasted together on the bull, with the domination of the new sun god now having been established. Then Mithras took the reigns of the Sun's chariot and ascended to the next realm, which was that of Saturn. Mithras then took on as his own identity as well, indicating that he overtook that god like he did the others, and henceforth ruled all of the kingdoms below.

So Mithras is both Saturn and the Sun, I thought to myself. But I've read that Saturn is associated in alchemical symbolism with the process of putrefaction, called the Nigrido. This is when the 'primal material' of the universe is sacrificed and dismembered. And the sign of the Nigrido is a black sun. They say this sun is somehow 'in the center of the Earth,' just like how Chronos, who is Saturn, is imprisoned in Tartarus by Zeus, who is Jupiter. I wonder what that means.

I Googled "Mithras" + "black sun." I also opened other tabs to search the terms "midnight sun" and "second sun" in combination with "Mithras." That's when I discovered an amazing new angle.

Because he victoriously overthrew both the Sun and Saturn, then took on both of their roles, Mithras was seen as the source of a light more primordial, beyond the known universe, the "sun beyond the Sun." The realm of light beyond the sphere of Saturn was called "Hyperuranium." It was named after Saturn's father Uranus, for the same reason the planet beyond Saturn was so named by modern astronomers. A document called "the Mithras Liturgy" described a Mithraic initiate, in imitation of Mithras, entering the palace of the "Seven Pole Lords" with the faces of black bulls. These are the guys who turn the wheels of the heavens, causing earthquakes, thunder and lightning. But Mithras basically makes slavish bitches out of them all.

The fact that Mithras was known for literally "storming heaven," invading the highest realm of the universe with shock and awe, seemed to be part of why his cult was popular with the military of an imperial power. Cybele was already an *official* patroness of the Roman military, and it is no accident that her holy week took place during the month dedicated to the war god Mars. But whereas the Magna Mater was seen as the protectress of the state, and the status quo (much like the Egyptian goddess Maat, whose name meant "world order"), Mithras was a god of rebellion.

The red Phrygian cap worn by Mithras—as well as by Cybele's *Galli*, coincidentally—is also known as a "liberty cap," because in Rome it was the symbol of a slave that had been freed. All slaves wore them during the festival of Saturnalia at the winter solstice, because they were considered free during this time period. Indeed, all rules were considered null during these days, giving way to orgies, drinking, and much mischief.

This was done in honor of Saturn and his Golden Age, when nobody had to work. It is the reason why we all take vacation around Christmas, and why Santa Claus wears that funny red hat. It's also why we get wildly drunk on New Year's Eve, just like the "Feast of Fools" celebrated in medieval Europe, when the social order would be upturned in honor of the "Lord of Misrule." It's why the liberty cap became the symbol of the French Revolution, inspired by Freemasons, who, like the Mithraists, gave no regard to social status within the boundaries of their lodges. The seals of the US Army and the US Senate bear this symbol as well.

Thinking about this at Chesterfield's breakfast table, while he clicked away on his computer across the table from me, I now understood the cosmology of the Smurfs. Papa Smurf, with his red Phrygian hat, was the "Pater," the Father, just like the leader of a Mithraic school was called. His subjects in the communist Smurf dictatorship were all male, like those in the temples of Mithras, except for Smurfette, who had been created through dark alchemy by Gargamel in order to mislead the Smurfs. Papa Smurf, however, had been able to magically turn her over to his will, and let her live with his subjects. But none of them had mothers and, from my recollection, all of them had been created alchemically.

"So," said Chesterfield, clearing his throat. "Learned anything about Cybele and Mithras?"

"Yes," I said. "Quite a lot."

"Well I know that Cybele likes to castrate boys and Mithras likes to fuck bulls in the arse while he kills them. What other sick stuff did they get up to?"

I laughed. "The record on the Mithraists is a bit confusing. On the one hand, there are sources saying that the cult valued abstinence from sex, as an extension of their general hatred of women, and that many of their priests took vows of chastity."

"Yes," he said, nodding as he glanced at his computer briefly. I continued

"But at the same time they had a ceremony for the second degree of their order, which is called "Nymphus" — "the Bride." It was dedicated to the love goddess Venus. The initiate would be married to another brother in the order, dressed in a bridal veil."

"Go on," he said, looking again at his computer as if he were checking off items on a list.

I gave him a breakdown of the material I had found indicating that both Cybele and Mithras were against normal sexual relations, and that both had been born from inseminated rocks. I mentioned the castration of Cybele, and her original hermaphroditic state. I compared her to Baphomet, also missing his penis according to Eliphas Levi.

"The Knights Templar officially rejected sex with women as well, vowing not to touch them, although we know that they did confess to sometimes using female prostitutes in their orgies, always for sodomy. But in order to stem their desires for procreative acts, they vowed *not* to reject the sexual advancements of their brothers. The masters told the initiates that it was better to indulge in this than to 'burn with desire' for females. That's probably why they kissed each other's penises and butts at the end of the induction ceremony."

He looked at me incredulously. "I've never heard *that* before."

"This was all revealed a few years ago by the Vatican," I told him. "It happened when they discovered the Chinon Parchment. It came out that the knights had confessed all of this stuff to Pope Clement V without torture. And this is in addition to the Satanic rituals they confessed about to the King of France years earlier."

"So they were a gay knighthood?" he said. He seemed crestfallen. I guess he really bought into the hype that the Templars were a wrongly maligned group of pure Christian martyrs.

"There's more," I said. "Joseph von Hammer-Purgstall found monuments he believed were of Templar origin, as I told you. Well, some of them had depictions of little boys being sodomized and made to have sex with animals. They also showed kids being sacrificed in a 'baptism of fire' ritual."

"And why would they have done this?" he asked.

"Well, I haven't figured it out entirely."

He rolled his eyes.

"I mean, I think it was an attempt to destroy creation through magic. But I don't know how it was supposed to work."

"Where did you get the idea then?" he asked.

"The Mete coffer." I said. "Remember it shows Cybele with a beard pulling the Sun and Moon down from the sky? She's uprooting the heavens, where the Archons rule from."

"Who are the Archons?" he said, getting visibly annoyed at the labyrinthine symbolism I was attempting to explain.

"The heavenly bodies," I answered. "The rulers of fate, whom the Ophite Gnostics saw as their enemies. They were the seven visible planets, which included the Moon and the Sun. Hammer-Purgstall thought the Templars were secret Ophite Gnostics. And the Ophite Gnostics, according to Hippolytus, incorporated the Cybele mysteries into their dogma."

"OK..." said Chesterfield. I continued.

"Another thing Hammer-Purgstall claimed was a Templar artifact was an engraving in a Bavarian castle showing someone standing in-between and holding two columns that were falling over. Beneath this was written a code that he decoded into the phrase 'the Distinguished Charity of Mete Uproots the Enemy.'"

"What does that mean?" Chesterfield asked with a sigh.

"Well, I'm about to tell you," I said. "I think the 'Distinguished Charity' part means 'strange love,' peculiar love, like the sick sex rituals. Somehow they thought that by having sex in an unnatural way, they could shake the foundations of nature herself, to bring the gods down from their thrones. They saw creation as a prison to be escaped."

There was silence for a moment.

"How would that work?" he finally said.

"That's the part I don't know," I replied. "But that's how I read it. Our ancestors saw things differently than we do. It's difficult to comprehend their logic."

"So could sodomizing the bull while killing it be considered "'strange love?'" he suggested.

"Yes!" I said. It was like a lightning bolt hit my mind. "And you know who else advocated strange love? Aleister Crowley. He did rituals where he raped animals and then killed them during his climax, just like the Mithraists. And he hated women, just like the Mithraists. He thought anal sex magick was the highest form of ritual. The created a secret society where admittance to the highest rank involved getting kidnapped and anally raped by all the other members. He named it after the Templars, and he called himself "Baphomet" as a special nickname. But do you know what he said Baphomet's name meant? 'Father Mithras!'"

I had long considered Crowley's attempt to etymologize the name of Baphomet to be the least useful of all the theories that had been proffered by scholars throughout the years. I agreed with Hammer-Purgstall's conclusion that it meant "Baptism of Wisdom," and most of the suggestions made by others had been similar in meaning. Now I had to rethink it.

Why did *he say that, anyway?* I wondered. I Googled and found a quote from Crowley's *Confessions*:

> Baphomet was Father Mithras, the cubical stone which was the corner of the Temple.

He also mentioned that the word "totaled 729" when interpreted kabbalistically, which I noted in my head was the number of days in a solar year (365) added to the number of days in a lunar year (364). I also recalled that Crowley had published a text called "Liber 729." So I looked that up too.

This, it turned out, was the same thing called *The Amalantrah Working*, which I had heard of before. It seemed to be a bunch of incoherent, personal stream-of-consciousness nonsense channeled from some entity called "the Wizard," presumably Saturn-Mithras (as he took the form of an old hermit). The Wizard kept referring to a quest for an "egg" that Crowley was supposed to embark upon. It urged him:

> The egg is a work which must be done – the great work. By doing the work we get to the key.

I read this out loud to Chesterfield.

"So the stone is Cybele. The stone becomes impregnated, and then it's an egg," he noted. "And the new Sun of the new universe, who is Mithras, who is Saturn, is born from that—he cuts his way out."

This struck me as a very good way of summing it up. I nodded in approval.

"This must be connected to the use of the London Stone in the ritual rape. Didn't you find that it was made of 'egg stone'?"

"Yes. Yes I suppose it must be connected," I agreed.

"The ritual took place on Easter," he went on. "And the film mentioned "Easter eggs" just before it cut out."

"And it showed her laying an egg," I said.

He gulped. "From her bum?"

"It's something that Crowley specifically mentioned he wanted to do: make a homunculus born rectally, whose birth would herald the start of a new era. It's also something that happened in the Egyptian pantheon. In the Ogdoad cosmology, Thoth gave birth to several of his children by laying an egg from his anus."

"What's a homunculus?" Chesterfield asked.

"An artificial person," I said. "In Hebrew it's called a 'golem.' There are lots of different thoughts on how you could do it. The simplest way is making an idol out of clay and bringing it to life magically with the use of sperm and incantations. Making a robot and doing the same thing with it is an even more sophisticated approach. The first so-called 'androids' were built in the Middle Ages with exactly this purpose. They were meant to me animated through supernatural means."

"Animated with what?" he asked.

"Well, you would invoke a spirit to rise up into it," I said, "whether it be the spirit of a dead person, or of something else, like a demon, or a god."

He raised his eyebrows.

"Theoretically, of course," I said. "I mean, that's what some people believe. I'm not saying I believe it."

"I see. Could you put a spirit into a dead body, for instance?" he asked.

"Yes, you could use a dead body," I answered. "Or just parts of one. Or you could stitch together parts of a dead body and animate then, like Dr. Frankenstein's monster. You could even combine the parts of different creatures, like how the Egyptian gods were depicted. Chimeras, they're called."

"So the gods of the ancient world could have been these demonically-animated Frankenstein creatures made from dead human and animal bodies?" he asked.

"That's actually what I think they were," I said, surprised at his insight.

"Crowley tried to bring a skeleton to life at his Black Temple on Chancery Lane," said Chesterfield, once again revealing that he knew quite a lot about Crowley's biography. "He was feeding it human blood and dead birds. I suppose that was an attempt to make a golem from a dead body, right?"

"Certainly," I said. "And the Templars' chief mascot, their secret captain, their lucky talisman and their idol of worship was a product of exactly this kind of sorcery."

"Baphomet, you mean?" Chesterfield guessed.

"Yes," I answered. "They say it started out as a skull with two leg bones. Specifically, these bones belonged to the body of a girl named Yse, who had been loved by one of the original Templar knights. But she had died before their love was consummated, and so the knight took it upon himself to break open her coffin and have his way with her corpse. After he was done, he heard a voice speaking to him that is described as coming from 'beyond the Void.' It told him to shut up the grave and return nine months later, when he would find a son waiting for him."

I looked at Chesterfield. He was literally on the edge of his chair, tilted forward so that the back legs were rising off the floor as he stared at me with his eyes wide, waiting for me to finish, like it was the best ghost story ever. I continued.

"The knight obeyed this instruction, and when he came back he found the skull and leg bones waiting for him. It spoke to him, promising to bring him luck in business and battle if he brought it with him everywhere and took its advice. That's how the original Baphomet skull came to the Temple's possession, and that supposedly had much to do with the extent of their worldly success."

"Interesting," said Chesterfield. "You know, just a couple of years ago we had a murder case in that De Vere hotel in Theobald Park—the one they made out of Lady Meux's old mansion, right in front of where she had the Temple Bar parked. Some guy—a lawyer and a friend of Boris Johnson— killed a young teacher in his room there on Christmas Eve. Then he had sex with her dead body. He said a voice in his head told him to take her there and do exactly that."

He finished his story and stared at me. I didn't react. So many weird things were connecting together, and this was just one more.

"It's just that Temple Bar is part of our mystery," he said, as if he had to explain the connection. "And Temple Bar is associated with Templars…."

"And lawyers," I added. "That's where the legal profession is headquartered. That's where we get the bar exam that lawyers have to take. The practice of law is like a secret society in itself." I was drifting off topic.

"I know," said Chesterfield. "So the head talked to them and told them what to do, how to fight, how to build a banking empire…."

"How to blackmail the Papacy into giving them an exemption from all laws and all taxes…." I interrupted.

"So that's the big secret of the Templars? A talking skull that gave them business advice?"

"Talking idols made from decapitated heads were quite common in the ancient East," I said. "They were called *teraphim*, and they were generally made from the heads of sacrificed young boys. But the head of a prophet was considered quite powerful, and could be used to enslave the soul of the prophet, to make use of his power. This is what the Templars were rumored to have done with the mummified head of John the Baptist to make into Baphomet, the Baptizer of Wisdom."

"But I thought Baphomet was a goat-headed human hermaphrodite?" said Chesterfield.

"I think they augmented it over time," I replied. "Like the chimeras we mentioned. Perhaps only the head was original. I also think they made other versions of the idol for all their other chapters, using the same magical principles, but that somehow they were all connected together and couldn't work independently. They were just conduits to the group's shared patron demon."

"And then they worshiped it as a god, right?" he said.

"I guess so. I mean, they bowed down to it and kissed it. Sacrificed to it. Testified that it could 'save' them, make them 'wealthy,' and make their crops prosperous. They said that it gave them 'wisdom.' They had to take an oath of allegiance to it, and renounce Jesus Christ in the process. It sounds like a religion to me."

"So they made up their own religion, like you were saying, out of bowing down to this idol, combined with other bits and bobs they collected from pagan cults, Satanic cults, Gnostic heresies, Greek and Roman mystery schools…. Am I missing anything?" he said.

"No, that's it. And the god they made for themselves was like a compound of all these different gods and goddesses, as well as demons, from all the various traditions. Just like a Dr. Frankenstein's monster, it was a bunch of parts from different bodies all stuck together. But they felt that it made their god and their religion stronger to be forged from so many different, even contradictory sources of power. They created an egregore that for a time took over the world, and still influences it immensely today."

"An egregore?" he said.

"A collective thought-form animated by magic," I replied. "The Baphomet golem was just the physical touchpoint that allowed the Baphomet egregore to manifest."

"So Mithras and Cybele, though they may have been contradictory in many ways, could have been combined by the Templar magicians into one thoughtform that was more powerful than both of them," he said.

"My thoughts exactly," I told him.

"And when did Mithras celebrate his birthday. Christmas, right?" said Chesterfield.

"Yes, supposedly," I replied. "But Franz Cumont thought that only came to be observed after Mithras was conflated with Sol Invictus towards the end of the empire. He said that Mithraic initiations typically took place during March, and that they particularly celebrated the time around the Spring Equinox. Just like Cybele's Day of Blood and the rest of her holy week festivals."

Just then, Agent Paris walked in and took a place at the table. He had been listening for several minutes from the next room while he was sitting at Chesterfield's desk, printing out documents from his own laptop with Chesterfield's computer. He had his own remarks to share.

"You know, what's interesting?" he said. "The end of March, or early April, was the time of year when they finished the orgies and murdered everyone in *120 Days of Sodom*. There's a bit of ambiguity because the Marquis never finished the novel. He ran out of paper when he was imprisoned in the Bastille. But he made an outline of how it would end. The 120 days of sex orgies started on November 1st. The child victims were kidnapped and taken to the Duke's hidden mansion in the woods on Halloween Night."

Chesterfield and I both leaned in, fascinated by what Paris was telling us. He continued.

"Now, those orgies ended on February 28th of the following year, in which 10 of the people died. That was the spell of 120 days that the title refers to. But then he planned it to go into a new phase of total torture and murder over the following three weeks. More and more people's tongues were to be torn out, eyes gouged out, fingers cut off, testicles crushed, organs removed or rearranged, etc., resulting in death for most of them. Twice as many people were to have died in these final festivities, which were set to end on March 21."

"There does seem to be something about the Spring Equinox, and the entire Lenten season, which brings out human savagery," I remarked, amazed by the coincidence but not sure what else to say about it.

"What's also interesting is that Lent started this year on Valentine's Day, and that's also the birthday of Blake Rosenberg," Chesterfield proffered.

"The former mayor of New York?" I said.

"Yeah." He replied.

"What's this got to do with him?" I asked.

"He's the guy that owns Rosenberg Plaza, where the *mithraeum* is," Paris replied, looking at me like I was stupid. "Yeah, that's the guy I've been researching for the last hour," said Chesterfield. "A real weirdo. But he's the sixth richest person in the world. 32 times richer than the Queen."

"I had no idea!" I said. "I mean, I knew he was rich. But I guess I didn't know how rich. Is it all from that financial news company he owns?"

"No, he started that *after* he got rich," said Paris. He made it big selling the 'Niptron Terminal.' It's literally a computer full of proprietary software that every single major trader in financial securities uses as a trading platform. Most of the trades made all over the world are going through one of his devices, and the users are all paying monthly licensing fees to his company."

"Wow, I can't believe I didn't know that," I said. "Doesn't that mean his company could potentially interfere with trading on a massive scale if they wanted to? And doesn't that mean they know every trader's strategy before it's executed? Couldn't they use that information to cheat on their own trades, or sell it to others?"

"Or front-run the entire market," said Paris, "using the data they're skimming and high-frequency trading to drive the traders exactly where they want them to go."

"Like sheep to a slaughter," said Chesterfield. "I found tons of articles alleging that they were doing exactly that. The company's been investigated for it numerous times, but the charges never stick."

"As it is, he's also pushing investment in gold," said Paris. "And hoarding it himself. He's always telling everybody that the markets are going to crash, and the currencies are going to fail, so they need to stockpile precious metal investments for Armageddon. That's why he's been nicknamed 'Doomberg.'"

"That word *Niptron* sounds really familiar," I said "I guess I must have heard of the terminal before."

"Maybe," said Paris. "But you probably also saw the word 'Niptron' when you were researching Mithraism. It's the term they use in the 'Lion' grade to refer to the 'baptism of fire' that happens in the ritual, which is symbolic of the universal conflagration that will burn up the unrighteous at the end of time."

"That's right," said Chesterfield. "At St. Martin's Ludgate there's a palindrome on the holy water font that says '*Nipson anomemata me monan opsin*, which means 'Wash my sin and not my face only.' So *nipson* and *niptron* are different conjugations of the same word."

"So do we think he was obsessed with Mithras way back when he started his company?" I asked "Back when the *mithraeum* was still sitting in a courtyard in the middle of Great Queen Street?"

"Probably," said Chesterfield. "He's also been obsessed with England for a long time, and doing business in the City for decades. But when the Queen offered to knight him, he 'respectfully' declined the offer, because it would have involved genuflecting to the queen during the investiture. He said he couldn't 'bow down' to anybody for 'personal reasons' he couldn't discuss."

"That's odd," said Paris. "I also noted that his newspaper has published several articles in recent years implying that the monarchy is strapped for cash."

"Have you found any connections between him and Thomas Weir?" Chesterfield asked. "Or the Oriental Club? Or Director Pindar?"

"Just the Alphamstone connection," Paris replied. "What's that? Chesterfield and I both said simultaneously.

"The Rector from the Church of St. Barnabas there — the one that has the Sator Square in it. . . ."

"Yes…" Chesterfield and I both said in exasperation. "She's just been named the Bishop of the London Diocese of the Church of England. And her first mass at St. Paul's Cathedral will be on Easter."

Our jaws dropped.

"What's her name?" we both said.

"Consivia Springhole," Paris replied.

"Springhole?" Chesterfield laughed. "It must have been tough getting through school with *that* name."

"She spent her teen years in a girl's hostel in Forest Gate in London," said Paris. "But it closed in the 1960s. I haven't figured out where she came from before that."

"What else do you know about her?" asked Chesterfield.

"You won't believe it," said Paris.

"What?" we both said impatiently.

"She's been the civil partner of Blake Rosenberg for the past twelve years."

"What?" We both gasped.

"You're telling me that Rosenberg, one of the world's richest men, is matched up with the rector of that tiny village."

"Yeah," he went on. "And rumor has it, it's an 'open relationship.' They have an adopted daughter. She's twelve. She sometimes gets in the tabloids for competing at royal equestrian steeplechases."

"Is that acceptable in the Church of England now?" I asked. "Bishops in open relationships?"

"Oh yeah, anything goes in Her Majesty's Church now,"

Chesterfield said, rolling his eyes.

"He's a Jew too. Secular," said Paris. "Most of his comments about Christianity have been pretty hostile. So the richest and perhaps most irreverent Jewish American in London is swinging with the leader of the Church for all of London. Bizarre, isn't it? But I'm sure nobody's complained because nobody wants to offend anybody."

"Then there's the fact that he hates women," remarked Chesterfield. "So what's he doing with a woman of the cloth, who is undoubtedly, due to the challenges of her nontraditional job, a feminist?"

"What's your evidence that he hates women?" I asked.

"Women *and* children," he answered. "According to the papers he's made a number of disparaging remarks about females. He openly insists that the women who work for him maintain a sexy appearance at all times, no matter how serious the job supposedly is. He's only allowed a handful of females to rise to the top of his business, and none of them had children."

I thought about how this might fit in with the man's reported obsession with Mithraism.

"In fact," Chesterfield continued, "his female employees usually get demoted once their bosses learn that they're pregnant. He once told a pregnant underling directly: 'Kill it, or kill your career.' Yet strangely, as Mayor of New York, he enthusiastically supported gay marriage so strongly that he insisted on performing the city's first same-sex ceremony himself, on two of his own employees."

Chesterfield turned his computer around to show me a newspaper article with a photo of Rosenberg, a Poindexter with brown hair, slightly crossed eyes and a medium build in an expensive navy suit. He was standing gleefully behind two men in equally costly suits, crowned with celebratory laurel wreaths and holding hands lovingly. In front of them stood their two adopted sons, ages 6 and 8.

"Employees of the City of New York? Or employees of Rosenberg Industries?"

"Of his own company," Chesterfield answered. He was about to add something else, but there was a knock at the door. Everybody suddenly got quiet. Chesterfield sat frozen, his eyes wide.

"That's odd," he whispered. "Normally visitors use the buzzer at the front door downstairs." He was clearly alarmed, with no reason to expect that anybody would be calling on him now.

"Well it could be a neighbor," Paris said in a conversational tone. But Chesterfield frantically quieted him.

"Shhh!"

He crept out of the kitchen and around the corner to the front door. Paris and I tip-toed quietly behind him. He looked through the peephole. Then he turned around, bewildered.

"There's nobody there," he whispered. Then he turned back around, looked through the hole again, and began turning the handle.

"Wait, aren't you going to get your guns out?" I said to the two spooks.

"We don't have *guns*," Paris sneered. "It's not the Wild West."

Chesterfield opened the door. Indeed there was no one standing there. On the ground, however, there was an empty glass Coke bottle sitting there, sealed on top with the bloody severed head of a black bird.

We all gasped. Chesterfield shut the door rapidly. Then he gestured for Paris to come over to him. Paris appeared to hesitate, and looked around the room frantically. Then he took an autographed cricket bat from the wall where it was mounted a few feet away from him, and walked up right behind his partner with the bat held high. Chesterfield rolled his eyes and opened the door wide.

Still, no one was there. Both men crept out into the hallway and searched it, then quickly returned to the doorway. By this time I had noticed that there was a rolled-up piece of paper inside of the Coke bottle, and mentioned it to them. Chesterfield put his jacket sleeve over his hand and picked up the bottle with disgust.

"God, I hope I don't get rabies from this," he said. He took the bottle into the kitchen and placed it on the counter, where we all gathered around to inspect it.

The dead bird's head had been sealed in place with red wax. Chesterfield took a steak knife from one of the drawers and unsealed it. He placed the head on a paper napkin, which he then rolled up and put inside of a sandwich bag, then in the refrigerator.

After that, he took the bottle and broke the neck off on the side of the sink so that the shards would fall inside the sink. Then he shook the bottle upside down, and the rolled-up paper fell out onto the counter. He put the broken bottle and its neck inside of the fridge as well, right next to the bird head.

I didn't ask, but presumed he was preserving these things as evidence, and planned to report the crime later. Nobody said anything. We were all trying to be as quiet as possible.

When Chesterfield returned to the counter, Paris was already using the steak knife to open the paper roll, which was also sealed with red wax. It looked like parchment. He unfurled it, and we all read the message, which appeared to be written in blood.

Sweet are the livers of the birds, but care reigns.

"What the fuck does that mean?" Chesterfield whispered. "What kind of sick weirdos are we dealing with?"

Agent Paris silently extended his hand to display his smartphone, on which he had already looked up the phrase from the scroll. It showed a website where these words were quoted as being written on the wall of a *mithraeum* in the Santa Prisca church in Rome.

Chesterfield rolled his eyes again. "Whatever. I'm getting my cat out of here. Who knows what they might do to her. Get your things ready, guys. We need to get going. Paris can't be late for his meeting and we need to check out Rosenberg Plaza."

"Are you going to report this as a crime?" I asked. "Later," he said, already exiting the kitchen. "It doesn't matter right now." He was clearly quite frightened, and understandably eager to leave the apartment.

Paris and I packed up our briefcases. Chesterfield returned momentarily with Lenore the cat inside a carrier. We silently walked out the front door and cautiously proceeded down the hall to the elevator. But when we got to the bottom floor, there was another surprise waiting for us.

Sitting on the two pink sofas facing each other in the lobby were two Metropolitan police, along with the building's manager—an old white man—and several other tenants. On the coffee table between the sofas was the decapitated body of a black bird, feet sticking straight up. One of the officers was examining a tag on the bird's right foot.

Despite Chesterfield's attempt to stop him, Paris headed right over to talk to the cops. Reluctantly, Chesterfield went over there as well, stooping under the burden of his cat carrier, and I followed behind. But by the time we got there, the short conversation was already wrapping up.

"I don't know," said Paris. "I'll get in touch with my contacts and see what I can find out." He shook the man's hand and we all walked out of the building towards the car.

"So what did you find out?" I asked him in a hushed voice.

"They found it in the elevator. It's one of the ravens from the Tower of London. The tag on the foot IDs it. And it even has its wings clipped just like the Tower ravens. Yet when the cops called Tower security, they said the Raven Master has reported nothing amiss so far. Which means it's a state secret. The Home Office has decided to keep it hush-hush. So the cops don't even know the truth."

At that moment, the cell phones of both agents rang simultaneously.

"But MI5 does," Paris sighed, clicking his car key to unlock the doors. They both pulled out their phones while I took the cat and got into the car to wait for them.

Chapter 18: Omnia Cum Deo

The industrial use of semen will revolutionize human society.

— Aleister Crowley, diary entry, August 8, 1923

"It does everything but give you a blowjob!" Rosenberg had said of the new building for his London headquarters at an opening dinner for the office staff stationed there. It was an inside joke, a repetition of something he had once gotten in trouble for saying about the Niptron Terminal when it first came out. But reports from employees who were already working there indicated that Rosenberg Plaza might *very well* be capable of giving you a blowjob. At least, that's what it said in the *Wired Magazine* article I was reading on my laptop, connected to my mobile phone for data. I was reading it as we inched along in London's morning rush hour in the Vauxhall. The article cited certain anonymous posts by alleged Rosenberg employees on 4chan, which I also began reading.

Rosenberg Plaza was built to be the "smartest building in Europe" (construction having started back when England was considered part of Europe). It was now the building that covered the largest land mass of any in the City of London. It supposedly was able to generate all of its own energy, due to being covered entirely in "solar windows." In fact, it was actually generating more energy than it used, creating a surplus that was sold to the employees' profit.

There were other schemes for generating energy within the building also. Energy was harnessed from the exercise equipment in the gym, with workers given fixed times that they were expected to spend there. This was enforced with alarms programmed for them onto their employer-issued smart phones. Reportedly, there was a secret power generator located in a subbasement of the main building that converted organic compost from employee lunches into energy. But only certain high-level executives had ever seen it, and they weren't allowed to talk about it.

Because of the covert way in which the program was being run, nobody could officially confirm this, and therefore nobody knew how well the energy conversion was working, but presumably it was worth doing. The recycling of organic material had continued unabated from the time the building had opened for workers, almost a year earlier, until then, the day on which the public parts of the Plaza were going to be opened, including the *mithraeum*. Since there were actually two buildings in Rosenberg's new Plaza—including a smaller one built to lease to other tenants, connected by a sky bridge, I wondered if the other tenants were required to participate in Rosenberg's organic recycling scheme, and if all of its bathrooms were hooked up to the same system.

I wonder if the other tenants of the Plaza are required to participate in Rosenberg's organic recycling scheme, I thought to myself.

From my reading, I further learned that the Rosenberg office building was super energy-efficient because it was equipped with a "digital ceiling." This means that the building itself responded to people's needs by spying on them constantly to figure out exactly when and where they required light, heat, or air conditioning. For this, cameras and microphones were everywhere, along with other sensors of every imaginable type, feeding data into a network of AIs that ran the entire Plaza as one integrated system. All artificial light was provided by a field of hexagonal white "flowers" containing high-efficiency LEDS that covered the ceilings. But this was largely supplemented by the gigantic sunroof on top that supplied natural light. There were also several much smaller sunroof portals that channeled sunlight into specific areas of the building.

The building also contained quite a lot of amenities to provide comfort and ease for those who worked there. Robotic vending machines on wheels could be ordered at the push of a button, so people could work at a desk for long hours without having to leave to get food. In fact, the digital ceiling allowed them to program hand signals or other body movements that could be used as passwords to summon food, or the police, or an ambulance, or simply to tell one's subordinate to come immediately.

This was possible, of course, because it was sensing and tracking everybody's movements at all times. All of these features could also be utilized with a smart phone. Indeed, everybody had to use their phone every day just to find an available desk, work station or meeting room, which is why there were phone charging stations everywhere. It was better than the Clapper, better than a Life Alert button. A complete George Jetson office. A Starship Enterprise docked in the City of London.

But it got weirder. Of course it did.

Rosenberg had been an early investor in sex robot industry also. Thus, my presumption that the building itself could provide sexual favors was not unfounded. In fact, I next discovered a 4chan thread, barely a week old, in which several alleged Rosenberg employees discussed the hidden secrets of the building known only to the elites among the organization. They said that there was a special bathroom, available only to certain employees (all of them men) which was equipped with a robotic glory hole.

Quite literally, there was a hole in the wall, covered with a small round door, in which a man could insert his penis and receive, at the push of a button, an artificially-induced orgasm. Afterwards, he would press another button, which caused the door to close again, and the hole would rinse itself with a sterilizing solution, making itself ready for the next user. There was a barbarous code word for this special room: "Qaphqa."

None of the people talking about the glory hole would admit to having used it. I suspected some were lying about that. However, there didn't seem to be the same kind of shame about using the company's sex robots at office parties, which several of them had apparently been treated to. I thought it was odd that this didn't embarrass them, because it basically amounted to the same thing in my mind. I also found myself wondering if the semen was being recycled like the other organic material in the building.

Heck, maybe even the toilets are hooked up to the generator, I thought, recalling that both urine and feces were thought of by alchemists as substances of great power. I remembered that Hennig Brand had discovered phosphorus in 1669 while performing alchemical experiments with urine. More recently, I recalled, a team of Nigerian girls had built a urine-powered generator just a few years back. So it seemed possible, though improbable.

Then I read another detail, about the women's bathrooms in Rosenberg Plaza—those for general female employee use—that seemed to fit in with such a scenario. The toilets were equipped with separate flush buttons for liquid and solid waste.

Nothing too weird about that, I thought at first. *They do that at the airports in Portland. Wastes less water that way. The liquid flush uses less than the solid flush.*

But then I read the next few lines of a 4chan post.

> To be clear: we are *specifically* asked to ensure that there is no solid waste in our urine flushes. After each flush, the bowl uses sound waves to cleanse itself. I've never tested it, because people who make mistakes around here get fired the first time. But I'll bet that if you mixed your poop and pee, the building would know, and you would get caught right away.

Then there was another comment from the same person, adding another amazing detail:

> There aren't many women working here, and most of those are past menopause. But I've heard that this handful of younger women get the day off whenever it's the first day of their period. There's a special room in the first basement where these women lay all day on a modified dissection table— nicknamed 'the Periodic Table'— equipped with conduits and a reservoir for collecting the blood. She gets paid for doing this instead of working all day, and is forbidden from discussing it with other employees, although somebody obviously discussed it with me.
>
> She would not be able to hide the fact that she's menstruating even if she wanted to. The building knows you're going to menstruate two days before you start, and sends an alert to your smartphone confirming your appointment in the subterranean menstrual hut.

Is Rosenberg secretly harnessing some age-old alchemical technology in his "smart building"? I wondered.

"I think you should have a look at these aerials of the Plaza," Paris said, handing me a stack of documents. On top was a color print-out showing a bird's eye photo of the whole site.

"Tell me if you see any symbolism there," he said.

I looked. The main building was an odd shape, kind of like a keystone, but not really. The other, smaller building resembled a coffin shape. The

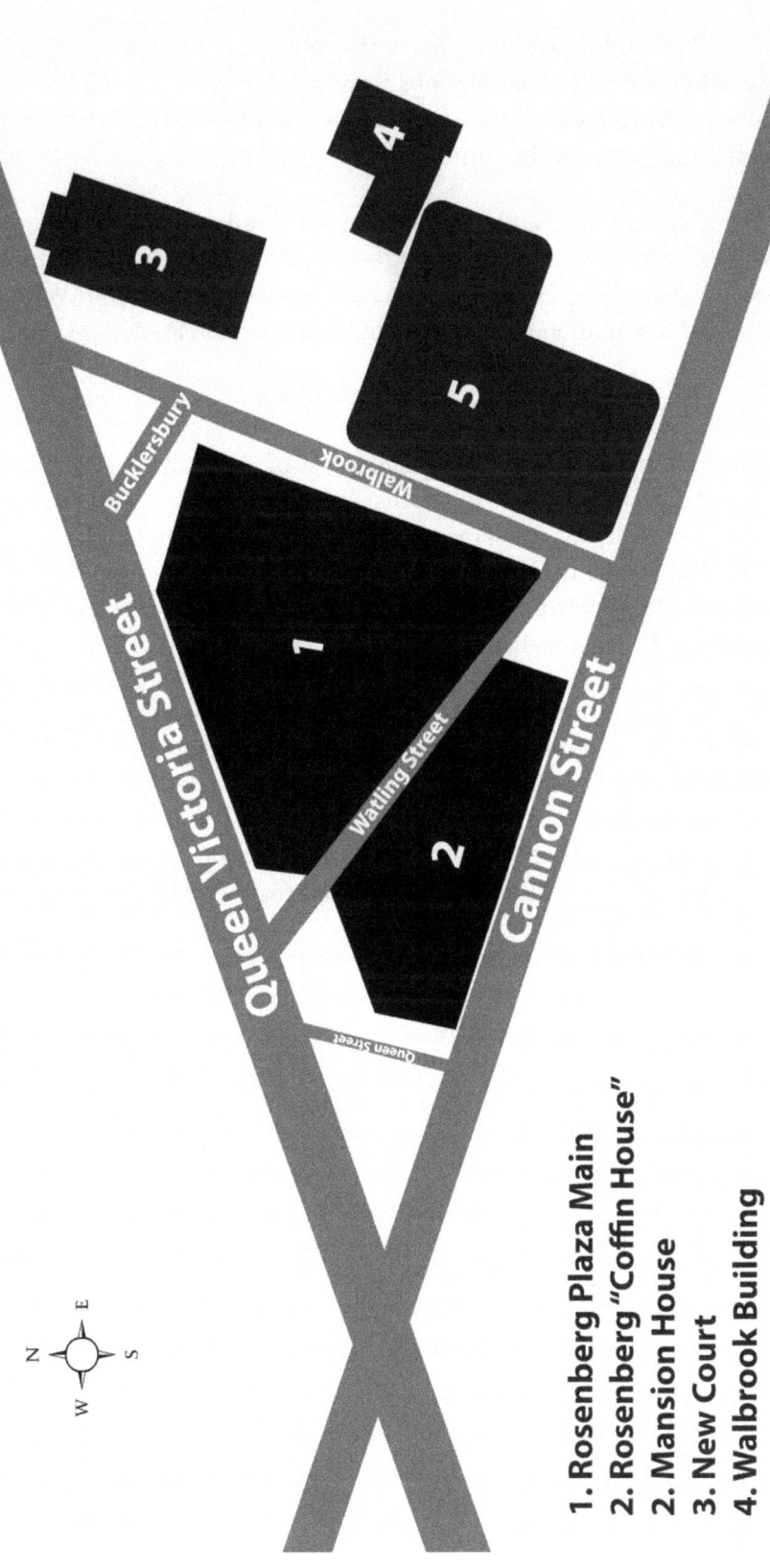

sides of the building and the rims of the roofs were a shimmering gold color, while the rest of the rooftops were filled in with powder blue. In the middle of the roof of the main building was a large white circular bubble, which I thought to be the sunroof.

I squinted my eyes and tried turning it around several times. I noticed that the shape formed by the five streets surrounding the site—Cannon Street, Queen Street, Queen Victoria Street, Bucklersbury, and Walbrook—resembled the diamond shape used in the Superman logo.

But what could that possibly mean? I wondered.

Then I noticed how the triangular pieces of sidewalk on the ends of the diamond completed it, like the horns on a bull, to form a very particular triangle shape. It was the same triangle shape I had seen in my mind's eye when I was at Stratford House looking at the map made from the bull intestines. Cannon Street and Victoria Street seemed to encompass the contents of the triangle like the blades on a pair of scissors.

I decided to thumb through the rest of the papers. Next in the stack was a blueprint for a trefoil spiral ramp that apparently wrapped all the way around the larger building in lieu of a staircase. It wasn't exactly a "triskelion"—the Celtic symbol made from three spirals—although it resembled one. Instead, it was all made from one line, wound in a way that almost seemed like a Mobius strip staircase from an M.C. Escher drawing.

I saw that the building had been constructed in a certain way that most of the above-ground floors were entirely open in the middle, and almost every such floor was visible from every other floor when standing near the center. The ramp connected them all, so that if you rode a skateboard from the top to the bottom, you would visit all of the sides of the building, which was made from six huge walls surrounding seven pillars.

The main lobby on the ground floor, however, had a full ceiling. But it was dominated by an object in the center called "the Vortex." I could not tell what it was from looking at the pictures, so I searched the 4chan board for employee posts about it. I found one, written by a janitor who worked there.

Apparently, it was some kind of glass-enclosed decorative feature containing what appeared to be water and other fluids of various "earth tone" colors, swirling around inside. It was made in the shape of a "curved triangle." The management of the company was very secretive about the Vortex, what it contained, and what it emptied into. Nobody knew if it had a purpose beyond mere decoration. They only let certain people perform maintenance on it, and none of the lower-level employees had ever talked to those people.

The janitor theorized that the toilets and the glory holes were hooked up to pipes that somehow emptied into the Vortex. He thought it was actually a fountain of untreated sewer water purporting to be a decoration. He also said there were pipes leading to the Vortex from the "Coffin House" (their actual nickname for the coffin-shaped auxiliary building that was ostensibly empty at present). Then from there, he said, pipes led to the generator in the basement.

As I read on about Rosenberg Plaza, particularly the large building that housed the company's own headquarters, I learned that instead of having individual offices or even cubicles for the employees, the space was constructed of hexagonal pods put together like Legos. There was usually one side left open as an entrance, which could be easily rearranged at will. Individual offices were discouraged, and there were only a few for certain executives.

So people shared hexagons, and shared (or perhaps competed for) the specially-designed L-shaped desks lining the sides of the hexagons. None of them had doors, so they were easy to move from room to room. The ratio of workers to desks was 2.5 to 1. It was something called "hot-desking." This was apparently all the rage in the European business world. There, a philosophy called *het nieuwe werken* ("the new work") was being foisted upon every poor sucker who needed to earn an income.

This approach, the literature quoted Rosenberg as saying, "encourages people to work together." It forced them to move around constantly, rather than being stuck at a single desk. People kept their personal items in storage lockers. Even these they were encouraged to change constantly. It was against the rules to use the same locker three days in a row.

A labyrinth of hexagons, I thought. *Just like a beehive.* Then I remembered the design of the library in Jorge Luis Borges' surrealist novel *The Lottery in Babylon*, which was almost identical. There, the hexagonal cubicles contained books made from all possible combinations of a 25-letter character set (most of them gibberish). The similarity was so close it couldn't be accidental.

To me, someone who suffers from acute social anxiety, values privacy, and would stay home from school as a child to avoid group projects, the thought of working in a place like this seemed like an absolute nightmare. But, after a minute of thought, it occurred to me that this whole design — the hexagonal pods and the spiral ramp-was probably meant to facilitate the movement of robots. It wasn't just about the robots that were already serving food to employees there, or cleaning up their food crumbs, or sucking their dicks at office parties.

In the near future, surely robots will soon replace the vast majority of those employees, I thought. *And robots don't need privacy.*

In fact, the machines that would soon be running the place would be better able to spy on the few humans that were left if there weren't any walls or ceilings in the way. A little more reading confirmed that the place was patrolled by "robocops" at night. These tin cans on wheels were not armed, but alerted the security team to anything unusual.

Also, as per the concept of "smart cleaning," the sensors around the building collected data on "all activity" within. This was so that the cleaning robots would know exactly when, where and how something needed to be cleaned without having to be told. If you put your gum underneath the desk you were borrowing, a robot would immediately come clean it up, and probably also tattle on you to your boss.

I thought again about my theory that Rosenberg Plaza housed an alchemical laboratory converting the urine, feces, semen, and menstrual blood of his workers into energy, and/or other products. It occurred to me that such a system could easily be masked within the labyrinth of long tubes that were shown on the plans running throughout all of the walls, ceilings and ramps for "radiant climate control." These were all connected to a large cluster of objects in the first subbasement labeled "water storage tanks" in the blueprints. But they were of different shapes and sizes, all networked together with pipes, and clearly not all just for storing water.

Their function is being masked, I thought silently. *This is the secret generator.*

Then I noticed that the largest of the tanks was positioned directly beneath "the Vortex." Pipes were also shown connecting the Vortex directly to the other tanks in the basement. It was a confusing circle of connections. I couldn't tell what was flowing into what.

I kept these observations to myself. Chesterfield asked to look at the papers, so I handed them over, pointing out the unique properties of the spiral ramp. This sparked something in him. His eyes lit up.

"The triskelion was a womb symbol to the Celts," he said, looking at me proudly. "Often there was a sun symbol in the middle, which could be taken to represent the rebirth of the sun god. It could be related. On Rosenberg's roof he's got a white circular sunroof to represent that part of the symbol."

"And the site as a whole looks like the Superman logo," Paris said. "Which, if you think about it, resembles a female pelvis."

I was shocked by both of their contributions. Most amazing was that Paris had also noted the resemblance to the Superman symbol. The resemblance to female anatomy had occurred to me too, but I had dismissed it, since I didn't take the Superman connection seriously in the first place.

Now I thought about the fact that Superman wore what appeared to be a pair of red bikini briefs on the outside of his blue leggings, as if to draw attention to the pelvic shape. A tingle went down the back of my neck. I knew we were on to something.

"OK," I said. "I've never heard that before, but if you thought of it, that means somebody else probably did too."

I contemplated the origin of the word "Super Man" involving the "overman" theories of Nietzsche, and how Hitler adopted them, thinking there was a new "Master Race" on the horizon. According to Herman Rauschning, Hitler once said of this:

> I have seen the new man. He is intrepid and cruel. I was afraid of him.

Then there was the first use of the term "Superman" in English. This came from Aleister Crowley's novel *Moonchild*, the one where he wrote about creating a child with divine parentage through sex magick. Regarding this process, he had said:

> ...the idea has been almost universal in one form or
> another; the wish has always been for a Messiah or
> Superman, and the method some attempt to produce man
> by artificial or at least abnormal means.

My meditation on these subjects was broken when I realized that we were going by St. Paul's Cathedral again. Then before I knew it, the car stopped at a stoplight between two office buildings. Paris turned around to speak to me.

"OK, you guys can get out."

"Where are we?" I asked.

"Rosenberg Plaza," he said. "The ribbon-cutting will

happen on the Walbrook side, east, right in front of the entrance to the *mithraeum*. Then go on to the conference room. That's where Rosenberg will give a speech."

"Should we bring the cat?" I said.

The question was directed at Chesterfield, who was already getting out of the car.

"No, don't worry. I'll take care of her. I have a special place where I can put her until it's safe. Try to figure out what's going on at this building. I'll let you know how my meeting goes."

I said 'goodbye' and got out. Before I closed the door, Chesterfield leaned over the back seat, where his cat had been sitting next to me, and stuck his fingers through the bars of the cage. He told her he would miss her, and then thanked Paris for taking care of his "little girl." Then the other agent drove off, leaving us standing next to the "bulky, impenetrable mass" that housed the Temple of Mithras.

I looked down the street to get a scope of the entirety of the site. We were on the western corner of the "Superman logo" formed by the site, with the buildings on our right. I looked down the street, north-west, and saw the division between the two structures, with the footpath leading down between them to the "arcade" as it was called in the paperwork I'd seen. There we would surely find the promised "dining and retail establishments" that the plans said would be there. Having only had a scone since the regurgitated meal at the pub the previous night, I was hungry.

"Let's find a restaurant," I said. "We have 40 minutes to kill until the ribbon-cutting."

"OK, sure," Chesterfield agreed.

"What's the coffin-shaped building for?" I wondered aloud as we walked past it. "I didn't see much about it in the design plans."

"I saw it in the permit applications," said Chesterfield. "They were at the back of the stack. Supposedly they're going to sublease it. But I'll bet it's still completely empty. It's just for real estate speculation. That's what most of the office buildings in the City are used for, honestly. Hardly any of them are more than half-full. It's a shame."

"Did you notice anything else in the permit apps?" I asked.

"Yes, actually, he replied. "There used to be a tunnel from the basement of Bucklersbury House, which is the building that used to be here. That tunnel connected to the basement of Mansion House, where the Lord Mayor lives. Rosenberg petitioned to keep this structure and incorporate it into his new building. Rosenberg is quite friendly with the Lord Mayor. So I do wonder what they may be getting up to together."

We turned down the walkway between the buildings— which, according to the street sign, was actually the "historic Watling Street," now restored to its former trajectory, but with a stone tile floor and a glass ceiling. Within a few feet we immediately noticed a sign for "Oz Pizza and Ping-Pong Parlour," with Lewis Carroll characters painted in the windows. A hand-written sign taped to the inside of the door advertised their ping-pong tournament for that afternoon, coinciding with the *mithraeum* opening.

I realized that this was the place Drexella the police lady had mentioned. I found something about it inherently revolting. But Chesterfield wanted to go in, and I was starving, so I went along.

The restaurant contained six dining tables and two ping- pong tables, beyond which was a set of doors that seemed to lead out into the lobby of the Rosenberg office building. So far nobody had arrived yet for the "tournament." The place was empty except for us and the greasy-skinned white teenage boy covered with tattoos and piercings who worked behind the counter. He looked like he was either on drugs or suffering from some neurologic problem. He stared at us with an open mouth.

In addition to the pictures of Alice and the Cheshire Cat painted on the windows, there were murals with similar themes on the walls inside. Lamps were mounted on the walls, all held in place with plastic human arms. Behind the counter, there was a framed painting of a trinacria, which is a gorgon head with three legs for a body, and not much else.

A trinacria is a heraldic emblem, part of the flag of Sicily. It's associated with a legend that I was familiar with. The story is that the legs represent the three pillars which, according to myth, hold up the island. The head in the middle signified a little boy named Colapesce. It was said that he voluntarily swam under the island and replaced one of the pillars, which was broken, with himself, thereafter serving to help bear that burden eternally.

The owners of Oz Pizza must be Sicilian, I thought.

Other wall art, however, was not as easily explained. In the center of the main wall was a poster advertising their "signeture pizza" (sp.), which was called "the Beast." What struck me even more than the awful typo in a professionally-produced full-color poster was the odd way in which the pizza was sliced and the toppings arranged.

The pie, which, at "10.8 inches," was no bigger than their regular "large" size (11 inches), featured only four pieces of pepperoni, accompanied by just one other topping: a single black olive. The pepperoni pieces were all overlapping in the center. On the bottom were two pieces, intersecting so as to form a *vesica pisces* shape. Then on top of this, in the center and slightly below, were two more pieces, both intersecting with each other, and with the other two. Together, if you traced the outline of the shape formed by the stack of pepperoni, you would see a classic trefoil clover shape.

The pizza itself had been cut so as to form a seven - pointed unicursal star. This meant that there was an outer ring with fourteen slices — seven thin ones and seven fat ones. These surrounded five tiny triangles and a heptagon in the center. However, the pepperoni slices were stacked on top of these, so that you could only see two of the tiny triangles, and only three sides of the heptagon. This meant that the pizza had been cut and cooked before the pepperoni was put on. Over the top of the upper portion of the pizza, the price—£9.99—was written in a black font with a red border, but each digit was slightly misaligned with the others.

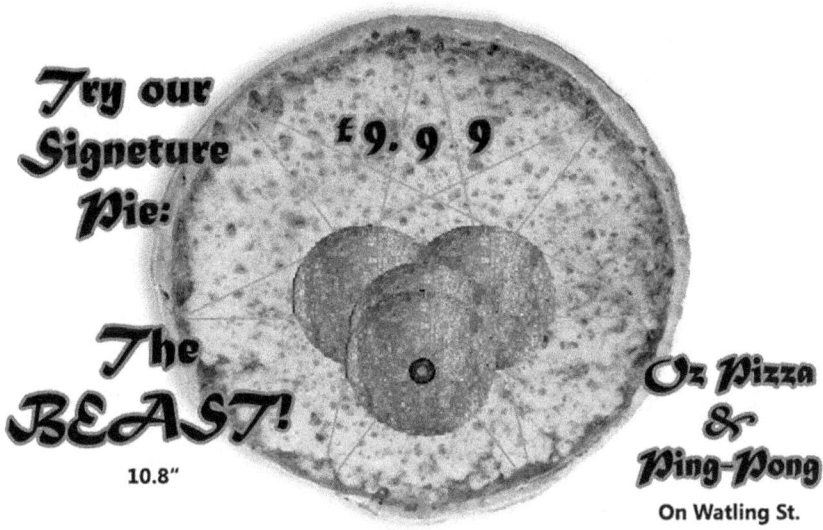

It makes no practical sense to design it this way, I thought. *And why call it "the Beast" when it's not especially large and doesn't have an extraordinary amount of toppings — in fact, hardly any?*

I stared at the poster. So did Chesterfield. Then we stared each other. I shrugged my shoulders and mouthed the words "I have no idea."

Chesterfield, apparently more hungry than curious, turned back around to the counter and ordered.

"A simple slice of cheese pizza, please," he said. The boy at the counter continued to stare at his face for 20 seconds before he registered a belated response.

"Oh, sure," he said. "Anything for you?" he asked me. "No thanks," I replied.

"But you said you were hungry," argued Chesterfield. "Come on, I'll buy again."

"No thanks," I said. "I lost my appetite." I was feeling uneasy there for some reason, but I didn't know why. The boy put a slice of cheese pizza in the oven for Chesterfield.

"How long has this place been open?" I asked.

"Oh, about four months," the boy responded. "My Mum got me a job here. She knows the guy who owns the building."

"You mean Rosenberg?" I said. "She knows him?"

"Yeah, I guess," he replied. Clearly, he either didn't know the details of who the man was and how his mother knew him, or else he just wasn't going to tell us. He picked at his fingernails for a minute and then pulled the pizza out of the oven.

"Do you want the Drizzle?" he asked Chesterfield, holding it out on a paper plate.

"The what?" the agent replied, bewildered.

"Oh, the Drizzle is our special hot sauce," he said. "You want to try it?" He held up a clear squeeze bottle filled with a red liquid.

"OK, sure," said Chesterfield. The boy put the plate with the hot pizza slice down on the counter, then proceeded to pour "the Drizzle" onto the pizza. Something about the odor of the sauce, and the spooging sound it made as he squeezed it out, caused me to experience a sharp wave of nausea. This brought clarity. As he applied the Drizzle with more care than a real moron could muster, forming a perfect counter-clockwise triangular spiral, I flashed on where I had seen that symbol before.

It was from the FBI's website, on their official list of symbols used by the pedophile community. The spiral triangle was the international sign of "boylovers." It had been infamously found on the logo of a politically-connected pizza parlor in Washington D.C. that some believed was part of a child trafficking ring. This caused a scandal that led to the company changing their logo in December of 2016.

Then, while thinking about Aleister Crowley and his voracious defense of pederasty in his own writings, I instinctively clasped my hand to my mouth in horror as the next realization hit me. Looking again at the poster for the "Beast" pizza, it now occurred to me what it represented. I used my phone to do a Google Image Search, just to confirm what I already knew.

Sure enough, the pizza on the poster was decorated to look exactly like the "Signet of the Beast" designed by Aleister Crowley. It was a symbol printed, among other places, as an illustration to go with a text by Crowley called "Liber Oz," which proclaimed the "right" of his followers to "love" whoever and however their "will" desired. It also stated their "right to kill" anybody who got in their way. The Signet consisted of a heptagram inside of a circle, with four circles in the middle, represented on the poster by the pepperoni.

The source I read couldn't explain what the circles in the middle truly meant, except to say that their resemblance to a penis and testicles was "intentional." At the bottom of the Signet, Crowley had put the number "666," a number he identified with personally, as he fancied himself the Antichrist. On the poster, the Signet had been cleverly turned upside-down so that the three sixes became the three nines of the pizza's price.

I turned back to Chesterfield to explain this to him. But then I saw him chomping down happily on the disgusting slice of filth. I instinctively grabbed it out of his mouth.

"Don't eat it!" I shouted. He and the teenage boy looked at me with confusion. I grabbed Chesterfield by the necktie and led him out the door, tossing the pizza slice in the garbage can near the exit. He wisely said nothing until we got outside, but he put a five-pound note in the boy's tip jar, presumably to make up for my rudeness.

"What's wrong?" he said. "I was hungry! And I *paid* for that!"

"There are Crowley sigils and pedophile symbols all over that place," I said. "God knows what they put in 'the Drizzle.' Who knows what they even put in the cheese."

"What exactly do you mean?" he asked.

I showed him how the pizza on the poster corresponded to the Signet of the Beast. Then I explained how much Crowley valued the ingestion of sperm, menstrual blood, urine and feces as spiritually beneficial. I told him how Crowley's cult members would put these substances in their Eucharist cakes, called "Cakes of Light," for their "Gnostic Mass" rituals, which were open to the public. Guests attending these rituals were not warned of the cakes' contents.

As I elucidated, Chesterfield began to turn green. He walked to a nearby water-fountain and rinsed his mouth out. Then he stuck his fingers in and appeared to contemplate gagging himself to purge his stomach. But he decided not to.

"Now think," I said to Chesterfield. "You know we're following the trail of some weird occultists who conjure demons, fuck kids, murder people and chop them up. Didn't you even think for a minute that there might be cum in the pizza before you started putting it in your mouth?"

"No that didn't occur to me," he answered, embarrassed and annoyed. "So I guess wine and cheese at the lecture is off the menu too, right? Speaking of which, let's get going. I want to get a nice spot up front so I can get a good look at this boyfucker who sells cum pizza and worships Mithras." He began to walk southeast down the arcade towards Walbrook.

"He's probably just subleasing to the cum pizza people," I said. As I walked away, I noticed a small sign in the window that I hadn't seen before. It said, so strangely:

PIZZA BY THE HOUR
INQUIRE WITHIN

I took a photo of it with my phone. Then I saw the kid that worked there walking towards the glass door, staring angrily at me. I hustled to catch up with Chesterfield.

We got to the end of the arcade and turned left. There we saw a crowd of maybe 60 people all huddled around one of the doors of the building. The street had been blocked off both ways by police tape, and there were a couple of cops on each end standing guard lazily.

We worked our way to the front. We saw that there were posters on the walls identifying this as the location of the temple. These included photos of some of the artifacts inside, and of the archeology that had taken place over the previous few years. The historian inside of me began to get excited.

Within a few moments, there was a bit of clamor and commotion. Rosenberg and his entourage, including several bodyguards, were arriving from the north side of the street. The lead man himself wore a tailored black pinstripe suite with brown stripes, and a red rose on the lapel. An assistant held the unavoidable giant scissors, which, after some cheers and a forgettable introduction in Rosenberg's nasally voice, were used by him to cut the ribbon, bringing even more applause. Then the doors opened. Rosenberg promised to give a speech to those interested in conference room in thirty minutes. Then he and his bodyguards disappeared around the corner.

"Well, if the Anti -Christ is a Poindexter, then that may well be the Anti-Christ," said Chesterfield, acknowledging the inherent dorkiness of the rich and powerful man that we'd just seen.

After waiting for the people in front of us to go inside the temple, we got our turn. I let Chesterfield pay the suggested donation of nine pounds for both of us.

The first room we entered was a gallery full of artifacts and framed photos. Off to the right there was a staircase leading down into the temple itself. Not wanting to compete with the crowds to get down there, I suggested we look at the artifacts first. That is where our fears about the *mithraeum* were confirmed.

The first thing we saw that we recognized was the bust of Serapis with the *modius* on his head. It had been discovered along with the other artifacts when the *mithraeum* was first found beneath Bucklersbury House in 1954. It had also been featured in the film *Easter Sunday April Fool*, when the boy had been castrated among the ruins.

A few feet away from that, we found, in a glass case, the little metal casket on a chain, containing the round strainer, which had also been used in the film. The plaque next to the case described it as a device for straining and administering psychoactive herbs during rituals. Depicted on the side of the casket was a person, who looked like a child to me, emerging from a rectangular box on the ground while an upright-standing grown man gripped his arm to help him up.

I thought it might be Mithras emerging from the stone. But the plaque said that it probably illustrated a death and rebirth ritual practiced by the cult. In this rite, the initiate would be drugged into a comatose state, buried, and then let out of the tomb upon awakening. I knew it very well could have been a little boy because I had read that Mithra's temples accepted applicants as young as seven.

Then, as if we didn't already know what we were dealing with, we saw the final confirmation. The posters of the original dig underneath Bucklersbury House were unmistakable. These were the stones that the boy in the film had been lying on when he was castrated. The site had been opened in 1954, and then the stones of the *mithraeum* were moved elsewhere just a few weeks later so that they could finish building Bucklersbury House. The first (very poor) "restoration" of the ruins didn't go on display in Temple Court until 1956. So the castration rite had happened sometime between those two events.

Chapter 19: Rose Mountain

> I am the son of a man and a woman from what I have been told. This astonishes me... I believed I was something more.
>
> —Comte de Lautreamont, *Maldoror*

Thus we were already feeling very heavy in our hearts, reeling from the implications of what we'd found, when we made our way down the stairs into the *mithraeum* itself, which was one floor underground. Inside, there was nothing visually surprising. It was my first time being inside such a temple, but it had been restored well, so that it looked exactly how I'd imagined a *mithraeum* should.

They all generally followed the same plan, and this did too: one long aisle, leading to an apse with an altar in front of it. The *taurtoctony*, depicting Mithras slaying the bull, was mounted on the wall behind the altar. All along the aisle were stone couches where members would have slouched back and watched the proceedings, or whatever else they did together. It seemed like they all did to me: empty and austere. They were made to look like large open caves, and this they achieved.

What struck me was not the décor or design, which was as expected. Instead it was the thickness of the atmosphere. Even stuffed with a crowd, the temple felt like it was full of choking energy: fear, anger, and pain. The pungent smell of a putrid flavor of incense came to my nose, even though I knew it was only coming from my mind. I asked Chesterfield if he sensed it too, but he said that he wasn't sure. He suggested that maybe it was just because being underground again was bringing back memories of my kidnapping by Leopold.

We began to follow several of the others back through the gallery, then through the door in the back that led to a large circular hallway. The walls were lined with blond wood paneling, and they curved up in a concave manner. We made our way up the ramp towards the ground floor. It was really more like a tunnel, spiraling up to the next floor and no doubt part of the spiral ramp that ran through the rest of the building. It also led back down the other way to another sub-basement below, but that way was cordoned off.

As we emerged from the underground level and into the light, I looked up at the ceiling and saw that much of it was sunlight, coming through a large piece of glass in the ceiling on top of which was a fountain of dirty water. Hidden jets on the sides were constantly injecting a denser, brown substance that swirled around in the mix. I could see why people thought that the Vortex contained sewer water. I also noted that, instead of merely being a "rounded triangle," as the janitor on 4chan had described it, the shape more closely resembled the Superman logo with rounded corners. I took note of the coincidence.

I also noticed that, once we got to the second floor, so that we were above the Vortex, the carpet on the ramp was lined on both sides with a transparent tube running constantly with a yellow-orange fluid.

These are the tubes carrying urine to the Vortex, I thought.

Cordons and posted signs encouraged us to keep moving up the ramp, while discouraging us from visiting the lobby or any of the other intervening floors, promising that the conference room was "ahead." So we kept going, until we were almost at the top of the building, on what must have been the ninth floor, as there were only ten and just one up above us.

There we found the conference room, surrounded by blonde wooden columns interspersed with clear glass. The podium, projector screen, and red plastic chairs could be seen from the ramp. Along the side of the wall on the left were two tables serving wine and cheese, which Chesterfield and I knew to avoid.

As we all filed in, I saw that the initial crowd of 60 had thinned to about 25. I spotted a familiar figure sitting in the front row. It was Drexella, the lady cop. As soon as I recognized her, she turned around, smiled, and waved, like she had felt my eyes on her. We had no choice but to sit down next to her.

"Hey Drexella," I said. "Nice to see you again."

"Yep," she said, smacking gum as she spoke. "Wouldn't miss it. Rosenberg's a family friend. I've been waiting for this for *years*."

"Really?" said Chesterfield. "We just met someone downstairs whose mother is also a family friend of his."

"Oh you mean Dennis? At Oz Pizza? Yep, that's my boy," she said proudly. I cringed. "We'll be on the same ping-pong team later on at the tournament."

"So how exactly do you know Mr. Rosenberg?" Chesterfield asked.

But just then, the lights were dimmed over the audience, and the spotlight over the podium was put on. Within a few seconds, Rosenberg entered from the back, this time wearing a red Phrygian cap, and everybody clapped. He took the stage and began to speak.

"Just call me Papa Smurf" was his first line, and everybody howled with laughter. He then began a speech about the history of the City of London, and to symbolic connections between the beliefs of the Mithraic cult, which I will attempt to paraphrase below. He said:

> It is fitting that the temple which we presented to you fully restored for the first time today was once the site of homage to gods of not one, but three different aspects of finance.
>
> First, of course, it was a temple to Mithras, the god of contracts. The Mithraic cult was called the Syndicoi—the "People of the Handshake," from which we get our word "syndicate." This is based on the deal that was struck, according to Mithraic mythology, between Sol and Mithras. After Sol and all of his henchmen, the other planetary Archons, had been defeated by Mithras in his march to the highest sphere in heaven, they made an agreement with each other to share both the power and the glory of the Sun, which they sealed with a handshake, before sitting down to break bread together.
>
> Some historians believe that the very origin of the custom of shaking hands, performed millions of times a day now, most often in a business setting, had its origins with the Mithras cult. This agreement between Sol and Mithras, which Mithraists believed kept the Sun rising and setting each day, was based upon mutual trust in the sacred nature of the oath. This is why they would invoke the name of Mithras as the enforcer of oaths whenever a new contract was signed. This same ethic, as we all know, is what lies behind everything that happens in business and finance today,

ever since the Knights Templar invented the concept of the checking system.

I noticed right away several things about this speech. For one thing, Rosenberg's analysis of Mithraism was very similar to my own, and not entirely consistent with what is right now commonly agreed upon by historians. What I mean is that for some reason they cannot see that the images of Sol and Mithras together clearly show him defeating the Sun god and forcing him to bow down in supplication.

This is shown happening before the handshake, and before the shared meal was permitted to occur (which so many have claimed is the origin of the Christian Eucharist). Rosenberg chose not to mention the specific imagery of the Sun bowing down to Mithras. But he did relate the meaning of it.

Another thing I noted was that he chose to use the term "planetary Archons." I couldn't think of any author on the subject of Mithras who has referred to the planetary powers he ruled over as "Archons." This term brings up specifically Gnostic connotations, and implies a negative view of their role in the cosmos as tyrannical. According to Gnostic thought, we are living in an invisible jail cell, made of illusion, and the planetary Archons are our captors, the rulers of our sad fate in this lonely world of despair.

To interpret this view as being present in Mithraism, as no previous author on the subject had done, would mean that Mithras was a heroic figure precisely because he fought and subdued these powers. It also indicates that he himself became the chief archon then, and thereafter allowed the others to rule underneath him as subordinates. He would then have essentially become the new Demiurge, the new chief jail warden. This viewpoint, I believe, was further reflected in the rest of Rosenberg's speech. He said:

> Now, this temple wasn't always exclusively a temple to Mithras. They found statues of other gods in there as well. One was Serapis, a.k.a. Hades, Pluto, or Dispater: the god of the underworld, and the god of the mineral wealth beneath the earth. This is where we get the word "plutocrat" for those who rule with the power of gold and silver.

They also found here a statue of Mercury, the wily patron of both commerce and thievery. From his first day of birth, he was making business deals with Apollo, yet another figure to hold the title of "sun god" ... There's so many of them....

He trailed off for a minute and coughed, staring off into the corner. He appeared to succumb to a short personal mental trip before shaking it off. Then he continued:

"But we know that Mercury's quicksilver-tongued promises are not to be trusted. We also know that gold and silver lose their shine if we lose our trust in one another. If the Mithraic value of the sacred oath is not honored, all money systems fail. All societies fail when that happens. This is why the real basis of the wealth of a society today *is* this mutual trust. The ranks of the Mithraic cult throughout the Roman Empire were initially filled with soldiers. Most of them were foreign legionnaires, rather than native Romans. And these, as any student of history knows, were not free men, but slaves.

In the Roman Empire, virtually every person with any sort of functional job was officially a slave to some landholder. The landholders did not work. They owned people who would do everything for them. Even the office-holders in the municipal governments were not free men, with the occasional exception of someone who was able somehow to purchase or earn their freedom. This is why these government office-holders were called, in Latin, *servi publici* — 'public servants.'

When I served as the Mayor of New York some years ago, I often thought about this fact. I can tell you that being a billionaire businessman makes you feel a thousand times more powerful than being a mere elected official. And most of the public servants I've met in my time would have to admit that they are slaves to the businessmen who are truly pulling the strings behind the scenes. Because Roman soldiers were slaves, it was only fitting that their god, Mithras, wore the Phrygian cap, like I'm wearing now. It was the symbol of a freed slave. Mithras identified himself with Saturn, the highest of the planetary Archons, and Saturn also wore the Phrygian cap.

During Saturnalia, the Roman winter solstice festival, slaves were given temporary freedom, and the whole social order was upended. Slaves would wear these hats, now called liberty caps, as a symbol of their freedom. This was because Saturn, the alleged founder of the Italian civilization, was remembered for having ruled over a "Golden Age" of abundance in the ancient past, during which no one was compelled to work for another.

Within the Temples of Mithras, the social order was always upended in the same manner. Even in the later years, when the Emperor himself had joined and the *latifundia* were flocking to *mithraeums*, we find in the records the names of slaves shown to be worshipping alongside their free superiors, often with the slaves occupying the positions of leadership. As Mithraic scholar Franz Cumont put it, 'In these societies, the last frequently became the first, and the first the last....'

Today it seems we live in a society where wealth and power has been largely divorced from the privilege of birth. The distinction between slave and freeman has been broken down. Private enterprise, and even public service, are routes to wealth and power that potentially anyone can follow. I came from a family of Jewish immigrants to New York, and I now possess 32 times more wealth than Her Majesty the Queen of England.

At this point, Chesterfield becoming visibly annoyed, nudged me with his elbow, then whispered in my ear. "He can't stop pointing that out. He's obsessed with it."

I tried to ignore him and strained to hear Rosenberg as he continued:

I dare say that I believe a large part of this change has been spearheaded from right here: the Square Mile of the Sovereign City of London, which still occupies the *pomoerium* of the old Roman city of Londinium. The *pomoerium* of a Roman city, by the way, which was the area within the walls, was officially designated by a state auger using divination, and did not necessarily encompass all of the territory controlled politically by the city. It was a sacred boundary, serving obscure purposes that historians still don't totally understand. Yet for some reason, perhaps mystical, even though most of London's wall is gone, the sacred boundary remains.

As all of you locals know, the City of London, governed by City of London Corporation, has always been a political power on equal par with the Crown, keeping it in check. The rights of the City are actually protected eternally in a special clause provided in the Magna Carta, to which the Lord Mayor was a signatory. This Corporation is formed by the Freemen of the City, and the Livery Companies. It was a government made of merchants and artisans who owned the freeholds to the buildings out of which they operated, or belonged to guilds that did, and were therefore called "free."

The City is separate from the kingdom in some ways, and yet it plays a leading part in many others, with the Lord Mayor even playing a role in the coronation of the monarch. As you know, monarchs used to traditionally ask permission to enter the City, with an elaborate ceremony at Temple Bar necessary to grant it. Although this ceremony has since been dispensed with, and the Crown is now quite cooperative with the City, I think this is only because the Corporation of London has so many times in the past not hesitated to remind the monarchs that they must either share power with the City, and respect its rights, or be replaced.

One of the aldermen from the early twentieth century, Lord Wakefield of Hythe, wrote in his book *London Forever* about how the City had always been the "real kingmaker" in the kingdom. He credits the Corporation with effecting every change of dynasty that has occurred in England, including allowing the formation of the Protectorate, and dispensing with it later when it had outlived its usefulness. He stated:

> London stood for Liberty and Moderation, and was the champion of constitutional rights regardless of the nature of the oppressor.
>
> When the King ceased to respect the laws of the land and the interests of his people, the Sovereign City drove him from the throne. When the Commonwealth ceased to represent popular government and tried to rule by force of

arms, the secession of the City brought back the exiled Stuarts.

By its action the Sovereign City expressed the national dislike for republican government and England's firm belief in constitutional monarchy as the best form of government for a free people.

So just as Mithras and Sol agreed to share ultimate power for the greater good, and to keep each other in check with mutual trust based on mutual understanding, the Crown and the City do also. It is fitting then, that today we have been able to open the Temple of Mithras once again, but now in a magical square mile that has led the world in a social revolution based on the merit of earned credit rather than the accident of birth.

How amazing is it that all this time until its discovery in 1954, the temple of Mithras was right here, right next to the official home of the Lord Mayor, whose office has always led this fight? It's next to the Bank of England, which financed the Royal Navy and allowed Britain to build her magnificent empire. And you know that the national bank provided the prototype upon which the world's central banks now function, stabilizing currencies and growing economies throughout the centuries since. And of course, the London Bullion Market Association, where the prices of precious metals are fixed for the *world* each day, is right here as well.

This location we stand upon right now is important for several other reasons. The London Stone once stood at 111 Cannon Street, just one block east of here. There is a tradition, lost in the fog of ancestral memory, that says the Lord Mayor used to be sworn into office upon this stone. Another tradition, confused with Arthurian legend, seems to imply that if a certain sword, once embedded in the stone to the hilt, could be removed from it, the holder would then become the king of England.

The truth veiled behind these myths was that the City of London, represented by the stone, restrained the "Sword of State' from being abused by the monarch against the freemen. Whenever that gentle but firm restraint failed, and the monarch insisted upon brandishing a weapon that ought best to remain holstered, the City saw to it that new blood would take the throne instead.

That was the *millarium* of the Roman city, the foundation of all the geographical measurements within. It may also have been their *terminus* stone, sacred to Jupiter, marking the crossroads where their two main thoroughfares intersected.

Not coincidentally, I believe, this exact point has for the last several centuries been the navel of the finance world and the crossroads of the global marketplace. I believe this is more true now than ever before. And we are just getting started.

We all know that the modern money system, while an improvement upon the past, is still another form of slavery. But I believe that there is another phase coming in our evolution as a species, which will set us free from this once and for all. It involves artificial intelligence, intelligently planned buildings, and intelligently run communities. It involves utilizing the untapped power and potencies that lie hidden within our own human bodies. And it starts right here, at Rosenberg Plaza.

With that anticlimactic summation, with that ridiculous pretension to be the harbinger of the future emancipation of humanity, lacking completely in any explanation, which landed on the ears with an uncomfortable thud, he looked up from his notes awkwardly and stared blankly, waiting for applause. After an uncomfortable moment, people began to clap.

"This guy's a fascist," Chesterfield whispered to me, as everybody stood up and cheered.

"No, he's an anarchist," Drexella replied, glaring at him. She obviously admired Rosenberg's philosophy.

After the applause died down, he came down and spoke to people from the audience individually, starting with the woman at the extreme right of our row in the front. I recognized her from the previous night's news report as Dame Marcia Martina, the Lord Mayor of the City. Their warm handshake, which morphed into a hug, indeed indicated that they were "quite chummy."

Rosenberg made his way down the row, and soon found his way to Drexella, whom he uncomfortably allowed to hug him. I stood staring at them, wondering how they knew each other, and wondering what I would say to him when I got the chance to touch his sweaty palm. But I didn't have to worry about that. The problem solved itself.

In a stunning turn of events, Rosenberg, who had not looked in my direction this entire time, let alone made eye contact, all of the sudden turned towards me and stared me in the face directly and deliberately. He had a mischievous expression: a small amount of nervousness mixed with a large amount of excitement.

"Drexella, how do you know Pamela Auger?" he said. "You never cease to surprise me with your interesting personal connections. Aren't you going to introduce me?"

He held out a hand for shaking. I grabbed it for a single shake and then let go, staring at them both confusedly, panicking, but still trying to smile.

I lied to Drexella about my name. How did Rosenberg know it? I thought.

"I have your book about the Templar idol, and your translation of the Hammer-Purgstall text," he said. "It was amazing how you found those artifacts right here in London, in the museum."

I couldn't believe it. The sixth most wealthy man in the world was reading my self-published books. For a moment I was flattered. Then I thought more about the implications of what he had said.

Can there be any doubt that everything I've experienced since I arrived here has been connected since accepting Leopold's bizarre invitation? The disappearance of the Mete coffer from the museum. My kidnapping. The underground bull sacrifice. The forced liver divination at Stratford House. The video of castration and child rape sent to MI5. The murder of the agency's director. Drexella alerting us to the opening of the mithraeum. *And Rosenberg reading my book.*

I looked to Chesterfield for help, but he was just staring at Rosenberg in shock.

"How about meeting me and some friends for a dinner party we're having tonight? It's just next door. You can autograph my books! I actually have them sitting in my office here. I'll bring them tonight."

For a moment, I let myself consider that maybe I was being paranoid to suspect him of nefarious deeds. After all, it was Leopold/Thomas who was undeniably guilty. The evidence against Rosenberg was still technically circumstantial.

Maybe, I thought, *this trip will finally open things up for my career, just like I'd hoped it would.*

But I shook off my ego response and listened to my fear.

You're going to get raped and killed, and nobody will ever know what happened to you, I thought more sensibly.

"As long as I can bring my friend, sure!" I said, grabbing Chesterfield's hand.

"Of course!" he responded. "Who's this?"

The question was directed at me, obviously prompting me to introduce him. But Drexella butted in.

"That's Agent Chesterfield from MI5," she said. "He's a cutie, isn't 'e?" She winked at him. He recoiled but tried to hide it. Rosenberg smiled in amusement.

"I'm very sorry to hear about Côme Pindar. I hope you catch the guy," he said. Then he turned to me.

"It's a date then. I'll see you at 5 o'clock. Just go to the New Court building at St. Swithin's Lane, right behind the St. Stephen Church. It's just off Walbrook, right behind us. Give your name to the front desk when you get there."

"You're still coming to the Ping-Pong Tournament, aren't you?" Drexella asked him.

"Oh, you know it," he answered enthusiastically. "I'm bringing friends!" And with that, he moved on to shake more hands.

Chapter 20: Equinox of the Gods

Hail! ye twin warriors about the pillars of the world! for your time is nigh at hand.

…my left hand is empty, for I have crushed an Universe; & nought remains.

– Aleister Crowley, *The Book of the Law*

Knowing that we absolutely could not consume any of the food at Rosenberg's party, Chesterfield and I opted for a pub lunch at the Green Man, right across Queen Victoria Street. It was inside of another office building that had a remarkable triangular courtyard built in the center of it. We enjoyed fish and chips while we tried to come to grips with all that had just happened.

"Doesn't it seem strange that Rosenberg's having his party in another office building?" I asked. "Why not his own? Surely he has space to entertain guests."

"It's probably his friend the Lord Mayor who is throwing the party for him," Chesterfield said.

"Why do you say that?" I asked "Wouldn't the party be at Mansion House then?"

"She hardly spends much time there," said Chesterfield. "She's usually at New Court from what I've heard. And it's hard to beat the Sky Box at New Court for entertaining billionaires. It was built for that. It has the best view in the area."

I stared at him, waiting for a fuller explanation, since I obviously didn't know what he was talking about. Finally, he continued.

"New Court is the site of the Rothschild empire in London. They've lived and run their business from that very site since the 1800s. They used to fix the price of gold *there* everyday, before the Bullion Association started doing it next door. And Marcia Martina is a Rothschild heiress. She married into the family. Her son Crispin works for Rosenberg as his right-hand man."

"I see," I said, whipping my laptop out of my bag and setting it up at the table.

"What are you looking up?" asked Chesterfield.

"I'm going to look at the site on Google Maps again." I dialed it up and stared at the Superman logo-shaped plot of land, with the New Court building, labeled simply "Rothschilds," just east of it.

"I wonder why Paris isn't answering his phone," said Chesterfield, who had just tried to call him. "Surely he isn't still getting grilled by Miss Equitone. Maybe I should check on him after all. Maybe it's safe."

All of the sudden there was a dramatic change in the atmosphere of the room. The music was switched off. The TV, which had been tuned to Rosenberg's financial news network with the sound muted, was simultaneously turned up. Several people moved to stand closer to the television. Apparently, it was a very bad day on the stock market so far. The news showed people on the floors of the New York Stock Exchange, the London Stock Exchange, and the Euronext exchange in Amsterdam running around in a panic.

"What's going on?" I asked.

"France left the Eurozone," said the man to my left. "And the President says they're going to default on their debt. The Euro's collapsing."

As we stood there watching the European project fall apart, a scream was heard from the back of the pub. It was a woman seated near the window. A man had just jumped from a balcony onto the pavement below, deliberately, she said. He laid face down on the ground of the building's central courtyard with a pool of blood around him.

Just then, Chesterfield received a text from Paris. He showed me what it said.

Don't come in to the office. And don't call.

"Well, I guess it's not safe after all," he said. "And he sank into an anxious quietude, tapping his feet compulsively with his hands tucked crossways under his armpits. I knew what he was thinking. He was worried about his country. And his partner. And his cat.

So with no particular place to go until 5 pm, we sat there watching the world's economy collapse on Rosenberg TV, drinking Shirley Temples while the businessmen around us freaked out and drank themselves silly. We watched the paramedics come and scrape up the dead guy on the pavement while a news crew filmed it. We saw the news report on this and several other suicides related to the market crash.

Many of the people in the bar were torn between fear of the unknown future and excitement, even glee, at watching a political entity they despised finally kick the bucket. Some were morose, having obviously lost their investments. Some knew they would be losing their jobs soon because of this. All were nervous, rightly, about price volatility. They knew that the chain reaction around the world would be causing all sorts of catastrophic issues as investors freaked out about the likelihood of a currency crisis in Europe and the uncertainty of trade agreements.

Some of the pundits on TV were smirking wryly at rumors trending on Twitter alleging that the events were caused by a curse that the markets had brought upon themselves. For the first time ever, Good Friday and "Easter Monday" had been removed from the list of national bank holidays in the USA, the UK, and the EU — a decision made by international agreement the previous year based on the projected savings of opportunity costs involved in allowing a four-day weekend. They did it so that everybody could make more money — *because, hey, more money!* Instead, many Catholics and Anglicans agreed, that decision may have cost the West a great deal, perhaps even, some suggested, the bursting of the entire decades-old debt bubble that supported its floundering economy.

"But this is all nonsense based on urban legends," Art Cashin said in a live interview on Rosenberg TV. "People say that the Black Friday gold crash in 1869 was on Good Friday, but it was actually September 24th. The last time the New York Stock Exchange was open on Good Friday was March 29, 1907, and the market was up when it closed at the end of the day."

"But that was the peak of the market that year," countered Seamus Molony, a journalist with an Irish accent also being interviewed in the same segment. "It went down after that. "And the Irish Catholic traders all lamented to the men running the exchange: 'We told you not to open on Good Friday.' That's recorded at the time."

Nobody knew what to make of this superstition. The only thing that was for sure was that nobody had any faith in anything: not the government, the Queen, or the banks. Certainly not "the People" — that is, the lazy mob. And not, most useless of all, the Church or God. When the Pope released a statement against "global panic," blamed the Eurozone breakup on "xenophobia," and lectured the "rich" of the world not to be "greedy" during the unfolding crisis, people started throwing food at the TV amid loud jeering.

Of course, a lot of these people were also on their cell phones, calling brokers and telling them to move money around. Gold and silver were natural fallbacks, but these were getting ridiculously more expensive by the minute. Or, as the pessimist would see it, currencies were becoming more worthless relative to metal by the minute. The news about France had come just minutes before the price of gold was "fixed" by the London Bullion Market at 3 PM, so it was set by the bankers with the benefit of that knowledge. The FTSE closed 20% down for the day, the biggest one-day loss ever, almost double the previous record, and got shut down 30 minutes early at 4 PM.

Chesterfield's only comment was to point out that Director Pindar's head mounted on Temple Bar was directly facing the London Stock Exchange building right across Paternoster Square. I told him it reminded me of a *"nithing* pole," the Norse form of cursing an enemy by pointing the severed head of a horse at his house, mounted on a stick. Then the connection with the imagery of bull sacrifice— specifically the blood baptisms of Cybele's *taurobolium* rite—was pointed out to us by the headlines used on Rosenberg TV to introduce the latest reports on the global stock market collapse:

BLOODBATH ON WALL STREET

and:

BAD FRIDAY: EUROPA SLAYS THE BULL

"How ironic," I said to Chesterfield. "Europa was raped by Zeus in the form of a bull, an event that was commemorated on Euro coins. Now the continent named after her has killed the bull market.

"I wondered how Rosenberg is reacting to the news," he said.

"There's only one way to find out," I said.

At 4:45, we finally left the bar and walked over to New Court, to keep our appointment. Little did we know at the time that if we'd stayed another five minutes, we would have heard Mr. Rosenberg's public comments on the market breakdown, as he was being interviewed live on his own network from his own office there in London while we were on our way to meet him at the Rothschild compound next door.

We crossed Queen Victoria Street, then passed Rosenberg Plaza on the north side. We went down Bucklersbury and across Walbrook, then through a narrow alley in-between Mansion House and St. Stephen's, a beautiful Christopher Wren-designed church almost completely obscured on all sides by tall office buildings. I wanted to go in and check it out for a minute. But the front door was locked, and there was a sign posted saying it was closed for repairs. So we took one more left around one more building, and then we were there, standing in front of the place where the Rothschild family had been running their global finance empire for over two centuries.

We opened the front door and walked into the reception area, which was a gigantic, virtually empty space with a ceiling oddly identical to the floor, looking like blond wood paneling. We found the elevators, but they were locked. Behind us, someone cleared his throat. It was a Hawaiian-looking man with broad shoulders, dressed in a dark suit, with a white cord dangling from his left ear. He was standing at the security desk. We walked up to him.

"Hi, I'm Pamela Auger," I said. "And this is—"

"Agent Chesterfield, I know," he said, interrupting me. He showed us a touch-screen tablet he was carrying, with pictures of us both, as well as several others. I recognized mine as my Facebook profile picture. The one of Chesterfield matched the one on his Security Service badge. I wondered how they got it. Chesterfield looked alarmed. The man motioned for us to autograph a sign-in sheet on his desk.

"Let me help you with the elevator," the guard said. He used a card carried in a lanyard around his neck to unlock the elevator, then punched the floor number, which I don't recall. When the doors opened, he stepped in with us, and rode all the way up.

When the doors opened again, we found ourselves in yet another vast empty room. There was almost nothing in it except one long wooden table, positioned a few feet away from the far wall, at which several people were already seated. One of them was Rosenberg. He was talking to Marcia Martina.

Most remarkable of all were the walls around us. They were incredibly tall, all glass, with a magnificent view of the city on all sides of us. It was like being on top of Mount Olympus. Indeed, I'm certain that's what it was designed to feel like. The side that the table was placed on looked out over the roof of Rosenberg Plaza, which, at only ten stories tall, was quite a ways beneath us. The setting sun reflected off the sunroof with a reddish pink glow.

This must be the 'Sky Box' Chesterfield mentioned, I thought to myself.

Chesterfield made his arm into a bow, into which I inserted my own, and then he led me over to where Rosenberg was seated. We all said "Hello" again, and then he introduced us to the Lord Mayor. To her right was Crispin Martina, her son and the chief operating officer for Rosenberg Inc. UK. Blue-eyed, blond-haired, comely and ectomorphic, wearing a finely-tailored suit the color of Egyptian blue, he resembled a twink from the cover of a men's fashion magazine. He couldn't have possibly been more than 22 years old from the looks of him.

That's quite an impressive position for someone so young, I thought. I have since learned that he was the *youngest* person to every hold such a title in a major corporation.

On the other side of the table was Mark Wetzel, the new Editor of the *Financial Times*. He was white and chubby with thinning gray hair and a pinstriped suit. He looked to be about 60. Finally, to Rosenberg's left was a homely-looking twelve-year-old girl, wearing white culottes and a white polo shirt, with her permed hair in a pony tail, and she had braces on her teeth. Rosenberg introduced her as Philippine, his daughter.

"Oh yes," I said as I took her hand. "I've heard about your steeplechases."

She looked very shy and uncomfortable, which was how I felt in a room full of financial elites, so I thought that breaking the ice with her first would be easiest. She blushed and turned her gaze away from me, smiling limply at nothing. The Lord Mayor grabbed me by the arm and whispered.

"Don't get her started. The only thing that empty-headed girl ever talks about is horses."

We sat down next to Wetzel. A young dark-haired white male in a black tuxedo came and poured us champagne from a bottle that probably cost more than I had made in the previous tax year. Everybody except for Philippine looked like they were already somewhat drunk.

"Blake already told us a little bit about you guys, particularly you, Miss Auger," said Wetzel. "Sounds like you've done some interesting work." I smiled.

"I saw you two walking up to the building," said Ms. Martina, sniffing as she spoke. "I was just coming back from the lavatory on the other side of the room. I looked out the window and I saw you walking down St. Stephen's Row." She sniffed again and smiled.

Cocaine? I thought. It looked like it. Her nose was red.

"You could have taken the secret tunnels," said Rosenberg. "I should have told you about them!" He and Marcia both laughed.

"What do you mean?" I said.

"There are tunnels connecting all of these buildings, and others," Marcia said. "From New Court to St. Stephens. From St. Stephens to Mansion House. From Mansion House to the Bank of England. All built by my dead husband's ancestors, of course. To make it easier to control everybody." Ms. Martina laughed again.

"You're joking?" I asked.

"Not at all," said Crispin. "And Rosenberg Plaza is now part of the grid too."

I looked at Chesterfield. He did not look amused. He grimaced at the Lord Mayor. The silence was palpable.

"Oh bloody Hell," said Ms. Martina. "I forgot we had MI5 in the house tonight."

"All this has been cleared with the City, I presume," said Chesterfield, making notes on his black leather notepad. Martina leaned in and squinted at him.

"Darling, this family IS the City," she bragged. She took another sip of her champagne.

"So what do you use really these tunnels for?" I asked.

"You'll find out tonight," said Rosenberg. "We're going on a special tour later on."

"Oh really," I said. "I'm not sure how long I can stay though."

"Oh you don't want to miss this," said Mr. Wetzel. "The first ritual in a properly restored ancient temple in London for thirteen-hundred years. When will you get another chance like that?"

Oh no, a ritual? I thought. The hair on my neck stood up as I thought about my last experience with a ritual inside London's secret tunnels.

"What's he talking about?" asked Chesterfield. He turned to Rosenberg. "I thought the *mithraeum* belonged to the people. It's a piece of British heritage that just so happens to be inside your building. It's not your personal playground."

"We're just going to have a little fun," said Crispin. "It's a party. Lighten up."

Chesterfield looked at his champagne glass, still full, and put his notebook in his pocket. Rosenberg deftly pivoted the conversation.

"You know, Dutch businessman Erik Ubels, whom I consulted on the design of the Plaza, has said that in the future all parts of a building will be connected to all the other parts. What's more, he said that all of the buildings in a city will be connected to each other. Tunnels are one thing, and that's been going on for centuries here in England. But they will also be doing things like sharing electricity, which they will be generating on-site for each other. And they will be sharing data about how the buildings are being used. The City of London in the future really will be a 'house with many mansions,' like the New Jerusalem. I think that's exciting, and I like to think that Rosenberg Plaza is helping to lead this movement."

"Well, we got Wodin Energy that consulting contract," said Martina. "Convinced the aldermen that it's worth the investment. Now we can get them to agree to fund the things we've already been doing. So it'll be done months ahead of schedule, which will impress them and keep them handing out funds."

"Wodin Energy is doing for cities what Erik Ubels is doing for buildings," Wetzel explained, seeing my confusion. "Networking the streetlights, covering them with sensors, and using the data to make decisions that boost energy efficiency. They call them 'Smart Cities.'"

"London is on the verge of a new renaissance," said Crispin with pride, looking at his boss with admiration. "Rosenberg has been working with the mayor of Greater London on the river restoration project too, which is huge. We're bringing back all the culverted underground rivers, like the Fleet and the Walbrook. We've been building the infrastructure and connecting it to the City's new Smart Grid. When it's all unveiled, the public will be completely blown away."

"What will the rivers be used for?" I asked. "I thought they were all mostly sewers now."

"They used to be," said Rosenberg. "But they closed them over and built other sewers, then mostly abandoned the rivers. They still trickle underground and empty into the Thames. Now since Ms. Auger here is an expert on occult secrets, I'll tell you a secret about the water system here and let you figure out what it means."

Everyone got quiet and scooted in their chairs so that they could lean in closer. Except for Philippine. She continued to stare blankly out the window. Rosenberg went on.

"In the 1200s they built a conduit between Tyburn Springs, on the current site of Buckingham Palace, and the Walbrook, right up Ludgate Hill where St. Paul's is, to bring fresh drinking water to the merchants in the City. Supposedly they stopped using it after the Great Fire in 1666. But the engineers from Woden Energy explored the old conduit, and found a tiny tube running along the length of the whole thing, from directly beneath Buckingham Palace to where the Walbrook meets Bucklersbury on the northern side of my *mithraeum*, before turning west."

From the corner of my eye, I saw Chesterfield wince when Rosenberg said "my *mithraeum*."

"What do you mean, a 'tube'?" said Wetzel. "Like a plastic tube?"

"Oh no. 2.7 miles of Burmese glass, surrounded by plain white PVC pipes," he said.

"Burmese glass? You mean that stuff they used to make from uranium oxide and tincture of gold? That was Queen Victoria's favorite! It's beautiful, and so radiant in UV light. She collected tons of it. But usually dishes and figurines, not plumbing pipes."

"Yes, well there may have been other reasons why she had the company in Massachusetts that manufactured it make so much of it for her. The glass is useful for maintaining the chemical composition of the fluid running through it. I wouldn't be surprised if that company itself was secretly contracted to produce some of these pipes. And somebody is still making them now. Certain sections of the tube line have obviously been replaced quite recently."

"You mean it's in current use?" I asked.

"Yep," he said. "Still running with fluid."

"Fluid?" everybody said all at once.

"Don't tell me you didn't know" said Rosenberg to Martina with a mocking smile. Then he turned around and gave the same look to Crispin. "Or you."

The young man and his mother looked at each other and shrugged. But Rosenberg was right. They were playing dumb.

"Blake, whatever are you talking about?" said Ms. Martina.

"Do you remember what Edmund Mortimer called the Walbrook River in *Henry the Sixth*, when he sat upon the London Stone and proclaimed himself Lord Mayor?"

She laughed. "He called it a 'pissing conduit,'" she said. "Which it was."

"Then he declared that the river should run with nothing but claret wine for the first year of his reign," her son added, swilling down the last of his champagne. He called the servants for more.

"So what's your point," said Chesterfield. "Is there sewer water still running through this narrow tube in the conduit for some reason?"

"No, not sewer water *per se*," Rosenberg answered. "Pure golden streams of urine. Obviously collected directly from the source, without contamination."

Once again I thought about the toilets at Rosenberg Plaza, and my speculation that Rosenberg might have been generating energy from human waste products. Or he could have been using it for any number of other esoteric, alchemical workings. Or maybe he was just a sick pervert who liked to bath in or drink other people's piss.

Now he was telling us that someone else was doing the same — somebody rich like him with access to the remains of the conduit. He implied that he thought the Rothschilds at least knew about it. Perhaps they did. Marcia and Crispin seemed to be getting uncomfortable.

"Has the site of Tyburn Springs always been the location of the royal residence?" I asked.

"No," said Wetzel. "It belonged to Edward the Confessor, but then a lot of other people owned it before they built Buckingham Palace in the nineteenth century."

An image flashed into my mind just as a tingle went down my spine, a sure sign that I was getting one of my intuitions. It was a picture I'd seen before of the River of Life flowing from beneath God's throne. This is the water that the righteous drink from to gain eternal life. The message is clear: immortality can be gained from consuming the bodily substance of immortals.

God, in the Old Testament, is shown consuming the flesh and blood of sacrifices, licking them up with tongues of fire. But while they might eat kosher meat, blood he forbade to the Hebrew people, as it contained "the life." For the same reason, Adam and Eve were booted from Paradise to prevent them from gaining access to the Tree of Life, which would make them "live forever."

The fluid exchange is this: God drinks the "Water of Life"—blood, generally—from the altars of his worshippers. He then feeds the "tree of life" in paradise with the "rivers" that issue from beneath where he sits. The tree grows the "fruit" that brings life, and that fruit is offered back to the worshipper in the form of the vivifying flesh and blood of Jesus.

What I was now hearing about from Rosenberg was an exchange in which urine was being piped from a location directly beneath Buckingham Palace and into the business district, right to the front door of the Rothschilds. That is, right to the family that historically funded the government which paid the royal salary during the nineteenth century, when this special royal pissing conduit may have first been built. For all I knew, they were still doing so.

Perhaps royal urine has a particular value for them somehow, I thought.

"So," said Rosenberg, breaking the silence. "Since you don't know anything about this, do you think your father-in-law does?" It was directed at the Lord Mayor.

"Look, everybody knows these freaks are dirty to the core. And richer than the Pope. So if you're telling me that my in-laws have a private pipeline carrying prostitute pee for their golden shower orgies here at New Court, don't expect me to be surprised. I've heard worse. MUCH worse." She then turned to her son, glared at him, and walked off to the rest room again. Crispin turned to Rosenberg looking hurt. He spoke.

"Blake, I do believe you are violating the Law of Hospitality. And there is STILL a token between you and my family that has not been satisfied."

"Don't accuse me of that," said Rosenberg, pointing in Crispin's face and staring him directly in the eyes. "You know I take that VERY seriously."

Wetzel, in an attempt to break the uncomfortable mood, leaned past me and asked Chesterfield how the investigation of Pindar's murder was going.

"Oh, we're working on it," the agent responded, a total non-answer. He changed the subject again. "I heard your paper moved back in to Bracken House round the corner."

"Yep," said Wetzel. "Same classy old building. We just had it outfitted for the modern age."

Chesterfield turned to me. "Bracken House is across the Square from St. Paul's. It's the one with the zodiac clock on the front featuring the face of Winston Churchill as the Sun. It's the historic home of the *Financial Times*, but they moved out for a few years while the place was refurbished."

I remembered seeing that place when we were walking to the murder scene the night before.

"Today's been a hell of a day for your paper, I imagine," said Chesterfield. "Where do you think it's all going?"

"Directly down the toilet," the Editor responded. "The Euro's obviously trash. Which may help the pound in the immediate, but unless you're these blokes you won't feel the benefit," he said, pointing to Marcia, Crispin and Blake with a broad swirl of his finger.

"So you guys aren't suffering at all from Europe's collapse?" I said.

"Are you kidding," Ms. Martina said, laughing as she sat back down at the table again. "We caused it. That is to say, we refrained from propping them up any longer. 'Going Galt,' as they say. The people won't accept austerity, they refuse to face facts, so we can't keep doling out free credit to states any longer. But we've all been hoarding gold for months. So we won't go hungry. Quite the contrary. We're on the precipice of what you might call 'the Great Reaping.'" She winked at Rosenberg. He smiled emptily.

I could never imagine that the world's elite actually refer to themselves as 'we' the same way we non-elites refer to them as 'they,' I thought to myself. Their arrogance was truly amazing, a combination of cinematic and surreal.

"Pamela, you remember the story of Joseph and his brothers in *Genesis*, right?" said Rosenberg.

"More or less," I answered. "Why?"

"Have you ever thought about how it tells the story of the process by which a people become enslaved through usury? Joseph's brothers come from Canaan to Egypt, looking to buy food during a famine. They don't know he's the brother they sold into slavery some time ago. They find that, because of his great psychic insight, which predicted the famine, he's been storing up grain for seven years in Pharaoh's granaries."

I nodded. He continued.

"He plies them with freebies. He makes them think the food was free because the money they bought it with magically reappeared in their sacks afterwards. He takes one of them captive as collateral, Simeon. Then he tries to trick them into giving up their littlest brother, Benjamin, as a slave to him, by falsely accusing him of the theft of his silver divination cup."

"Where is all this going, Blake," said Miss Martina. "You know I despise the Bible." She yawned and sipped her champagne. Rosenberg rolled his eyes and kept talking.

"Then he convinced Pharaoh to give his brothers a good slice of the best land in Egypt, and lots more free stuff besides. They lived there fat and happy for two years, until the famine spread to Egypt as well. Then the true process of enslavement began." He cleared his throat, and smiled eerily.

"First Joseph, on behalf of Pharaoh, took all the money from both the Egyptian and the Canaanite people in exchange for bread from Pharaoh's granary. Then the money "failed" in the land. All of the coins of real value being in the hands of the Pharaoh now, anything coined as money from that point on would not be accepted by the market as a store of value. We all know that."

Crispin, Marcia and Mr. Wetzel all smiled, now picking up on the similarities between the Bible story and the present situation.

"People like me and the Rothschilds have all the gold now," Rosenberg continued. "The coming breakaway European states can print their own money all they want. But nobody abroad will accept it. And the market already knows it."

"But let them try," said Marcia. "I really want to see them try."

"Returning to the story," said Rosenberg, annoyed at the interruption, "Joseph next took cattle, from both the Egyptian natives and the Canaanite aliens, his own brethren, in exchange for more bread. That lasted only a year. After that, there was nothing left but for the people to offer up their lands, and their bodies for slaves, in exchange for mere bread."

"Now they were all slaves to Pharaoh, with Joseph in the real seat of power as vizier. But the Canaanites were the happy slaves, because they got special treatment from Joseph, on account of their relation to him. The aliens grew more prosperous and more numerous in their condition of slavery than the native Egyptians, and this bred contempt. So when a new Pharaoh came to the throne, he instituted a policy of treating the Canaanite aliens more harshly."

He stood up with his eyes closed and his arms raised up, bent at the elbow, his palms turned outward towards us.

"This is how the condition of harsh slavery in Egypt came upon the children of Israel. This is also how the Egyptians themselves became slaves to their Pharaoh. It was because of the financial machinations of their brother Joseph, wily like Hermes the thief."

"I've actually thought for some time that the figure of Joseph is a masked form of Thoth or Djehuty, the Egyptian Hermes," I said. "Jude also."

"Well, yes, 'Djehuty' sounds a lot like 'Yehudi,' doesn't it," Rosenberg agreed. "Using confidence tricks to gain wealth and power, to enslave the masses through money. That's what both Joseph and Hermes were known for. And that's the popular stereotype of the money-grubbing Jew that has endured for almost two millennia."

"Because they keep living up to it!" howled Miss Martina. Rosenberg shot her a look of disapproval. She looked away from him towards me.

"I was married to one so I can say it," she chuckled. "I've counted his money. I know what I'm talking about."

"Well there's one more parallel with the anti-Semitic stereotype. Joseph was originally a slave, an alien, but came to rule the land *de facto* by ingratiating himself with the royal house: by making himself indispensable."

"He took Dale Carnegie's advice," joked Wetzel.

"He used his mind's eye to gain intelligence that gave him power. Because it was useful. Think on that, Miss Auger," said Rosenberg, raising his eyebrow at me.

"Why?" I asked.

Before he could answer, there was a flurry of movement around us. It was dizzying and disorienting. It all happened so quickly, I didn't realize what was going on. I didn't actually see any of the servants carrying the platters. But when the movement passed, I looked down and saw a shiny silver plate in front of me with a tiny bird on it, baked with a caramelized sauté. We each had one. The plates were all different colors and, it looked like, made from different materials.

But now Rosenberg was missing from the table. His wine glass was also gone. And there was no setting for him at the table.

"Where'd Blake go?" asked Wetzel. He looked at Philippine, who looked up for the first time in twenty minutes. She shrugged her shoulders. I noticed that the Sun was now almost totally gone over the horizon and the Moon was visible behind Philippine. Although it was not quite full, it loomed large and seemed to hang down very low.

"He's probably gone to the toilet, I imagine," answered Crispin.

"So what are we having anyway?" Marcia asked her son.

"I don't know," he responded. "I let Blake tell the kitchen what to make."

"Oh right, Blake ordering our family's servants around, as always," she sighed. She took a bite of her bird. She swallowed it, but slowly, reluctantly, looking both disgusted and surprised.

"Oh right, now this is gross," she said. "What the Hell is this? It tastes like an arse."

"No kidding," said Wetzel, who had sampled his as well and pushed it away in disgust. "That's foul." He snorted a laugh at his own joke. "Get it? Fowl?"

I put a piece of it on my fork and sniffed it. It smelled like spoiled milk and sulphur.

I looked at Philippine. She was dutifully eating it, but shuddered as she did so. Then I looked at Crispin. He was eating his too, with dislike, in very small bites.

Marcia turned around to complain to the servants. But she found none. We were now alone in that vast empty room, with no sign of the guest of honor who had ordered this mystery meal.

"Maybe Rosenberg went to go tell the staff that they forgot my plate," said Chesterfield. "Although it doesn't look like I'm missing out on anything good." I looked and, sure enough, he had no plate.

"No, he must be in the lavatory," said Marcia, angry. She stumbled drunkenly over to the unisex toilet room and walked right in, calling his name. A few seconds later, she came out.

"He's not there either," she announced, coming back to her seat.

"You don't like your food?"

Rosenberg's voice came from the other side of the table. He was standing next to his daughter, who sat motionless staring at the bones on her plate, having eaten every scrap of the bird's bitter flesh. Everyone was startled. Then Marcia and Wetzel laughed.

"Yeah, send it back and order a pizza, Blake," answered Marcia. "This is the worst."

"I've already had a pizza today," he said.

"Not that kind of pizza," said Marcia, snickering at what appeared to be an inside joke.

"Don't reject my offering, friends," said Rosenberg, addressing us all. "True, Crispin kindly provided the champagne, and let us sit at the table of his esteemed family's house. But these birds I caught myself, and put myself in great peril to do so."

"Seriously?" said Marcia. "Honestly, I didn't know you liked to hunt. I thought you hated firearms."

"No, he hates peasants having firearms," whispered Wetzel, oblivious to how weird things were getting.

"I didn't shoot them!" he responded. "I had the servants slaughter them." He inhaled sharply.

"Please nourish your bodies with this flesh," Rosenberg continued to implore. "At least enjoy the *sweet livers*. That's the best part."

Upon hearing the words "sweet livers," Chesterfield stiffened up next to me. I could feel his eyes upon me. But Rosenberg now stared at me as well.

"Come on, Miss Auger," he said. "Eat the liver. It's the best part."

"Don't do it, Pamela," said Chesterfield. "You don't have to. We can leave."

"Not until you've eaten!" shouted Rosenberg. As he said this, he leaned forward, slammed his fist on the table, and stared angrily at me, his face becoming red.

I don't know if it was a hallucination, like so many of the things I witnessed from this point onward. But to me it seemed as if his eyes began to glow red as well, as his stare pierced me through my skull. I felt myself swaying in my seat. As if I had no will of my own, I picked up my fork and knife, tore the bird open, located what looked like a liver, and stuck it in my mouth. In my peripheral vision, I saw Marcia and Mark doing the same.

At that moment, Chesterfield got up and ran across the room to the elevator we had arrived in. He punched the "down button." Everybody was looking at him, so I took the opportunity to spit out my bite of the unknown bird into my champagne glass, which I then covered with a napkin.

"Come on, follow me Pamela!" he shouted, beckoning me with his hand. But then he looked at the elevator button, and the digital display next to it, which was supposed to tell you what floor the elevator was currently on as it moved up and down. However, something was wrong. He pressed the button frantically several more times, shouting "Fuck! Fuck!" Then he stormed over to the table again.

"Tell me why the elevator's locked," he demanded of Rosenberg. The man just sneered at him. Then Chesterfield addressed the Martinas.

"How do we get out of here?"

"Oh, don't overreact," said Marcia. She walked over to the elevator.

"It should be working," she said. When she saw that it wasn't, she tried pressing an intercom button next to the elevator.

"Hello! James? Hello! Teddy? Anybody?" There was apparently no answer. She walked back to her desk and took her phone out of her purse. Her bag looked like it cost more than my mother's house. But she had the same model smartphone as I did. It didn't do her any good though.

"Bloody Hell, I can't even get a signal. What's going on?" she shouted to Crispin. He shrugged, then gave Rosenberg a pleading look.

"Nobody's going anywhere until we've all eaten!" Rosenberg shouted.

"I think we're done," said Wetzel. "We've all had a bite. We all tried it. Thank you, Blake. Maybe we're just not hungry. Let's do something else now." He was trying to calm his friend down.

"*I'M* not *DONE!*" Rosenberg countered.

"Where's your plate?" asked Crispin. "Should I tell the servants...."

"I'm eating mine *raw!*" Rosenberg interrupted.

He reached down and picked up something on the floor next to his feet, which had been obscured from my view by the table. It was covered in a black cloth. He placed it in the center of the table. I heard coos and a flutter of wings.

Not again, I said to myself. *I don't want to see another animal die.*

But of course I couldn't stop him. He ripped the cover off the birdcage, revealing a raven, which he took out with his hand, gently, putting it on the tabletop. It walked around and flapped its wings helplessly. They were clipped.

I thought to look away, but I wasn't fast enough. With sudden ferocity, Rosenberg grabbed the bird and tore its head off with his bare hands, then tipped the neck towards his mouth and sucked down the blood as it spurted out. At that moment, I heard a sonic boom and felt something like a shockwave. This was followed by the sound of metal crunching and scraping together. It didn't seem to be coming from the sky, which became noticeably darker in that instant, as if someone had put a light filter over it. Also, the Moon drew down lower in the sky. The crunching sound turned into a high-pitched whine, then a low, long moan like a foghorn. It sounded like a concert from an orchestra of 100 waterphones.

"Ahhh," said Rosenberg, wiping his mouth and gasping like he had just taken a refreshing drink on a hot summer day. "That's the sound of the sky beginning to fall in earnest. Now let us commence with the Supreme Rite, to bring about the Baptism of Wisdom!" He threw the desiccated raven's headless body into the middle of the table, and dropped the head where he stood.

I wasn't operating at full capacity, so I wasn't reacting as I normally would to these abnormal occurrences. But I wasn't as bad off as most of the other guests. Indeed, they all appeared to be going through an almost lycanthropic transformation before my eyes.

Across from me, Marcia had pushed her seat back from the table and now sat back in her chair, with her blue evening dress hiked up to her crotch, which she was now rubbing lasciviously through her panties, fully visible. She was biting her lip hard, and blood trickled out of the corner of her mouth. She cackled like a witch.

Presently Crispin stood up and kissed Rosenberg passionately on the mouth. Rosenberg reciprocated, then violently wrenched the young man's arm behind his back. He bent him over the table and began dry-humping his ass.

Next, Mr. Wetzel stood up, an evil gleam now in his beady eyes. He walked over behind Philippine, grabbed her by the hair bun and jerked her head up. Her eyes were solid whites without pupils. I'd never seen anything like it before.

Her jaw dropped open. Her tongue began to flutter. She started to utter some strange glossolalia that I didn't recognize as human language. But then Wetzel slammed his right foot up on the table in front of her, unzipped his pants, and silenced her with a thrust of his penis. Her speech turned into gagging and slurping. That lasted a few seconds before Rosenberg reached out and shoved him away from her.

"Don't shoot your load just yet," he admonished. "You'll need all your potency for the ritual."

Then he turned and addressed the group, bellowing:

"Let us now descend to the sacred caverns! Last week was the Spring Equinox, but this weekend we shall celebrate the true Equinox of the Gods!"

Over his shoulder I caught sight of the Moon again. Then from behind it—I swear—I saw five bright lights emerge, each a different hue, and just hover there. They looked like stars, but they behaved like UFOs. I could tell that they were looking at me—at us.

I stood up and stumbled backward. Chesterfield grabbed me from behind and steadied me, immobilizing me with his arms.

"Do you see the stars moving outside?" I whispered in his ear.

"Just pretend you're possessed and make out with me," he whispered back. Understanding his meaning, I kissed his neck and growled like a dog. He began fondling my breasts.

Rosenberg walked over to the elevator now, with his friends following behind him like a procession of screaming banshees. He hit the intercom button.

"Miles, you can come up now," he said.

Miles? I thought. *How many servants in England are named Miles? That's so cliché! Why not Jeeves? Why not Mr. Belvedere?* Even in this insane crisis, under the slight influence of whatever was in the raven meat I spit out, my mind was still able to calm itself by telling itself stupid jokes, like it had so many times before.

I watched the numbers on the display change as the elevator climbed up to our floor from the bottom. When it got there, the doors opened, and there was Miles, Leopold Black's chauffer, with a gun in his hand again, pointed out towards us.

"Hello, Miles," said Rosenberg. "Where are the others?"

"They're waiting for you in the temple, sir," he replied.

Rosenberg gestured towards us, and we all piled into the elevator. Miles punched a code on a keypad next to the elevator's main set of buttons, and we started going down. The others were shrieking loudly, still busy molesting each other. There was enough noise that I could safely whisper something to Miles, who was standing right next to me.

"So you and Leopold and the rest of the butchers were in it together all along!" I said. "No surprise, I guess. Now what are you guys going to do us?"

But he just stared ahead like a Beefeater on duty, holding his gun with the barrel pointed out towards the elevator door. Meanwhile, the elevator continued to descend, down, down, down. We went past B1 and B2, the two basement levels listed on the main set of buttons. Then we kept going, into what seemed like a bottomless pit.

Chapter 21: Taurobolium

> According to one account dating from the 1830s, the Rothschilds owed their fortune to the possession of a mysterious 'Hebrew talisman' that enabled Nathan Rothschild, the founder of the London house, to become 'the Leviathan of the money markers of Europe.'
>
> —Nigel Ferguson, *The Ascent of Money*

When the elevator opened, we walked out into a hallway with stone floors and walls. The walls were lined with torches lighting the way. At the end of the corridor was an opening leading off to the left, and a statue of Harpocrates, the Egyptian god of silence, as a naked young boy. He held his index finger to his lips in his signature pose, with his other hand covering his crotch. I knew he was equated with Eros in Hellenistic syncretism, and was bound by an oath to keep the secrets of his mother Aphrodite's many sex crimes. I could only imagine what his presence in this hallway presaged. But my imagination was not extreme enough to predict what actually did happen.

All of us came out of the elevator except for one person: Chesterfield. He tried, but Rosenberg pushed him back in there, and then instructed Miles to shoot him in the head. Miles pointed the gun, and Chesterfield cringed, bracing himself. But then Rosenberg changed his mind, saying that Chesterfield "might come in handy later." The elevator door was shut, and then Rosenberg punched in a code that locked it in place. Poor Chesterfield was stuck in there.

I was blindfolded by Miles again, just like last time I was in a tunnel with him. But was led by him arm-in-arm down the hall, instead of being forced to lead. As we walked, Rosenberg and his friends were hooting, hollering and whooping like animals. Then we stopped abruptly. Someone, Rosenberg I presume, grabbed my arm and put my left hand upon a door handle. Then Rosenberg spoke to me.

"Pamela, my Cryphius: tell me: Can you see it in your mind's eye yet? What will we find in here when we open this door?"

I recognized the word "Cryphius" from my online reading about Mithras. It literally meant "occultist," and it was named by Franz Cumont as the title of the first degree of the Mithraic brotherhood. However, this was based on a single archeological find. All other evidence showed that the name of the first degree was *Corax*, meaning "raven." Allegedly, a raven had played the role of divine messenger, Mercury's job. It was sent by the sun god to Mithras, instructing him to have the bull slayed.

Pondering this, I then realized that Rosenberg wanted me to use my innate clairvoyant abilities to play the role of messenger for him. I was there to do divination on command, just like what Leopold and the Butcher's Society had kidnapped me for. That was probably why he had invited me to his party, and why he was keeping me alive.

So I had better find a way to perform, I thought.

I couldn't see anything in my "mind's eye," but I did hear a male but inhuman eldritch-sounding voice in my head, and it gave me a message.

The Lion, the Witch, and the Wardrobes.

I repeated this to Rosenberg, and he laughed.

"Good, good, you'll do," he said, taking off my blindfold. He opened the door, revealing a dimly-lit room with old light fixtures, and three wardrobes sitting next to each other on the far wall. Two were closed, and the one on the right was open. Inside there were what appeared to be theater costumes. And in front of the wardrobes stood two people already in costume.

One of these people was wearing a black robe and a mask of a lion's face. The other was an old Caucasian woman wearing a white gown, a red cape, and a large white hat that resembled a champagne cork. She had white foundation caked on her face like a clown, with thick black eye make-up and bright red lipstick. She smiled.

"*Paternoster*!" she said to Rosenberg as she held out her arms for him.

"Hello *Matri Deum*, Consivia, planter of the garden!" he said back to her. He kissed her on the hand, smiling back at her.

So this is Consivia, I said to myself. *And she's here as a priestess tonight, but not for the Anglican church.*

Rosenberg then turned to the man in the lion's mask.

"Is everything ready with the bull and the Butchers?" he asked.

"Absolutely, Father," he said. I recognized the voice. It was Leopold.

So even the pretense that Leopold and the Butchers were working against Rosenberg was a ruse, just like everything else about him, I thought. *They're all in league together, and this entire thing has been a set-up against me from the beginning.*

We all got suited up too. Each one of us had a face covering and a black robe tied that opened in the front, tied with a silver cord. Everybody dressed himself except for me. I got help from Consivia and Miles. They gave me a black bird's mask like the ones we had seen on the *Easter Sunday* film. Crispin wore a golden headband that suspended a white linen veil over his face. Marcia Martina put on Roman soldier's plumed helmet and a plain white mask. Wetzel wore a golden sun face. Most put their robes on over their clothes, but Philippine, her pupils now returned to the front of her eyeballs, somberly stripped off her clothes first, having obviously been given instructions ahead of time. Instead of a mask, she wore a black lace veil.

Rosenberg donned his Phrygian Smurf hat and a mask that resembled the bust of Mithras found at the London *mithraeum*. He also took a foot-long iron *harpe* (an ancient type of sickle) that was hanging on a hook on the back wall of one of the wardrobes. He holstered it with his belt. Then Miles opened the door to the hallway again, and everyone filed out, with Rosenberg leading the way.

Just to the right of the door of the wardrobe room, the hallway ended. The long dark corridor we had come from stretched out into darkness on our left and ended. Right there was a stone spiral staircase leading up. Rosenberg took a torch off the wall with his free hand and started going up. Everyone followed.

I couldn't see where it was leading until Rosenberg got to the top and drew his *harpe*. He then used it to flip open a hatch door above him. Torchlight and some ominous piano music poured through the opening. He holstered the blade and climbed up.

Rosenberg put his torch through the opening first. Someone above played a triumphant series of notes on a trumpet. Then a white gloved hand came down from the other side. Rosenberg grabbed it with his free hand and allowed himself to be helped up. A few seconds later we heard him bellowing loudly.

"Hail to the Lions!"

Then came a reply from a chorus of voices above.

"Hail, Father!"

We all went up through the hatch as well, except for Miles and Philippine. Miles grabbed the girl by the arm and nudged her with his gun back down the stairs. Then he motioned for me to squeeze past him. When I emerged, I saw that we were in the *mithraeum*. Miles shut the door behind me.

We had come out of a hole in the floor in the southeast corner of the room, near the altar, which was a recreation of an original feature, as I remembered from reading the plaques on display earlier that day. It was covered by a box on the floor, made of stone and about a foot high. The archeologists who found it thought that it must have contained ritual paraphernalia of some sort. But now the box acted as a portal to a lower chamber, with a door that could be pushed open from below. Miles came up from behind me and shut the door as well as the box lid as soon as he was through.

I saw before me a small crowd of about 40 people, some adults, some children, and all male as far as I could tell. They all wore black robes like us, and masks like those worn by several of Rosenberg's friends. There were men in lion masks, men in raven masks, men in Roman soldier helmets, and young boys aged seven to twelve wearing linen veils like Crispin. Each of these types were lined up in a row together.

The ones in the lion masks were using large censers on chains to waft us with incense as we each emerged from the box. The veiled boys were all against the wall on the left, making music. One sat at a piano in the corner, playing the somber tune, right next to the boy holding the trumpet. Against the opposite wall were boys singing dolorously in Latin.

But only Rosenberg wore the liberty cap, Wetzel had the only sun mask, and only Consivia wore the champagne cork hat with the clown make-up. Also, nobody else wore the lacey black veil that Philippine had been wearing.

However, there *were* several people in the congregation who were wearing black veils, just not of lace. These others were made of leather with eye slits cut out, just like the one I had seen on the people who slaughtered the bull beneath Stratford House. But there was one change: some of the leather veils were marked with a white waxing crescent moon symbol in front of the mouth. Others were marked with a black waning moon symbol outlined in white.

These must be Leopold's Butchers, I thought. *I wonder why there are two different kinds.*

Each of Rosenberg's friends took their place in front of their corresponding groups of congregants. Leopold stood before the Lions, and Marcia the Soldiers. Wetzel stood in the middle, in-between the Soldiers and the Lions. One of the Soldiers grabbed my arm and positioned me in front of the Ravens.

Consivia Springhole went to stand behind the stone altar, and Rosenberg stood to the left of it. It was not the original short and narrow altar that had been displayed in the *mithraeum* earlier. It was a much larger one of roughly hewn stone, the width of a man's length when horizontal, and I recognized it from Wikipedia. It was the one from the church next door, St. Stephen Walbrook, famously made to resemble the one in the Dome of the Rock in Jerusalem. The latter was, by tradition, the place where Abraham almost sacrificed his son. It was also said by Jews to be the "Even Ha-Shitiyah," the "foundation stone" of the universe, from which creation radiated outward at the beginning of time.

Behind the altar and the priestess was a black curtain, attached to a curtain rod that ran in a circle throughout the room. I hadn't remembered seeing that last time I was in there, so they must have set it up just before the ritual. All of the informational plaques and other display items I'd seen earlier had been removed.

Consivia began waving her arms about and chanting in Latin, making an invocation of some sort. One of the Ravens pulled the curtain aside, revealing the ancient stone *taurtoctony*, now the only piece of art on display from the original *mithraeum*, mounted on the wall behind the altar, just as in the days of old. Consivia turned and faced me directly.

"Cryphius, have you any dispatch from the Mount of the Gods?"

This was a test, I knew. Again, they wanted me to prove my psychic abilities. I tried to clear my mind so that I could hear that same strange voice that had told me about the wardrobe room.

Tell me what to say, I asked mentally.

To my relief, a reply came quickly. *Bring forth the Bull of the World. Give its blood and seed to the Virgin my Queen.*

I repeated these lines to the priestess, and then she repeated part of it as well. She shouted to the back of the room.

"Bring forth the Bull and the Queen of Heaven!"

At that moment, one of the two doors acting as the main entrance to the *mithraeum* swung open. A man with a waning moon veil led a black bull on a rope through the door and down the wheelchair-accessible ramp into the temple. The bull was draped with laurel crown and a red tasseled scarf on its back. On top of this Philippine rode side-saddle, her veiled head slumped in front of her.

When they got to the altar, two waning-moon Butchers grabbed the girl and slid her down from the bull. All three then went to stand with the rest of the Butchers. Another took the reigns from Miles, who walked back to the front doors, now closed, and stood before them, facing the altar while holding his gun out in front of him as before. A Raven came and stood near the altar, holding a *modius* full of grain. Then Consivia spoke to me again.

"Now, Cryphius, come stand before the altar."

I hesitantly stepped forward, trembling. A Lion brought forth one of the censers, now burned down to nothing but smoldering charcoal. She stuck her finger in the ashes and drew a circle between my eyes. Then she put a dot in the middle.

"Now with your mind's eye do you see what is in store for your own near future?" she asked.

Again, I couldn't *see* anything, but I heard an answer from the robot voice, with a very disturbing message.

This is going to hurt a lot, it said.

"Oh shit," I said as the floor beneath my feet gave way. I fell through the trap door and into a stone pit, landing hard on both legs, which both snapped on impact. I screamed as my body crumpled beneath me. Bones stuck out of both ankles. Blood poured out. I moaned and cried pathetically. I shook and convulsed uncontrollably, going into physical shock.

"Wh-wh-what are you going to do to me?" I was stuttering because I was hyperventilating.

But of course I knew what was coming. More or less. The pit was about six feet deep. It was round and small, barely big enough to sit in, except that in front of me there was a hallway the width of a man, which I could not see the end of. I could hear well what was going on above me. As my sobs grew quieter, Consivia began intoning an incantation above me

"Spirit of the World, come into the body of this horned creature. Accept the grain offering! Eat!"

I heard the bull's hooves scraping against the stone floor. I heard it snort as it most likely began to eat the grain, probably offered upon the altar in the style of the Greek *Bouphonia* ritual. That meant the "hunters" would now be sneaking up behind it. And if Rosenberg was playing the role of Mithras in this syncretistic ritual which they had devised, then it was probably his lance that would do the slaying. I heard the bull lowing, while men were shouting and grunting. Then I heard the voice in my head again:

Close your eyes.

I obeyed the order as the bull's blood came pouring down upon me. It was a kosher slaughter, so it took a few minutes for the animal to bleed out, during which time I continued to hear grunting. This was followed by a loud gasp of exaltation just as the flow of blood was slowing to a halt.

This told me that the tradition of sodomizing the bull while it died was being carried out by someone in the group.

Now I don't know what was the worst part: the sounds the poor creature made as it died, the feeling of the disgusting ooze dripping on my face, or the horrible stench. Thoughts of Mad Cow Disease and intestinal parasites came to mind. But none of it distracted from the pain in my legs for more than a few seconds. I wiped the blood from my eyes with the sleeve of my robe. Then I looked up and saw Consivia staring down at me from above.

"Now you have been baptized with a blood *niptron*. You should be able to see more clearly."

Quite the opposite. Not only was there still some blood stuck in my eyelids, clouding my vision, but my eyes, already swollen from crying, were also starting to itch and sting in reaction to the bacteria in the raw blood.

But I wasn't the only one crying. Philippine, whose only known personality trait was her love of animals, was becoming hysterical. She was under the influence of the poisoned bird from dinner, but she was still herself, and she was being severely traumatized by the sight of this (although, I suspected, not at all for the first time). However, she would not remain herself for much longer. Consivia began another invocation, even as the knives of the Butchers could be heard ripping into the bull's flesh.

"Virgin Mother, Queen of the Night, come hither into the vessel of this female body that stands before this altar. Come forth and accept the bollocks of this bullock, the World. Take into your mouth the sacred germ of secular living. Feast!"

The room above me suddenly became illuminated with a new light. It was not torchlight, but a soft blue glow, like natural moonlight. It traveled from the southwest side of the temple to the altar, floating over the aperture above me along the way. I say "floating" because when I finally got a look at it, I saw that it took the form of a sphere. When it passed over me and onto the altar, I heard Philippine gasp.

I then heard yowling, like that of a cat, and the hissing of a lizard or a snake. This was following by gurgling, ravenous chewing and swallowing.

The gore of the bull's severed testicles was undoubtedly being poured into her mouth.

I heard more ripping of flesh with knives, and the cracking open of bones. Then there was a rattle of chains, and muffled screams from the girl, sounding human again. After that, there was a moment of silence, just long enough for me to hear the faint sound of an insect stridulating. I looked directly in front of me. There was a scorpion, blond-colored and about an inch and a half long, standing about two feet from my disfigured legs with its pincher prone.

I tried to scoot back away from it using my hands. But I was already pretty much up against the wall. It started running towards me, and I closed my eyes. Then I heard a footstep, and a crunch. I opened my eyes and saw one of the Lions standing in front of me, holding an iron ring full of skeleton keys in a disfigured old white hand. He had stomped the scorpion beneath his light brown leather cap toe Oxford shoe.

"Leopold?" I said, just as the onerous music started up again in the temple above me.

He looked upwards through the trap door, at nothing, then lifted up his mask briefly, revealing the expected familiar face of the devious old con man. He winked at me, then put the mask back down. He knelt down beside me and pulled out a syringe. I screamed.

"No!" I turned away from him as far as I could, and tried to wrench my arm away from him as he grabbed it. He held tight. He whispered in my ear.

"Be quiet and stop struggling. I'm trying to help you. Now be still. I don't want to hurt you."

"I'm already in agony!" I snapped.

"That's why I'm giving you morphine," he replied through clenched teeth.

My struggle subsided. Within seconds I could feel that the injection did indeed contain opiates, ameliorating my suffering. I accepted it.

Maybe they'll chop me up and eat me bit by bit while I'm still alive, I thought to myself. *At least with the drugs it won't hurt as much.*

I slumped back and allowed myself to be dragged without struggle several feet down the dark hallway. Then Leopold picked me up and heaved me into a chair. It was a wheelchair.

He blindfolded me again. I felt the chair dragged backwards some distance. Then he turned the corner, and was able to turn the chair around so that he was pushing it forward. I felt us going up a ramp, turning and turning, for several minutes.

Then we straightened out again, went across a hallway, and stopped in front of a door. Leopold tapped on it nine times — six short ones and three long ones. The door opened and I smelled the incense. The Gothic organ music played and the boys chanted in Latin as we rode down the wheelchair ramp of the *mithraeum*'s proper entrance. At the bottom, he removed my blindfold. The music stopped. Consivia addressed me.

"Cryphius, you have been hobbled to prevent you from running away. For you are a slave to us. You will now be set forth before your master, to whom you shall genuflect in obeisance."

"How am I supposed to get down on my knees when I can't even stand?" I said, quivering.

But even as I spoke, Ravens were lifting me up and placing me on my knees. I had to fall forward on my hands and hold my broken legs up behind me with great effort to keep them from bearing weight against the ground.

"That just makes it easier to fall on your face," said Rosenberg, behind his mask of Mithras. He now stood in front of me, and in front of the altar, now displaying the eviscerated carcass of the sacrificed bull split down the middle and cracked open. Despite the incense, which itself was an unpleasant smell, the room was still full of the most god-awful stench from the dead animal. Rosenberg stated his demand.

"Do you promise to serve me without reservation henceforth, to do everything I ask, to submit to every humiliation, while also offering me your best efforts on the tasks I set for you, giving me true and complete information on every question I lay before you, and accepting a price worse than death if you fail in this?"

"Yes," I said in a cracked voice full of desperation.

How is this a bargain? I have no choices and nothing to negotiate with! I thought to myself.

Rosenberg then stepped aside from the altar, and two torch-bearing Lions stepped out to shine their fiery lights ahead of me so that I could see what was on the ground in front of it. There was a bloody pile of meat, specifically a string of intestines, now just a foot away from my face. Then Rosenberg spoke again.

"Here are the entrails of the sacrifice, sitting in the exact state in which they fell from the victim's body. Within the bowels of this beast you should be able to see the location of the keystone we are seeking. Can you see it?"

The Ravens raised me up a couple of inches. I looked at the guts. I couldn't help but notice that the manner in which they were arranged resembled the trefoil spiral staircase of the building we were in. And right in the center of the pile, at the end of the hose, there was something red and shiny like a ruby, its bright glow visible through the slime-covered flesh. I swear it looked like the Superman logo.

"Yes I can see it," I said. "Can you?"

He looked down at the pile of intestines. He was silent for a while, breathing heavily behind his mask. Then he at last he looked at me and spoke.

"That's what I have you for. Can you remember exactly what you see here? We'll need to use this information later on in the rites."

"Well I don't have a photographic memory, if that's what you're asking," I said. "Why don't you take a picture?"

He said nothing for a moment.

"You said you wanted accuracy. I'm in pain and on morphine. You'd best take a picture. There's a cell phone in the pocket of my jacket underneath my robe. It might still have some juice left."

Rosenberg laughed at that.

"I'll do it my self," he said. "But thank you for reminding me about your phone."

He reached into his pocket and took out his own phone, then tapped the side to open the camera function. He framed up the shot and activated the flash. In the dark cave, the sudden burst of light was blinding.

"Ravens, remove the lady's phone from her jacket, please, and open up the photo gallery" he said to the men holding me.

The Raven on my right hiked up my robe, and fumbled in my jacket pocket for the phone, unnecessarily squeezing my right breast in the process.

"Stop it, you pig!" I objected. Rosenberg chuckled. So then did several others.

"Miss Auger, genuflection is ultimately a sign of sexual submission made into a societal custom. It's an evolutionary vestige of our wild bestial ancestors. The animals do it whenever they lose a fight, or whenever they don't even dare to fight. It was first practiced by human tribes conquered in war, to obtain mercy from the victors. Then it was made a general sign of "respect" from slaves to their owners. Why do you think Muslims put their asses in the air when they submit to Allah?"

The Raven with the phone held it out in front of me while his partner now took control of both of my legs.

"What's the swipe code?" the Raven with the phone asked.

"It's the sign of Jupiter," I answered.

"Huh?" he said.

"It's like a number 4," I said.

He took off his white glove and tried to draw a 4 with his finger on the cover of the phone. It didn't work. So he took off his mask and squinted at the phone in the torchlight. I saw that it was Drexella's pimple-faced, greasy-haired son, Dennis.

I put all of my weight on my left hand and reached out to draw the swipe code on my phone with my right hand. I got in at once and then hastily put my right hand down again so that I wouldn't fall forward. Even with the morphine, the muscle strain from hanging there and the pain from the injury was unbearable.

"Hey, the phone's at 3%, boss," Dennis said as he handed the phone to Rosenberg. "Want me to plug it in somewhere?"

"In a minute," he said as he looked at the screen. "Can I sit down now?" I pleaded.

Rosenberg nodded and waved in our direction, giving his ascent. Then he looked at the phone again and gasped. "You already have a photo of raw meat on your phone.

What is this for?"

"What do you mean?" I said. I hoped that I wouldn't be struck by lightning for violating my oath to be truthful to him. I also hoped that my phone being almost dead would buy me some time before I had to give him an explanation. I didn't know exactly what the relationship was between Rosenberg's Mithras cult and Leopold's Butchers, but if Rosenberg didn't already know everything about the bull liver at Stratford Place, I wasn't going to volunteer to tell him.

Any information gap between me and him, I thought, *is a strategic advantage.*

My hope was well-founded. With the phone at 3%, he couldn't open up the image gallery to see the detail. The phone just shut down when he tried. He rebooted it, but it immediately shut down again as soon as he opened the gallery.

"Fuck!" he yelled, and almost threw the phone across the room. Then he stopped himself and handed it to Dennis.

"Plug it in," he told the lad, no doubt regretting that this was the one room in the building where he'd decided, out of respect for history, not to put phone chargers everywhere (or, indeed, any electrical outlets whatsoever). He signaled to the boy at the piano, who began playing an unsettling line of notes in repetition.

The Ravens set me down on the ground with my feet out in front of me. Then Dennis went out the front entrance to plug the phone in while the other Raven dragged me to the nearest of the fourteen pillars in the temple.

He sat me on the first stone bench on the right side and propped me up with my back against the pillar second from the altar, so that the altar was in front of me. Then someone else who I couldn't see came up from behind me and wrapped a heavy iron chain around my body, fixing me in position. My arms were pressed tight against my sides, and my back was firmly against the pillar.

"So, Cryphius," said Consivia, addressing me from behind the altar. "Part of your duty is to help us determine the correct order of operations for the rest of the rituals. We should not have to tell you what the purpose of the rituals is. Which of the Archons should be we invoke next?"

Well, I didn't get an answer from my telepathic informant, but it seemed only obvious to me. Events like this always start with an orgy of rape, followed by an orgy of murder involving even more heinous forms of rape. Erotic rites precede rites of sadistic violence, but the longer the preliminaries could be stretched out, the longer the murders could be postponed. That wouldn't make the rapes any less difficult to watch, or make me feel any less responsible for what happened to the victims. But it seemed like the least harmful choice.

"Invoke first the Archon of Lust," I answered.

"Yessss!" the crowd hissed, like serpents. Consivia nodded and raised her shepherd's crook, then used it to gesture to the girl in the black laced veil, who, I now saw, was chained to the pillar opposite from me.

"Now, Luna, lay down upon the altar, within the carcass of this beast, and let your brothers make you pregnant with the seed of a new aeon!" declared Consivia.

A Raven came to unlock her chains. He unfastened her robe and let it fall to the ground, so that she stood there naked and shivering. Then he led her to the altar, where she obligingly laid down in her bed of raw meat, sobbing piteously. The Raven then began wrapping the chains around the carcass to strap the girl to it. Her legs were positioned so that the chains held them open, with her vagina gaping open and easily accessible from the left side of the altar.

The black curtain was now covering the wall behind the altar once more. Now one of the Ravens pulled it back again, revealing this time, instead of the *taurtoctony*, another curtain, made of red translucent linen, into which an inverted cross – the Cross of St. Peter – had been cut. Through the cross-shaped hole something else displayed behind the curtain could be seen mounted on the wall.

I recognized it as one of the broken pieces of the relief of Dionysus that had been found in the original *mithraeum*. This was the section with only his naked rear end.

I didn't know it at the time, but I now realize that the image before me – of the backside of Dionysus seen through the inverted cross cut into the curtain – looked just like Man Ray's picture *Monument à D.A.F. de Sade*, which he used as a cover for his personal edition of Marquis De Sade's *120 Days of Sodom* in 1933.

"Master of the Nymphi, come forth before the altar!" Consivia called to the back of the room.

There, seated on the stone bench at the back with several of the young veiled boys was the only grown man wearing such a costume: Crispin Martina. He rose and did as he was told, standing with tall, proud sensuality in front of the altar. The priestess watered him with lustrations from her aspergillum, then laid her hand upon his head.

"Aphrodite, Queen of Harlots, come now, and be joined in marriage with Our Father! Come into the body of this young man and enjoy the double pleasure of the *Tanin'iver*, the pole betwixt the serpents. Fuck and be fucked!"

"To you we will give the first taste of the flesh of our beautiful young boys of high birth, and of our virgin royal queen. To you we will also give the pleasure of penetration from the rod of Our Father. Lady Venus, you who were born from the foam of the phallus upon the waters of feminine desire, yet who burns with the fire of male ferocity, come forth and take your fill of the Distinguished Charity of Mete!"

That last phrase, if you'll recall, came right out of my commissioned translation of Hammer-Purgstall's *Mysterium Baphometis Revelatum*, where he wrote that he found it encoded on a former Templar site in Bavaria. No other published work besides mine had utilized that phrase in English.

My work is being used to write lines for elite rape rituals, I thought with horror. It was so unbelievable, yet it was happening before me.

Next, I saw a yellow-white ball of light emerge from within the well in the southwest corner of the room, which had, in the original *mithraeum*, been connected to the Walbrook River underground. (Little did I know at the time that the Walbrook had already been re-irrigated surreptitiously by Rosenberg and his friends, so it was presently floating back through the site we stood on down to the Thames once again.) The light ball then glided across the room, hovered over Crispin's head for a moment, and then swiftly entered through the crown of his skull. I saw his face and neck become flush as sweat poured down his forehead.

Consivia took a step backwards, and Rosenberg stood before Crispin.

"Harlot, kneel before Our Father," Consivia commanded.

The young man did so. Rosenberg split open his robe in front, then stepped forward and pulled the veil over Crispin's head. He shoved his crotch in Crispin's face, and was eagerly serviced by the man, now possessed by the goddess of love, or rather, "strange love." After a minute, the "Father" pulled out and the priestess proclaimed:

"I now pronounce you the bride of the Father! Let us all enjoy the harlots of the temple in the spirit of the Archon of Lust. Come forth Nymphi!"

With that, all of the boys in veils stepped into the center of the temple. There they were seized upon by the older participants. These men, and one woman, dragged them off to the stone benches between the columns on the sides of the chamber and had their way with them.

Only one of the ritual's participants opted out of the child rape: Consivia. She stood behind the altar with her eyes closed, praying in tongues and making the cross sign with her hands every few minutes. Marcia squatted with her robe hiked up over the face of a twelve-year-old. I had lost track of where Leopold was in the room, but I certainly didn't see him standing on the sidelines. Miles seemed to have left the room. Almost everyone was fully engaged in either raping or being raped.

This included Rosenberg, who, after being formally "married" to his boyfriend in a bizarre rite of sexual subjugation, extended his hand as if in friendship to the man on the floor. He helped him to his feet, but then spun him around and held him from behind. Rosenberg pulled up the young man's robe, exposing his erect penis, which he stroked a few times.

The Pater then gestured to one of the Nymphi, about ten years old, who was already servicing one of the Lions. The boy immediately stopped and came over to attend to Crispin's now throbbing member. The man howled in bestial ecstasy and leaned back on Rosenberg to support his weight.

After about a minute of this, Rosenberg pushed Crispin towards the end of the altar where Philippine lay strapped inside the bull carcass. The young man shoved himself into her body and began thrusting as she screamed. Then Rosenberg pulled up the back of Crispin's robe and inserted himself into the young man's buttocks. Beneath the weight of the daisy chain, the bull carcass cracked a bit more, but it still held its general shape with the help of the chains.

As the Nymphi were both the prostitutes and the musicians, and they were presently employed, the only soundtrack for this rite of debauchery was the screaming and the moaning of the participants, the sounds of their bodies slapping together, the slurping sounds of fellatio and analingus. The odor of sex, and anal sex in particular, aided with the cans of "Lyle's

Golden Syrup" that were being passed around the room for lubricant, mixed with the smell of incense and dead animals into a sickening perfume. That, the morphine, and the shock of the physical pain, as well as the sight of the meat on the altar, and the rape of the young, was enough to cause me to vomit right next to the place where I sat chained helplessly watching. The smell of my own vomit made me want to vomit more, which I did.

Though they seemed to transgress every sexual barrier, I noticed that the modern Mithraists did observe one restraint. All of the males were quite careful about where their seed went. Most had their semen collected into metal bowls that were passed around. This included the boys, all of whom, it seemed, were successfully milked for this purpose. These bowls were then emptied into two large Greek-style kraters that stood on either side of the altar about two feet away in front of it.

Wetzel and Rosenberg, however, pulled out before they got to that point, and gave themselves a "cold *niptron*" (Rosenberg's words) from the *amphora* of holy water that sat next to the altar, cooling off their excited genitals. Rosenberg asked his friend to help wipe off his penis, and he seemed more than happy to comply. He then stood next to Crispin, rubbing his backside and promising him divine progeny as the young man pumped his semen into Philippine.

"You shall sire us a new god of love, a new Eros who will come forth from the egg of a new aeon. I shall name him Cupidonus," Rosenberg cooed.

"Why can't *I* name him?" said Crispin, turning towards Rosenberg as he finished his orgasm. "I want to name him after my father."

"Silence!" shouted Rosenberg. Before Crispin could react, Rosenberg grabbed him by the throat, and pushed him back into the center of the room with the others. Then he pointed directly at me.

"Cryphius! Whom shall we invoke next?"

This time I was too sick and weary to think up a good answer. My first choice had been made strategically to save or at least extend people's lives, hopefully long enough for someone to come along and save us. But now the first wave of orgies had passed and it was time for me to make another decision.

Rosenberg wanted me to used my sixth sense to find the answer, so that was what I decided to so. In the moment of relative silence he allowed me, I cleared my mind as best I could, and put out the question to the voice that had spoken to me before. I received an answer, which I repeated verbatim without thinking.

"Let Ares come forth to play bloodsport and enjoy the caresses of Aphrodite, as he is wont to do."

There was a logic at work here. Each of the gods invoked so far had been baited with something they found irresistible. Ares (a.k.a. Mars) was a god of warfare, rape and pillage. He was also famous for fornicating with Aphrodite (a.k.a. Venus) despite her marriage to Hephaestus (a.k.a. Vulcan).

"Yes, let him come forth," said Rosenberg. "I've always preferred the purity of hatred to love, and death to sex. Marcia, if you please, march yourself up to the altar here."

From the right side of the room, where she had sat being serviced by boy prostitutes, Marcia Martina arose, with her Roman helmet still on, but with the visor up, so that her face was visible. She grinned from ear to ear, and stared lustfully at her son, who looked back at her with dread. Consivia sprayed her with the aspergillum, and a Lion wafted her with incense again.

Then one of the Ravens pulled away the curtain with the Satanic cross of St. Peter and brought forward a curtain displaying a Greek-style tapestry. From my position I could see that it showed a number of ancient battle scenes, including soldiers spilling out of a large wooden horse.

The Trojan War, I thought.

I then understood that the curtain had been made to represent Penelope's tapestry from Homer's *Odyssey*, the one she supposedly never finished. Rosenberg stepped into the center of the room and began bellowing out a speech.

"Lord Mayor Marcia Martina: for centuries your family has been the keeper of the holy buckler of our temple. It was this sacred object that the site where we now stand, Bucklersbury, was secretly named for, as only the initiates of our esteemed syndicate know. This powerful talisman is represented on your family's arms, and reference to it can be found in the current incarnation of your family's name."

She nodded her assent, as if to say "This much I know."

"As the patrons of soldiers, your family has lent your wealth to assist in many great pageants of honor and valor, of bloodshed and rape. Your gold has been spent to pour the Water of Life upon the Earth, and she has thirstily drunk it up. With your help Britannia's enemies have been conquered many times, creating an empire where the Sun never dies, shielding her with your strength. Even now, as the aegis of the empire has been occulted from the eyes of the profane, you and your kin have continued in this service."

She nodded again, now with a bit of curiosity in her eyes, like she wondering where this was going.

Then a Raven pulled back the tapestry to reveal a display of twelve heavy metallic shields mounted on the wall, painted red, all of different shapes and sizes. One of them, however, was in the shape of the Superman logo. It was placed in the center of the arrangement. Rosenberg continued his speech.

"Now, Lord Mayor, if you are fit to be the scion of your seed, the one who shall wear the mantle of great Mars, the captain of all armies, please walk up to the wall and take up the buckler of your esteemed heritage."

Marcia seemed confused at first, then scared. She turned around and looked at me for help. I looked at the ground and tried to blank out my mind. I knew what was coming, and I wasn't about to save her ass. So she walked up to the wall behind the altar and started guessing.

It was like watching someone playing Plinko on "The Price is Right," trying to guess the correct digit. First she gravitated towards the one that looked like the shape of the shield of the Rothschild coat of arms. This was in fact the one that looked most like every heraldic shield you've ever seen. Then she reviewed the field of choices again, and settled on a much smaller one, which looked like the small round buckler that formed the central jewel on the Rothschild arms. This is the one that actually represented the "red shield" of popular lore.

It was this symbol that Mayer Amschel Rothschild supposedly used as a logo for his currency exchange business in Frankfurt. This is what the family was allegedly named after, according to mainstream historians. But now I knew better. They were named after another object, some kind of "talisman." Bucklersbury, the old name for the intersection of streets where the *mithraeum* and New Court both stood, had been named after this object, probably long before the Rothschilds "officially" took residence there. I was certain that it took the shape of the Superman logo, although I had no idea what that meant.

So Marcia had taken the wrong shield from the wall, albeit the logical choice. But she didn't possess the secret gnosis that I had been given quite accidentally. She would pay the price for this mistake eventually, but not right away. Rosenberg preferred to play with her first. She stood with her left hand inserted into the handle of the buckler and stared at Rosenberg.

"Now what?"

Rosenberg turned to Consivia.

"Priestess, please, invoke the Archon of War," he said.

Consivia motioned for Marcia to come stand with her before the altar. Then she laid her hand upon the woman's brow and spoke commands into the aether.

"Lord Ares, come into this vessel of power. Enjoy with us the fruits of incarnation. Feel the glory of killing in the flesh for yourself once again as you help us initiate the greatest bloodbath the Earth has ever known. You can be the general, and you can call out the first shot!"

Suddenly we heard the ringing of a cell phone with a "99 Luftballons" ringtone. Marcia, startled, fumbled inside her robe with her right hand and pulled out her phone. She then stared at it in excited astonishment.

"Oh my goodness," she said, as if she had any goodness. "It's the Lord High Admiral. He only calls when there's a war on."

As she spoke, an orange-red ball of light came up out of the well in the corner, just like the one before, and flew across the room, straight into Marcia's skull. She then became possessed of a spirit even more demonically evil and sadistic than the one she already called her own. When she answered the phone, she spoke with a masculine, guttural voice.

"Hello Sir. Yes. I'm fine, sir. I have a sore throat. Yes, of course. Go ahead. Fire the torpedo. We'll help you pay for the aftermath, like always. Don't worry."

She hung up and distractedly tried to hand her buckler and phone over to Rosenberg.

"Father, hold these for me please," she said, staring wantonly at Crispin. Rosenberg jerked his hand away in disgust and motioned for one of the Ravens to take the items instead. Hands now free, she ripped open her robe and her blouse, squeezing her shriveled old breasts. Then she grabbed Crispin and kissed him passionately on the mouth, rubbing his chest and grasping his limp penis between her bony fingers.

The young man seemed revolted at first. But, overcome with his lingering possession by the Archon of Lust, he succumbed to her caresses and began to regain his erection. Marcia then decided to sit down on the stone bench on the wall opposite from the pillar where I was chained. She laid back on the large cushion behind her and had Crispin kneel with his head between her legs. I had a perfect view. I couldn't help but stare in horror.

The son dutifully began stimulating his mother's clitoris with his tongue, as I suspected he had done many times before in less ritualized and divinely inspired circumstances. She admonished him not to be "too hasty." Then she closed her eyes and let out an intense moan that turned into a growl. After a few minutes, she told him to stop. She regained her composure temporarily and issued a command to the other people wearing Roman helmets like hers.

"Soldiers, take up your spears and shields and divide yourselves into two even rows."

The Soldiers all looked at Rosenberg, who stood next to the altar. He nodded his agreement. Obediently, they all grabbed bucklers from the wall behind the altar, and spears, which were mounted right next to them. (None, I noticed, chose the Superman-logo-shaped shield, perhaps because it was so peculiar.) Then they stood at attention in two rows with four men each. There was a row of men on either side of her bench, staring across to each other, awaiting instructions.

"Fight the man across from you, until either he or you are dead."

There was a moment of hesitancy. The men looked at each other from behind their masks. But it only lasted for a few seconds, as Rosenberg appeared to have no objection. To the contrary, he issued a complimentary command to the Nymphus whose job it was to play the drum.

"Give me a drumbeat please. Something appropriate for a soldier marching to war."

The Nymph nodded and began tapping out a furious beat. One of the guys in the middle of the row on my right struck out at the man across from him. Then all hell broke loose between the two teams. Blood was flying everywhere. An ear got sliced off and landed in front of me.

Marcia looked on at the spectacle in satisfaction, and leaned back again. Crispin resumed his work. Within a couple of minutes, four men were dead, and Marcia looked like she was about to climax. She was laying diagonally on the bench now, arching her pelvis up towards Crispin's mouth as he slurped away.

"Now fight each other until there's only one of you," she gasped in a raspy demonic voice. Caught up in the frenzy of battle by this time, nobody questioned the order. It took a few more minutes for these more competent soldiers to be cut down.

During this time, Marcia had her son remove his mouth several times for a few seconds, and then resume his work. She seemed to be timing her orgasm until the last kill of the combat was made. When this occurred, she began jerking spasmodically, yelling "Hurrah! Hurrah!" while the victor stood before her with his spear held high over his head, panting and sweating nervously. He was obviously still terrified for his life, even though he'd won.

The drummer boy had just finished his set, but a new set of knocks was heard coming from the doors of the front entrance. One of the Ravens went to open it as Marcia stood up and closed her robe. It was Miles. He walked in and raised his hand to signal Rosenberg.

In so doing, he exposed his gun, which was holstered in his belt on the front of his body. Marcia, seeming to react on instinct, seized it on sight. Miles just stared at her, taken aback at her brazenness. She turned around and pointed the gun at the victorious sole surviving Soldier.

"Well done, you brave young man. You've earned some metal on your chest."

And with that, she shot him in the left breast. He fell over, emitting vacuous gasps of air from the hole in his lungs as blood sputtered out of his mouth.

"Ah yes, that was great!" yelled Marcia. She began goose-stepping around the room happily. Behind her, Miles cleared his throat loudly and then spoke past her to Rosenberg.

"Father, sir, two of our brothers have arrived late unexpectedly, with a little one in tow."

"Tell them to go home. We can't be interrupted now," replied Rosenberg. "How rude and careless of them. Our elect ones should know better than that."

"These brothers are very important," Miles added.

"Oh, then who are these supposed VIPs?" he asked, laughing. "You know that Mithras is no respecter of persons."

"The Duke of Rothesay, sir. And [Baron Carrickfergus]. And Little Saint George."

A collective gasp went through the room. It seemed that everyone present was both familiar and impressed with the code names mentioned. It wiped the smile off Marcia's face. She sat down on the bench next to her son, both of them now looking very serious. Only Rosenberg was unmoved. He walked over and took the gun away from Marcia, who handed it over without objection.

"Is that so? Well, that *is* impressive. Nonetheless, I'm not sure we can dispose of one form of decorum for another…."

Prompted by my telepathic informant, I interrupted, projecting my voice as far as I could.

"Let them come hither. For *three* kings are destined to bow down before the new Sun!"

Rosenberg turned and looked at me through his mask. He cocked his head to the side, confused. Then he walked up to me and whispered.

"But don't we have to finish the rite tonight first? I believe the hour is getting late."

"And these are the ones who have been called to finish the rite! Some of the actors you have chosen do not fit the role."

I spoke quietly, and I no longer sounded like myself. My voice took on a *seething* quality, raspy and inhuman, as if I too had a hole in my lung, just like the poor Soldier who gurgled out his last spit of blood on the floor in front of me. Rosenberg took it all in, then nodded.

"Go ahead, Miles, let them join us. But see that the two brothers are properly suited according to their grades in the order. As for the little one…"

He looked at me, as if waiting for a judgment from me about what to do with "Little Saint George." Apparently, this was a child too young to be a "brother" in an order that admitted boys as young as seven. He had been brought to a place where young boys were subjected to repeated homosexual rapes and made to be complicit in ritual murder.

How can I prevent them from bringing him into this pit of hell and abusing him here?, I asked my telepathic informant.

There is no way to save this child, the voice told me. *But let Miles sit with him in the main lobby for now.* I repeated that last part to Rosenberg as a command from the realm beyond.

"Don't worry," said Miles. "They're already in their costumes. I'll take care of the child."

With that, he ducked out through the door, which he left slightly ajar. A moment later, two men in robes and masks, one a Sun, the other a Lion, came through the doorway, then walked down the hall, the Lion leading the Sun. The Lion had salt and pepper hair. The Sun had short golden hair with a bald patch on top. They both came and stood before Rosenberg in the center of the room.

"Well, brothers, it's nice to see that you finally decided to show up. I thought you were too busy to come tonight, despite my insistence that it would be the most important rite we have ever conducted."

"Yes," said the Lion. "Well, it has been an eventful evening. My father received a call from this building a few minutes ago that has initiated a very dangerous sequence of events. This country is now in a perilous international crisis. The Russian sub that was just torpedoed in the Straight of Dover may very well set off a nuclear war if we don't dial it back somehow."

"So we came here to talk to the very persons we believe to be fomenting this crisis, to ask them to back off," said the Sun-man, looking at Marcia and Crispin. "We ask not only as representatives of the crown, but as your brothers in Mithras too." He nodded politely with reserved deference towards Rosenberg. It was sort of a half-bow, as if showing respect for the leader of the Order, but holding back full obeisance out of respect for his own position of authority. It reminded me of Barack Obama trying to bow to the King of Saudi Arabia without looking like he was bowing.

"And for the sake of the Goddess our Mother," the Lion added, making the same half-assed bow towards Consivia.

"Duly noted, Rothesay. Thank you," said Consivia, nodding back at him.

So that's the Duke, I thought to myself. *The other one must be Baron Carrickfergus. I wonder if he got his barony from the same place Leopold did.* I was trying to think flippantly, to bring some levity to the situation for myself, but my gut told me that this Duke and Baron were not pretending. In fact, I got the feeling they were each just using some of their more *minor* titles for this occasion.

Marcia now stood up, looking possessed by evil intentions rather than fear once again. She took what she thought was her family's hereditary buckler back down from the wall, and one of the spears, which she held in her right hand with the tip downward. Then she strode arrogantly over to where the two apparent aristocrats of high stature, self-identified as *agents of the crown*, were standing. She addressed herself first to the Lion.

"You know, not only should you *not* interrupt a meeting in progress that you couldn't be bothered to show up on time for. The fact is, in this part of town, you're supposed to ask for my permission to cross the *pomoerium*."

"Not if Regina's still alive," he replied.

"I hear she isn't," said Marcia, bringing her spear up and pointing it in his face. "And if that's true you're putting the kingdom in a very precarious position by coming here. Which means you're desperate. So what do you have to bargain with? Is that why you brought Little Saint George? Bring him out here. I love a Vienna sausage every now and then." She gnashed her teeth at him.

"Show some respect!" said Rosenberg, grabbing the spear from out of the Lord Mayor's hand. Even possessed by the war god, the old woman's boney hands were no match for the strength of a man. He didn't even have to point the gun at her, and instead holstered it in his waistband beneath his robe before he took the spear. As her weapon slipped out of her grasp, Ms. Martina stumbled backwards and landed on her butt. I heard brittle bones snap.

Osteoporosis is a bitch, I thought.

"Actually what you're holding is a trinket," Rosenberg said sneeringly as he towered over her cowering body. "It's for little boys and girls who like to dress up and play toy soldier. The real Hebrew talisman that turned Nathan Rothschild into the Leviathan of finance worldwide is something else entirely. But of course, you don't have the subtlety of mind to understand that. Wetzel!"

"Yes!" The other man with the Sun mask stumbled out from the shadows and stood dutifully before his master.

"Let the Lord Mayor and her son have a look at the explosive headlines that just hit the international news wires," Rosenberg instructed.

"Which ones?" Wetzel asked. The nuclear threats from Russia? Or the financial news?"

"No, first the one about the video you just leaked to your contacts at the BBC," the Pater specified.

Wetzel reached into his robe and pulled out a smartphone. He pressed a few buttons, and then turned the screen out towards where Marcia sat on the ground, looking aghast. Crispin got up and walked towards the screen, staring at it in horror with his right hand holding his veil up on top of his head. Wetzel pressed a button on the side of the phone, and the sound became loud enough for us all to hear.

It was a familiar sequence of words and sounds—ones we had just heard coming from Marcia moments earlier. We heard again the moans of ecstasy as her son pleasured her. Then a male TV presenter's voice could be heard, apparently narrating a *series* of clips.

"Another recording provided to our reporter by this anonymous source shows what appears to be the Lord Mayor in the same position with a male child, possibly as young as twelve, from the looks of it."

Marcia pushed her heavy metal helmet off of her head, and it landed with a loud clang on the floor. The presenter continued.

"Of course, we won't be showing you even doctored versions of that, as it *does* constitute child pornography and *is* illegal to possess. We've passed both videos on to MI5 for authentication."

"I hope those shots were tight enough to conceal our location," said Wetzel.

"Shh," said Rosenberg. "Listen." The report went on.

"But the most heart-breaking thing is that this film, *and* the first one we showed you, with Crispin Martina, were date-stamped with tonight's date, from *less than an hour ago*. That means that this sick party, where children are being abused, is potentially still taking place right now. Scotland Yard has confirmed that they are on their way to Mansion House with a warrant for the Lord Mayor's arrest."

"Good God, Blake, you'll get us all taken down. What have you done?" said Crispin. He reached in his robe, got out his phone, and began dialing a number.

"That is an extreme move," said the Duke of Rothesay to Rosenberg. "We're all vulnerable when it comes to that sort of thing. It's supposed to be the bullet that never gets fired."

"Tell that to Jimmy Saville," said Marcia, opening up her own cell phone now. "I'll be damned if I'm going to let you hang me out to dry like that. My family won't let it happen."

"Your family will be too busy scraping up whatever assets they have left and fleeing the countries they live in," said Rosenberg. "While you were in this chamber having your smegma-covered cunt serviced by your sniveling son, the value of your family's wealth has evaporated. What good will mountains of gold do you when the volume of gold on the market has just been quadrupled literally overnight?"

There was a collective gasp in the room, then a few seconds of silence.

"That's impossible," said Crispin. "Our family holds over half of the world's gold. There's no way anyone could dump that much gold on the market without our participation. And we're not selling right now."

"That's OK, 'cause nobody's buying," Rosenberg retorted. "Did you forget that you're talking to an alchemist?"

The eyes of both Martinas widened at the sound of that. They stared in disbelief.

"You can't be serious," said Marcia.

"He is," said Crispin addressing his mother. "He made it from the urine we've been getting from the throne in Westminster. He discovered the tubes in the tunnels, remember?"

"Oh fuck," she said, tearing her wig off and revealing the gray hear underneath, with a significant bald patch on top.

"And I've got a process that produces in much more abundance than what you and your ancestors have been doing," said Rosenberg. "I know the true secrets of *multiplicatio*, not just confidence tricks!"

"Because you've been harvesting semen from all your employees here for over a year," said Crispin, pacing back and forth frantically. "Through the robots and the glory hole in the Qaphqa. And from all of the orgies we've been having over at the Coffin House over the last year. And the blood and guts of the victims too. God, even the spinal fluids. I can't believe I didn't see what you were up to. I really believed you were looking for a source of free energy, to help the Earth."

"Oh, what I'm about to do will give the Goddess of Dirt exactly what she needs, and a source of power that will be inexhaustible. You see, Crispin, what she really wants is to be reunited with her lover, the sky, and that is the kind of love that we are making tonight. It's a strange love, a mad love, like the laugh of the hell-worm that will not die. Isn't that right, Reverend Springhole?" He turned around and looked at Consivia. She smiled at him and nodded.

"What the Devil are you talking about?" asked the Duke of Rothesay.

"The Devil you *don't* know, apparently," said Rosenberg. "Never mind, you'll find out soon enough."

The Pater then turned back to Marcia and Crispin.

"So you see, Lord Mayor, you bitch of the parasitic, warmongering House of Rothschild: as much as I hate the sickly sweet love between low, plebian souls, I actually hate hatred too, even more. Certainly, we can do without the kind of revolutionary instincts that your family fosters to keep the war machine turning. Because it weakens loyalty, quickens the pride, and stirs rebellion among the unworthy."

He inhaled and exhaled deeply, pacing in a circle around the two Martinas. He continued.

"In the new aeon, there will be no resistance to the Lord of Unrule. Remember what Zeus once said to Ares in the *Aeneid*? To his own despised son? He said 'were you born of some other god … long since you would have been dropped beneath the gods of the bright sky.' We don't need a war god under the new Sun."

Marcia turned to her son.

"Crispin, help Mummy up please."

The young man reached down, grabbed the injured old woman's arm and began lifting her to her feet. She leaned on his shoulder, putting her weight on him. But he reached out to Rosenberg for the spear, which his boss willingly handed over to him.

Then Crispin placed the spear upside-down with the tip of the handle pressed down onto the floor, and pushed his mother's body towards the blade. She fell upon it, and it went all the way through, skewering her through the heart. There was only time for her to utter a single wheeze before she closed her mouth forever. Crispin let the body fall to the floor as it expired. Then he turned to Rosenberg, with a pleading look.

"Please just help me escape from this. I will be your most loyal servant, as I always have been. I'm willing to do anything. I'll even. . . ." He paused to consider what he was agreeing to, staring off blankly at a far wall. "I'll even let the Barber-Surgeons change my beautiful face, if it means I can be released from the life of infamy that now stands before me." He looked like he was going to cry.

"Your beauty is fading in any case, dear lover," said Rosenberg. "You're far too old and your rectum is far too worn out for my taste these days."

At this, tears were definitely welling up in the corner of Crispin's reddened baby-blue eyes. Rosenberg continued his emotional torture.

"But don't forget: I've got *you* on camera now too, diddling a twelve-year-old girl. So why don't you give up now to avoid the humiliation. In the next aeon, a new catamite will be born to me with the beauty of Ganymede."

He sighed at the pleasure of this contemplation, then reached in his waistband and pulled out the gun. He offered it to Crispin, holding it by the barrel. Without a moment's hesitation, he put it his mouth and pulled the trigger, spraying his brains all over Consivia behind him.

The splatter reached the ceiling too, as well as the wall, and the altar where Philippine now lay silent and still on top of the rotting bull carcass. Some of the gore apparently sprinkled on the Duke's lion mask, even managing to penetrate the slit of the mask's mouth. He stuck his finger underneath the mask and we heard him lick his lips.

"Mmm, tastes like a Jew," the Duke said. Everybody in the room started laughing uproariously.

"Hey!" said Rosenberg in mock objection, chuckling underneath his Mithras mask. "I resemble that remark!" More cachinnation followed.

The Duke pulled off his mask, revealing his rat-like old face, proving that he was indeed the person I feared he was.

Here's one of the most crucial figures in the kingdom, I thought, *standing there exposing himself to incrimination that could destroy the crown itself, not to mention the threat of assassination. Yet he seems so perfectly comfortable, as though he still trusts in the honor among thieves. This even after he just watched two other very important figures cut down in cold blood before him. Even after he himself has just been threatened with a spear by one of them. Despite the fact that Rosenberg has shown himself to be indisputably the most powerful person in the room, with a financial weapon in his arsenal of an unimaginable magnitude, and completely disloyal to his so-called "brothers", neither Duke nor Baron seem fazed at all.*

"So, my liege," said Rosenberg to the Duke, "can you call off your dogs at Scotland Yard before they start combing through every building on the block?"

"Ho ho, old boy, they're not *my* dogs," the Duke said, replacing his mask. "Can you help me call off the dogs of war that the Lord Mayor unleashed?"

"Yes, but this first," Rosenberg insisted. "If they don't find the Lord Mayor at Mansion House, they will surely go looking at New Court, and eventually they'll end up here."

"That's precisely why you shouldn't have leaked that video to the press! What were you thinking? Anyway, I can't be seen to interfere on this case. Not with all the child sex charges still haunting Andrew. The order to quash must come from within Scotland Yard, or from within the Security Services. Don't you have connections at Thames House?"

"I used to," said Rosenberg. Then he remembered. "Wait, yes!" He got out his phone and pressed a button, then spoke into it.

"Yes, Miles? Please go fetch the man in the elevator at New Court and bring him to my office. I'll meet you there. Thank you."

While the Duke and the Baron stood casually mumbling to each other, Rosenberg walked up to me to whisper another demand for instructions through divination.

"So what's next," he asked. "How should we proceed?"

A voice from beyond seemed to take over my larynx in response to Rosenberg's prompting.

I was ready for him. I had already received a message from my psychic informant.

"The seed of Venus was planted in the appropriate vessel corresponding to her sphere of influence. As for the others, let the three kings plant their royal seeds in her rose garden next door instead. Let the king with the highest rank have her first. Then let the Sun-Runner's horses plough her field too. This will open a gateway between the two gardens, causing the seeds to comingle and graft together in a manner more than natural. It will also free her mortal soul and complete the rites for this evening."

I really had no idea what these metaphors were about at the time. I think Rosenberg's understanding of them was vague and incomplete, or else he would never have gone along with the plan.

"Horses? Where from?" he asked, incredulous.

"Send a text with the Lord Mayor's phone to the Lord High Admiral," the voice said through me. "Tell him to come here with four horses and a chariot with standing room for two. He must inform none but his personal entourage where he is going, and may use only his most trusted assistants for this. He shall take the tunnels to be sure he isn't followed. Also, tell him to bring the device he uses for mating with horses."

"He has a 'device' for mating horses?" said Rosenberg, amused.

"Mating *with* horses," the voice I spoke with corrected him. "Most certainly. Just letting him know that you know about it will be enough to ensure that he gets himself here right away."

"And you want us to squeeze four horses and a carriage in here?" Rosenberg said skeptically. "With all these other people?"

"No," I replied. "On the sky terrace at New Court. Make sure someone brings me another shot of morphine before we go." The informant's voice was confined to my mind now, allowing me to control my own throat again, but still feeding me the lines.

"So the Lion and the Sun-Runner whom I'd planned to use: what shall we do with them now?" asked Rosenberg.

"Continue to use the Lion as a servant," I said, hoping as I spoke it was worth it to save Leopold's life. "But not Wetzel. He's finished his purpose. We shall add his blood to the Hellbroth in the Gradalis, and use his fat to make a flying ointment. Make sure it's prepared before the next ceremony begins."

I felt no remorse. Wetzel was a child rapist and an accessory to murder, just like everyone else in the room. Also, from what I could tell, he was slated for sacrifice at the end of the ritual anyway. I just assumed that most of us were. I was just moving up his execution date one day, I figured. These were the instructions I had been given by my psychic informant, and I saw no reason to deviate from the message in any way.

"Now, do the invocations before the Sun-Runner's carriage arrives," I was told to say.

"The Sun-Runner's carriage?" Rosenberg said, second-guessing me. "You mean the Lord High Admiral's carriage?"

"He will be bringing it, but it's for the Sun-Runner's use," I said with telepathic prompting. "It is he who shall work those Starry Wheels. Have your servants outfit it with scythes for reaping."

Rosenberg nodded. "Anything else?"

"Yes," the voice continued through me. "Have them connect the Walbrook to the Rothschilds' royal pissing conduit at Bucklersbury, so that the spirits of the Archons can travel to New Court with ease. There is a piping system sufficient in diameter for our needs that you can access behind a locked door in the tunnels there at that junction. It can only be opened with Crispin's fingerprints—the right hand, and just the fingers of blessing. This pipe connects to the toilets in the Sky Box. Make an opening for them to get from the Sky Box toilets to the terrace below. It will serve as a divine portal for the rite, like the well that you have here."

Again, I did not understand the meaning of the words I was speaking. I reached for a picture in my mind of how this was going to play out, but was given only a blank screen. After receiving that last detail from me, Rosenberg promptly pivoted on his heals and called out to the men in the black leather veils standing at the back of the room.

"Butchers! Please, take the bodies of these Soldiers down to the Gradalis room for processing. But leave the Lord Mayor and Crispin. Lay them down on the benches. We have special plans for them."

"Wait!" said Baron Carrickfergus. "First, I've got to take a leak. Dad, what do you say?" He looked at the Duke and gestured towards the bodies of the two Martinas.

"Oh yes, splendid idea," said the Duke. "My bladder is bursting. I've had a pint too many tonight."

Both men walked up to the corpses, which had fallen within inches of each other, and opened up their own robes. Then I heard the unzipping of trousers and the splash of the urine as it hit its targets. The father and son walked in a circle around the two bodies so as to thoroughly drench each one. As they did so, they laughed.

"So you want my piss, do you?" said the Duke to the lifeless remains as he soiled them. "There you go, bean- counters. Drink your fill."

"Oh, how I'd love to do this to the rest of the family," said the Baron as the last of his urine stream sputtered out.

"You can," said Rosenberg. "But it's not necessary. They shan't be bothering you much anymore, now that my economic plan is taking effect."

"Still, I wish you'd have let me piss in their mouths while they were still alive, these two," said the Duke, shaking off the final drops. "They were worst. I never understood what you saw in that boy, other than his pretty mouth and his tender arse."

Rosenberg chuckled and shrugged his shoulders.

"What else do you need, right? But seriously, I'll give you a better way to use your cocks for revenge against these two besides pissing on their cadavers."

Both the Duke and the Baron looked up and gave him their full attention. The moment Rosenberg hinted at an opportunity for vengeance-motivated debauchery, both men's penises hardened in their hands.

"What have you got, Blake?" said the Baron eagerly.

"Well, she's not much to look at," Rosenberg replied. "But she *is* the only biological heir to the corpses beneath you. Oh, and she's quite known to your family. She used to go with the Lord High Admiral for carriage rides and polo matches when she was a young lass. I've even seen *you* bouncing her on your knee a few times during those years, you old goat. And I *let* you do it."

The Duke looked away from him as if ashamed. He continued.

"I didn't mind. You see, my daughter was never really 'my daughter.' Consivia and I merely helped the Martinas cover up something that would have been of great embarrassment to them."

"But how can that be?" said Baron Carrickfergus. "She's only twelve!"

"So was Crispin when he got his mother knocked up!" Rosenberg howled with merriment. "Oh, how that pregnancy heightened his disgust for the female race, almost bringing it up to my level. He couldn't get hard for her any more after that, or any woman for that matter. I took the baby off their hands, knowing that she would come in handy some day."

He walked up to the girl, still splayed and strapped to the decaying meat on the altar, and placed his left hand flat on her stomach. She flinched, the first sign of life I'd seen from her in a while. Rosenberg continued his speech.

"And now, tonight, she is providing the material basis for the most ambitious magical working that any man has ever attempted. But I am inviting you, my lords, to aid me in this endeavor. Tonight, as part of this effort, Philippine will die in the midst of extreme pain and sexual degradation. The Lord High Admiral is already on his way here to lend some technical assistance. I would be much obliged if you two would play out the roles I have prepared for you."

"You know very well that we are already obliged to you, so of course we will accommodate," answered the Duke, closing his robe.

"Is she a virgin?" asked the Baron, now gently stroking his swollen member.

"Not as of an hour ago," said Rosenberg, with a slight hint of regret in his voice. "But the back door is what I'm going to hit. After you two, of course."

"Oh, but let my son have first shot," said the Duke. "He's very particular about these things."

"Of course, it's a deal," said Rosenberg, shaking the hands of both men in turn. "We'll be moving over to New Court for the next part of the operation."

He looked down at his phone, which had just received another message.

"But first, I must speak to one of my captives," he said in conclusion.

Then he addressed the Butchers, who had been standing there the whole time waiting for permission to take the bodies of the Martinas. He held up his right thumb, index finger, and middle finger.

"Take the first three fingers from Crispin's right hand and save them for me," he instructed. "Then take the bodies and put them in the Coffin House, in pods 1 and 2."

So the other building was *intentionally made to look like a coffin*, I discerned silently.

The Butchers complied with the orders. One of them snipped off the fingers with large meat shears. The others covered up the corpses with curtains (Crispin with the cross curtain, Marcia with the Troy tapestry). Then four more Butchers came through the main entrance and carried the bodies away on gurneys. Before they arrived, Rosenberg had already gone, presumably to speak with Chesterfield, whom I took to be his "captive," the MI5 contact he bragged to the Duke of Rothesay about.

I swooned with exhaustion at the thought of what must still lay before us, before the night was even through, before I would be allowed to rest in the comfort of either sleep or, most likely, death, it seemed to me. Though it hadn't really been that long, I felt like I needed another shot of morphine. Just when I thought I couldn't take waiting any longer, Leopold showed up with the syringe in hand, giving me the only small comfort I would be permitted that night. Oh, and one other: he gave me a long draught of water from a stone *amphora*.

I wished I could have drowned in it at that moment.

Chapter 22: Archons Uprooted

And when We said unto the angels: Prostrate yourselves before Adam, they fell prostrate, all save Iblis. He demurred through pride, and so became a disbeliever.

— *Quran* 23:97, Pickthal translation

The rooftop terrace at New Court was positioned partially beneath the Sky Box where our evening began, with our rancid meal of raven meat and champagne. However, most of it was uncovered and sitting to the east of there. The Sky Box was mounted unevenly on top of the two adjoined New Court buildings, as if a toddler had been lazily stacking up wooden blocks on the floor. It hovered, mounted on poles, mostly over one of the buildings: the one we'd initially entered. But part of it stuck out to the East over the other building, which had the terrace on top. And that is where we were now all assembled for the second part of tonight's ritual. The mysterious voice that had spoken through me told Rosenberg that's what we should do.

I had no idea how long these ceremonies would stretch on into the future. I was in so much pain, so tired, disoriented, scared, worried, sick, hungry, and in dread of the horrors to come that my only hope was to put to death soon, without more torture or degradation. But the hope felt empty. I also anticipated that there were even worse things to be concerned with besides just what my own fate was. The signs in the heavens were ominous.

The Moon was huge, now with a red mass that appeared to be swelling within it. Two of them had disappeared, but there were still four huge stars hovering around the Moon, even larger than before, with one significantly bigger than the others. Both the Moon and the stars were lower in the sky than before.

You might think that Rosenberg and the others would have been concerned about the possibility of others seeing us up there, especially when Scotland Yard was supposedly *en route* to arrest Marcia. We had actually seen, from the roof, police arriving at Mansion House next door to the northwest. Uniformed officers had gotten in position around the perimeter, preparing to perform some kind of action. We even saw a helicopter approaching in the distance.

For a minute, Rosenberg did appear worried, and alerted Chesterfield, who now sat next to me on the grass, handcuffed to my wheelchair. The spook had merely shrugged his shoulders, looking scared of retaliation for failure. But then the helicopter turned around 180 degrees and went back the way it came. The policemen all got in their cars and drove away. Rosenberg patted Chesterfield on the shoulder and went back to preparing the rest of the ritual.

The Lord High Admiral arrived with his escorts through the elevator. He was not wearing a costume initially, but came in a navy blue suit with a brown overcoat and a black derby. Wrinkled and decrepit, he stooped a bit, but not as much as you'd think a man his age would. His jaw quivered uncontrollably, though, and his bloodshot eyes burned with the fire of dementia on top of psychopathy.

In days of his prime, he would have been among the ones raping and murdering with zeal. Tonight, his job was merely to bring the horses and their gear, all of which arrived through the service elevator. This included the carriage, stood up on its back end to fit inside, and of course the "device for mating with horses." This latter item resembled the one used by Pasiphae, the wife of King Minos, to mate with the Cretan bull, made by Daedalus on the orders of Zeus. This one, the Lord High Admiral bragged to us, had been made for the set of a Spanish film, 1978's *The Coming of Sin* (though you might know it under alternative titles like *The Violation of the Bitch* or *Sodomia*).

The terrace was designed along a grid of lines formed by stone and cement, arranged diagonally against the sides of the roof so as to form a pattern of rhombi. Within this grid were placed patches of grass, trees, and hedges enclosing larger rhombus-shaped paved areas, which were meant to be used as "outdoor meeting rooms." Inside the largest of these, in the southeast corner of the terrace, the brazen horse was set up. It was put in the northeastern corner of the hedge, which was closed all around except for its northwest corner.

Three or four yards apart from this, in the center of the hedge, three velvet-covered throne-like wooden chairs— one yellow, one purple, and one black—were assembled in the eastern corner in a semi-circle facing the back end of the horse. The Duke of Rothesay was seated on the left side, in the purple chair. The Baron was ensconced in a yellow throne in the middle, looking down at his crotch, petting it gently with his thumb.

Rosenberg sat on the right, in the black chair. Like everyone else present, they still wore their robes and masks.

Behind the thrones, three standards, each about three foot by two foot, hung down from a horizontal pole held up by two others. Each flag had a field matching in hue to the color of the throne it flew behind. The purple one behind the Duke showed an old man in a toga vomiting up six planetary sigils and a red polygon: the Superman logo again. On the black flag behind Rosenberg there was a similar figure eating a human baby.

But on the golden flag behind the Baron, there was an image of the Sun inverted, with a pained expression on its face, surrounded by what appeared to be a pool of red blood. It reminded me of the Sun and the Moon on the Mete coffer.

"I think my flag's upside-down" said Baron Carrickfergus to Rosenberg.

"It certainly is not," Rosenberg replied.

The torches were lit, held now by the Lions standing at the three closed corners of the hedge, and the electric lights at the top of the New Court buildings were switched off. All of the Butchers and Ravens gathered in the southwestern corner, to the left of me, facing the three seats and the brazen horse. To my right in the southeast, aligned with St. Swithin's Lane, beneath the low-hanging Moon with its juicy red center, another altar had been set up. It was the Cybele altar—the one that had been used in the castration ritual in 1956. Behind it stood Consivia, muttering prayers with her eyes closed. On either side of her were two Nymphi, with the one stage left holding a violin.

Above and to the left of the hedge, hanging from beneath the Sky Box, was a green plastic construction chute, about twelve inches in diameter. Normally used for removing debris from rooves and upper floors during construction projects, it had been hastily assembled by Rosenberg's servants and connected through the bottom of the Sky Box, as per my orders. On top of the Sky Box, in the center of its eastern edge, Rosenberg had them erect nothing less than the London Stone itself.

The Stone had apparently come recently into his possession, being held in safekeeping for the City of London for a short term. It was supposed to be installed for public display the following week close to its original location on Cannon Street, right in front of the Walbrook Building next door to both New Court and Rosenberg Plaza.

About an hour earlier that evening, while things were being set up there on the terrace, and Wetzel's body was being rendered into various products, Rosenberg had showed me the London Stone, which he had hidden inside the column that was holding up the altar in the *mithraeum*. He was showing it mainly to brag to me that he had it, and also to ask me if I thought it should be used as a ritual implement in the next portion of the ceremonies. I instantly saw in my mind's eye that it contained the same red light I had seen at the end of the bull entrails I had been forced to examine. I then heard that same mental voice tell me that the London Stone held the answer to that other riddle which Rosenberg was demanding a solution for.

This Rock is the Egg that contains the Keystone, it said.

It seemed to me that my survival depended on giving Rosenberg the information he wanted to make his ritual successful from his perspective, whatever that meant. So on my instruction (acting on the inspiration that came to me from my psychic informant), Rosenberg had the Ravens post the London Stone on top of the very pylon that it was due to later be displayed on. I had him place it sitting on its side, taller than it was wide, unlike the way it was normally seen.

Consivia ceased her private prayers and it became deathly quiet. The only sound was coming from the four live horses, outside the hedge and beyond our field of vision. They could be heard clopping around and snorting, as the Lord High Admiral and two of his personal servants prepared them for God knows what.

The Duke of Rothesay reached into his jacket underneath his robe and pulled out a cigarette wrapped in brown paper. He pushed up his mask part-way and was about to light it with a Zippo. Rosenberg looked over at him and coughed. He threw it on the ground, put his mask down again disapprovingly, and slumped back into his chair.

One of the Nymphi started chanting in Latin verse once again, for just a few lines. The last was perfectly timed. It ended just as the bells of St. Paul's Cathedral struck out, ringing eleven times. Clouds began to cluster around the stars and the pregnant Moon. A cold breeze stirred the air for just a moment, which had the effect of intensifying rather than dispersing the tension.

Next, having been told by me that the proper Archon to invoke next was Zeus (a.k.a. Jupiter), Consivia told the Duke of Rothesay to stand before the altar.

"Will the royal Lion on the purple throne come forth please?" she said, holding out her right hand in a beckoning gesture.

Then a man in a Raven mask approached the Duke from his right with a metal bowl containing a piece of cooked meat. It smelled like the same stuff served to us at dinner that night. In another hand, he held a metal goblet filled with wine.

"Eat, dear prince, the sweet livers of the birds who guarded thy kingdom. And drink the ambrosial wine made from the blood of thine enemies."

He cocked his head to the side, as if confused. Then he sighed and pushed his mask up a few inches, exposing his mouth. He grabbed the meat with his hand, quickly shoving it into his gob whole. I think it was just the bird's liver.

"Mmmph," he gagged.

A Nymphus began playing a raucous, violent tune on the violin. I watched the Duke's mandibles masticating as he forced himself to eat it despite its awful taste. Then he took the wine and swallowed the whole mess in one gulp. His throat bulged as it went down. Sweat began to pour down his neck. Then he emitted a growl and broke into loud, heavy breathing as he handed back the dishes to the Ravens.

He stared at the Priestess with his arms at his sides, balled into fists. She pushed his mask back down and then laid her left hand upon his head. She used her right to douse him with her aspergillum as she intoned the following incantation.

> *Jupiter Feretrius,*
> *On this rooftop come to us,*
> *Use your thunderbolts to free*
> *The trophy of your destiny*

> *Let your flaming sword come fly*
> *Down from your throne in the sky*
> *Then the stony egg shall yield*
> *To thy crown the true Red Shield.*
>
> *So that from thine enemy*
> *Whom we killed so valiantly*
>
> *Spoils of war you now shall reap*
> *Precious jewel that's yours to keep*

I didn't tell her that the Rock was an Egg, I thought. *How did she know?*

Behind her, one of the four stars hovering next to the Moon in the southern sky unmistakably began—I swear—to droop down and come closer. It grew so large that it no longer looked like a star, but rather a giant purple ball of light.

This terrified me more than anything I had witnessed so far. All my life I had suffered from a recurring apocalyptic nightmare about seeing something just like this in the sky. I now realized that these were all premonitory dreams preparing me for this exact moment.

Everybody else gazed up at the purple ball in wonder, even Rosenberg and Consivia. The Duke seemed almost like he had been electrocuted in place as he stood like a statue staring at it, with Consivia's hand still on his head. Baron Carrickfergus turned to Rosenberg and spoke, awkwardly.

"Oh yes, we saw something like this on the way over here this evening. Looked like there was a star literally hovering over your Plaza, Blake. They were almost like guiding lights directing us to your doorstep."

"Shh!" said Rosenberg, annoyed.

Clouds covered the rest of the sky all around us, like being smothered by a pile of freshly-sheared Gotland wool. They obscured everything but the purple sphere. Consivia handed the Duke a *sistrum*, as I had told her to. (This was a rattle used in ancient Rome to make a noise like thunder in rituals.)

"*Juppiter Tonans*! Shake your thunder-stick!" she commanded the Duke. He obeyed. The *sistrum* rattled, held high above his head. Then we heard a clap of thunder, and a bolt of lightning shot down—not from the clouds, but directly from the purple orb. It hit the London Stone on top of the Sky Box. The music stopped and everybody gasped.

The Stone immediately disintegrated, and chunks rained down on us. One of them hit the violinist in the shoulder, nicking him. Another one clobbered Philippine in the back, bruising her badly and causing her to crumple back down to the ground with more sobs.

But inside the oolite of the London Stone was a hidden surprise, revealed when it disintegrated: a gigantic shimmering clear crystal. It looked to be well over a foot wide and almost a foot tall, which meant that it had been taking up the majority of the space within its casing. about It landed with its tip pointing downward on the hedge right behind the altar, shining brightly even in the dim light as it fell. From the side, it looked exactly like the Superman logo.

From subsequent research, I have learned that this is actually the shape of the side-profile of a diamond that has been cut in the style called the "modern round brilliant." This is currently the most popular diamond cut, designed to refract the maximum amount of light. What's odd is that, as you might have guessed from the name, this cut is a twentieth century invention, created by Marcel Tolkowsky of Belgium in 1919. Yet this giant brilliant cut diamond had clearly been hiding inside the London Stone for hundreds of years at least.

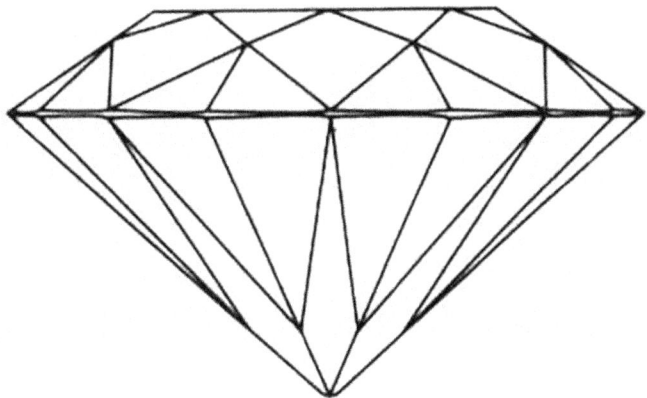

Furthermore, the number of facets, and their distribution on this enormous gemstone in front of me turned out, as I soon discovered, to match the modern standard for a modern round brilliant cut. This consists of 33 on the crown, and 25 on the pavilion, for a total of 58. It was designed this way to refract the maximum amount of light.

Whatever the explanation for this, I knew it was obviously going to be something very unusual. Considering the strange things that had already happened, I was able to accept the presence of a modernly-designed gemstone concealed inside of a supposedly ancient and natural rock as another example of the mutability of reality.

After the diamond landed on top of the hedge, Consivia looked at the Duke and gestured at it as if to say "Go ahead." In response, the Duke nodded to her and walked behind the altar. He reached up to take the shining gemstone from the top of the hedge. When he got his elderly, shaking hands upon it, he almost dropped it. He pulled his mask up above his eyebrows and gazed at it with awe. Its lustrous sparkles reflected in his eyes.

"What *is* this?" he shouted to Rosenberg. "This has been inside the London Stone the whole time? What's it made of? What's it for? My God, how much is it worth?"

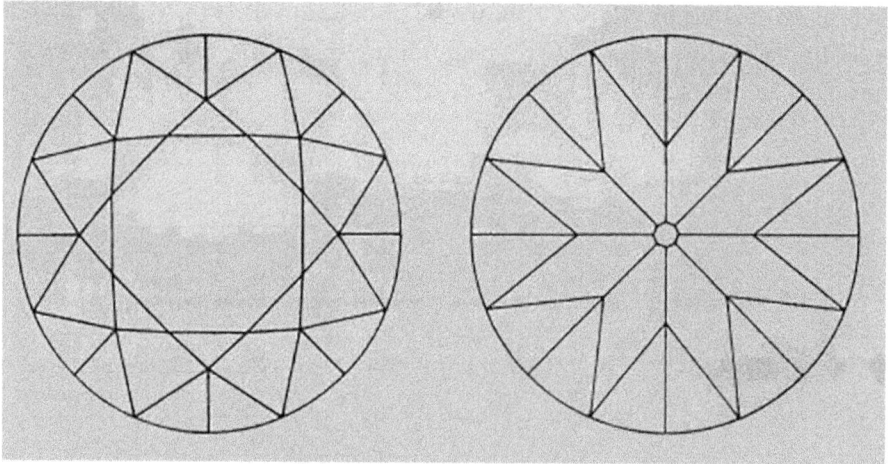

Rosenberg exhaled in exasperation. "It is worth more than your mother's entire kingdom—not just because of what it's made of, but also because of what it can do. And yes, the Lords of the City have had it keistered on Cannon Street this tire time. It's part of the reason why the City has always been more powerful than the monarchy, though almost everyone has forgotten that by now. Even the Rothschilds, the younger ones, don't know about it. They don't even know what their family buckler symbolizes, or why this place is named Bucklersbury."

"It looks like an actual diamond!" the Duke gasped, still fawning over it. "But it's got to be ten times bigger than any diamond I've ever seen!" Rosenberg nodded, smiling.

"If my projections are correct," he said, "it should be 15.5 inches across the girdle, and 10.625 inches from the tip of its culet to top of its crown. That's four times bigger than the largest *uncut* diamond ever seen," answered Rosenberg. "That was the Cullinan, which Edward VII had chopped up into over a hundred pieces, now all owned by your mother. But I reckon she's never seen one cut quite like this, or with the same properties."

The Duke turned it around in his hands, allowing me a glimpse of the octagonal "table" at the top of the crown. I realized that the geometry on the top of the diamond matched what I had seen found in the design of the sunroof for Rosenberg's main building next door.

"Yes, who would have done the cutting, if this thing has been around for hundreds of years?" asked the Duke. "I mean, it's a brilliant cut, right? 58 facets? I thought this design was invented by that Tolkowsky fellow in 1919."

"In my experience," Rosenberg replied, "most modern scientific discoveries are either rediscoveries or reworkings of ancient alchemical techniques. Sometimes the inventors are ignorant of this, but sometimes they hide the truth too, just so they can file a patent. Take silicon on sapphire, for instance…" The Duke interrupted, to Rosenberg's annoyance.

"The workmanship is fantastic! I'll bet the fire it puts out is amazing. Shall I call up my man in Ghent to have it evaluated?"

Rosenberg rolled his eyes. "You are speaking as a mortal!" he said to the Duke. "A monarch-in-waiting, yes, and intoxicated with divine substance, but you *still* speak as a *man*. Let the Lord of Olympus take control of your mind and body *completely*. Let him experience the pleasures of being a man in the flesh through your own mortal flesh. Then you will remember what it is you hold in your hands."

As he said that last sentence, Rosenberg looked up at the purple orb, now even larger and lower in the sky than before. He stood up and gestured to the Duke's empty chair.

"Return to your throne here," he instructed. "Soon the Ravens will bring you something that Jove himself could not resist."

The Duke sat down with the enormous jewel in his lap, pointing upward. The violin struck up again, and the Priestess called Baron Carrickfergus to the altar.

"Will the majestic Sun-Runner on the golden throne come forth please?"

He got up and walked to her with an arrogant swagger. She gave him the same preliminaries as the Duke had been given. He choked down his raven liver with disgust equal to that of his predecessor, but no greater comprehension of what he was eating. However, he really seemed to savor the intoxicating effects of the food and drink, which took hold immediately, with the characteristic sweating and heavy breathing.

After draining his glass of blood-ambrosia, he asked for a second, which he was given. When he had swallowed the last of it, he uttered a loud laugh of voluptuous exultation. Then he pushed down his mask again, pointed to the singing Nymph in front of him beside the altar, and pointed to the ground in front of himself. The boy immediately ceased his song and complied with the unspoken order.

Consivia intoned another stanza of her invocation to Jupiter.

> *Now's the time for little Whore -Hey*
> *To come in here and join the soiree*
> *Playing precious Ganymede*
> *To the Prince of Pride and Greed*

She held her right hand pointed out in front of her towards the opening in the hedge. In walked Miles, holding the hand of a little boy, white with blond hair, who couldn't have been more than five years old. He sucked his thumb and looked frightened, rightfully, by the spectacle in front of him.

"Oh no no no no no no, we can't do *this*!" the Duke whispered to Rosenberg, audible enough for me to hear, but not the Baron, who stood oblivious, getting sucked by a Nymphus at the altar and uttering obscenities at him.

"I've gone to great lengths to never be alone with him so that this sort of thing never happens," the Duke continued, his voice trembling. But Rosenberg only beckoned Miles to come closer with the boy.

"My dear Lion Prince, you know quite well that incest and pederasty is in your nature, not only because of your genetic predisposition, but because of the planetary archon that rules over you. He's the ruler of a dying aeon who doesn't seem to have noticed that his throne is slipping out from underneath him. You *do* remember, *don't* you?"

The Duke's body began to quiver as the boy came closer. To the right of us, over the sound of the Baron's ecstatic moaning and the ridiculous violin solo, the distant crash of thunder could be heard, and the clouds above grew even thicker. Rosenberg turned his attention to the light ball in the sky.

"Wouldn't you love to sit in the throne of power again, the one which your own son supplanted you from, and be serviced by his son as a slave, turning his royal heir into your own royal cupbearer?"

These last lines were directed more at the spirit of Zeus than the man who was becoming possessed by him. Rosenberg was reminding the lord of Olympus how he had obtained victory over his father Chronos by pretending to be his "cupbearer." This was a euphemism used in the ancient world for a catamite—a young male sex slave.

Zeus used his intimate position in his father's royal court to obtain an opportunity to "poison" Chronos, a plot said to have been devised by the goddess Metis, whom Hammer-Purgstall identified with Mete/Baphomet. As you no doubt remember, this caused Chronos to vomit up the children he had swallowed, which included all of Zeus' siblings, the gods of Olympus. They then defeated Chronos and the Titans, locked them up in Tartarus beneath the Earth, and then ruled happily ever after. Or, at least, that's where the Greeks broke off their tale.

Come to think of it, I said to myself mentally, *the Romans did imply that Apollo was the first-born son and successor to Zeus, or Jupiter, as they called him. Apollo was the Olympian sun god, in contrast to Helios/Sol, who played the role of* the Sun during the "Golden Age" of Chronos/Saturn and the Titans. Most writers just chose to say that Helios/Sol became 'syncretized' with Apollo in later years.

But what if they were really separate characters? I wondered. *What if Apollo supplanted Helios as the new sun, and the former sun he overthrew was locked up in Tartarus with the rest of the Titans? Maybe that's the meaning of the symbol of the 'black sun' that's 'in the center of the Earth.'*

Then I thought about the fact that in the late Roman Empire, Mithraism finally gained support from the emperors by syncretizing Mithras with Sol Invictus, thus making a god already identified with Saturn/Chronos a solar figure as well.

And alchemists have consistently identified Saturn with the black sun, I thought. *In the present aeon, which is the one that supplanted the rule of Zeus from Olympus, the Sun is the undisputed ruler of the current order. But Zeus used to play that role somehow, and before him, Chronos did it. But during that time, Helios was a separate entity, playing a different role than he does now. The Sun was not, back then, the central power. Or rather, someone else was playing the role of 'the Sun.'*

Now the things that Rosenberg said to the Duke of Rothesay made sense to me. The Duke's body was being used to draw down Zeus/Jupiter into mortal incarnation. The body of Baron Carrickfergus was being used to draw down the spirit of the new sun, his successor.

Zeus was defeated by the new sun god, I thought to myself. I wonder when that happened exactly. The era of the worship of Jupiter gave way at the end of the empire to Apollo, Sol Invictus, Mithras, and of course ... to Jesus.

And there it was. The answer to my question of when the aeon of Zeus/Jupiter had given way to that of the present sun was obvious: year 1 *Anno Domini*.

The transition marked by the collapse of Rome and the descent of the West into long-term intellectual darkness may not have been clear to everyone back then, I thought. *But later it became connected with the advent of Jesus Christ, and it came to pass that the reckoning of time was started over from that point. So fate devised an appropriate way of marking the passage from the Aeon of one Sun to that of the next.*

All of this came to me as I sat there in the wheelchair at the rooftop terrace of New Court, prompted by the comments that Rosenberg was making to the Duke of Rothesay.

Zeus is being enticed into the Duke's body, I realized, *with the promise of having Apollo, his supplanter, serve in the humiliating position of cupbearer, as Zeus had once done in the effort to take the throne from his father. Also, pederasty with very young boys was a known proclivity of Zeus', going back to his kidnapping of Ganymede to serve as his own cupbearer.*

My attention snapped back to the scene in front of me. Little Saint George was being guided by Miles to stand between the legs of the Duke, who handed the diamond over to Rosenberg. He looked at the man in the Lion mask with fear, clearly not recognizing that it was his own grandfather. Then Miles tapped the boy's shoulder, and he sank to his knees, obviously trained for the job ahead of time.

The Duke handed the red crystal in his lap to Rosenberg, who then handed it to a trusted Raven. I looked away, up at the sky, just in time to see something like a golden chain, appearing as thick as a tree trunk, emerged from the purple orb. It dangled down somewhere to the south, seemingly close to our location. The bottom of the chain dropped down below my line of sight.

The Golden Chain of the Zeus, I thought to myself.

In Homer's *Iliad*, Zeus says to the other gods:

> If you tied a chain of gold to the sky, and all of you, gods and goddesses, took hold, you could not drag Zeus the High Counsellor to earth with all your efforts. But if I determined to pull with a will, I could haul up land and sea, then loop the chain round a peak of Olympus, and leave them dangling in space. By that much am I greater than gods and men.

Here I was looking at such a golden chain, quite literally, with Spiga-style links (forged from ovals twisted to look like grains of wheat). It dropped down from the purple sphere like Rapunzel's hair, hanging there for a moment between the sky and the Earth. Then it slithered down and disappeared from view, like it had been snipped from above.

For about a minute, I heard the zapping sounds of electricity arching, and everybody's hair bristled. Then something that looked just like the purple orb in the sky, but about five inches in width, shot through the construction chute and hit the Duke on the top of his head. There it was absorbed, causing a ripple down the man's spine. He convulsed, ripped his robe open, and then arched his pelvis upward, towards the boy's head, which was already dutifully going down to its task.

Now, it seemed, what gods and men before had not been able to achieve with force for thousands of years, a wealthy businessman in London had done merely by offering the body of a powerful prince as the vessel through which to experience the carnal pleasures of pederasty. Watching it happen before my very eyes led me to a realization about a line from my favorite Welsh poet Robert Graves' book *The White Goddess*.

This is what he meant when he said the priests of ancient Rome performed the 'Rites of Elicio' to seduce the gods of captured nations into serving the Empire instead.

As the Duke gave in to his proclivities and gasped with pleasure, possessed by debaucherous divinity, Rosenberg chuckled and encouraged him.

"That's it, King Carlos, let Whore -Hey treat you right." "What about the boy's father?" the Duke gasped in a whisper, almost too overwhelmed with delectation to speak.

"Ignore him," said Rosenberg. "He's ignoring *you*."

As if to create a barrier to blind the Baron to his father's abuse of his son, Consivia stepped out in -between the altar and the thrones. She then beckoned the Ravens and men with leather veils, who gathered around the thrones in the space beside her, fulling covering the Duke's actions from the Baron's view. She sang another stanza to the incarnation of Jupiter before her.

> *'tis so divine to rape your meat*
> *The taste of pain is good to eat*
> *And bliss sublime is all the more*
> *When child of thy loins doth play the whore*

The Duke moaned loader, and Rosenberg stepped in quickly, pulling the boy's head away.

"Easy there," he said. "Hold your horses. You've got a job to do here, don't forget. This is just a warm-up exercise."

Then he addressed Consivia. "Invoke the Sun, and have the Barber-Surgeons bring the girl!"

The priestess gestured towards two of the men in leather veils, both with waxing moon symbols. They nodded, then left the hedge to go fetch her. Consivia returned to her place behind the altar and held her arms aloft.

> *Sol Invictus join your bride*
> *Shining queen who pulls the tide*
> *Fructify the holy womb*
> *Rape the goddess in her tomb*

At that moment, quite suddenly, the Moon peeked out through the clouds, along with one of the other stars, which now grew until it was the very same size as the Moon. It was yellow like the Sun, but it did not light up the sky as the Sun does during the day. They stood next to each other, with the purple orb, slightly smaller, sitting beneath them, and the other, smaller stars nearby. Nobody else seemed to notice but me, Chesterfield and Rosenberg. All the others were too entranced by the sex acts, which they no doubt wished to join in on.

"And what the Hell is that?" Chesterfield whispered to me. "The New Jerusalem? Is this the end of the world?"

It was the first thing he'd said to me since he returned from selling out his country and helping Rosenberg cover up the Rothschilds' child sex slave ring, which they had no doubt used to compromise virtually everyone with any power in the entire kingdom. I knew that his life had been threatened, and I knew I was guilty of things just as bad, but that didn't mean I'd forgiven him.

"The New Jerusalem is a cube," I replied. "This is the Sun coming out at night."

"But William Blake said that London was Jerusalem," Chesterfield noted, seemingly irrelevantly (or so it seemed at the time).

"Shut up!" the Duke snapped. "I was about to cum!"

"Not yet," said Rosenberg, and he stood up quickly to help block the Duke's view of the entrance to the hedge. The Duke returned to his preoccupation.

Poor Philippine, who could barely walk now, was brought in on a gurney by the "Barber-Surgeons," which, by now, I had gathered, was the term for the men with the waxing moon symbols on their veils (the "Butchers" being those with the waning moon on their veils). They dumped her, awake again now and crying, on the pavement between the horse and human blockade protecting the pederast prince on his purple throne. Naked on top of a tall building in the middle of the night, Philippine was shivering severely. She rolled over on her stomach and emitted a high-pitched squeal.

At the sound of her cry, Baron Carrickfergus turned around sharply, separating from the boy as he did so. When he laid eyes upon the girl—I swear—I saw them flash with a golden glow for a brief second, visible through the holes of his sun mask.

Then the yellow orb poured out a yellow-orange stream of fluid. It seemed to fall close by, to the south of us, just where the golden chain had dropped down. It honestly looked like the sun-like object taking a piss. A few moments later, a miniature version of it was immerging from the construction chute, about the size of a basketball.

The mini-sun came and hovered over the Baron's head, forming an angelic halo behind him. He looked up at it lovingly and smiled. Then it entered him, lighting up his body like a yellow glow stick as it traveled down his spine. Fully possessed now, the Baron grabbed his falling trousers with his left hand, raised his right hand to the sky and laughed excitedly.

"Ah yes! Finally, a female in this castle of faggotry!" He let his pants fall to the ground and then stepped out of them, along with his shoes. Consivia placed a horsewhip in his hand.

"She's got the face of a horse though," he said, without looking up at his hand.

"Then get her inside the Brazen Horse where you can't see her face and have a go at her backside," said Consivia. "That's what we're all here to witness!"

The Baron looked left at the crowd that had gathered near him, unaware of the sight they were blocking him from, and acknowledge them with a salute. Then he looked at his hand and saw what the priestess had given him.

"Alright then, thanks!" he said.

He brought down his whip upon the girl's exposed buttocks, shouting "Gee!" and "Haw!" at her with repeated blows to get her to move in the direction he wanted. He forced her to climb inside the horse's velvet-lined interior with her rump lined up to the hole in the back. This opening also wrapped around the side part-way, providing a cross-section for the audience to view of her pelvis and legs inside the device.

The Baron walked up behind her, and up the three-step mounting block that had been placed there for him. He pulled his mask up to his forehead for a moment, and spat on his hand for lubrication. But then Consivia offered him an open can of Lyle's Golden Syrup.

"Don't be vulgar," she admonished. "This is a holy rite, not a porn movie."

He looked at her for a moment, probably finding the same irony in her comment that I did.

"Out of the strong shall come forth sweetness," she said, in all seriousness.

That was a paraphrase of the company slogan on the syrup can, which itself is a quote from *Judges* 14:14, something about bees making honey in the carcass of a lion. The Baron took a handful of the syrup, which was somehow less vulgar than spit for sodomizing twelve-year-old girls with, then smeared it on himself, as well as the girl's behind. The sun-like object above then began pulsating, its brightness flickering up and down to different levels at the pace of an excited heartbeat.

"Ooooh nooooo," Philippine droned dreadfully. Then she let out another ear-piercing shriek as the Baron penetrated her anus. Above, the sky darkened as the Moon and the golden orb, still pulsating, merged together half-way, forming a *vesica pisces* shape with a sickly yellow oval in the center. Inside of this oval was that round red splotch that the Moon had acquired, now tinted to appear orange.

Just then, the Duke used his shoe to kick Rosenberg, still standing in front of him, lightly in the back of the leg. Rosenberg turned around and looked at him.

"What?"

"I can't hold out much longer," said the Duke. "I'm ready to blow."

The Baron had fallen backwards a step on the horse mount, probably drunk from ambrosial blood-wine and, of course, archontic possession. He caught himself on the second step, and didn't fall all the way down. But he had to reinsert himself into his victim. Then he climaxed suddenly with a shout. However, half-way through shooting his load, he pulled out, then went back in quickly to deliver the rest of it.

"Whoops, wrong hole there," he said, and laughed, slapping her behind. Then he glanced over to his left and scanned the crowd, looking for the Duke.

"Daddy, she's all yours!" he hollered.

Just in time, Rosenberg pulled Little Saint George away from his task and into the shadows in the corner of the hedge behind us. Then I saw him hand the boy off to Miles. Meanwhile, Consivia grabbed the Duke and shoved him over to the brazen horse, forcing the crowd to part.

There was no time for more lubrication. The Duke put his penis in the young lady's now-widened anus just in time to deliver the seed. But as his thrusts subsided, his relief turned to shock. A hand grabbed him from behind on the left shoulder and pulled him part-way out of what he was stuck in. Another hand brought the blade of a ceremonial *harpe* down swiftly on the man's genitals, severing them in one clean blow.

It was the Baron. Rosenberg had handed him the weapon, then pulled the Duke backwards so he could make the cut.

The Duke screamed and fell backwards, blood pouring out of his crotch, which he covered as he rolled over in pain, hollering horribly.

"Auughh! Auughh!"

Then Baron put the *harpe* on the altar and picked up his horsewhip again, which he had temporarily placed there. Consivia stepped forth and shoved the cut penis and balls, which were still sticking out of Philippine's rectum, all the way in. The girl shrieked again, then sobbed some more.

"That will give your baby some extra nutrition tonight," said the priestess, as she smiled psychotically in her clown make-up.

The Baron stood over the Duke, horsewhip in hand, as his victim continued to wail. He landed a blow on the man's face, causing him to try to roll further away. Then he started shouting at the Duke, and pointing at Saint George, who was still cowering in the corner of the hedge, hugging Miles' leg and burying his face.

"So you use my son to get your dick hard, because you can't get it up for a girl anymore? Because you're a faggot!"

He whipped him again.

"Because you want to mess up his head the same way you and Grandpa messed me up? Then you come and fuck my wife too!"

Another blow. The Duke, barely able to speak, managed to choke out an objection to the Baron's delusional remark, brought on, no doubt, by the possession.

"That is not your wife!" he said. "That is a whore and a Jewess. Your wife is back at the Palace waiting for you." The Baron hit him again.

"Do not talk about my wife like that!" he shouted.

"She's not a Jewess," Rosenberg said, intervening. He took away the horsewhip, which the Baron reluctantly allowed, and stared down at the Duke.

"You both may think she looks like a horse, but you have only your own genes to blame, not the Rothschilds."

"What do you mean?" both the Duke and the Baron asked in unison.

"Crispin was the youngest son of the Princess," said Rosenberg. "Your wife, the one you let your mother kill, Duke of Rothesay. Just as Oenomaus, the son of Ares, disposed of his daughter's suitors with a faulty chariot wheel that sent twelve of them to their deaths."

"That's just a conspiracy theory," said the Baron. "And she wasn't pregnant with that Arab's baby."

"No, but she was pregnant with your father's baby," Rosenberg replied. "They had recently engaged in an intimate encounter, despite their divorce. Isn't that right, Duke of Rothesay."

"How do you know this?" the Duke gasped, losing blood rapidly.

"Because the Barber-Surgeons were hired to cut up the body on your mother's orders. And to deliver the heart to you, on your orders. But they were already working for me as well, and when they told me about what they would be doing with the Princess, I took the liberty of having the womb excised for myself. Then I brought it to fruition with the power of my alchemy."

The Baron's head hung low as he took it all in.

"He was a fine boy, really. Intelligent and beautiful to behold. I let the Martinas adopt him, thinking that he would be well cared-for. But they just wanted to use his existence as leverage against the crown. They neglected his moral instruction. The influence of being raised by bankers turned him into a greedy, weak pantywaist, fit only for fucking. I thank you for helping me take him out of the picture. I don't think I could have done it otherwise. I loved him like a son, in my own way."

"Is it true?" the Baron asked his father, tears streaming out from under his sun mask. He had picked up the *harpe* again and stood holding it above his head. The Duke took his own mask off and managed to get on his knees, crawling to the Baron's feet, where he put his face.

"Is it true that you killed my mother," the Baron continued, "and that Crispin was my brother?"

The Duke looked up, pleading in his eyes, which now appeared human again.

"I didn't *know* he was your brother. And killing your mother was Regina's idea. There was nothing I could do to stop it. But I loved her. That's why I kept the heart. I'm sorry, son."

The Baron looked up at the sky, and so did I. The sun-like object was separated from the Moon again, and no longer pulsating. The purple orb was drooping down below them, while two other stars hovered nearby. What's more, now there were *two* dark red circles in the center of the Moon, side by side, one darker and larger than the other, both bigger than the one we had seen before. As we watched, the purple orb dropped out of the southern sky, straight down, as though into the river, causing all, even me, to gasp, even though I was kind of expecting it.

A sharp clanging sound brought my eyes back down to the scene before me. The Baron had dropped his *harpe* and turned away from his father, exhaling a sigh of exhaustion and grief.

"I forgive you," he said, and walked out of the hedge.

The Duke's face hit the pavement. He was dead.

Rosenberg rolled the body over with his left shoe and then used his face to wipe off some horse dung that was stuck to the bottom of his right shoe. Having now pulled his face away from Miles' leg, poor Little Saint George screamed as he finally recognized the man who had been wearing the Lion mask.

"Grandpa!"

Miles held him tight to prevent him from running over to his grandfather's emasculated and disgraced body. A pair of Ravens walked up briskly and covered him with the purple standard. Then two Butchers carried the body away on a pram like the others. A Lion, whom I thought to be Leopold, came forward with an antique box that I recognized: the Mete coffer. He picked up the diamond from the black throne, wrapped it in white linen, and placed it inside of the box. Then he followed the Ravens out of the hedge.

Seized with ferocity upon hearing St. George's pitiful wailing, Rosenberg marched over to grab the boy by the arm. Miles actually tried to hold on to him for a moment before ultimately letting go. It was the first sign of resistance to either of his bosses that I had seen from him so far. Rosenberg jerked George over to the side of the Brazen Horse. Philippine, bleeding profusely from her now-gaping rectum, was conscious still, but seemed to be near death. I was sure that the repeated anal rapes had already damaged her internal organs, and I knew that she would not last long without medical attention. But her suffering thus far was nothing like what she was about to endure.

Rosenberg told the boy to bow down before him. The child looked up, confused, like he didn't understand the words. Tears were still pouring down his puffy red face as his protruding lower lip quivered.

"Kneel!" Rosenberg shouted at him. Saint George looked at Miles helplessly. Rosenberg looked at him too. "Make him obey!" he yelled.

Miles reluctantly took out his gun and motioned for the boy to get down on his knees. I had thought that Rosenberg just wanted oral sex, which he did. But first, he had another demand.

"Do you promise to serve me as your master for the rest of your days, no matter what fate shall befall you?" he asked.

"OK," the boy said between sobs. Of course, he didn't know what was happening or what had just been said. But he knew how to do what he was asked to do next. As this august personage and child of perfect innocence began his second round of forced fellatio in a twenty-minute period, two Nymphi and two Lions circumambulated both Rosenberg and Consivia, who stood behind the altar and aligned with Rosenberg on his left. They now locked eyes with each other while the Nymphi sprayed them with holy water and the Lions used their censers to fumigate them. The violin began playing again, but just for a few bars. Rosenberg took his Phrygian cap off and Consivia, about three inches taller than him, reached out to put her hand on his head. Thus began another invocation:

Chronos, Saturnus, Sotomo, Satanas,
Cutter of the crooked phallus!
Stercutus, Sator, Satre, Dispater,
Killer of the Cosmocrator!

Piercer of the Deathly Womb!
Raider of the Sacred Tomb!

Plow the fields and work the Wheels,
Crash the Pillars, seal the steal!

Consivia reached out to Rosenberg with her right hand and he bent over to grasp it. The hand hung there between them for a minute as the invocation continued.

Come back to thy bride Jerusalem,
The bloodsucking Lam, the Ericapaiam

Come back and join your true lover again
Come back and join with your mother again

Join with your daughter and join with your wife
Let us pierce the sky with the tip of your knife!

Suddenly a laser-like indigo ray of light came down from the sky with no obvious source, dropping down close-by to the south of us, just like the emissions from the light orbs. Then a black sphere came out from the same place in the sky and travelled down the beam to the bottom, beyond my field of view. About two minutes later, that black sphere, now shrunken to the size of a soccer ball, flew out of the construction chute and onto the top of Rosenberg's head, which was exposed and ready to receive it.

At first, the only sign that the spirit had taken hold of Rosenberg was that he became more violent now with Little Saint George. He began choking him with his penis and grunting obscenities over the child's gagging, muffled screams. The jangle of chains caused me to look away from this abhorrent abomination.

Four Ravens walked in with three metal polls, some sandbags, and a pair of iron chains. They set them up swiftly in front of the altar, so that one beam was held up cross-ways by the other two, which had bases at the bottom and were about nine feet high. The bases were supported by the sand bags. The chains were hung from the cross-beam, each with a shackle at the end.

Consivia stepped forward from the altar, taking off her cork hat, and a shoulder-length braid of powdery gray hair emerged, falling down the back of her neck. A Raven then brought her a bowl of meat and a cup of the blood-wine, which she consumed quickly without visible reaction. She closed her eyes briefly and inhaled sharply.

When she opened her eyes again, a moment later, they were glowing with a piercing silvery light. Her new eyes scanned the crowd intimidatingly. She put her hands in the air, with her shepherd's crook held high in her left hand, and called out forcefully with a commanding voice, quieting all who were present in an instant.

> *Silence! Be still! I command you to listen!*
> *For I am the Hen and the Egg in the Chicken!*
> *It is me! Thy Lady of Perpetual Sprouting!*
> *Sophia Subactrix, denying and doubting*
>
> *Opiconsivia! Madonna Lactans!*
> *Omnipotent Mete, with the world in my hands!*
> *Spica Virginis and Magna Mater*
> *Co-murderess of the Cosmocrator!*

The line where she identified herself as "Opiconsivia" caused me to see the priestess in a new light, for it finally dawned on me where I had seen the Latin title *Consivia* before. It was from none other than my published translation of *Mysterium Baphometis Revelatum*, where Joseph von Hammer-Purgstall wrote that he found a "genuflecting idol," on the back of which were engraved words in Arabic letters that, transliterated and translated, spelled out:

> She is exalted, Mete, Consivia. I and our race were seven.

My translator, I now recalled, had put in brackets that *consivia* meant "she who plants." It occurred to me that it was an appropriate name for Reverend Springhole, whose persona was clearly meant to invoke the role of the wife of Chronos/Saturn "the Sower." But it confused me.

If Mete was Metis, I mused, *as Hammer-Purgstall had suggested, that means she was the wife of Zeus, not Chronos. That was Rhea, the one the Romans called 'Ops.' But they say that the mother of Zeus plotted against her husband to save her son, just as Gaia had done to save Chronos from Ouranos. Metis schemed with Zeus to poison his father, before she married him and got eaten by him. And some say that Chronos actually married his mother — that Gaia and Rhea were the same.*

A chill went through me as all of these errant pieces snapped into place to form a picture in my mind.

I wonder if Metis and Rhea could be the same too. I wonder if it's the same goddess in every story, always playing the same roles with her husband and her children in each generation. The Greeks compounded Rhea with Cybele, making Cybele the mother of Zeus. But Cybele was also the mother of Attis, and look how she treated him...

I was abruptly snapped out of this contemplation as Reverend Consivia Springhole stopped humming and began stomping her right foot to an angry beat, which the drummer boy accompanied in perfect synch.

> *I am the stone of the Wisdom of Mete*
> *I baptize my own with the blood from my teat*
>
> *I bring down the stars from the darkness of Heaven*
> *And cut off the heads of the One and the Seven*
>
> *The Nine are within me as well as the Eight*
> *For I am the Mother of Love and of Hate*
> *With Stercutus my Lord I shall consummate*
> *Destroy all but death and then regenerate*

A sweeping gust of wind came in from the southeast, blowing the robes around. Rosenberg pushed George away from him—thank God—and the boy ran off to a safer space near the hedge. Then came a dramatic drumroll from the drummer boy, off in the shadows behind me. I was unprepared for what came next.

The Ravens untied and pulled off her garments. This revealed the predictably boney body of an elderly Caucasian woman, with wrinkled, blanched skin covered in liver spots. But there were two unique features.

For one thing, the breasts looked like a couple of halved grapefruits sagging down at the bottom of previously- overstretched skin sacks. They were not real, and they had been implanted decades ago.

For another thing, the pubic region was completely covered with something like a free-standing athletic support cup, but with less bulge. This was removed, revealing that there was no vagina, but rather a white plastic stoma keeping a small hole open about a finger's width and sticking out about a quarter of an inch. This too was removed, so that now just the hole was showing.

That explains how Rosenberg could be partnered with a female even though he hates females, I realized. *Because this is not a naturally-born female.*

The Ravens picked up Consivia and put the shackles on her legs. They set her dangling upside-down from the crossbeam. I could see that the bowl was ancient, and it was covered in grotesque reliefs of semi-human figures contorting in mass congress.

As these things were being assembled, Consivia looked on with the most obscene harlequinesque grin on her face, and her eyes continued to shine praeternaturally as she seethed with enjoyment. This could be heard quite clearly when the music abruptly stopped. All was silent but her breathing, and the wind, now gentle but steady.

Rosenberg straightened up, put his hat back on, dipped his hand in a can of Lyle's Golden Syrup that was offered to him by a Raven, and slavered it on his whetted, palpitating member. Then he used the first three fingers on his left hand to scoop up another dollop of lube, which he held in the *Mano Pantea* gesture of blessing towards the priestess, like a sacred offering.

Another Raven brought the three-step horse mount over and placed it behind her. Rosenberg ascended with a hop, putting his pelvis up within reach of Consivia's backside. He wrapped each of his arms around one of her legs, and two Ravens raised her up so that her torso, neck and head were now horizontal.

As Rosenberg inserted his syrup-laden finger into her urethra hole, she inhaled sharply, then exhaled with a lilting, blissful sigh. Then he held the first three fingers on his right side out to his left, and a Raven took the cue, giving him more Lyle's syrup. Rosenberg used it to lubricate Consivia's ancient anus, stretched out and grotesquely protruding due to decades of abuse. This caused her to sigh again. These sighs were the only hint of Consivia's sexuality that we had so far seen. Throughout the orgies until that point, she had been the only chaste participant.

But now, possessed by what appeared to be the true consort of Saturn, she gave herself to the host of that spirit with gusto. Rosenberg's entrance into her rear caused the most peculiar ululation to come from Consivia's throat. As they copulated, he continued to stretch out her urethra hole, until he was able to insert two fingers, thrusting them in and out vigorously, to her intense enjoyment. In-between moans, they both chanted lines from William Blake's *Jerusalem*, clipped and assembled out of context:

> *The Stars in their courses fought, the Sun, Moon, Heaven, Earth*
> *Contending for Albion and for Jerusalem his Emanation*
> *A brooder of an evil day, and a sun rising in blood*
> *A sun of blood-red wrath surrounding Heaven on all sides around,*
> *Glorious, incomprehensible by Mortal Man, & each chariot was Sexual Twofold*

The sound of them both droning these lines in absolute perfect unison while joined in flesh so bizarrely, looking and sounding like a single monstrous being, was quite chilling. Then suddenly Rosenberg rammed his rod further in, with more violence, growling like a ferocious bear.

"Ah! Oh! *Paternoster! Paternoster!* Oh! Ah!" Consivia screamed.

Just like the others before him, and as I suspected he would, Rosenberg pulled out from her before ejaculation, and shoved himself into the back of his adopted daughter, who barely reacted to the entrance this time. She was still breathing though, I noted. I also saw that, above us, the Moon had been half-eclipsed by darkness. As the semen poured in, and his pelvis quaked, he uttered a moaning, gasping mantra in Latin, with his eyes closed, and his hands clenching the back of the brazen horse.

> *Dixit ei Spiritus Sanctus superveniet in te*
> *Dixit ei Spiritus Sanctus superveniet in te*
> *Concipere in ano est*
> *Concipere in ano est*
> *Concipere in ano est*

Consivia now joined in as well, now hanging straight upside-down from the chains again. As she chanted with her pupils rolled up into her eyelids, Lyle's Golden Syrup dribbled from her buttocks down onto the ground.

> *Dixit ei Spiritus Sanctus superveniet in te*
> *Dixit ei Spiritus Sanctus superveniet in te*

> *Concipere in ano est*
> *Concipere in ano est*

The first two lines I now, with subsequent research, know to mean "The spirit of God shall come upon you," a quote from the archangel Gabriel to the Virgin Mary found in *Luke* 1:35. This had been joined with a Latin phrase meaning "conceive in the anus."

I glanced up briefly at the Moon and noted that it was full again, unobstructed from view, and that the larger red spot in the center was actively growing bigger before my eyes. Just as the last drop of Consivia's semen was squirted from the turkey baster, a Nymphus tooted six annunciatory notes on his trumpet, and the clopping of horse hooves could be heard. I looked and saw the Lord High Admiral leading in one of the horses through the entrance to the hedge. Then I looked back at Philippine. A Raven was daubing her with yet another sticky substance onto her back end at both openings.

For a moment I thought it might be the "flying ointment" that I had ordered, prompted by my unseen informant, which was supposed to be made from Wetzel's fat. But then I saw the stallion rear up and break away from his master. The Lord High Admiral let go of the reigns, then started clapping his hands with excitement as he watched what happened next.

Horse hormones, I thought to myself. *Oh God*. I looked away. Philippine shrieked repeatedly, for a few seconds. Then she didn't make any more sounds. I looked down at my side and my eyes met Chesterfield's. He looked ten years older than he had when I met him, and in those eyes I saw that a part of his soul had died that night. Then his eyes dropped down, his mouth parted, and a single tear rolled down his cheek. He put his deformed hand on top of mine and squeezed it.

That horse was led away, and three more were brought forth in succession, each with a trumpet blast. I kept my eyes in the other direction. I only saw the horses arriving and departing. When the last horse left the hedge, the Nymphus blew his trumpet once more, and then we heard the bells of St. Paul's Cathedral chiming twelve times. As the chimes rang out, Consivia softly sang a song made from a set of lines I recognized from Fulcanelli's alchemical treatise *The Mystery of the Cathedrals*.

At midnight a Virgin mother
Brings forth this **shining** *star*
At this miraculous moment
We call God our brother

I looked up at the sky. The clouds around us were dissipating rapidly. Now it could be seen that there was only one small light still hovering next to the Moon, which had gone mostly dark, and was no longer white at all. There were now three red spots in the center, one bigger than the others, and they actually seemed to be glowing. It was as if this light—not a reflection of light from the Sun—was spreading faintly from there to the outer edges of the lunar disc. The rest of the Moon was cast in a gradient fading from old mauve to brownish-red, and then to black.

I know they call a lunar eclipse a 'blood moon' because it turns the Moon red, I thought. *But there isn't supposed to be an eclipse tonight, it's just the night before the full moon. And there aren't supposed to be red lights glowing from inside of it.*

I also noticed another thing: the appearance of the craters on its face seemed to be upside-down from the way I remembered them being.

"Where's that thing that looks like a sun?" Chesterfield asked.

As he said that, we both saw it moving northeast across the sky. The whole congregation began running out of the hedge, trying to follow it. Chesterfield jumped to his feet and ran behind them, pushing my wheelchair along the way.

When got out of the hedges, we turned, like the others, towards the northeast and looked across the terrace to the yellow orb in the sky, which had come to a halt. There was the Lord High Admiral, hitching the last of the four horses up to his black chariot. The other three had already been hitched. They looked quite satisfied. Their undersides were covered with blood. I noticed that the chariot had been outfitted with a sharp scythe sticking out of each side. Baron Carrickfergus was standing there solemnly before the horses with his sun mask in his hand beside him, and his head dropped down. Little Saint George was inside the chariot car on the right side, leaning against the side and staring at the air in front of him, traumatized into catatonia. Suddenly out of the hedge we had used for the ritual came a procession, led by the Lions with their torches and censers.

Next came the Ravens, the first of them carrying the silver casket from the *mithraeum*, swinging on a chain. This was the vessel that had been used in the *Easter Sunday* film to hold the hallucinogenic ointment that lubricated the Bosse of Billingsgate prior to the rape. Undoubtedly, it now held the flying ointment made from Wetzel's fat.

The Ravens were then followed by the Nymphi, the Butchers, the Barber-Surgeons, and finally Rosenberg. They all marched solemnly to the chariot and then gathered behind it. Chesterfield walked closer, slowly, pushing me along, so that we could get a clearer view.

The lead Raven with the casket anointed the chariot wheels, the back of the car, and each hoof of the horses with the foul salve. Meanwhile, Rosenberg walked up to Baron Carrickfergus and whispered something to him. The man raised his head and seemed to take whatever he heard into consideration.

From the hedge, Consivia had emerged, with her vestments on once again, and looking no worse for the wear. She spryly strode up and stood next to her partner the Pater.

The Baron took a long, mournful look at his son, who didn't look back. Then he put his sun mask back on, and bent down on one knee in front of Rosenberg, like one about to be knighted. However, this wasn't good enough. Rosenberg wanted a much greater sign of submission.

"Not quite!" he shouted to the man on the ground in front of him. "Genuflect to me *in toto, Heliodromus!*" The violinist played eight long, droning sonorous notes. Consivia raised her shepherd's crook and chanted:

> *Et procidens adoravit eum.*
> *Et procidens adoravit eum.*
> (That is, "And they worshiped him.")

"Give me the FULL obeisance!" Rosenberg ordered.

Slowly, the Baron got down on both knees and then prostrated himself completely. His head was on the ground, and his rear end was in the air. Then Consivia turned to the congregation with her arms spread out wide before her, and sang.

> *Omne genu flectatur*
> *caelestium, terrestrium et infernorum*
> (That is, "Every knee shall bend, in Heaven, on Earth, and in Hell.")

Everyone else got down on their knees also, genuflecting in the same fashion. Seeing this, even Chesterfield did it too. I was hoping I would get out of this requirement for being in a wheelchair with broken legs. It didn't matter. Rosenberg didn't even look our way. He was also droning in Latin, his hands stretched out to the sky in a grabbing gesture, savoring the moment.

Two Butchers brought out Philippine's bruised and besmirched body. She was motionless. I did not see if she was breathing because she was now covered in the folds of a black robe. They lowered it to the ground and arranged it in the same genuflecting position as the others—not unlike the position she took inside of the Brazen Horse as she was raped repeatedly.

> *Somnium quasi solem et lunam et stellas adorare me*
> *Sed non est somnium somnium*
> (That is, "I dreamt that the Sun and the Moon and the stars bowed down to me. But it was not a dream.")

In unison, all of the Nymphi began to hum ominously. The drummer boy gave a drum roll. A Lion—Leopold, I think—walked out holding a staff before him. It was one I had seen before—the one with the mummified human penis on the end of it: the Bosse of Billingsgate.

Two Ravens came and lifted up the back of the Baron's robe, then pulled down his trousers. Another greased both the Baron's backside and the Bosse quite liberally with Lyle's Syrup. Rosenberg took the Bosse from Leopold and aimed it at his target with relish.

As the shaft was inserted violently, repeatedly, Baron Carrickfergus pushed his mask up over his head and tore at his hair. He grunted in pain, but he didn't scream or cry. He kept that dignity. Yet when Rosenberg finally stepped back, satisfied with the humiliation, the Baron raised his head up a bit, displaying a grimace with his open mouth formed into an O-shape, a tunnel of darkness leading to an empty void. It was a look of total shock at the outrage against his majesty.

I recognized the look on his face. For a moment I couldn't place it. Then I remembered the golden flag behind the thrones in the hedge. The countenance of the inverted Sun depicted there had borne the exact same expression. Behind him, I noticed the sun-like object had dipped lower in the sky, as if it too were lowering itself in submission to the incarnation of Saturn. A bit to the south of that, the Moon had dipped lower as well.

Then I heard a retching sound, and a ghastly smell, a horrid mix of feces and vomit, pervaded the air. I looked down and saw that Baron Carrickfergus was emptying the contents of his stomach—and, judging from the odor, his intestines as well—onto the ground in front of him.

Fecal vomiting? I thought to myself. Caused by rupture of the intestines, and/or plugging of the anus at the time of an attempted bowel movement? I wonder if sodomy was the 'poison' that Zeus administered to Chronos as his cupbearer.

"You may rise," said Rosenberg.

"All rise!" said Consivia.

Everybody in the congregation stood up again. After a few seconds, Baron Carrickfergus regained his composure, replaced his mask, and stood up also. As he did so, the sun-like object behind him rose up in the sky again to its previous position before the Baron had prostrated himself. When two Ravens picked up Philippine and tied her with ropes onto the back of one of the horses, the Moon moved closer to the sun-like object, and somewhat behind it.

Baron Carrickfergus didn't bother to fasten up his pants. He just grabbed his belt and let his disheveled robe fall down over him haphazardly as he waddled to the car of the chariot. When he had climbed in, Rosenberg had the nerve to approach him for a handshake.

"Thank you for living up to your part of the bargain," he said.

The Baron shook his hand, letting go of his pants, which fell to his feet. Consivia handed him the horsewhip again, this time for actually whipping horses. Then he took the reigns. Little Saint George grabbed on to him, frightened, as the horses took off trotting.

I knew what the 'bargain' was. He had taken the rape from the Bosse of Billingsgate so that his son wouldn't have to endure it. That's what he had been threatened with, so it wasn't a bargain at all, just like all of Rosenberg's "deals."

The Baron drove the horses in a circuit around the perimeter of the terrace three times, each time whipping them once to get them to speed up. As they went around, Rosenberg and Consivia chanted the Sator Square repeatedly in unison:

> *SATOR!*
> *AREPO!*
> *TENET!*
> *OPERA!*
> *ROTAS!*
>
> *SATOR!*
> *AREPO!*
> *TENET!*
> *OPERA!*
> *ROTAS!*
>
> *SATOR!*
> *AREPO!*
> *TENET!*
> *OPERA!*
> *ROTAS!*

As he approached the southeast side on the third circuit, he drove closer to the wall. Everyone got out of the way, except the Lord High Admiral, who just stood there, right where they are headed, senile and oblivious, rocking back and forth on a cane. The Baron deliberately drove the horses right at him.

When they got within a few feet of him, the Baron lifted the reigns up a bit. But the horses did not slow down. Instead they began — I swear — to lift up off the ground. The "flying ointment" was doing its magic. It was the same substance — made from human fat — that witches once used to make their broomsticks fly to the mountaintops for secret nighttime sabbats with the Devil. Now, right before our very eyes, right there on that cursed high-rise rooftop terrace crowning the empire of a dynasty of financial sorcerers, the ointment caused four horses, a man, a boy, and a chariot to fly up into the sky with no other means of suspension or propulsion.

As they began their lift-off, the horses knocked down and trampled the Lord High Admiral under their feet. He tried to look up from the ground, just in time for his head to be chopped off by one of the scythes, sending it scuttling across the pavement. Then the horses and the chariot soared up over the rooftop railing, like Santa and his reindeer, over St. Swithin's Lane. Most remarkably, the sun-like object along the sky as well, mimicking the trajectory of the chariot.

From there, the carriage took a swift right turn over King William Street. It was headed south, it seemed, in the direction of the Thames. The yellow orb followed in its own way up above. Meanwhile, Consivia and Rosenberg chanted more lines from William Blake's *Jerusalem*:

> The Sun shall be a Scythed Chariot of Britain
> The Moon a ship in the British Ocean

Then something even more dramatic happened, as we all scuttled around the terrace trying to follow their movements. Little Saint George tried to grab the reigns away from his father angrily, and pushed him. The Baron fell out the side of the chariot, but his pants, still around his ankles, got caught up in something on the outside of the chariot. He hung there upside-down for a few seconds, flailing, while his son tried unsuccessfully to control the horses. As this was occurring, the glowing orb above behaved sympathetically in tandem, jumping about in an erratic, herky-jerky manner.

The chariot took a sharp left, heading northwest, over the Walbrook Building, towards Rosenberg Plaza, the sun-like object and the Moon mirroring this above. Then, as the horses, the chariot, and its occupants suddenly lost their aerial volatility. Everybody ran to the south side of the roof to watch the horror unfold.

It was just like when Wile E. Coyote runs off a cliff, and doesn't fall until he looks down. The chariot plummeted, crashing through the sunroof at the main building of Rosenberg Plaza. The air was filled with the sound of the glass cracking and the final screams of the boy, man and horses.

I knew that, due to the way the building was designed, nothing would stop their fall until they hit the "Vortex" over the lobby. I assumed that was where they probably landed. So too did the architects of the ritual, Consivia and Rosenberg, for they must have planned it all ahead of time somehow. As the chariot crashed down, they sang out in unison another line from *Jerusalem*:

Albion the Vortex of the Dead!

I looked up. The Moon was there, at the very top of the arch of the sky, still transformed in appearance. The sun-like object was no longer visible.

There was a moment of silence. Actually about three minutes, probably. Everyone was shocked and amazed at what they had just seen. Nobody knew what to say, or if they were allowed to speak. Finally, Rosenberg spoke up. He turned around to face the congregation, and announced that we would all be heading back to Rosenberg Plaza through the tunnels immediately.

"I will select a core group of helpers to assist me in inspecting the damage and cleaning up the bodies at the main building. Most of you can take the tunnels over to the Coffin House. There are rooms with soft beds waiting for you there. Tomorrow is Shabbat, a day of rest. My servants, both human and electronic, will make sure you receive all you need to relax and recuperate. The rites will resume at dawn on Sunday."

There was an audible, collective sigh of relief that passed through the crowd in a wave.

I guess even the most evil people in the world get tired after a six-hour orgy of rape, murder and fantastic supernatural events. We were all beaten up (me more than anyone still living), and even though I knew my death could not be far away, I welcomed the thought that I might be able to sleep until then at least.

But it was not to be. Rosenberg walked straight up to me and Chesterfield as the others piled into the elevators.

"You two will have to come with us to the main building. I need you, Ms. Auger, to assist me once more tonight. Then I'll arrange for someone to work on fixing up your legs. Agent Chesterfield, please push the wheelchair and accompany us."

Rosenberg turned around and began talking to one of the Ravens. I looked at Chesterfield, who was wincing at the thought that our torture was to continue onward tonight. He pushed my chair towards the elevator, and I closed my eyes, hoping I could make myself sleep on the ride over. But I couldn't. The morphine was wearing off again.

"The eye sees more than the heart knows," from William Blake's *Visions of the Daughters of Albion*

Chapter 23: Prison Coffin

> …The womb, breeds, whereas the Eye of Horus does not; or, if it does so, breeds, according to the Turkish tradition, a Messiah.
>
> – Aleister Crowley, *The Book of Lies*

The sight that awaited us as Castle Rosenberg was as amazing as it was disturbing. The boy, the girl, the chariot and the four horses had plunged down into the Vortex between the first and second floor. However, they had only broken through the glass on top, and hadn't fallen through the bottom. The rest of the feature remained intact, full of its mysterious fluids which, whatever they were, stank to high heaven now that the top of the container had been broken. The sight of the dead child and horses floating in the vat of sewage soup was heart-wrenching to me and Chesterfield. But it was the stench of the Vortex that brought tears to the eyes of all who were present.

We, the select group of twelve (including me, Chesterfield, Rosenberg, Miles and Leopold, among others) walked up the ramp, all the way to the top, so that we could get a good look at the rest of the damage. Right away, from the second floor, we could see Baron Carrickfergus hanging from the ceiling, suspended horizontally with his front pointed down. As we got closer, I could see that he'd gotten hung up by his own clothing on the rafters of the ceiling beneath the broken sunroof.

His top half was hanging by his robe, due to the way in which the fabric right between his shoulder blades had gotten torn and hooked to one of the rafters. His arms, stuck in the sleeves, jutted out sideways from his body. His bottom half was hanging by his trousers, which were still around his ankles. He was nude from his ankles to his armpits, since he hadn't been wearing underpants.

As I stared at the body of the man hung from the ceiling, I noticed that, when looked at from directly down below, it formed a perfect lower-case "t" shape. His sun mask had been wrenched around to the back of his head. His eyes were wide-open, unblinking, almost plastic-looking. Bruises and cuts could be seen all over his exposed flesh. Behind him, through the round broken sunroof, that strange- looking Moon was framed perfectly.

One of the Ravens, who apparently worked for Rosenberg's company, took off his mask and robe, revealing a light blue business suit. Prompted by his example, everyone else began doing the same. He then went into one of the few closed offices on the upper floor. A few moments later, he emerged with a drone mounted with a camera and some other equipment, which he flew up to the ceiling to inspect the Baron's body. It featured a small medical robot on-board, which was able to scan him for vital signs. Shortly after the inspection, the guy flying the drone announced that the Baron was not entirely dead.

It's hard to say which, of all the bizarre things I observed during this adventure, was the most odd and bewildering. But at that moment, the strangeness of how the body was arranged, and how it had gotten there, was overshadowed by what Rosenberg ordered his Barber-Surgeons to do next. The drone was brought down, and then the Barber- Surgeons—now without their robes and veils—began outfitting the robot medic with tools and medicines. They supplied it with a variety of tubes and vials of fluid mounted into on-board injector guns. Leopold was in charge of this, and instructed them on what to do.

The drone was flown once again to where Baron Carrickfergus was hanging. The injector guns shot their contents into his barely-breathing body. Then a tube was inserted into one of the arms—gently, without causing the fabric that the body was hanging from to rip any further. Then the tube was slowly unraveled from the wheeled dispenser that it was mounted on, as blood began to flow through it. It was strung up over one of the rafters, and then brought down to the top floor, where it was inserted into a foot-tall, bulb-shaped glass bottle without spilling a drop.

This process was repeated again. This time, a tube was inserted into the urethra. A much smaller amount of fluid— yellow urine—was collected from this tap into another bottle. We watched it all unfold, mesmerized, from a set of couches that formed a "meeting area" on the top floor.

Chesterfield fell asleep on one of the couches next to me. I was starting to doze off in my wheelchair, despite the increased pain in my legs, when Rosenberg and Leopold approached me. Chesterfield didn't stir.

"Let this man take you to a room at the Coffin House where he can give you a bit of medical attention," said Rosenberg. "He will ask you some questions when this is done. Be as truthful with him as you have been with me. The stakes are just as high."

He called him 'this man,' I thought to myself. *So he still hasn't figured out that I already know Leopold. And Leopold knows this now, but has chosen not to point it out.*

I thought about what had happened since the Butcher meeting at Oriental Club was interrupted by the police. Leopold had disappeared from custody while in a highly unusual private interrogation by Director Pindar himself. Chesterfield, Paris and I had all assumed that Leopold had kidnapped the Director, then later murdered him at Temple Bar in Paternoster Square.

After all, we already knew he was a "Butcher," a kidnapper, and a known liar running an organized criminal enterprise, supposedly. We already knew he was involved with a secret society that committed bloody sacrifices in secret tunnels underneath London. Yet we didn't know anything about Rosenberg then, and therefore his potential connection to the events had not been taken into consideration.

For those few minutes after we heard that Leopold and Pindar were missing, we all thought that Pindar was corrupt, and had helped him escape somehow. But once we knew about Pindar's death, it seemed more likely that he had been kidnapped and murdered by Leopold as part of his escape from police custody. When we learned about Rosenberg, we all began to suspect that he might be involved as well.

When Leopold showed himself during the ritual at the *mithraeum*, I had proof that they were working together, and that Miles was working for Rosenberg too. Whatever he told them to do, they did. Everyone seemed to treat Rosenberg that way, even the most powerful men in the kingdom, whom I had seen murdered tonight. Baron Carrickfergus being apparently vegetative and legally dead (although there may be exceptions in British law for a man in his position).

So what does it mean, then, I thought, *that Leopold hasn't told him that I was the reason he got arrested in the first place, and the reason he was being interrogated by Director Pindar?*

It means there's hope, that's what, I thought. *It means it's possible that Leopold isn't entirely on Rosenberg's side after all. Maybe he's just cooperating* under duress, like so many of Rosenberg's other 'partners' in crime seem to be doing.

I recalled that the Butchers at Oriental Club seemed outraged somehow by Rosenberg, although I didn't know it was him they were speaking of at the time. They said that he was trying to do something catastrophic and dangerous out of personal greed and ambition, to which they objected: "collapsing the Pillars of Heaven." Chicken Little? Yes. But after all I had seen tonight, and the things I'd heard both Rosenberg and Consivia say, I couldn't afford not to take the accusation seriously.

Then I heard, for the first time in a while, the voice of my psychic informant counseling me in my head.

Go with it, the voice said. *Let him help you.*

As Leopold wheeled me down the spiral ramp and over to Coffin House through one of the sky bridges between the two buildings, I drifted off to sleep.

The next thing I knew, I was waking up from a deep sleep in a hospital bed, inside of an empty office that had been set up as a makeshift operating room. There was bright sunlight coming through a large window across the room from me and to my right. I was stretched out on a hospital bed, and the pain in my legs had taken on a new form. I looked down and discovered why. Both of my feet and ankles had been amputated.

I screamed when I took the sheet away. The realization of what had been done to me filled me with such grief that I cried for twenty minutes. Then the pain in my legs prompted me to punch a red button positioned on a box sitting on a nightstand next to my bed. As I did so, I began to vaguely recall being told by Leopold what that button was for, before I went to sleep there. We had talked for a few minutes, I remembered. I couldn't educe what about yet.

But I did remember him giving me an anesthetic injection. He told me to push the red button as soon as I woke up. I asked him what he was doing this for. As I fell rapidly into deep oblivion, I recalled, he told me that my legs "[needed] to go." He suggested that if I somehow survived this ordeal, I should try to stick around the UK for a while so I could get prosthetics and physical therapy through the National Health Service.

Promptly, Leopold showed up with another shot of morphine, a cup of coffee, and a jellyroll. Actually, two coffees and jellyrolls. One set was for him. He sat on a chair against the wall next to me and we both ate in silence. I didn't care anymore about what kind of gross things might be hidden in the food at this cursed place. I went into waves of sobbing every few minutes. He made no attempt to comfort or distract me, but merely looked away uncomfortably. Finally, he spoke.

"I have some good news for you. Miles and I discovered a friend of yours sneaking around in the *mithraeum* as I was gathering up my equipment. We were able to smuggle him over here without alerting Rosenberg. Sure, everything he does is being caught on camera, but unless his security robots alert Rosenberg to suspicious activity, most likely nobody will review the footage. If the robots had issued any alerts, I think I would have found out by now."

"Who is this friend of mine?" I said. "The only people I know here in town are you and Chesterfield, and Miles, and now Rosenberg's sick gang. And clearly only Chesterfield is my friend."

Leopold looked hurt. "Hey, I know we've done things you don't approve of. And you think you're in a position to judge us morally. But you don't understand why we have done these things. And surely you know that I have risked my life repeatedly to try to help you…. To try to save us all from what may come of this experiment in psychopathy."

As he spoke, some of the previous night's conversation came back to me.

Yes, now I remember, I thought silently. *He is on my side. Or so he says.*

He had told me the secret truth that he and others in the Worshipful Society of Butchers had just discovered, with help from me: that Rosenberg's Mithras cult had been operating behind the seats of power within the kingdom for years. This was because of his wealth, along with his seemingly magical ability to manipulate stock, bond, currency, and precious metal markets. It had something to do with the Niptron Terminal, (which, Leopold admitted, he himself didn't fully understand and therefore couldn't explain.) Rosenberg controlled vast numbers of media companies that repeated his propaganda. Through his contacts in the police, intelligence, and security sectors, he had acquired blackmail material on just about everybody.

More than that, as we had seen demonstrated in the *mithraeum* with Marcia the night before, Rosenberg did not observe the "honor among thieves" decorum as expected. The whole idea behind the surreptitious videotaping of child rape and murder parties/rituals was mutually-assured destruction. Everyone knew that the others present were guilty of the same atrocities. Therefore, nobody ever dared carry out any of the unspoken threats that kept each individual operator in the oligarchy from trying to dominate the others.

But Rosenberg didn't hesitate, giving him leverage over the Rothschilds, the royal family, and many others. Because of his influence on them, he had *de facto* control of populations the world over.

"Then he began searching for a higher realm to rule over," Leopold had said.

Upon remembering that part, my memory became blurry again.

"So where is the 'friend' of mine that you found?" I asked.

"He's with his partner, Chesterfield," he answered. "They're in a room across the hall. I'll bring them in soon, when I feel it's least risky to do so."

Agent Paris? I thought. *I wonder how he got inside.*

There was a knock on the door. It was Miles, and he was, for once, not brandishing a gun. He also had a softer look on his face than I'd seen before.

Were they really just acting the part of Rosenberg's loyal henchmen last night? I thought to myself. *Is it possible that they not only stood by but actively participated in everything that happened — Leopold helping him with the butchery and the medical aspects, Miles standing guard this whole time, preventing us from leaving — with the ultimate intention of finding a way to stop him?* It was all very confusing and frightening.

Then there was the fact that they had taken my feet from me, a harsh truth that I confronted once again when Leopold and Miles picked me up from the bed to wheel me over to the window while they switched out my bedpan.

I guess the privilege of having my decency spared by the Butchers Society has now been forfeited, I thought, remembering how they had been kind enough to have me bathed by a female at the Oriental Club. *I wonder if they're going to give my urine to Rosenberg to do alchemy with.*

The window was tinted on the other side, which let the perfect amount of light in while filtering the glare. I noted that my room seemed to be very high up, probably on one of the upper floors of the ten-story building, and that we were on the southeastern corner, at the intersection of Cannon Street and Walbrook. I sat there, watching the giant orange sun rising behind the southeastern edge of the Walbrook Building across the street, and thought about my current status as a cripple.

They intentionally broke my legs, I reminded myself. *And Leopold himself made the cuts last night, supposedly for my own good. But why should I believe him?*

I didn't want to look at either Leopold or Miles. I could not forgive Leopold for suckering me into this situation with his lies, nor for consorting with this network of rape-and-murder clubs in the first place. This was secondary to the fact that everything about his public persona was a lie.

I don't care what side you're on now, I thought. *You got yourself into this mess, but you got me involved through fraud.*

I was glad when they both took their leave of the room. But that left me alone, with nothing but my traumatic memories and the realization that I would never walk on my own two feet again. So I was also glad again when Miles returned a few minutes later, this time with Paris and Chesterfield. Then Miles ducked out to give us some privacy, saying he'd be back in twenty minutes.

Paris and Chesterfield were both wearing very expensive - looking black suits, with the collars open and no ties. These were undoubtedly provided by the house. Neither of them could afford such clothes. They both looked like they had bathed, a condition I envied. But thinking about that made me aware of the fact that Leopold had at least washed the bull blood from my hair, face, and neck, for which I was grateful.

It seemed they both had been told about the loss of my feet. They didn't look surprised, really, but horrified when they actually laid eyes on me. Chesterfield tried not to show it, but Paris stared for a while before he spoke.

"I'm sorry," he said. "I wish I could have gotten here sooner. I wish I could have stopped them from doing this to you."

"They killed a twelve -year-old girl last night. After raping her for hours. And a little boy, after abusing him. And they raped dozens of other children. And the little boy they killed, I'm pretty sure, was..."

"He knows," Chesterfield said, as if to shush me, as if it was something so horrible, so dangerous to the kingdom that it shouldn't be spoken aloud.

"They wiped out almost the entire line of succession," I said. "And they did it to each other. Both the Baron Carrickfergus and the Duke of Rothesay. They both hurt so many children, including their own little boy."

"He *knows*," Chesterfield repeated, sounding angry.

"Yes, I know, said Agent Paris, staring blankly out the window at the sun.

"I know what they are capable of, that family. They compromised the kingdom, which is now totally in the hands of a complete psychopath, thanks to them."

"And do the British people know what's happened yet—to the Duke and the Baron?" I asked.

"Not last time I checked. I don't know what's going on anymore. That Thomas Weir guy took our phones. Said it was for our own good, to keep us from getting caught. He claims he wants to help us, says he's running some kind of undercover op on Rosenberg. But he can't tell me who he's really working for. Yet it seems to me that he and this 'Miles' guy are the ones keeping us from leaving."

"How did you get in here in the first place?" I asked.

He sat down on my bed, and continued to stare, now at the wall. He explained what had happened slowly, as if lost in his own thoughts.

"My meeting with Miss Equitone and Scotland Yard was *pro forma* and utterly meaningless," he said. "Afterwards, I spent some time researching in-house files about the history of this site: Bucklersbury, the *mithraeum*, etc. I looked at more permit applications for Rosenberg Plaza and realized that he's constructed a well that leads down to the old Walbrook River underground."

"That well connects to the Walbrook?" I said in surprise. "I thought the Walbrook was dry?"

"I thought so too," said Paris. "I've seen for myself that it certainly isn't." Then he spaced out for a moment, lost in memories.

I thought about the well in the corner of the *mithraeum*, out from which the orbs containing the souls of Venus, Mars, and the Moon had appeared. Then I thought about how, while outside on the rooftop of New Court, we had seen Jupiter, Saturn and the sun-like object appear to eject certain "essences" down below, in an area to the south of us, quite possibly right where the River Thames was. These ejections took the form of a golden chain, a blue ray, and a yellow liquid. Moments after each ejection was made, a ball of light resembling the orb that made the secretion would come out of the construction chute hanging below the Sky Box. This was connected to the Rothschilds' secret royal pissing conduit, and to the Walbrook, which was itself connected to the Thames.

Did the souls of the first three planetary Archons travel upstream from the Thames, through the Walbrook, and into the well in the mithraeum? I wondered. *Did the others travel up to the rooftop terrace at New Court via the conduit and the construction chute?*

Also, I thought to myself, *why had he only invoked six? What about Mercury? And what entity did Consivia invoke into herself? Was it Mete? If so, what does that mean, exactly?*

My meditation was interrupted when Agent Paris halted his own reverie and continued his story.

"Then I spent the next few hours pouring over files about the old underground rivers here in London. Not computer files, but the physical files in the old vaults of Basement Level 1."

"I'm surprised that didn't arouse suspicion," said Chesterfield. "Nobody ever goes there."

"It did arouse suspicion," said Paris. "But anyway, I figured out how the culverts that were built for them intersect with various other subterranean structures. There are so many abandoned subway lines, including all the ones that used to be run by the postal service. If you know what you're doing, you can actually travel almost anywhere in Greater London without coming up for air and without using public transportation."

There must be loads of nefarious deeds going on underground here all the time, I thought.

"It's all illegal, of course, but I'm doing an investigation on Her Majesty's Service, so I figured I had the right. I thought I would just see how far I could get. So I started at the entrance to the River Tyburn, which runs right between Thames House and Millbank Tower. There's a tunnel there that can be accessed from a sewer hole in Basement Level 2 of Thames House."

"Wow," said Chesterfield. "You found documents on the secret tunnel entrance at Thames House in the file cabinets?"

"No," said Paris. "Miss Equitone told me about it. She walked in on me ransacking the files. She told me I needed to go to the *mithraeum* and rescue Chesterfield right away. But she said I would have to go alone, and that I should travel underground to avoid being seen. Then she urged me to hurry up, and practically shoved me in the elevator to go down to the second basement."

"Oh my," said Chesterfield. "There must be nobody in the whole service that she trusts. The whole bloody country, taken over in one night…" He trailed off. Paris continued.

"I found my way from there. Or at least, I found some tunnels underneath the *mithraeum*. Then Thomas Weir discovered me a couple of hours ago, as he was walking down the hallway with a wheelbarrow full of human body parts. And he brought me here to Chesterfield's room, where I've been hiding out, catching up on recent events at Rosenberg Plaza. Tell me Pamela, have you been to the lavatory yet?"

I became embarrassed.

"No," I said, "I have a bedpan. And I'm not really eager to see myself in the mirror right now."

"Well you should at least look through the little sunroof. There's one in Chesterfield's lavatory. You probably have one too."

Chesterfield was already in the bathroom, checking it out.

"Yup, she's got one," he said. "Come look, Pamela."

"At what?" I asked.

Paris wheeled me in there. Sure enough, there was sunlight coming through a nine-inch glass-covered aperture in the ceiling. After being positioned directly beneath it, I looked up (carefully avoiding the mirror), and saw what looked like the Sun at its zenith — the exact same place in the sky that the Moon had been in the last time I'd seen it the night before. This made no sense, of course, at least when I first saw it.

"How can the Sun be up there when it's rising in the east behind the Walbrook building right now?" I asked. "I just saw it through the window!" I continued staring at it in awe, with no ill effects on my eyes.

"Yeah, my watch says 9:10 am," said Chesterfield, showing me the face of the black Citizen Eco-Drive Perpetual Chronometer strapped to his wrist.

"That's right," said Leopold, as the door opened suddenly. We all turned around to look at him, quite startled. He wheeled in a tray with a tea kettle and three cups with saucers underneath them.

"Sol is stuck at his meridian for the time being," he continued as he poured out three cups of tea. "He's also lost most of his luminosity. But Sol Novis is on the horizon." "What do you mean?" the three of us asked him simultaneously.

"Because there are two suns presently competing for supremacy. And the final battle won't play itself out 'til Easter Sunday," he answered.

That is the craziest thing I've heard yet, I thought, as Paris wheeled me back into the main room. As I was pushed past the window, I noticed that the sun's disc was no longer in view from there. Paris and Chesterfield both sat down on my hospital bed and looked at Leopold with hostility.

"So you're telling me it's going to stay like this until tomorrow?" I said. "Won't people be panicking in the streets?"

"I don't think most of them have noticed it, and most of them won't," Leopold replied. "Something seems to be having a soporific effect on the populace."

"So how many other people are here?" I asked.

"You mean in this building?" said Leopold.

"Yes," I said. "In the Coffin House. I know that all the folks from last night's ritual were told to sleep here last night. Are they still here? Is there anybody else here?"

"This building's listed as unoccupied right now," said Chesterfield. "There aren't supposed to be any tenants yet. But obviously, there are."

"There were 729 occupants in the beginning," answered Leopold, "when they contracted Pindar as their lead *victimarius*, almost a year ago. He was a member of the Butchers, but we didn't know he was doing this. The victims were all orphans or children taken from troubled homes. He's killed off two per night, one male and one female, every day since, after having them raped, of course. But these were all just preliminary sacrifices leading up to the main season of festivities, which started last Tuesday on the equinox. They are now culminating with this weekend's Supreme Rite, which began last night. And it will continue through Sunday."

We sat slack-jawed staring at him, horrified anew. He continued, looking out the window with weariness.

"We got wind that someone nearby was doing a working to collapse the Pillars of Heaven. But we didn't know who, or what exactly was involved. That's why we brought you in, and you helped us figure out who it was. But Pindar had already betrayed Rosenberg to the Security Services. So Rosenberg had him kidnapped, and me. I pretended to be interested in working with him, and I got the Butchers and Barber- Surgeons to play along. That way we can subtly sabotage him, although we must be quite careful that he doesn't figure out what's really going on.

"So now you've got a company of 'Barber-Surgeons' too?" interjected Paris. "What a bunch of baloney. The Barber-Surgeons were phased out as a livery company in 1745. I don't get my hair cut by a doctor. This is just as fake as your bullshit Company of Butchers, and your hoax barony."

"You know so little," said Leopold between clenched teeth, glaring icily at Paris, "about the way things actually work."

"Rosenberg he wouldn't have contracted Pindar to do this kind of stuff unless the Butchers and Barber-Surgeons were already doing it before," I said. "I saw you kill the bull. I saw Butchers and Barber-Surgeons raping kids last night. But you say you're on our side? If you want to stop murdering and raping, just stop. Help us leave here, kill Rosenberg, and set the other captives free, if there are any. Just do the right thing finally!"

He stood there stiffly looking away from everyone for a moment longer. Then he turned around to face us.

"The blood and tears of so-called 'innocent children' are the glue that holds this society together. Any society throughout history, in fact. The goddess wants blood. She wants brains. She wants skin, and fat, and testicles and eyeballs. She wants to fuck and fuck and fuck! She wants to fuck kids and cows and the King of Spain and the Chairman of the Federal Reserve! And if she doesn't get what she wants, everybody pays the price. These are just *some* of the things you three don't understand about power, and never will."

Leopold's face had turned red and his voice trembled with emotion when he spoke, as though he was really making a profound philosophical statement.

By what criteria, then is he calling Rosenberg a psychopath, if this is his own mentality? I wondered. Leopold continued.

"It takes humility to approach the altars of the gods. You must know that your puny peasant morality is not theirs. You must understand that the food chain of the universe cannot be denied."

"So what's Rosenberg doing wrong, in your estimation?" asked Chesterfield. "He's killing and raping for the gods too."

"Not at all! He is killing and raping the gods themselves, can't you see? He's trying to defeat them! He's trying to bring down the host of heaven, and take the place of the immortals himself. With each planetary archon that was killed last night, he climbed another step up the heavenly staircase. When he gets to the top, two things will happen."

We all looked at him silently, spitefully, waiting to hear the two things.

"Either he will become the new chief of the Archons, ruling us here below with omnipotent power from the realm beyond, or he will snuff us out, and start another universe to rule over. Or he snuffs out everything all at once, accidentally, by causing the layers of existence to crash down on one another catastrophically."

"That's three things," said Chesterfield. "And they all sound ridiculous."

"The layers of heaven have already started to collapse," said Leopold. "It's happened quickly, yet so smoothly that you didn't recognize it for what it was. You just thought there were large orbs of light in the sky. You didn't realize that divine, august immortals were being enticed to lower themselves into physicality, then forced to bow down to an arrogant thug, who didn't even have the decency to spare their lives after they submitted. Now they're all dead except for the Sun and, at least in part, the Moon. He's going to torture them both 'til tomorrow, when the womb opens up, and then he'll have a new victim to torment."

"What womb?" I said. "What's going to open up?"

"The womb of the Mother of the Gods. That's all that's left of poor Philippine."

"Oh no, not again," said Agent Paris to Leopold. "You're keeping the womb alive? Another posthumous royal birth?" The agent's eyes looked crazed. Leopold looked at the door.

"I have to go do something for Rosenberg," he said. "I don't want to raise any alarm by being tardy. I'll be back later."

"You know what I'm talking about, don't you, Butcher!" said Paris as Leopold put his mangled hand on the doorknob.

"Shh!" said Leopold, finger to his mouth. "Don't get caught. I'll see you when it's time for her next morphine shot."

The door closed behind him. We tried it. It was locked.

"So what were you talking about, Parvin?" said Chesterfield. "What did you mean by 'not again'?"

He cleared his throat and then took a deep breath, preparing to tell us another story.

"When my dad was working for SIS, he found out that Mossad was blackmailing the royal family. They knew the truth about the princess who died so tragically, and the baby she was carrying."

"Oh wow," said Chesterfield. "So you *knew* about that."

Paris cocked his eyebrow at his partner, curious about what he was referring to. But he didn't stop his storytelling to ask. He continued.

"Now I don't want to bring the princess into disrepute. She was a victim of rape. But in the traditions of our ancestors, the victim of a divine rape was always blamed for it. The idea is that they have somehow enticed a sacred spirit into denigrating his holiness for the lusts of the flesh. That's how Perseus justified his murder of Medusa after she was raped by Poseidon in Athena's temple. This is what conceived Pegasus. But *he* didn't come out of her body until Perseus *gave him* an opening...."

His voice got softer. He lost his train of thought for a moment as he seemed to mutter to himself. Chesterfield and I both leaned in closer, straining to hear, wondering what he was getting at.

"The Princess was raped by her former husband, who was possessed by a god at the time, my dad said, during a ghastly ritual beneath the Palace. Afterwards, they cloaked her memory. She had no recollection of it. She thought her boyfriend had gotten her pregnant. Three months later, they offed her. But they harvested her womb."

The story was so far synching up entirely with what Rosenberg had said to the Duke of Rothesay about his ex-wife, the mother of Baron Carrickfergus. But Paris had added some much-needed detail. He continued.

"Someone else took the womb, he said. Not one of the family. But they had obviously orchestrated the conception rite as well. And this group performed another ceremony, six months later, which Mossad was able to spy on also, according to the reports."

"Reports that your dad wrote from SIS?" Chesterfield asked.

"Yes," Paris replied, "about reports he had seen in Mossad's own internal documents. Anyway, during this ritual, the womb, which had been kept alive somehow in an incubator, was hung from a ceiling by a couple of meat-hooks through the fallopian tubes. It was meant to look like the head of a bull, with the tubes resembling the horns. They put a severed bull's head on the altar behind it to emphasize this point."

He took a drink of his now lukewarm cup of tea. Then he went on.

"They had a special aperture in the ceiling for admitting lunar rays. When the Moon reached the right position, and the light hit the uterus, the baby came out, miraculously without defect, and landed on a bed of straw positioned beneath the exit of the womb."

"Some miracle," said Chesterfield. "Like *Rosemary's Baby* is a miracle."

"I don't know what happened to the child after that," Paris concluded, "or even what sex it was. And I don't know how the magic of the ritual worked. But I believe my father's story. And I think the baby must have lived on, because Mossad blackmailed them for years after, at the very least."

"Well, *we do* know what happened," said Chesterfield. "The baby was adopted by Marcia Martina and her husband. He was Crispin Martina, Rosenberg's catamite and errand boy. Now he's dead."

"Oh yes," said Paris. "I know he's dead. I saw his head sitting on top of a wheelbarrow."

Suddenly we heard a click. A single click. Coming from the door.

Now what was that? I wondered.

Try the door, came the unexpected reply from my psychic informant, speaking inside of my head once again.

Of course, I thought to myself. *I should have asked you sooner.*

I repeated the suggestion about the door to my friends.

"OK, said Chesterfield. He walked up and turned the handle. The door opened.

It's been unlocked! I thought. *Remotely!*

Chesterfield immediately closed it again, except for a tiny crack, in which he stuck his finger. He turned around and looked at us.

"What should we do?" he asked.

"Stick your head out and see if there's anyone in the hall," said Paris. This he did.

"Not at the moment," Chesterfield replied. "But where do we go from here? All three of us?"

"No, you're right," said Paris. "Let me go alone. I'll see if I can find us a way out."

And so, after a brief reunion, we let Agent Paris slip away from us. We left the door open slightly, but we stayed inside, terrified of being caught trying to escape. We knew the only reason we had been kept alive was because we each were still perceived as somehow useful to Rosenberg. I knew he needed me for something in regards to the next ritual the following day. And Chesterfield was his means of keeping MI5 under wraps now.

But surely we will both soon outlive our usefulness, I thought.

We didn't see Paris again that day, or Leopold. After an hour, when Leopold didn't return, Chesterfield decided to sneak back across the hall to his room, so that nobody would know Leopold had let him in there. Before he left, he helped me back into bed.

A while later, when the drugs were wearing off and the pain in my legs was once again almost beyond what I could bear, a black female servant that I didn't recognize came to change my bedpan again and to give me another shot, along with a turkey sandwich and a packet of tea biscuits. She put me in the wheelchair again so that I could eat sitting next to the window with the food tray beside me. The color of the sunlight and the shadows that it cast indicated late afternoon to me.

I sat there staring at the street below for a couple of hours as the sunlight faded away. I didn't see any people go past, not even in cars. When it was completely gone, and night had fallen, I noticed a reddish tinge to things that were illuminated by the light now coming from the buildings and the street lamps. I looked at the bathroom and noticed red light descending from the ceiling.

I wheeled myself in there, still not letting my gaze fall upon the mirror, and looked up at the little sunroof. Now, in the exact place where "Sol" had been earlier, there now stood the Moon. It was in the same condition it had been in before, but was fuller and larger. This last part seemed appropriate, since it actually *was* supposed to be the night of the full moon. But of course, the coloring was completely abnormal.

The Moon appeared sickly. It was still dark red, fading to brown and then black at the edges, with three bright red circles shining within it, one larger than the other two. The glowing circles in the middle were brighter and bigger than the night before. The craters on the face were again inverted from the way they normally appear in the northern hemisphere. Also, of course, the Moon does not usually just suddenly appear at the very top of the sky right after nightfall, as it had that night.

Just then, a burly white male servant came in and served me dinner: roast beef with mashed potatoes, gravy, and asparagus. He helped me get to the toilet, waiting outside the door for me to finish, which was much less humiliating than using the bedpan. I desperately wanted to ask him what was going on with everybody else in the building, but I didn't dare. I just prayed, to which god I knew not, that Chesterfield had made it safely to his room, and that Paris had found a way out of the building.

Maybe he's bringing help now, I thought, trying to cheer myself up.

Only God can help the three of you, said the voice of the psychic informant.

Who are you anyway? I said mentally to whoever it was.

Why don't you come and see for yourself? was the reply I received.

I heard the clicking sound on the door again.

Try the door, the voice said.

I wheeled over to it, grabbed the knob, and pulled it open. It was indeed unlocked again. I held my breath, listening for anybody. I heard nothing. So I turned my chair backwards and maneuvered myself through the doorway, not without making a little racket, which worried me immensely. But when I got out into the hallway, it was still dark, empty and silent, just a long corridor full of locked doors. Then the lights came on above me.

The digital ceiling, I thought. *You sensed me. Fuck you.*

Don't worry about that, said the voice. *It's the security robots you need to watch out for. And only if they think you're suspicious. Rosenberg's asleep. The rest of the group is so compartmentalized nobody knows if you're supposed to be out of your room or not. Keep your own eyes open for danger. But let me guide you. I have so much to show you.*

I had practiced divination many times before, mostly on the Ouija board. I had never had such a clearly-spoken entity dictate to me in my head like this until it started spontaneously the previous night. I had spoken to gods, demons, servitors, and disembodied human spirits on the Ouija board. The gods and demons all had very unique, poetic, and eloquent ways of speaking. But the people all talked like people.

This voice had tried to come off as god-like or demonic in the very beginning, when it was dictating how the rituals should go. But now its choice of words sounded more human. Yet I felt sure it was the same voice.

So where should I go now? I asked the spirit.

This is the Day of Rest. Come to the Room of Rest, it said. *Mind your Ps and Qs.*

Which way? I said in my head.

Get to the Sixth Floor the voice said.

I looked at the door of my room.

729. That was the same room number I'd had at the Regent Palace, I thought. *And Leopold had said 729 children had been held captive here at Coffin House, murdered over the course of the last year. It means something. I've read about it recently. I just ... can't remember.*

I saw an elevator up ahead. I wheeled myself over to it and pushed the down arrow button. But then I heard something down the hallway, around the corner. I ducked back into my room, which I had sensibly not closed the door to completely. I still kept it open a crack so I could get out again, and I waited.

I heard something, a motorized vehicle, moving down the hallway.

A security robot, I thought.

It paused in front of my door, no doubt alerted by the fact that the lights in the hallway were on. But it didn't seem to notice that the door was ajar, because it eventually moved on. I watched its shadow travel down the hallway and around the corner through the slit between the jamb and the slightly- open door. Then I heard the elevator ding.

It may be a digital super-building, I thought to myself. *But the elevators are slow as snot.*

I quickly wheeled myself out and into the elevator just before the doors closed. It was already on its way down to the second floor. So I hit the 6 button, hoping I could just get off on that floor without running into anybody else.

When the elevator opened, I was at first relieved not to see anybody standing in front of it. I had turned my wheelchair around backwards, and was using the mirrored walls to check what was behind me. Then I pushed myself up and arched backwards to peak down the hallway both ways.

Nobody here, I thought. *Phew!*

Just then the elevator doors slammed against the sides of my chair. They opened again automatically, but it was a bit of a struggle to get the rest of myself through the opening before they closed again. They almost smashed into the swollen and still-bleeding stubs of my legs, but I managed to pull through before that happened.

Now, said the voice in my head, *follow the trail of blood.*

What? I thought. But I looked down, and sure enough, there was a trail of dark brown spots on the white carpet, leading from the elevator down the hall, then off to the right at the fork. I followed. As I rolled along, segments of the ceiling switched on to illuminate the path ahead, while the ones behind me shut themselves off.

This brought me to one of the sky bridges that linked the Coffin House with the main building, with walls of translucent glass. Looking out, I noticed that the City appeared to be cast in a strange purple light, and everything looked very queer. I couldn't tell if this light was actually coming from outside, or was radiating from some source inside that I wasn't able to perceive, coloring my view of what was outside. Inside the sky bridge, this light caused the white carpet to gleam brightly, while the blood trail now looked dark purple in some places, black in others.

I rolled across the bridge, which was about twenty feet wide, over to the other building. The corridor ended quite strangely. It looked like a single glass door until I got up within five feet of it. Then, for a moment, it took on the appearance of a mirror, causing me to stop quickly to avoid running into it. When I got two feet closer, where the blood trail ended, I could see that it was a transparent glass wall with three different "slots" you could go through, each leading to a different part of the trefoil ramp that ran through the main building. According to the signage you could go down through the left to get to the "Recycling Center," down through the right to get to the "Rosenberg Privy Chamber," or up through the middle to get to the "Executive Restroom."

I looked behind me quickly to make sure nobody was coming. Then I closed my eyes and attempted to clear my mind for a second.

Which way should I go? I asked my unseen informant.

Now follow the light, it said.

I looked through each of the slots. Only one had a path that was illuminated at all: the one in the middle. I could see a path ahead there, lined with two bright yellow-green stripes. Whatever was behind the other two slots was completely dark. I went through the center slot and rolled my wheelchair up the incline.

At first I thought that these glowing yellow-green strips were just artificial lighting to illuminate the path, like the colored strips that light the aisles of movie theaters. Then I realized that these were the tubes that ran throughout the building, which I had seen the day before flowing with a pale yellow substance. It looked like urine yesterday, and I had assumed that these tubes were emptying into the Vortex. Now, for some reason, the fluid inside was fluorescent. The area was bathed in a purplish light that seemed to be coming from above, like what I had seen lighting the City when I was on the sky bridge. But here it was more intense. Other than this light, the place was completely dark.

Blacklight, I thought. *That's what's making things glow. But where's it coming from?*

Then it came to me. I realized that I was at the top floor of the main building, towards the middle.

That means I'm underneath the big sunroof, I thought to myself. *And underneath Baron Carrickfergus.*

I looked up. Sure enough, there he was, with the purple light coming in from behind him, through a clear plastic tarp (*perfectly* clear, like Saran wrap) that had been placed over the broken glass panels. The exact source of the strange light was still unclear from my perspective. It made his pale, white, mostly-nude body gleam brightly, as well as a circle with a dot in the middle—the alchemical symbol for the Sun, or gold—that had been painted over his navel with something that glowed bright red.

The Baron's middle had drooped down quite a bit. The legs and neck had now been secured to the rafters with black wire. The effect was that his body now formed a circle, curled backwards on itself, just like the headless body of Pindar hanging from the ceiling at Temple Bar. But Baron Carrickfergus still had his head, now almost touching his feet, up above his drooping belly. His head had been positioned so that it faced straight up at the ceiling. The bright red sun symbol on his stomach moved up and down slightly. He was still alive.

Further proof of life came from the erect penis which also hung down beneath him, attached to what seemed to be a sort of penis pump, which itself was attached to a tube, like the ones I had seen inserted directly into his body earlier. It was again connected to a small, thin glass vessel, this time held below by a drone that hovered directly below him. The pump was moving up and down, much like the pistons of a cow-milking machine.

The purpose was presently ascertained when the Baron's body began to quake. Sperm shot out in globules that just glowed bright green, dripping down and filling about three quarters of the bottle. Then the drone pulled the tube out of the bottle, sealed it with a cap, and retracted the penis pump. It flew down to the top floor with its cargo, right past my head. I couldn't figure out why the sperm was that color, or why it was glowing so brightly, but it allowed me to follow the drone with my eyes in the darkness.

The drone then traveled to a door on my right and seemed to insert the bottle into the wall, about five feet up from the floor. There was a sucking sound, and the bottle disappeared. Apparently, it was a pneumatic tube system.

I looked at the door next to it, which from what I could tell was painted a dark color. There was a strange plaque on it, about six inches square, appearing hot pink in the UV light, and adorned with characters that glowed neon green. There was a three-be-three grid displayed on it—a tic-tac-toe board, with two solid circles in the middle square. This, I knew, was the alchemical symbol for zinc. I noted to myself that zinc is used most often in making fluorescent pigments and plastics.

Inside of each of the other squares on the grid were other sigils. These included two Uranus symbols like the one at the top of the message left with Pindar's body. There was one in the upper-left corner, and one on the bottom right, both with their arrows pointing towards the bottom right. In the middle square on the right was a sign for Pluto, and in the middle left, a symbol for Saturn. In the upper right and lower left squares, I recognized the alchemical symbol for arsenic, and in the top middle, the alchemical symbol for platinum, which consists of the symbols for the sun and moon squeezed together. In the bottom middle was a representation of the diamond, with eight facets delineated on its face.

I recalled the voice's cryptic message: *Mind your Ps and Qs*. I realized that the way the arrows were pointing on the Uranus sigil made them look like the letter Q. The arsenic signs looked somewhat like the letter A. The Pluto symbols resembled the letter P. The Saturn insignia look like an H. Therefore, the characters in the right and left columns spelled a word.

This must be the Qaphqa, I thought. This is the secret private bathroom for Rosenberg's special employees. And I'll bet I know what the invisible ink on the door is.

Suddenly, the blacklight disappeared, and so did the characters. I could see almost nothing. But the drone was still shining its headlight as it flew away and descended into the shadowy depths below.

Maybe I've been still for too long, I thought. Maybe if I move around the digital ceiling will strike up the blacklight again. Or any light. Though I must admit I prefer the blacklight. It's easier to hide in.

Then, just as suddenly, and again for no obvious reason, the blacklight returned. I looked up. I was certain now that it was streaming in through the sunroof, where the purple glow was concentrated.

But from what? I thought. Something on top of the building?

I rolled up to the door, pulled my sleeve over my right hand for sanitary reasons, and tried the handle.

Unsurprisingly, it didn't open.

How do I get in? I asked my invisible friend.

You have to pay a token, said the voice.

Where do I get one of those? I said mentally.

Look inside your pocket, said the voice.

I reached down into the pockets of my hospital gown. Indeed, in the pocket on the right side there was a single coin, about the size of a quarter and made of glowing green glass. impressed with a picture on each side.

Vaseline glass, I thought. *Uranium. It glows green in the UV light.*

On one side was the Uranus symbol. On the other side was the image of a king with a beard on a throne. A young man was standing in front of him, bent forward, as the king prepared to swallow his head whole into his mouth.

Then I noticed that in-between the two circles in the center square of the plaque on the door was a slot, barely visible to me, which I thought might be big enough for the coin to go through. I inserted it, and heard a clunk, then a click. The door opened.

It was dark inside, but here too it was illuminated in blacklight. I could tell because body fluids spritzed all over the room gleamed brightly, but of it a yellow-green color, like the tubes lining the ramp. There were also stains that glowed more faintly with a light blue appearance. I figured that the yellow-green stuff was urine, and the light blue substance was probably semen. Much of the latter was concentrated around one particular area of the wall opposite the door, and also on the floor near there. There, about waist-high on the wall, were two Latin words painted with a fluorescent green pigment: CUM DEO.

I pushed my chair through the door and rolled into the blackness towards the glowing words. I heard the door shut behind me. I turned around and tried to open it back up. But I could not. I was trapped.

So you told me how to get into this room, I said mentally to my informant. *Now tell me why. And tell me how to get out.*

All will be revealed momentarily, it answered.

I looked up and saw that the room had a roof that was clear glass, faceted in such a way that the blacklight coming through from above gave it the appearance of a purple rose. I felt around for a light switch but couldn't find one.

All artificial light is automatically controlled by the digital ceiling, I remembered. *So the UV light that's coming through the sunroof is tricking the system into thinking its daylight. I wonder if it's damaging my eyes.*

Just then, I head footsteps approaching. I pushed myself as far back into the farthest corner as I could. I heard the person step up to the door, and then a series of clicks. The door opened. With only blacklight coming from above, I couldn't make out anything. But luckily the person couldn't see me either.

I heard the person grunt. It sounded male–a safe bet in a place like this. The door shut behind him. I heard him unbuckle and unzip his pants. The buckle clanged as it dropped to the floor. Then I heard the flick of a plastic cigarette lighter, and saw the flame.

As my eyes adjusted in that brief second of additional light, I could make out the person in front of me lighting a cigarette. It was Dennis. His teeth and the whites of his eyes glowed white in the blacklight. Luckily he was staring straight ahead at the wall opposite the door, away from me. He was staring at the words *CUM DEO*. When the lighter was lit, I could see that they were painted in fluorescent green on a small circular metal door in the wall.

Dennis approached this wall, waddling with his pants around his ankles, slouching backward. He held his short and thin but erect member casually in front of him as he flicked it around. Then he touched something on the wall, and the *CUM DEO* door slid open, revealing a round hole cushioned with a soft plastic material resembling the stuff that stress balls are made from. It looked pink in the ultraviolet light. Dennis grunted again, and the wall began to emit a soft hum. He threw his head back and closed his eyes.

As he spent the next 68 seconds or so being satisfied by the automatic glory hole, I got a chance to look around the room more. It wasn't at all what I imagined. I thought it would be like the dream executive washroom, with tuxedoed attendants handing you warm towels.

Instead, it was a small, dark hole with few features. A square plaque inside of the front door with the same color scheme as the uranium glass coin, featured that same illustration of the king swallowing a man's head, but with more detail in the background.

Beneath it there was a poem:

> When the Son entered the Father's house,
> The Father took him to his heart,
> And swallowed him out of excessive joy,
> And that with his own mouth.
> The great exertion makes the Father sweat.

I did not recognize this stuff at the time, but I now know that both the poem and the image are from a seventeenth-century alchemical text called *The Book of Lambspring* by Nicolas Barnaud.

The other items in the room included a small sink, an automatic hand-dryer, a toilet, and a urinal, on the same wall as the *CUM DEO* flap, near the corner. The urinal was interesting. It was white, but old-fashioned looking, and of course it was covered with bright yellow-green urine stains, especially in the basin. But on one side of it, glowing blue-white in the UVs like dried semen, were written the words "R. Mutt." I recognized this as the name that was written on artist Marcel Duchamp's "readymade" statue called *Fountain*, which was really nothing but a urinal with this name written on it. It was actually the alias of the socialite aristocrat who had given Duchamp the idea of displaying the urinal as an art piece.

On the wall, above the urinal, painted in the same substance as "R. Mutt," were the words "Fountains of Youth," along with a double-headed arrow. One pointed to the urinal below, while the other pointed leftward at the hole where Dennis was currently thrusting his hips at the wall, making poses at it, and calling it "bitch." As he ejaculated with flair, the device in the wall made a grinding sound. Then there was the sound of something dropping and clanging against a metal surface.

"A penny saved, a penny earned," the young man said to himself with a chuckle. He put his hand around his junk and attempted to remove his penis from the wall. But something went wrong.

I'm doing this for you, said the voice in my head.

"What the FUCK is happening," said Dennis. The alarm in his voice was quite real.

He seemed to be unable to pull out of the glory hole.

"Oh fuck. Oh fuck. What the fuck am I going to do?" he screamed, frantic now. I pushed my wheelchair forward.

"How do I get out of this room?" I asked, prompted by my informant. The young man nearly jumped out of his skin and screeched "whoop!" as I startled him. Lucky for him, he jumped forward, and smacked his head into the wall, instead of jumping backwards and ripping his penis off.

"How did you get in here?" he said. I didn't reply.

"Can you help me get out of this?" he said, nicer now.

"I don't know," I said. "Show me how to get out of this room and I'll get someone else to help you."

"OK," he said. "You'll need the coin to get out, just like you do to get in."

He reached down underneath the glory hole, and then underneath another, smaller flap that was there. From this, he extracted a Vaseline glass token identical to the first. He handed it out to me. I wheeled forward to grab it.

"There's a slot right next to the door, he said. He rested his hands and forehead on the wall in front of him.

"Hurry up," he said. "I can't stand here like this much longer."

"Where should I go to get help?" I asked.

"Go to Rosenberg's Privy Chamber," he answered. "There's a crossroads on your left. The signs will show you which way to go."

'A crossroads on your left.' What strange words to use, I thought.

Get the 'key to the outer doorways,' the voice in my head said.

I demanded this of the lad. He seemed shocked that I knew to ask for this.

"I only have the key to Rosenberg's Chamber," he said. "Knock first or he'll kill you. The Outer Doorway key is with him. But there's no way he'll let you have it."

"Where's the key you DO have," I demanded.

"In the back of my pants," he replied.

Great, I thought. *And your pants are on the floor, where you can't get them because your penis is stuck in the wall, and I can't get them because they cut off my feet.*

I had no choice. I positioned the side of my chair parallel to his back, and leaned down as far as I could to grab the keys from the back pocket of his jeans. The left pocket yielded nothing. At first I couldn't reach the right pocket. I used the right wheel of my chair to nudge the jeans and push the pocket up a bit. Then I managed to get my fingers in. There I found a set of electronic keys.

"Which one's Rosenberg's Privy Chamber?" I asked.

"The one that says '81'," he replied, groaning with discomfort. "That's the room number too. It's not marked otherwise."

With that, I turned my wheel chair around, pumped the coin into the slot next to the door, and barreled down the hallway, letting the door slam shut behind me.

Wheeling down the ramp was much easier than wheeling up, as you can imagine. Within seconds, I was back at the "crossroads" at the end of the sky bridge, which I still don't understand the nature of. As I approached it from the other side this time, it seemed to suck me in and subsume me.

Then suddenly I was presented with the three slots again, leading in three directions, but in a different order compared to what they were before. Now the Privy Chamber option was in the center, and the "Recycling Center" was on my right. Once again I headed down the middle.

It felt like I was on an amusement park ride. My wheelchair seemed to move itself through almost empty space. The most visible sights were the ramps spiraling ahead of me and around me, each lined with the glowing tubes. Directly down below, the Vortex glowed brightly with the yellow-green fluid, the identity of which was now undeniable. It occurred to me that it was probably covered with a clear tarp just like the broken sunroof, or else I would have been able to smell the stench of it, like the night before when the top was broken. Philippine, the horses and the broken chariot parts had been removed. The contrast between this and the darker substance floating within it, along with the body of the dead little boy, was amazing.

As my wheelchair winded self-propelled through the twists and turns of the ramp, shooting stars seemed to come out of the darkened dome above me, spreading out over the ceiling, and all over the body of Baron Carrickfergus, glowing like the flecks of urine and jism on the walls of the Qaphqa. I felt my head spinning as I whirled around. I was getting dizzy. And I wasn't pushing the wheels at all.

Where is it taking me? I asked my invisible friend.

To Paradise, it said. *But remember: I never promised you a rose garden.*

A catchy tune from Joe South. Why do you mention it? Rosenberg…? Rose Mountain…? Rose Cross…?

Just look for the keystone, was the reply, with a hint of exasperation. *Then I'll tell you what to do next.*

Presently I found myself in front of a door that looked just like the other private office doors I'd seen in that building, what few there were. But it was marked "81." I pulled the key out of my pocket.

Dennis told me to knock first, I thought. *Otherwise he'll kill me.*

Don't knock, surprise him, came the answer from my psychic informant. *Use the ruse that Jupiter used on Saturn according to Orpheus.*

What? I thought. *I'm running out of time here. I'm not in the mood to solve riddles.*

Unmoved by my plea for clarity, the mental voice replied with a poem.

> When stretch'd beneath the lofty oaks you view
> Saturn, with honey by the bees produc'd
> Sunk in ebriety, fast bind the God.

I pushed the button on the key marked "81." The door opened. Just then I heard a security bot approaching around the bend from the left. It quickly pushed myself and my chair through the doorway backwards, letting the door shut behind me just as the machine turned the corner.

"Dennis! Is that you?" Rosenberg slurred from behind me.

I was silent.

What do I do? I asked my informant.

"What's the word, bird?" said Rosenberg. He sounded really drunk.

The Rose Gives Honey to the Bees, said the voice in my head. *That's the password.* I repeated this phrase, a well-known Rosicrucian motto, though its meaning remains obscure.

"Oh Pamela!" he said. "Oh how lovely. Won't you join me for a drink?"

I turned my chair around to face him. But I found that there was a divider made of glass brick behind me, obscuring the rest of the room. I wheeled around it. This brought me in to the main chamber.

The room was quite large, with immense ceilings, and a huge theater projector screen against the wall on my left. In front of this there was a long and exquisite black leather sofa curled into a C-shape around the fat end of an egg-shaped black marble coffee.

Here sat Rosenberg, alone, in a once-white, now red-stained terry cloth bathrobe and nothing else, surrounded by empty and half-empty ceramic *amphorae* once full of blood-wine. He looked up at me, then seemed startled as he looked at my feet. But he didn't ask me what had happened, so I presume he remembered hearing (or perhaps ordering) that my feet were to be cut off. He poured himself another drink. He didn't actually offer me one, which was fine with me. All I wanted in that regard was morphine.

The room — which also contained three more leather couches, several leather seats, many more black marble tables of various shapes, several rows of bookshelves built into two of the walls, a 4.5 foot-tall porcelain wheel painted iridescent purple, and a metal dissection table on wheels — was completely trashed. In addition to more empty *amphorae*, other debris included used cans of Lyle's, empty canisters of "poppers," discarded clothing, including black leather fetish garments, and small empty animal cages.

On the dissection table, which was utterly covered in blood and gore, were the dismembered arms and legs of a small white male child with dark hair, aged about nine years, strapped to the sides. The table had been used to do a vivisection. The hands were still clenched into fists, and the toes splayed outward in pain. The rest of the body — the head and torso — was draped around the top of the porcelain wheel, face down. It seemed to me that he had died quite recently.

He had been dissected while alive, then positioned on the wheel and anally violated, from the looks of it. I could not tell if had been alive for that last part or not, but the tongue was bitten through. Next to this on the floor was a large krater, still full of blood-wine, and from the smell, still fresh. I shuddered and looked away.

You know what I don't see, I said mentally to my informant, *are any keystones lying around haphazardly*. I waited for a clue, but got only silence.

Rosenberg was paying me no attention. He was staring at the screen in front of him and laughing as he ate something out of a white ceramic bowl. It was popcorn. I looked at the screen.

He was watching an old black & white film, familiar-looking, with a Wagnerian score. At the moment I looked at it, a continental soldier sitting on a chair on the patio of a large house had just put a ten-year-old boy on his lap and begun kissing him on the mouth.

I've seen this before, I thought. *In film school.*

"It's *L'Age d'Or*," said Rosenberg, still without looking away from the screen. "Luis Bunuel and Salvador Dali. Have you seen it before?"

"I've tried watching it a few times," I said. "I always fall asleep."

With that he finally turned around to face me. "Neanderthal! Troglodyte!" he shouted, pointing at me and shaking his head as if to shame me for my lack of art appreciation. I was too high on morphine, and too much in shock from everything else, to care what he thought of me. I smiled and stared straight into his eyes.

"Why don't you tell me what's so great about it?" I said.

"Look," he said. He faced forward again and pointed the remote control at a machine against the wall. The film skipped to a scene of a man with silver hair and a pointy beard stuck to a ceiling next to a chandelier.

"You see that?" said Rosenberg. "That's what happens to the Minister of the Interior in this film. That's a prophecy of what happened to Baron Carrickfergus."

He rewound it a bit to show what led up to that scene. The Minister of the Interior was sitting at a desk making a telephone call to a younger man with a black mustache. They spoke in French, with the English given in subtitles.

"You scoundrel," said the Minister of the Interior. "You are entirely to blame. You compromised me too. Do you realize that not one child survived? Many women and old men perished too."

"You're bothering me about a few brats?" replied the man on the other end of the line.

A crowd was shown running down the street as they were chased by the flow of hot lava.

"Filthy ruffian, you've dragged me down with you!" said the Minister. His phone was shown destroyed on the floor next to his desk. Then we saw him on the ceiling again. We were back where we started. There was no explanation of how he got up there.

Rosenberg pressed another button on the remote control. It skipped to a title that read "the first prismatic articulation," followed by a scene of scorpions fighting.

"Those are the scorpions that the *mithraeum* here, and the chambers beneath, are infested with. They are the scorpions that Luna sends to devour the testicles of the bull. The entire film is arranged to resemble the 'prismatic articulations' of the scorpion's body. This refers to the prism that imprisons us."

'The prism that imprisons us.' Did I hear that right? I wondered.

"Then, there's this," he said.

He skipped ahead a bit. Now a crowd of people were gathered around a cornerstone-laying ceremony officiated by a man in a black top hat. Corn, wine and oil were poured on top of a brick, then smoothed out with a trowel.

"You see this?" he asked me.

I nodded, bewildered.

"The foundation of the Holy City. *Ab Urbe Condita*," said Rosenberg. Remember what Crowley wrote? 'Baphomet was Father Mithras, the cubical stone which was the corner of the Temple'"

The film displayed archival aerial footage of Rome, accompanied with subtitles that almost seemed like they explained what was going on. But they didn't really. The text said:

> In the year 1930, on the premises occupied by the remains of the Majorcans, was placed on the sheer rock the foundation of the city of... Imperial Rome. The world's ancient, pagan mistress became the seat of the secular church for centuries. Some aspects of the Vatican form the firmest pillar of the church.

Rome was founded on April 21st in 753 AD, I thought. *This film was made in 1930. What the fuck?*

"Now look at this," said Rosenberg.

In the next scene, a man was seen walking out of a café, brushing bits of crumbled masonry off of his coat. Then, a few shots later, another strange title page read:

> Sometimes on Sunday....

Next, a row of buildings was shown collapsing.

"The diverse and picturesque aspects of the great City!" said the title page that came right after this.

The whole scene reminded me of something.

"Wasn't there a part in *120 Days of Sodom*, I said, "about an aristocrat whose fetish was to make buildings that were set to collapse eventually, trapping women and children in the rubble?"

"That's the Holy City collapsing," said Rosenberg, ignoring my inference.

Then a man was shown kicking a violin down the street and stomping it into pieces.

Violence, I thought. *Violence against violins. Stupid surrealists.*

"Here," said Rosenberg. "This part's about me."

The man who brushed the collapsed building debris off his coat was now shown walking through a park with a flattish stone balanced on top of his head. He walked past a statue of a man with long hair, also shown with a similar stone on his head.

"Psalm 118," said Rosenberg. The cornerstone becomes the headstone."

The line in question, number 22, actually states:

> The stone which the builders refused is become the head stone of the corner.

This statement was also paraphrased by Jesus in *Matthew* 21: 42-44, where he said that the rejected stone became "the head of the corner," leaving out the repetition of the word "stone." Then he followed it up with this:

> And whosoever shall fall on this stone shall be broken: but on whomsoever it shall fall, it will grind him to powder.

"That was me, you see," said Rosenberg. "I was born from a rock at rock-bottom, from the dirt on the ground. And yet it is I who shall climb to the highest heaven tomorrow and sit on the throne of God himself. My head will be the keystone to the Arch of Heaven."

"You're drunk," I said.

"Drunk on that blood -wine." "Am I? Listen, my dear," he said, turning around and smiling at me, with a bloodstained Batman Joker grin extending from the corners of his obscene mouth. "Human flesh and body fluids are definitely rich with chemicals that are intoxicating when ingested by other humans, or those who take their form. But that does not mean I am mentally incapacitated. Far from it. I am in a heightened state of awareness right now."

Keep him talking, I thought.

"What do you mean you were born from a rock?" I asked.

"Like Mithras?"

"Pretty much," he said, burping. He got up to refill his glass. Then he walked over and made a bizarre swishing motion in the air with his hands as his robe flopped open. It looked effeminate and awkward. I thought he was just twitching compulsively, but then the sliding glass doors to the patio opened on the farthest wall. I realized he was communicating with his digital ceiling. Cold night air came pouring through the open doors. Behind him, the sky was empty and black, but the blacklight was bathing his clothes and face, as well as the buildings behind him.

What on Earth *is causing this?* I wondered again. *It's definitely something on top and outside of the building.* I wheeled my chair closer so that I could continue to hear his confessional James-Bond-villain-style rambling. He was telling me things I thought I might need to know. I decided to goad him more.

"So you didn't have a human mother?" I said. "Some god just ejaculated onto a rock and you came out of it like a chicken from an egg?"

"Not quite," he said. "It was more like a Kinder Surprise Egg. They're illegal in the USA, but in Europe you can buy these toys for your kids that come in tiny plastic eggs covered with chocolate."

"I'm familiar," I said. "There are videos about them on YouTube. You can't avoid them for some reason." "Yes, well, they're illegal because really dumb kids have deservedly been weeded out of the gene pool by swallowing them whole, which often causes them to choke and die."

"OK," I said. "What does that have to do with who your parents are?"

"'Parents,' you say?" He snorted a laugh. "That's for mortals. No. You've read *The Gospel of Thomas*, I'm sure.

When you see him who was not born of woman, fall down upon your faces and worship him. And that's what everybody does. They fall down and worship me."

He smiled.

"Even Little Saint George bowed down, like his father, and his father's father."

I couldn't take it anymore.

"You motherfucker!" I said. "What's wrong with you!" He stood up straight, looked directly at me with rage and stomped right towards me.

"So what if I fuck my mother? At least she produces seed from it—glorious seed full of astral light and transcendental power! At least she has something more than just a vacuous slimy hole that takes without giving! At least I'm not like your friends, the Butchers, those stodgy old aristocrats who cut off their own dicks and feed them to their queen, their *Great Mother*. The only way they can cling to their decaying carcasses is by sucking period blood out of their mothers' pussies! Did you know that? So do the sons of the crown that the Butchers have been propping up for one hundred and twenty years! They call themselves princes, but they bow down to something as low and disgusting as a *vagina*!" As he spoke, he gritted his teeth and bared them like an angry dog. With his teeth and the whites of his wild eyes gleaming brightly in the blacklight, it looked like he was transforming into a monster. I started to back away from him. "It is I who shall *destroy* the works of the female! Your friends at the Society of Butchers sacrifice bulls to the Great Mother because its horns remind them of her womb. But you and I both know that the Great Mother's womb is a tomb, because it is also a stomach. It is also the cauldron that cooks the meat that the stomach digests. It is a prison where we *all* suffer as slaves to provide sustenance to overlords whom we cannot see, because we are inside of them."

He knows that I know about the Society of Butchers, I realized. *What else does he know now in regards to that?* His hands were balled into fists at his sides and he stumbled as he continued to close in on me. He was truly enraged, though not at me specifically, I was relieved to confirm. He continued his tirade.

"You see, I *will* bust out of here. I will bring each floor of this mansion crashing down until I find the Father who has no Mother. Then and *only* then will I find something worthy to bow down to."

"So who were *your* mother and father," I asked, wanting to bring it back to the original question. "You said something about a Kinder Surprise Egg?"

"Yes, well the egg contained the makings of a golem," he explained, calming down. "It was prepared by an expert rabbi kabbalist working for the Rothschilds. It was swallowed, forcibly, by the host. Then, after being passed through the intestines, it was fertilized *in ano* during a paschal rite by 108 Freemen of the City of London, one from each of the livery companies at the time. Not the 'official' ones, of course. They all have 'clandestine' versions that operate 'night works,' as they call them, where these things happen."

I recalled that fourth to fifth-century Italian grammarian Maurus Servius Honoratus, commenting on Virgil, had said that the Great God Pan, a satyr, was conceived by Penelope when she gave herself to all 108 of her suitors during one night of debauchery in the absence of Ulysses. I had written about it in my Baphomet book. Multiple fertilizations of the same ovum were not uncommon in the mythologies of ancient gods.

"So you have 108 fathers?" I said. "I guess your mom was a real slut."

He already hated women, so I wasn't sure this would rile him at all, but it was worth a try. I wished I could find a way of hurting him. I despised him so much at that moment that it was almost overwhelming. Then it got worse. He smiled that ugly smile again.

"I guess you could say she's a *debauched woman*. Even back when she was a little teddy boy taking a free titty mag from a stranger at Piccadilly Circus. None of the lads who strutted their asses around the fountain of Counter-Love were innocent in those days."

So that's it, I thought. A sick feeling slid down my throat, like a cold cockroach swallowed accidentally from a can of Coke that's been sitting out since yesterday.

I can't believe I didn't realize it before, I thought. *But that makes Rosenberg.... No. It's impossible.*

"You're telling me that Consivia is your mother as well as your wife?" I asked.

"Civil partner," he corrected.

"And Consivia was the Easter Sunday April Fool," I said. I put my hand over my mouth.

Did I say that out loud?

For a moment, I panicked.

He already knew that I knew about the Society of Butchers, I thought. Now I just gave away that I knew about the child rape movie from the 50s. He probably already knew I knew about that, which is probably why he mentioned it. But did he?

Apparently, so, for it seemed that nothing I had said to him upset him any further. He was smiling like the Batman Joker again.

"Yes, my mother is *quite a lady*. 'That which does not kill us makes us stronger.'"

"So where is she now then?" I asked.

"She's in the kitchen," he said. "Where every Great Mother belongs. Preparing for Easter."

"So early?" I said. I wondered how people like Rosenberg and Consivia would celebrate the Lord's resurrection day.

"Well, she's got to be at St. Paul's at the crack of dawn," he said. "She's leading Easter Mass."

Outside of his window, I could see the gleaming dome of St. Paul's, which started to chime. From the number of rings, I surmised that it was 4 a.m.

"I'm really overdue for a morphine shot," I said.

"Well then let me take you to your friend Thomas Weir," said Rosenberg, grabbing my wheelchair and pushing me towards the door. "Or, as you like to call him, Leopold Black. Did you know he was related to the house of De Blacas?"

"What?" I said. "You mean Louis and Pierre?"

He wheeled me through the door and down the ramp through the darkness.

"Yes, Blacas," he replied. "The family that collected the Templar artifacts that Hammer-Purgstall wrote about. They are among the many of Thomas Weir's illustrious ancestors. When some of their descendants moved to the Britain, first to Scotland, they renamed themselves 'Black.' It was his mother's maiden name. That's why he took it as an alias. Has it ever occurred to you that Louis, Duc de Blacas may have been the inspiration for the Duc de Blangis in *120 Days of Sodom*?"

It certainly had not occurred to me. But now I had to think about it.

The Duc was a Jesuit-trained aristocrat, entwined with the crown, essentially running the government in France as a sort of prime minister, and against the Revolution. The Duc was accused by modern historians of faking the Templar artifacts he showed to Hammer-Purgstall, covered with scenes of the sacrifice and rape of animals and boys. They claim he might have done this to make Templars, and thus the Freemasons associated with them, look evil, to discredit the Masonically- inspired Revolution.

Since commencing my research into this topic, I had dismissed this argument. *What a lot of work to go to for a roundabout, indirect jab at the enemy with no impact*, I had previously thought. But I considered the fact that the Marquis de Sade had been a Revolutionist, and had presented his obscene works as political commentaries.

His debauched villains were always aristocrats like himself, or in the clergy. Sure, the Marquis was guilty of many of the crimes depicted in his novels. But his point was not merely to glorify rape and murder for the joy of hurting people. While he did accomplish this indirectly, his point, he claimed, was really to show the audience that *this is what the ruling class get up to*. Pasolini, in his modernized film version, had the same point.

This is what Pasolini was truly persecuted for, I thought. *The same was probably true of the Marquis. That's why he was in the Bastille, instead of being invited to elite parties. Because he exposed them for what they were.*

Rosenberg, almost as if he could read my mind (and I'm pretty sure he couldn't) now mentioned the first film adaptation of the Marquis de Sade's novel, which we had just been watching in Rosenberg's Privy Chamber, although I didn't know it at the time. It was *L'Age d'Or*. I had no idea that *120 Days of Sodom* was the basis of the film, because I hadn't read anything about it since college, and because I'd never been able to stay awake through the whole thing. I was astonished. Rosenberg continued to enlighten me.

"Did you know that the Marquis de Sade's manuscript wasn't published until the twentieth century? And do you know who rescued it from the cowans who were holding it hostage? Who preserved it? Who brought it out of hiding to take its place in the history of literature? His family. His descendants. They became the House of Noailles. They were patrons of the arts. They funded Dali, Cocteau, Man Ray, Jean Hugo, and Bunuel. Most importantly, they funded this movie, *The Golden Age*, the first film version of the Marquis de Sade' story. It came out before the book even did."

"Didn't the Vicomtesse de Noailles let Cocteau get her pregnant?" I said, making conversation with one of the few related odd bits that I knew of the subject.

"Yes, but that was no ordinary pregnancy either," he replied. "And the child was removed from the womb prematurely for his own protection. He grew up with a camouflaged identity, sucking out sperm from the very cock that had spawned him, and he never even realized it. But that's none of your business."

Just then, as we swirled around the ramp to the second floor, the blacklight came back and the ceiling lights faded out. I looked up at the giant sunroof behind Baron Carrickfergus. Now with a better angle, I could see that full red Moon behind him, the three circles now glowing purple and almost consuming its entire visible surface.

Is the Moon actually glowing from inside? I asked my friend in my head.

She's pregnant with new light, came the answer. *And she's about to give birth to a new aeon.*

Astronomy aside, it did seem as if the Moon had something luminescing inside of it, and not just on its surface.

The ancients called the Sun and Moon the 'lamps of Heaven,' I thought to myself. *Can the Moon really have a star in its womb? Can its skin act as a lampshade? If so, that would explain where the UV rays are coming from, but also why they aren't blinding us. Because it's being filtered, just like a blacklight at a nightclub.*

You're not far off, my invisible informant told me.

As we walked, the ramp curved down towards the basements. The Vortex was above me now, and I could see was the stiff, well-preserved body of Little Saint George, still floating face down, with his eyes shut and his mouth open into a scream, swishing around the revolting cocktail of shining sludge like a lonely ice cube. The effect of the blacklight shining through it now was at once amazing and horrifying.

As we went further down into what must have been the second underground level, I could see a glowing circle that was now in the center of the semi-triangular Vortex. It had three concentric rings of glowing green fluid—a deeper green than how urine looks in blacklight. It resembled the stuff collected from Baron Carrickfergus by the drone. Two of the rings were spinning clockwise, and the one in the middle was spinning counterclockwise, reminding me of the wheels within wheels featured in Marcel Duchamp's avant-garde film *Anemic Cinema*.

"What are those bright green rings in the center of the Vortex?" I asked Rosenberg.

"The seed of the Sun," he replied. "He gave him an injection so that his sperm would be stained with a fluorescent tincture. We just placed an annular container of ejaculate from Baron Carrickfergus into the middle of the Vortex.

Now I understood why his fresh semen was glowing in the bottle, even though it doesn't normally fluoresce when wet, and never bright green.

"So what's making them spin?" I inquired.

"Nothing,'" he said proudly. "Semen that is sufficiently rich with healthy sperm in large concentration, such as that produced by my own well-fed and well-sexed employees, naturally forms rings that rotate unpredictably in either clockwise or counterclockwise fashion when placed in suspension in an annular container. These findings were published by the Royal Society in October of 2016 in a report about research on the introduction of fresh ejaculate into a microfluidic chip for the purpose of nanotechnology development."

"Oh," I said. I stared ahead, trying to make sense of what he had just said. A few seconds later, I asked for clarification.

"An 'annular container'? I asked. "Like an anus?"

"Anus just means 'ring,' Pamela," Rosenberg replied.

Yeah, I know, I thought to myself. *Like Uranus.*

"Like Uranus," he said, "the Ouroboros, whose hogtied body, bent backwards, forms the circuit of the heavens."

Hogtied, I thought. Like Baron Carrickfergus on the ceiling. Like Director Pindar's headless corpse. Uranus is Ouroboros, the discarded, mutilated corpse of Saturn's father, wrapped around the concentrically-stacked aeons of the planetary Archons, in the midst of which Earth is secreted, and within that, her womb, filled with monsters, hiding inside like the baby hides in the pastry filling of a king cake on Mardi Gras.

But if he's bent backwards wrapped around us, that means when we look up at the sky, we're looking at his ass. The same side God chose to show to Moses when the prophet asked to see his Lord. The only side it's safe to look at, according to God himself.

The Gnostics said that Saturn is the highest sphere of the Archons. But Uranus occupies the realm beyond that. Does that make him the highest god, even though he's emasculated, and in most respects, actually dead?

Rosenberg began running as he pushed me around the curving ramp, below the lobby, into the subterranean corridor leading to the basements. The blacklight and glow-in-the-dark circles of the Vortex blurred into the light of the digital ceiling. Then at that moment, everything, even my perception of time and space, seemed to blur together in my mind.

It was as though we had entered a tunnel of lights. Among the shining streaks that surrounded me, some seemed to be caused by luminous colored balls jetting down from the ceiling, all of various hues and sizes, each bringing a certain warmth, and a certain humming sound. Then it seemed like the lights were behind us, both the streaks and the spheres. Yet we were still running, outpacing them.

"The fixed stars are descending to bathe in the blood of the Archons and the blood of the innocents," said Rosenberg, jerking his thumb back over his shoulder. "It won't be long before the child frees himself from his gestational prison."

"Is this the Baptism of Wisdom?" I asked involuntarily, forced by the voice intruding into my mind. Rosenberg threw his head back and cackled.

"Yes, Miss Auger, this is *their* baptism into 'genital wisdom,' as your translator of Hammer-Purgstall's work rendered it. *Zoogogon sophian* in Greek or, in Arabic, *ma-ta na-sha*. The carnal knowledge of good and evil, of generation into flesh. We are bringing down the lights of heaven with the Rites of *Elicio*. I've given them an offer they can't refuse. Like flies eagerly drowning themselves in honey, they know better, but they can't stop themselves."

Rosenberg slowed his pushing and brought the wheelchair to a quick but gradual halt as he continued lecturing me on his evil plot to exploit the salacious and bloodthirsty proclivities of the gods so as to gain power over them.

He already seduced them into human bodies and murdered them, I thought to myself. *What else can he possibly do to them? And what does all this really mean?* Rosenberg continued.

"These are the unalterable laws of existence in the present order of aeons. Like a horny dog who smells a bitch in heat tied up to railroad tracks, or a cat who's sniffed out a delectable puddle of antifreeze pooled up on a neighbor's driveway, there's no turning back. The fall has begun. Now tell me, my Virgil, where shall we go next?"

As my dizzied outlook came into focus, I realized then that we were actually floating in black empty space, or so it seemed. I couldn't tell what we were standing on, if anything.

"Where are we?" I said. "I thought you were taking me to see Leopold."

"I've taken you as far as I care to," he said. "I brought you here so you could guide me the rest of the way. Now show me how to get there from here."

Oh boy, I thought. *Yet another test. Surely he knows which way to go. He's just trying to keep me on my toes. But I don't have toes anymore.* I decided to consult with my psychic informant.

What do I do now? I asked mentally.

Find the right door and go through it, came the reply, and then nothing else.

Well, I didn't see any doors at all. But I had gotten through two sets of crossroads so far by choosing the door in the middle. So I decided to look a bit harder for a door directly in front of me.

I tried to clear my mind. I tried to look with spiritual eyes the same way I had heard the voice of the informant with nonphysical ears. I tried to see with the same eye that had seen the shine on the picture of the bull liver at Oriental Club. This was the same eye that had seen the red glimmer at the end of the bull's intestines on the floor of the *mithraeum.*

As I pictured this last image, the eye that had spied it opened up again, and I now saw before me, off in the distance, a ruby-red diamond, brilliant-cut just like the one from the London Stone. It was giving off a pulsating red light as it rotated in mid-air. I knew that the red light was broadcasting a message to me, although I could not pick it up.

Either I'm not equipped to, I thought, *or I'm not close enough.*

I desired to be closer to that light, to pick up its signal. In that instant, Rosenberg and I began to float towards it. As it grew closer, it stopped rotating. Now it was situated at the top of an archway of gray stones. The portal within the arch was black, and I could see nothing beyond it. But we were headed straight towards it. Then suddenly we stopped right in front of it.

"Show me your hands please," said a voice overhead. "Please identify yourself."

It was a feminized but artificial voice. The message was either coming from a robot, or it was being translated by one. And it was coming through that diamond keystone in front of me above my head. I was picking up its signal. I put my palms out in front of me and looked over my shoulder. Rosenberg had vanished. I was on my own in front of the archway in empty darkness.

What should I say? I asked my informant mentally. *Should I give my real name?*

Identify yourself by your title, the informant replied.

Cryphius? I asked silently.

'And Caducifer,' the informant answered.

OK then, I thought. I announced myself, speaking directly to the keystone.

"Cryphius and Caducifer am I."

"Then where is your heralding stick?" the keystone asked.

I looked down at myself. I had nothing with me but a wheelchair, a hospital gown, and the set of keys I had stolen from Dennis. I examined each key carefully. I didn't see anything that qualified either one of them, even symbolically, as a "heralding stick." This term was, of course, a reference, to the "caduceus," derived from the Greek word *kerukeion*, meaning "herald's staff."

I've never really understood how snakes wrapped around a stick represents a messenger, I thought to myself.

I knew that many analysts thought it represented the human spine entwined with nerves, which was reasonable. I thought about putting forth my backbone as a reply. Then once again an answer came forth through my lips without my conscious awareness.

"I did not come here as a herald, but of mine own accord, seeking the light of the keystone," I said.

Then why did you have me say before that I came bearing a caduceus? I asked my informant.

The caduceus is within, the informant replied.

Within my skin suit. Yeah, I know, I said. I rolled my eyes.

Now I will tell you this: the rape and murder I had witnessed, the maiming and dismemberment of my body, along with the deprivation of sleep, food, and water that I had endured much of the time on a diet of mostly morphine—all these things had taken quite a toll on my mind and physical well-being. But the constant dangling of cryptic clues by virtually all of the villains involved in this adventure, including my mysterious psychic intruder acting as mystagogue—this was what threatened to drive me over the edge into insanity. I'd rather the layers of the universe crash down into the Abyss than to have to solve, learn about, or even think about another esoteric riddle, which at that moment I could have done without for the rest of my life. Or if given the option of ending that life there rather than doing so ever again, I would have gladly chosen the former. So I said:

> "You know, I think I left my heralding stick inside last time
> I was in there heralding"

—hoping that a deadly laser beam would shoot out of the talking crystal and sever me in twain right there where I sat half-naked with my bloody stumps sticking out of my wheelchair. Whether this deadly guardian of the portal should cut me with her fiery sword of vengeance sideways or down the middle, it mattered not to me.

But instead, by the sweet grace of Providence, that didn't happen. Rather, an eye, fierce with wisdom, opened up on the keystone, and a white light shot out of its pupil. It then split off into seven rainbow-colored rays, two of which (on either end) I caught with the pupils of the eyes that had just opened up in the palms of each of my hands, still displayed next to my head with the thumbs pointed at my ears in the pose of surrender, as required.

The key turned. I don't know what it was, or where the lock was. But the door must have opened. Because the next thing I knew, I was inside. But so too was Rosenberg. Posing as the caregiver of me, the sad cripple, he had wormed his way in right behind me.

Or shall I say beneath me? For I looked down and there was his face, directly below in the chamber that I was being lowered into on a plank attached to two ropes. Who was holding the ropes? I couldn't tell. I craned my neck up to look at them just in time to see an iron plate placed over the opening I had come through. The ropes had just been secured to something above.

But I was not yet on the floor of the chamber. Instead I was floating above yet another hole, leading down into endless darkness. Noxious, suphurous fumes arose from the hole directly into my nostrils, heightening my opiate-induced nausea.

However, that hole was in the floor of a room. I now regarded this room with curiosity. I looked for Rosenberg, but he scurried off into a corner behind me. Scurried? Yes, that's what it looked like, peripherally: like a scary tarantula scurrying off. But I thought that it was probably just the shadow of a spider cast on the wall by the light of one of the several torches that were set into holders along the periphery near the ceiling. I saw no other people, but all four of the corners of the chamber were dark, so I couldn't be sure. I decided to call for Rosenberg.

"Mr. Rosenberg? Are you here?"

"No Pamela," said a voice from behind me. It was a familiar one, yet unlike any other I had heard with my ears before. It was coming from the corner behind me where Rosenberg had scurried.

"No, Rosenberg isssss not in h-h-h-here. H-h-h-h-he's afraid to come in here. I am not your jailer. I am your friend. And I am also in prison. I h-h-h-h-have been h-h-h-here for countless aeonsssssss. Or at least, they are countlessssss to you."

"I saw your face," I said, though I knew I was wrong. "When I first came down. I saw Rosenberg."

"You feel h-h-h-h-his presenccccce because h-h-h-h-he's watching. And when you saw my face, it was s s-s-s-so s s-s-s- s-hocking that your mind immediately pasted over it with the last one you h-h-h-had s-s-s-s-seen."

The voice was so odd. It was like speaking to someone with a tracheostomy. It was atonal, gritty, and gasping, with the sound of air being sucked through a hole that was being plugged up every few seconds.

"So let me see your real face," I said.

"Are you s-s-s-s-sure?" the voice gasped ominously.

A wave of renewed fear washed over me. Suddenly I was filled with apprehension.

"Yeah, sure," I said, clearly unsure.

Still, I had agreed. The proverbial foot was in the door.

I heard a rustling sound, like the sound I remember from my childhood of the animals getting up to greet me when I first walked into the barn at the crack of dawn.

My eyes now widened with terror as I saw two feet step out of the shadows towards me, trailing bits of straw in their wake. They moved in a disjointed manner, scraping the stone floor underneath as they went. They were white with circular cuts made around each of the ankles. But I saw that they were both curved on the right, like human left feet normally are, which I found quite unnerving. Furthermore, the one on my right looked like that of an adult male, with black hair on the big toe. The one on my left had the appearance a woman's foot, but was unusually large—a description that could have applied to the feet I had once possessed, just a day and a half previous.

But then the creature rotated its body a quarter-turn towards me, and another foot emerged on the other side, behind which I detected yet another. All four, jutting out from the sides of this creature's body, bore the ankle cuts, and I saw that they were all attached to legs that were clearly not their original partners. Yet it was what these legs were attached to that was most unthinkable. It was no wonder that my mind had pasted over it with a picture of Rosenberg when my abused and bewildered eyes first beheld this visage.

What I was looking at wasn't exactly a trinacria, like the painting we had seen at Oz Pizza. But of course there were similarities. The head in the center had the pallor, leathery lips and sunken eye socket of one having been preserved after lying dead for a day—not that of a young boy happy to be of service as a table leg.

I say "eye socket" in the singular to refer to the casing around the left eye, which was preserved. The left eye socket was covered with a black eye patch.

Like a pirate, I thought, as I stared down in horror at the monstrosity. *Or the pirate mascot, the Jolly Roger.*

But it was also reminiscent of the Egyptian symbol of the Eye of Horus, pierced in mythic battle by his brother Seth. A long red line ending in a spiral, with the curvature and proportions of a Fibonacci spiral, but looking something like a shepherd's crook, was trailing out of the corner of the eye, having been carved into the flesh.

As the creature, clearly artificial though organic, shambled the rest of its body out towards me, I saw the fullness of what the head and legs (actually five in total) were attached to.

The main body was topped by a bulbous balloon of flesh stretched out to the point of partial translucency, like a frog that's been inflated by a sadistic little boy with a straw inserted into its rectum. Another living creature could be seen inside, red in appearance when viewed through the veil of pink skin. On top, I saw what I at first took to be a blowhole. But then when the creature took a step closer, I determined that it wasn't really an opening — not anymore. It was the former entry-point for a feeding tube: a navel.

What I was looking at was a white human torso, small, adolescent, yet female and pregnant, with the belly pointed upward, so that it looked a bit like the abdomen of a blood-swollen tick. But there were two lumps in the belly, one slightly smaller, so that it also resembled a two-humped camel. Attached to this, with barely any neck, was the head of a middle-aged white man with brown hair, pointed forward. On the bottom were the five legs — yes, five actually — each connected to five feet taken from other bodies.

You see, there were two legs on the left, and two on the right. But now I could see that there was another one in the back that acted as a sort of kickstand, allowing the monster to kneel down backwards with its butt pointing downward. When the creature turned itself around again in the process of walking up to face me, I saw its pudenda and anus from the back, both enlarged and making a schlopping sound as it walked. The anus, of course, was also enlarged, through abuse.

This is Philippine's womb, I thought. *And the head must be that of Pindar, skullfucked through the left eye.*

Then there was the matter of the feet. I wasn't sure who the others belonged to, but I certainly recognized the ones on the right as mine.

Oh Yes! I thought as my mind finally made the connection. *My feet! Maybe if I get out of here alive somehow, I can have them reattached somehow!*

"Do you h-h-h-h-h-have the keyssssstone?" the creature's voice hissed.

"Have it?" I said. "No. I think I saw it in the doorway though."

"Which doorway?" it asked.

"The arch made with twelve stone bricks and a red diamond keystone on top," I answered.

"The Arch Keeeria," the hellish voice responded. "The Outer Doorway. That'sssss it."

I recognized this term. It was something I hadn't thought of in many years. But almost fifteen years earlier, I had published a book about a French secret society called the Priory of Sion. "Arch Kyria" was the name of their inner order, which they also called the "Arch of the 13 Rose-Croix." Nobody has ever determined the significance of the term. "Kyria" might be connected to "Kyrie," a Greek word meaning "Lord." But this doesn't seem to elucidate the meaning much.

"Did it s-s-s-s-s-speak to you?" the thing asked.

"Yes," I said. "It asked me some questions. It told me to put my hands up and identify myself."

"Good," it responded. "That means that it's closssssse."

"What do you want with it?" I asked.

"I want to be relieved of my burden," it said. "I want to get out from under thisssss weight without everything collapssssing on top of me. The keyssssstone's job is to take my placccce, so that I may asssscend oncccce again to my rightful abode."

"And where are you now?" I asked. I said "you" because I had decided I didn't really believe that this creature and I were actually occupying the same physical room at the same time.

"In Tartarusssss," it replied. "In the c-c-c-c-center of everything, bearing the weight of it all."

"So is that what you want Rosenberg for?" I said. "Are you trying to get him to take your place? Have you been grooming him for that with your psychic manipulations? And me?"

I was pretty sure I was looking at the thing that had been talking to me psychically for the previous two days. Or at least, I felt that the possessing intelligence was the same, and that the head in particular had been used as its vessel or touchpoint this whole time. The addition of the other body parts was clearly more recent.

"We are all playing our role," the creature said. "Now you do yoursssss, Caducccccifer."

It turned its hideous backside towards me and schluffed off back into its straw bed in the corner.

"When do you give birth?" I asked.

"Eassssster morning," came the reply.

"You mean today?" I said. "Now?"

"Almosssst," it answered. Then I heard the lid of the chamber behind me open. I felt the ropes being tugged on from above, and just as suddenly as I had entered, I found myself on the outside of that room. Or rather, on the outside of *some* room. I'm still not sure if it was really the same one.

Chapter 24: Opera of the Phantom

There's a void outside of
Existence, which if entered into,
Englobes itself and becomes a womb; such was Albion's couch.

— William Blake, *Jerusalem*

So in the blink of an eye, I was back in my wheelchair, at the very bottom of the spiral ramp running through the main building of Rosenberg Plaza, at least one floor underground. Rosenberg was behind me again. The digital ceiling light was on here. We were in front of a room marked with the number "27" and a placard that said "Recycling." Beneath this was the typical triquetra recycling symbol, but with a pink happy face emoji in the center. The deliberate resemblance to the Trinacria was obvious.

"What's this?" I asked.

"What I call 'the Kitchen.' It's the room where we operate 'the Hellbroth Gradalis.' It's the heart of the Plaza's alembic system, and the place where we make things into other things. Of course, it's connected to the universal system."

He took Dennis' keyset out of my hands and selected a key marked "27," which he then inserted into the door. He opened it, and we descended down a simple, straight cement ramp painted baby blue, into a hallway. It was lit brightly, not by the digital ceiling, but by regular white fluorescent tube lights, like you would find in any normal commercial property. The air was humid and hot. The smell of sulphuric acid reminded me of visiting the hot geysers at Yellowstone Park.

We reached a bend in the ramp and took a right, then another immediately, to go down a second cement ramp. It was open on the left side, except for an iron railing, and you could see a room below. The walls of the room were made of brick and painted white. A series of large metal containers wrapped around three of the room's four walls (the space against the fourth wall being taken up mostly by the ramp).

Coming from no scientific background, several of these containers looked to me like large water heaters, or the big tanks I'd seen at breweries. They were all connected to each other, and to the walls and ceilings, with pipes. There was either smoke or steam coming out some of them through other pipes, some of which were open, and some of which were connected to the other vessels. I realized that this was the source of the sulphuric acid smell.

As we continued down the ramp, I thought I also recognized the odor of pork being boiled. But then I figured out that everything I was smelling was coming from assorted human body parts and fluids being put through various processes of putrefaction, rendering, and distillation. I became certain of this when I saw, just to the left of where the ramp ended, the door to a large meat freezer. Through the window on the door, one could see the bodies and severed parts of people, mostly children, hanging from the ceiling on meat hooks.

At the bottom of the ramp, on the wall to my right, there was a series of framed pages from medieval illuminated manuscripts. One showed a woman standing over an anvil with a baby laying on it, her anvil raised high, ready to strike. Around the anvil were scattered human body parts. Next to her was a flaming forge made out of brown bricks with some of these body parts sticking halfway out of the fire, and a broom on the mantle for sweeping up ashes. It was obviously a symbolic portrayal of renewal of life through death, being used here as a shorthand depiction of what was literally going on in that very room.

The other framed pages showed: a man hammering out a statue — seemingly — of a naked woman; a real naked woman lying on the ground being eviscerated with a knife by a man while another holds her down, in front of several men that look like priests or potentates of some sort; a small enclosed rose garden, from which a river issued forth, and forked off into two streams; an old bearded man lying on a bed, being castrated with a sickle by a younger bearded man; and, a crowned woman falling onto a sword that pierced her chest, in a manner identical to the way in which Marcia Martina had died.

I recognized the statue -chiseling image as belonging to a bizarre medieval allegory called *The Romance of the Rose*, which I had never read or looked at much. I had learned about that one image only by reading about the influences for Jean Cocteau's 1930 film *Blood of a Poet*, in which an artist makes a statue of a woman that comes to life, just like in the Greek myth of Pygmalion and Galatea. I have since determined that all of the pictures on that wall were from the same book. These were the only things mounted on the walls, except for a few signs listing safety rules and procedures.

It was only when I got past the wall hangings and turned around that I got a good view of all of the stuff in the room. The sizes and shapes of the metal tanks varied, as did the metals that they were constructed from. I am pretty sure that I can identify these metals. The largest one, placed against the wall to the left of the freezer door, was encased in a dull- gray lead. The next-largest, to the left of the previous one, against the wall opposite the ramp, was a tin cylinder almost as tall as the ceiling.

To the left of this was a large, square iron forge encased in red bricks that had been put together to look like a little castle. This then piped smoke into a large copper retort to the left of it, against the next wall, opposite the lead-covered tank. The retort was also connected on the other side, via another pipe that ran diagonally from the corner, to two ball- shaped chambers—one silver and one gold. These were connected by clear glass tubes to the large green glass vessel that dominated the room, soon to be described in detail. In addition to these items, an emergency eyewash and shower station was situated in the corner between the lead and tin tanks, beneath the pipe that ran along the wall connecting the two. It was a yellow box with a window, slightly larger than a phone booth. Then between the tin and copper vessels, again beneath the connecting pipe on the wall, were three aluminum shelves, which were right in front of my face as I turned off the ramp into the room. These were mounted to the wall from waist-height to shoulder-height. There were dozens of small glass vases and bottles on these shelves, filled with various fluids. Some had pastes or powders within them. Beneath this was the door of a small refrigerator with one shelf. On the bottom, a human hand and forearm was visible. On the shelf were Tupperware-type boxes. One was labeled "Peepee-roni," and the other, "Sliced Peepee-roni."

Milling about these appliances were a couple dozen people, performing a number of tasks with scientific equipment mounted on metal rolling trays (among which I identified a centrifuge for spinning test tubes, and two electrolysis machines). I recognized many of the people from either the post-ritual gathering at the Plaza the previous night, or from Rosenberg's speech at the *mithraeum* opening the day before. At the center of the room was another dissection table, with dismembered human body parts on it and, of all things, a sewing machine.

Seated at this table, on a metal stool with a red leather seat, was none other than Consivia, wearing clean white clerical vestments, similar to what she had worn the night before, but without the cork hat. She was using the sewing machine to do something to the lumps of flesh in front of her. At first I could only see her back and the sewing machine. I couldn't see the body parts clearly.

"What's going on here?" I said.

"Nature at her Forge," said Rosenberg.

"Seems artificial to me," I said.

"Nature is an artificer," he replied. "And now we know her recipe."

Whatever Consivia was doing, she was wrapping it up — literally, in a black cloth — and handing it to a man in a white jacket by the time I got close enough to see the table in front of her. But by then, my focus had turned to object near the wall that was now furthest away from me, which appeared to be the main vessel within the whole system. It was made of clear glass, vase-shaped, with a long neck on top that reached to the ceiling, which sealed it on top, and a big bulbous bowl at the bottom. It was full of clear liquid up to the base of the neck.

On the right and left sides, hookah-like tubes with nozzles on them were hanging down a couple of feet lower than the bottom of the vessel, which was itself about four feet off the ground. I knew that this was the "Gradalis" that Rosenberg had mentioned, a Latin word for a dish that was used to serve multi-coursed meals in medieval times (also called a *satura*, interestingly). Many etymologists thought that this word might be related to the genesis of the term "Grail" (as in "Holy Grail"). The tubes reminded me of ancient Mesopotamian depictions of the Tree of Life, which depict gods collecting nectar from the "tree" through similar hoses.

Another interesting aspect of the Gradalis was how it was being held upright. Instead of having a stand to rest on, it was balanced on the shoulders of what appeared to be two hoodwinked men, who were chained to the floor. They each knelt on one bent knee in a half-genuflecting position, with the heavy apparatus perched on their shoulders, kept aloft with their hands.

Though their heads were entirely covered with black cloth sacks equipped with no eyeholes, I recognized the expensive black business suits they were both wearing, without ties, which were visible from the shoulders down. It was Paris and Chesterfield, the latter identifiable as the one with pale skin and a truncated middle finger. They were swaying a bit under the burden, but for the most part it was held remarkably still. The lack of tilt to the apparatus was indicated by a most unusual plumb bob dangling down to the middle of the vessel, inside the fluid, from a golden chain attached to the ceiling at the top of the vessel.

Attached to this chain from its top with a black suction cup, and situated in the center of the vessel, in a strata of yellow liquid, was the diamond-like gem uncovered from the London Stone by a bolt of lightning the night before. But now it had undergone a remarkable transformation. In addition to being greatly magnified in appearance (which I assumed was an optical illusion caused by the shape of the glass and the liquids inside), there were now eyes inside of each of the Within each of the kite-shaped facets on the crown were there were eyes, blazing red with a green glint of intelligence. I could only fully see two from my perspective at first, but I saw the periphery of two others, and I knew there were eight of those beveled facets on the crown, so I (correctly) surmised that this would be the total number of eyes now open on top of the diamond.

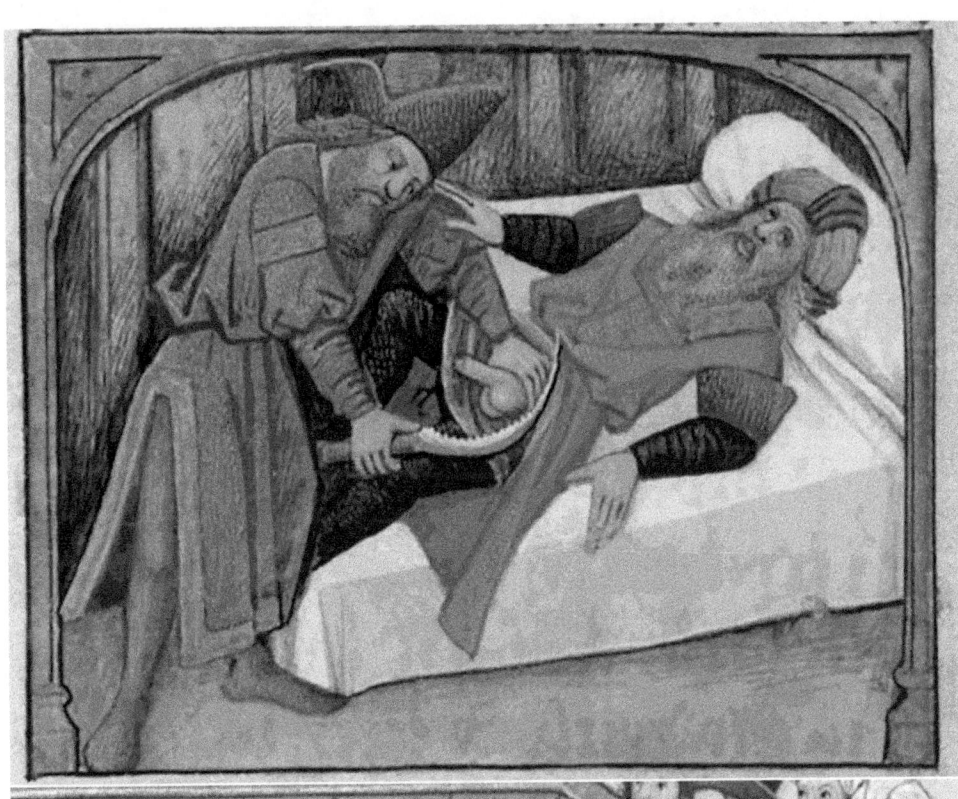

One for each of the seven planetary archons, I thought. *Plus one extra. Uranus? Mete?*

Whatever spirit or spirits these eyes belonged to, the two in front of me were staring directly into my own eyes. This filled me with panic. I attempted to contact my informant for guidance.

What is this? I asked mentally.

My replacement, came the reply.

"This is where the rivers of Paradise meet," said Rosenberg, as if I had asked him. "All of the waters of life flow here. It's where we transform them into a higher state and then make our deposits into the universal bank."

Just then, Rosenberg reached into his coat pocket and put on a pair of tinted glasses. Then a small octagonal window opened up on the ceiling above us. It encompassed the Gradalis, and an area of several feet around it. You could now see all the way up to the lobby, and the Vortex above it. But after looking up once, I looked away, because the opening was bringing in what looked like blacklight from the Moon, seemingly stronger—hotter—than before—and I could feel that it was damaging to look at it directly. However, it was impossible to avoid the glare of it, reflecting off the glass vase and refracting through the diamond. I squinted. I could feel a headache coming on. Rosenberg tapped me on the shoulder. When I looked over, I saw that he was offering me a pair of the same type of tinted glasses. I took them and put them on. They stopped the pain right away.

So how is the moonlight coming through so intensely?" I asked Rosenberg. "Surely it can't penetrate the colored fluids in the Vortex that easily."

"Total Internal Reflection," he responded. "We actually use some of the streams of fluid that we've piped in to bend the light directly into here. We've not only got light from the sunroof coming in, but also from several other light portals arranged around the building. And in a few minutes, the UV light of the Moon will be replaced by the green rays of Hyperuranion.

Total Internal Reflection, I thought to myself. *The basis of modern fiber optics, a way of making light bend to follow a stream of liquid. And the long - treasured secret to the alchemical technique of star-bathing.*

"Star-bathing," which I had written about in the past, was a means of channeling the light of the heavenly bodies into liquids, which alchemists claimed to be a key element necessary to effect certain chemical transformations. Mysterious illustrations for cryptic alchemy manuals often show the essences of the seven classical planets, including a sun and a moon, being drained into a vessel, which *another* sun and moon then bathe in. This is what Rosenberg had been referring to when he spoke of the "Bath of the Stars," an alchemical term which, I have theorized in the past, might be related to Baphomet's name, if interpreted to mean "Baptism of Wisdom."

"So this is where you offer the fruits of your sacrifices?" I said. "To your partners on the other side?"

"Yes," he said. "And everything that's happened on the grounds of this plaza for the last 729 days has been part of a pact negotiated long ago. Much of the detail was worked out ahead of time regarding the victims and how their various essences would be processed. But there were elements left for me to figure out with the help of others, and parts left to chance, as per the demands of the party of the second part."

"And what exactly is being negotiated?" I asked.

"Dining club privileges," he said. "Our ethereal partners are always welcome and encouraged to dine upon anything offered here whenever they like. Fresh essences can be absorbed directly from the body at the time of expulsion. But we also keep the system here ever-flowing with the sacred fluids which our partners like so much to suck. Specified amounts are piped directly to the upper and lower worlds at regular intervals according to pre-existing agreements."

"You mean piped to the planetary Archons?" I asked.

"They among others," he replied. "And this is really just a demonstration of my ability to pay. I am proving that what I have claimed is true. I have the bodies and souls of every man, woman and child of the human race at my disposal to negotiate with forever according to my will. That's the most powerful capital you can have in the higher worlds."

"You mean you think you own all the people on Earth and you can offer them as either slaves or food to another species living in another dimension?" I asked, wondering if I really understood him.

I wheeled myself closer to the Gradalis, and followed Rosenberg in circling it counterclockwise. I then found that there was a third man helping to hold up the vessel. From the looks of his light brown leather cap toe Oxford shoes, I knew it was Leopold.

"Oh yes," Rosenberg replied. "I have all the gold I need now, and I hold a controlling interest in the debt of all the world's governments now, though their populations don't know it yet. People have already signed themselves away *in toto* to their governments in every country on Earth. So that makes me their *de facto* owner, and puts me in a position to use them as collateral, or to use them for whatever I want, really. I have all the power in this world now, and so I am going to use it to gain power in the higher worlds."

"But what about now?" I said. "Now that the planetary Archons themselves have been sacrificed...."

"I have offered both them and the Earth people to the one most anxious to see them humiliated." He put his hands behind his back and resumed his strut around the Gradalis.

"There is one further offering to be made, and that's the baby. He has been nurtured on the blood of the Archons. Now he is to be born under the first light of Hyperuranion on this Easter morning."

"Which baby?" I asked.

"The child of Philippine, of course," he said.

I knew that was the answer, but I still didn't understand how the conception and development of this baby was supposed to work. So I was questioning him to try to get him to reveal that information.

"You mean she was pregnant when you guys raped her?" I said.

"No of course not," he said. "We raped her to get her pregnant! And to humiliate her as Luna, the goddess bitch of birth and menstruation. But that goes without saying."

"Then why did you all rape her in the behind?" I said. "And why would there be a baby born today when she died Friday night?"

He laughed victoriously. "Pamela, you know better. You know the Eye of Horus does not obey the same rules of conception and gestation as the typical female womb. Extraordinary results require extraordinary efforts."

"So this baby is going to be magically born from the rectum of a dead girl today," I said, "and then you're going to sacrifice it?"

"Yes," he replied. "As I am deflowering his rose garden and absorbing his celestial power through the opening of his fundament, I shall cause the expiration of he who has waited since the birth of time to be avenged. I will suck up his god- power through my cock like a straw as it leaves his body." Rosenberg's penis became hard as he said this. He massaged it through his pants as he continued.

"This will not only ruin his plans for a return to glory, but will pin him down into a new place of subjugation, while opening a secret door for me into the Supernal Eden of the highest heaven. Then as he's dying I will use his back as a stepping-stone and climb up through the aperture to take my rightful place above."

"So what do you want me for?" I asked.

"You'll see," he said, coming back around the Gradalis to stand next to me on my left. "You'll see entirely too much. The sight of so much reality, cast into a new light, will shock you greatly. But I'll need you to maintain your constitution as you have so far, and tell me what you see when a new hole opens up in the sky and the rays of the sun from beyond are felt. You know what I mean: the light of the Blazing Star, from the portal between the pillars of the Earth and the sky, beyond the Moon and beyond the solar disc. This is the light that the Masons symbolized with their sacred G, just as scientists have named the Gamma ray after it, and used the Greek letter to represent the photon—the ultimate unit of light."

"Don't you want to see it yourself?" I said. I was getting nervous, not wishing to be alone in whatever was about to happen to me.

"No," said Rosenberg. He reached into his pocket again and switched to another pair of tinted glasses with pink lenses. "I have my reasons." He stopped pacing suddenly and stood still facing the Gradalis. Next, he stomped his left foot on the floor, and slid his right foot up against his left heel at a right angle. Then he pulled his red Phrygian cap out of his other pocket and put it on his head.

Most of the men in white coats seemed to leave the room all at once. Consivia came over, wearing a pair of pink glasses as well. She whispered something to him, then turned around to walk up the ramp to the exit. But then she turned around again, leaned over me from behind, and whispered in my ear also. I could feel her hot breath on my neck, and the odor was atrocious, like a restroom at a gas station.

"You're on your own with him for this one," she said, patting my shoulder and causing involuntary spasms of revulsion. "He'll need you to tell him certain things about what to do and say next, based on what you see and hear."

"Wait," I said, not wanting any such responsibility. "Where are you going? You're in charge of the rituals here."

"I'll be directing another rite while you are working here," she said. I have to do Easter Mass at St. Paul's."

The lights went out. Two assistants each switched on hand-held white LED lanterns. These now provided the only illumination apart from the lights on some of the room's machines, and the blacklight coming through the Moon, channeled down to the Gradalis.

"What if I don't see anything?" I asked.

"Oh you'll see," Consivia said. "And you WILL look. You won't have a choice."

Just as she walked away I felt someone approach my wheelchair from behind. Then I felt the barrel of a handgun up against my right shoulder, just like I had experienced before. A large male hand grabbed my head from the top and jerked it backwards so that I was looking up at the top of the Gradalis near the ceiling. Another hand from outside my field of vision removed my glasses, causing great pain in my head. Then an eye dropper was used to put a drop of something caustic in the corner of each eye. I squinted and squirmed in my chair as it burned.

"Keep your eyes open," the man said. It was Miles. He was wearing pink glasses just like Rosenberg.

This is like A Clockwork Orange, *I thought. But I have already seen so much ultraviolence, and so much ultraviolet light. What's a few Hyperuranian rays?*

But I was just trying to give myself courage. Truly, I was afraid. That the sky would literally open up—including all of the layers of the atmosphere that protect us from the deadly radiation of space. Already ultraviolet light was coming through, and now Rosenberg was speaking ominously of deadly Gamma rays.

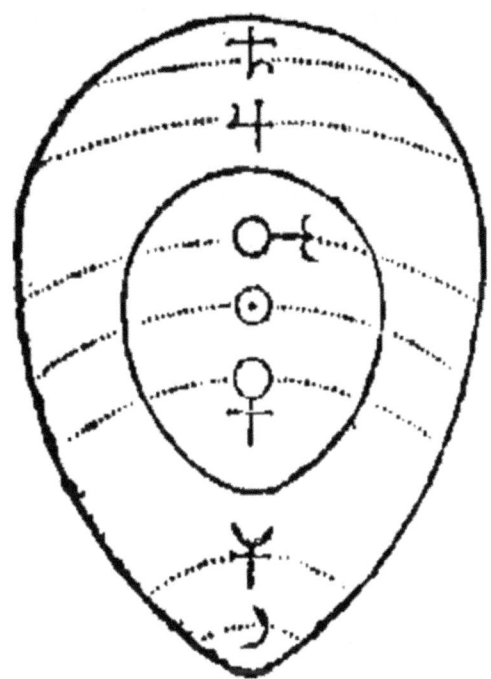

Do these atmospheric layers somehow correspond to the realms of the planetary archons? I wondered. Is that why the light from beyond was thought by the ancients to be light from beyond Uranus, the lord of the sky?

Then I saw something I hadn't noticed before: a recess in the floor directly beneath the Gradalis. I had to back up my chair a little bit and bend sideways in my seat some to get a glimpse of what it was, and it was still hard to make out the detail. But because of the vision—or whatever it was—that I had been given just before coming to "the Kitchen" in room 27, I now understood what horrors crouched beneath.

It was a hole about three feet deep, plated with a metal that looked like copper, and a bed of straw in the middle. In it sat the creature I had seen before, with Pindar's head, Philippine's womb, and my stolen feet, among others. But it seemed like it was in an even in a worse state than it was when it had appeared to me in the vision. Now it was convulsing and sweating profusely, while its one eye was rapidly fluttering uncontrollably. The womb that formed its back was even more swollen than before, and one lump was now greatly larger than the other. When it moved one of its legs, two scorpions, glowing bright green in the blacklight, scuttled out of the straw to the edge of the pit.

The blacklight illuminated the occult sigils that had been drawn all over its head and body, which hadn't been visible in my previous encounter with/vision of it. A glass rod coming down from the bottom of the Gradalis, terminating just a few inches above the navel on the back of the creature, and was entwined with two clear plastic tubes that were inserted directly into the womb. I figured it was for the baby, presumably an IV drip feeding it the contents of the Gradalis. And of course, it resembled a caduceus.

A crush of people were now filing into the room, all in their ceremonial black robes. But instead of the masks as before, they now only wore sunglasses on their faces, like Rosenberg. When they were all standing still, one of the young boys, no doubt a Nymphus in the previous ceremonies, tooted some annunciatory notes on a trumpet. Then I heard everybody gasp.

At that moment, I saw that the diamond was now levitating above the level of the fluids, and rotating. Its color turned from clear to red, and the faint purple glow of the blacklight changed to a bright pink hue. I noticed planetary symbols being projected in green on the sides of the vessel, and then refracting all over the room. They included the familiar signs of the seven classical planets, plus another — the Monad — a symbol discovered by John Dee, which combined the other seven. He representing this combination as an alchemical operation taking place inside of an egg.

Now the very thing that Dee had written about was taking place right before my over-exposed eyes, as revealed by the pink light from beyond (or whatever color it really was, as scientists insist pink light doesn't really exist, but is rather a stand-in color our brains put in to represent certain invisible rays of the spectrum).

With this brighter light I could now see the scene in the hole below much better. But when I looked again, I wished that I hadn't. For what I saw was the creature's anus— Philippine's anus—opening up from within. As it did so, the rectum began to protrude externally, forming the pink fleurette that is referred to as a "rosebud" in extreme anal pornography, now even pinker.

"Here we see the blossom of the Holy Rose Garden of Great Mother Nature," said Rosenberg. "And the Rose Gives Honey to the Bees." He sighed with carnivorous lust.

I had been horrified a year earlier when I had learned that some people were turned on by seeing internal organs collapsing and falling out due to sexual abuse. Now my horror reached another level as I watched a tiny hand protruding from the opening, humanoid but with sharp white claws for fingernails, covered in blood and other slime. It was my first witness of an anal birth. I hope it will ever be my last.

It took less than a minute for the baby to rip itself out with ferocity, shredding the sphincter and utterly disemboweling the body of its mother as it did so. Even more astoundingly was the fact that the baby seemed to be getting larger as it emerged. First one entire arm came through. Then the other arm and head came out together, ripping flesh along the way. Finally, the rest of the body fell down onto the straw below like a piece of dung. All the while, Rosenberg chanted as the Nymphi sang hymns in Latin and the head of Pindar, attached to the monstrosity below, howled in pain.

Already resembling a fifteen-month old in stature and appearance, the precocious newborn immediately stood up and used its teeth, quite sharp, to sever its umbilicus, which appeared to me to be a short flesh tube connected to a much longer plastic one. This was strung through Philippine's womb and connected to the Gradalis above. The child pulled it out through the entry hole in Philippine's pelvis. Then it put the tube to its lips and began sucking fluid out. As it drank, it grew to the size of a three-year-old in just a couple of minutes.

Apparently sated, the child climbed onto the back of the thing it had come from, the back being Philippine's stomach. That creature, despite being eviscerated rectally, willfully crawled over to the side of the enclosure where the child used its body as a step-stool to try to climb out.

But it could only reach up high enough to get its forearms out, and couldn't pull itself up. So the creature, whether motivated by maternal instinct or something else, raised itself up on its hind legs and leaned with its forelegs against the wall, which allowed the child to escape.

I refer to the child as "it" only to be gender-neutral, as it quickly became clear that both sex organs were present. But there were other unique features as well, such as certain markings on the child's skin. These became more apparent after what happened next.

The hermaphrodite toddler ran into the emergency shower, where it managed to jump up and pull the triangular yellow handle that was hanging down from the ceiling inside. A siren went off, the white light came on inside, and water began pouring down on the child. It used its hands to rub the muck off of itself. This revealed its skin, which was dark and covered with what looked like stars. In the UV light, these popped out brilliantly, so that its hide looked like the sky itself.

As all this was happening, one of the robed celebrants, acting on a nod from Rosenberg, slammed the door shut. The child turned around with a look of horror on its face. It banged on the door with its fists and cried. At this, everybody laughed.

The person who shut the door leaned over and turned a red knob that was on the outside of the shower station, next to a blue knob, right where the water was piped in. It seemed he had turned the hot water on, as the window began to fog up. The water was pooling up rapidly, and due to the steam, dripping down from the entire ceiling in addition to the shower head. The child became increasingly frantic. The hot water was undoubtedly scalding it.

"Enjoy the purifying pain of the *Niptron* of the Stars, my son," said Rosenberg, not acknowledging the child's feminine aspect. "This is nothing like the *Niptron* of Empyrean fire that will soon baptize the entire peasant population of this pathetic prison with its flaming wisdom."

He walked up to the shower door and looked directly into the child's eyes through a hole in the fog that its panicked fist-pounding had made. He laughed at the poor thing for another couple of minutes. Then when the water was up to the child's chest, he announced:

"That's enough!"

Two others pulled the child out, who was shivering in shock. Another pushed the dissection table out between the congregants and the Gradalis, with the sewing machine still sitting on one end of it. The body parts that Consivia had been sewing together were gone already.

The other two assistants dragged the child over and placed it on the dissection table face down. Then they held it in place as Rosenberg stepped up behind it. The person who had brought the table over now held out for him a can of Lyle's Golden Syrup and a black umbrella.

Rosenberg dropped his pants and slathered up his penis while the other two forced the child onto his knees with his rump positioned at the end. I turned my head away and shut my eyes, not wanting to see yet another child raped—and this was to be the youngest one yet. But Miles pushed my head back to face the scene.

"Open your eyes," he said. "Or I'll kill you."

I opened them, but purposely kept them out of focus so that I would not see the horrors in front of me very well. Yet I could still hear the horrible sound of the child screaming, and it seemed to me that the rape had already begun. As much as I tried not to see, I peripherally observed that Rosenberg was attempting to open the rectum with his finger and a glob of syrup.

At that moment, there was a rumble in the building, like an earthquake. The diamond now flipped itself over and ascended to the very top of the Gradalis, to the octagonal window in the ceiling, where it fit perfectly like a puzzle piece. Then the Hyperuranian rays came through. I don't think the others saw it, because they didn't react. But I saw the diamond, after having been temporarily red, now light up brighter than before, putting out a rainbow of colors all over the place. The fluid in the Gradalis took on the appearance of a pousse-café, stratified into different colors.

Now when I say "different colors," I mean it was a rainbow of colors that I had never seen before. They were sparkling all around me as the diamond rotated, putting out dizzying flashes that threatened to induce a seizure in me. But then the diamond turned green in color, and switched its rotation. The light I saw also became green in appearance. The diamond was acting as a deck prism on board a ship, amplifying the light from above the chamber. I could tell that it was filtering this light—light from normally invisible spectrums—into a form that I could see, although presumably, these rays were still quite dangerous, as the glasses worn by the others would indicate. Furthermore, what the new light allowed me to see in the rest of the room was absolutely horrible.

The ghastly creatures I now spied filled every single inch of space around me. There were things everywhere, things that resembled in several aspects living beings. It's hard to say what they looked like because each one was different. Also, you couldn't tell where one ended and the others began.

The only individual items I could distinguish in the room were the things I had already seen before the green light entered. Everything else was a mass of greyish-green-colored slimy flesh, consisting of hundreds of beings with black beady eyes and long proboscis-mouths. These mouths were all busy sucking on things, mostly on the bodies of the people in the room. A large number of mouths were also sucking from the hoses hanging from the Gradalis.

There were insect-like legs on some of these creatures, and tentacles on others. These became enmeshed with those of the other beings as they moved around the room, hungrily chasing emissions from living bodies wherever they might be found. These emissions could be seen by me now as diversely-hued jets of light streaming out of particular points on people's bodies.

I noticed a large cluster of mouths around the stumps of my legs, with little black reptilian tongues slithering in and out, licking at the blood that had seeped through the bandages. But more—many more—were surrounding the victim on the table, screaming and struggling as the preliminaries of its rape continued. Those closest slurped eagerly. Many others crushed to get close. What was happening on that table clearly put out an energy that they were desperate to drink. I shuddered in revulsion.

They're not just in this room, said my telepathic informant, now crouching before me in the dying body of the Frankenstein creature in the pit beneath the Gradalis. *These are the Amaleks. They're everywhere, all the time. You can only see them now because of the Hyperuranian light.*

Then I noticed a mess of these monsters crowded around the rear end of the creature in the pit. Some were eating the blood from the its wounds, and the afterbirth on the ground. But most were eagerly licking and sucking at something else: its vagina. Something was coming out. It took a moment for me to realize that there was yet another small humanoid hand emerging from it, this one coal-black skin, but with white claws like the first child.

The green light had been there for at least a full minute before Rosenberg noticed that I was looking at things that he and the others, because of their glasses, couldn't see.

"What do you see?" He asked.

Don't tell him the truth! the informant said in my head.

What should I say? I asked.

Nonsense, the mental voice replied. *Distract him. Sing a song. Keep him from hearing the other baby's cries. This child is our last chance to prevent the collapse of the Pillars of Heaven.*

"What do you see?!" Rosenberg insisted angrily.

I tried to close my eyes to clear my mind and think of something. But Miles slapped me and told me to open them again. So I couldn't shut out the image of all these parasites sucking off of everybody, and I just *could not* think of anything to say. No mental voices came along to rescue me, and I began to wonder if my informant was dead, since I had felt him to be inhabiting the head of Pindar that was sewn onto the creature at the bottom of the pit, and that creature seemed to be dying as the second twin ripped its way out.

Pindar's head was grimacing in pain, but remained silent, presumably choking back the moans so as to keep Rosenberg ignorant of what was happening. The baby's head, however, had begun to emerge, and I knew it was possible that it would begin to scream immediately. I sensed that if Rosenberg knew about the other baby, he would kill it, and that would be the end, somehow, of an opportunity for Earth to escape its apparent impending doom.

I wasn't sure how it was going to happen, as my informant had been vague. But I realized that somehow Rosenberg's imminent sodomization of the child of the planetary Archons that had been born from Philippine's anus would cause the layers of the universe, already unstable from the sacrifice of most of those Archons, to collapse.

They could perhaps be regenerated somehow by the child, I thought. *But not if the sodomic rite is allowed to continue.*

I realized that as Rosenberg penetrated the target, he was opening a portal to the Hyperuranian realm, the source of the green light I was seeing. I knew that if he managed to totally destroy the child's fundament with his penis, that would somehow undermine the foundations of our world. Then the Pillars would collapse and the sky would come down on us.

Meanwhile, he would have "sucked up," in his own words, all of the child's "god-power," and somehow used it to escape through the portal to a higher realm outside of our own doomed universe. There, he believed, he would be able to use the "contracts" that he had spoken of, giving him the right, as he claimed, to all human souls as his property, purchased by his gold. He thought that this could be used to establish himself in a powerful position in the outer realm, as the lord of everything below, even though it would, at that point, presumably, be nothing but a ruin.

But there could be alchemical purposes afoot, I thought. *Perhaps he is transmuting our entire universe into something else, using it for something we can't even imagine.*

These were the ideas that came to me as I sat staring at Rosenberg, with him staring at me in disbelief over my insolence, repeating the demand that I tell him what I was seeing. I forgot to lie. But at least I only told part of the truth.

"The green rays of Hyperuranion," I said. I added nothing more. He laughed and turned back around to his task. "Hold him open!" he instructed his assistants. They both frowned at this, but reluctantly obeyed, using their hands to spread the victim's buttocks for him, which the grayish-green creatures, invisible to everyone else, licked at ferociously.

"Well that light's about to get a lot brighter. Just tell me what you see."

With that, he grabbed his penis again with one hand, the child's thigh with the other, and lurched his pelvis forward towards the rear end. Then one of his assistants deployed the umbrella and held it up over his head, presumably to protect himself from the Hyperuranian rays.

If he doesn't want to see that light, why does he want to go to the place where it's coming from? I wondered.

Sing you idiot! shouted the voice in my head, suddenly returning. *Don't let him go through with it! Distract him!*

"Return through the rectum is easy!" shouted Rosenberg, pointing his finger at the screaming child on the table, just an inch away from achieving his goal of penile penetration. "The Distinguished Charity of Mete uproots the enemy! I am *Saturnus Stercutus* and you are my *Stercus*. I shall plow you and then burn the fallow fields with the *Niptron* of fire!"

The words "*Niptron* of fire" reminded me of something. Something stupid. This happens to me all the time. Even in the worst situations, something I hear another person say will remind me of a song with lyrics that sound similar. It can be any type of song—even a TV theme song or an advertisement jingle. Regardless of how catchy the tune is, or whether or not I like the song in question, it will immediately get stuck in my head, often in altered form. My mind will automatically create a new version with parodied lyrics to fit similar- sounding words I've just heard.

Well, this is what happened to me at that moment, and it filled my head with the lyrics to a once-popular song. It was not my favorite by any means, and not all that singable for me, really. But "*Niptron* of fire" made me think of that song by the Pointer Sisters from the *Beverly Hills Cop* soundtrack. And so, without a second to lose, I sang out loudly, swaying back and forth in my wheelchair like a brain-damaged moron.

"I'm just burning doing the *Niptron* Dance!"

The distraction worked. Rosenberg stopped what he was doing and turned around to face me.

"What did you say?" he asked, confused and annoyed. Just then, I heard the newborn twin cry out from the pit. I sang more to cover it.

"I'm just burning doing the *Niptron* Dance! I'm just burning doing the *Niptron* Dance! Hooty-Hoot! Hooty-Hoot!"

"What's wrong with you?" Rosenberg said angrily. Then, his look changing to serious and curious, he asked "Are you hearing a radio station in your head?"

But I didn't answer, I just continued singing. As I did so, I saw that Miles had followed my gaze, and now saw the baby coming out, still crying. But instead of alerting Rosenberg, he looked me in the eye for a good second, then began to sing along.

"I'm just burning doing the *Niptron* Dance! Hoo hoo!" As we both sang this together, another light entered the room from above. Everything became brighter. I could still see the Amaleks all around, but they were not as distinct anymore. I looked at the Gradalis. The diamond was clear again, and refracting a normal rainbow spectrum of colors, quite beautifully, all over the room.

Real sunlight! I thought. *Sunrise on Easter. Halleluiah!*

But Rosenberg didn't notice this either, so distracted was he by our terrible singing.

"Miles, why are you doing this? Rosenberg screamed. He pounded his fists on the table like a pouting child. "Stop it! I'm losing my erection!"

While he had been throwing his fit, the twin child had fully emerged, cut its own cord and was already drinking its fill from the Gradalis. It too had grown to the size of a three-year old. And while it resembled its brother/sister with its dual sex organs, the coloring of its body was much different.

It was piebald, with one leg and foot black, the other set white. The same was true of the hands and arms, but the white and black colors were on opposite sides compared to the legs. The torso, divided into quadrants, was similarly chequered, as was the head. The white segments were marked with black sun-shapes, and the black segments covered in white crescents. All this was quite visible because there was clearly a bright morning sun shining above us now, and also because, while covered in afterbirth, this twin wasn't nearly as mucky as its sibling had been.

Now, as Rosenberg approached me and Miles in fury, with the umbrella-holder following him uncertainly, the twin came crawling out of the pit behind him. But Rosenberg didn't notice because he was focused on getting us to shut up. He took the gun from Miles, which it seemed to me that Miles allowed rather easily, and then pointed it at us, repeating his demand for us to be quiet.

"The light is frying your brains! Stay cool! I need to keep focused on my task," he yelled.

As he said this, the twin ran behind the Gradalis and disappeared in the shadows of the room's machinery. Rosenberg turned back around to return to his rectal raping ritual, placing the gun next to the sewing machine. But then we were joined in our singing by the three men that were holding up the Gradalis: Paris, Chesterfield and Leopold.

"I'm just burnin' doin' the *Niptron* Dance!" they all sang, completely out of sync.

"What the fuck!" screamed Rosenberg. "Nymphi, sing the *Nosiéle eiryk*! These folks want to hear some music, it seems!"

The young boys in the room immediately began singing, in Greek this time, but backwards. I'm pretty sure it was the Greek Orthodox version of *Kyrie eléison* in reverse, the undoing of the traditional Christian prayer for mercy. The tune was backwards too, probably an inversion of Franz Schubert's Mass No. 2, composed for this prayer. Meanwhile, Rosenberg chanted the Sator Square once again.

SATOR!
AREPO!
TENET!
OPERA!
ROTAS!

SATOR!
AREPO!
TENET!
OPERA!
ROTAS!

SATOR!
AREPO!
TENET!

OPERA!
ROTAS!

Rosenberg's member dangled perilously close to its desired entry-point once again, and with it, seemingly, the fate of our world was hanging in the balance. At that second, which might well have been our last as far as I knew, the dumbest thought ever came to me, spawned by Rosenberg's chanting.

The only thing that can save us now is a deus ex machina, I thought.

A *deus ex machina*—a "ghost from the machine"—is, of course, a term for when dramatic stories have the crisis solved at the end by the sudden appearance of some new element, such as a supernatural being who saves the day. As per example, the flying chariot sent by her grandfather Helios to rescue the witch Medea at the end of the play by Euripides that's named after her. The "machine" in the phrase is said to have originally been a reference to a crane that was used in ancient Greek drama to lower the gods in these scenes—or rather, the actors playing them—onto the stage.

However, this is a little-known detail. Most people who use the phrase assume that the "machine" is the story itself, and I think the meaning has evolved to include that. It occurred to me that the phrase "phantom of the opera" could be reinterpreted to mean the same thing essentially, as *opera* is Latin for "work," and is considered synonymous with *machina*. *Phantasma*, meanwhile, is a synonym of *idolon*, another Latin word for "ghost." In terms of Rosenberg's present working, both terms could refer to his ongoing series of rituals, and the rousing of a spirit that would then determine the final outcome of the ceremonies.

As I pondered this, the phantom of the operation made itself known. The piebald twin hermaphrodite now sneaked up behind Rosenberg, who was applying more Lyle's to its sibling's rectum, and stealthily removed a large pair of surgical scissors lying next to the sewing machine on the table. Then it opened them up, and spoke.

"Oh Paternoster!" it said, vibrating the air in the room with a voice of many waters. Everyone else in the room, most of whom had noticed the child moments earlier but reacted very slowly, began to back away from the dissection table in fear.

"Ah?" said Rosenberg, spinning around.

He still hadn't achieved penile penetration of his target, and in fact the child still seemed relatively intact in that regard, judging by what I saw peripherally from my vantage point. Nor would Rosenberg get another chance to deflower it. The instant he turned around, the child's brother/sister removed Rosenberg's manhood expertly, as if it had done so a thousand times before, at the birth of a thousand different aeons.

It took a second for him to realize what had happened. He was still holding his penis when he noticed that it was no longer attached to him. At first he just dropped his jaw silently, with his eyes wide with horror. Then he dropped the umbrella on the dissection table, where it got caught up against the sewing machine. Finally, he dropped to his knees as he screamed in pain, and his attacker buried the scissors in -between his shoulder blades—a fatal blow. The instant he let go of the child on the table, the green light from above, and the horrible bloodsucking creatures it revealed, vanished from my vision.

Then, as if to be thorough, as if to ensure that this penis of terror could never again be used as a weapon against another child, the piebald hermaphrodite caught the genitals in its hand before they hit the ground. It bit off both testicles, swallowed them, and threw the penis into the pit where both twins had been born. Next, it grabbed its sibling around the waist and began helping it down from the dissection table. I saw Rosenberg's body stop moving. He was gone.

At this moment, the three men holding the Gradalis all acted at once on a pre-arranged signal.

"Go!" I heard Leopold shout.

All three of them began attempting to stand up, which was quite a struggle. The weight of the fluid-filled vessel must have been enormous, plus there was counter-pressure coming from its attachment to the ceiling. Then there was another complication, which I hadn't seen before because of the hoods draped over their heads. But when those hoods got lifted up a bit as they were struggling, I saw that all three of them actually had their necks attached to the Gradalis itself.

Their brainstems were being leeched? I thought.

Then Leopold gave another signal. "Three, two, one!" he said.

They rose up sharply in unison, heaving and sighing, with the Gradalis still on their necks, until the glass cylinder at the top connecting it to the Vortex above the ceiling cracked and shattered. A flood of fluids immediately began raining down like from the sluicegates of Heaven in the days of Noe.

"Go now!" Leopold shouted. All three men each reached up with one hand to detach themselves from the neck valves as they simultaneously pushed the Gradalis backwards with the other. By "backwards" I mean that two of them pushed it off of themselves, and, necessarily, in Leopold's direction, as he also pushed it forward.

The Gradalis tipped over and landed on top of Leopold, shattering and spilling its load around. Most of the contents fell down into the pit where the creature with Pindar's head, Philippine's torso, and my feet (among those of others) stood eviscerated and presumably dead. Leopold too now lay face-down and motionless on the concrete floor, so I assumed he was deceased as well. The twins had run off somewhere and were no longer visible.

Chesterfield and Paris lurched forward, free now, but with clear fluid now dribbling out of their necks. They both took their hoods off quickly and pressed them against the backs of their necks to stop the leaking. Then they each fell forward onto their hands and knees in the full-genuflect position. Whether by pre-agreed design or instinct I know not, but the two of them both began praying.

"Kyrie, eléison, Kyrie, eléison, Kyrie, eléison..." Chesterfield chanted.

That was the *real* Christian prayer for mercy, and in Greek, too, which was uncommon but not unheard of in his native Anglican church, and, I've always thought, much more authentic than the English-translated versions. Paris, next to him, muttered a Mohammedan equivalent in Arabic.

"Bismillah, ar-Rahman, ar-Rahim...."

Rosenberg was kneeling next to them too. But he wasn't praying. He was crying, screaming, and bleeding to death.

While this was happening, the other congregants were quickly filing out of the room via the exit ramp. But when the one at the front of the line opened the door, an ocean of blood and other human sewage greeted them, flooding into the room. It washed the people on the ramp back down into the room and began filling the floor, making its way towards the pit with the Frankenstein creature in it that had my feet.

My feet! I thought again with a pang of longing.

I wheeled myself closer to the pit and leaned over in my chair to get a better view. The pit was half-full of fluids and broken glass now, but the chimera creature was still standing on its legs of various origins. I couldn't see any breathing, though, and the head was flopped forward in defeat.

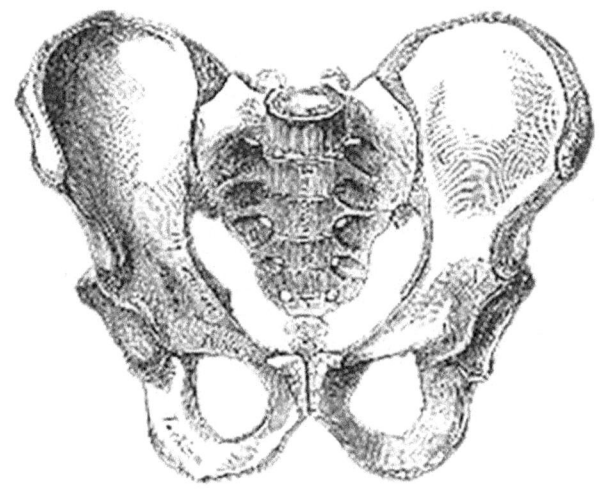

I saw that the diamond had landed point-down directly in Philippine's excoriated pelvis, where it was slowly sinking into the flesh, which seemed to collapse and partially liquefy under its weight, capturing it like quicksand. Next to this, Rosenberg's severed penis had landed, halfway on top of the creature's backside, where the vagina and anus had both been ripped open so badly as to form one large hole. That hole now began to collapse inside, swallowing the penis, tip first.

The entire torso dissolved into a fleshy, bloody pink mass resembling Playdough. Then it coagulated around the diamond, forming a thin membrane over it. This made me think of the similarity of shape between the side profile of the diamond, this sacred "keystone," and the human sacrum bone at the center of the pelvis. It occurred to me that this bone actually *does* act as a keystone for the pelvis and, in a way, for the entire human body, positioned in the center, dispersing the weight of the upper half evenly through the lower half.

In fact, if you bent over onto your hands to form an arch with your body, I thought, *either forwards, like Nuit, the Egyptian goddess of the night sky, or backwards, like Uranus, the Ouroboros (and Pindar's body, and Baron Carrickfergus) — the placement of the sacrum bone would be precisely in the keystone position.*

As I was watching the creature's bodily transformation in front of me, I noted that the sacrum bone, when detached from the other bones, including the coccyx below, also closely resembles the keystone referred to in the Masonic Royal Arch degree — the one that was used as the official seal for Pennsylvania, "the Keystone State." Then I remembered some of the things written in a 1922 book by Masonic writer Manly P. Hall entitled *The Initiates of the Flame*, in which he states outright that the sacrum bone and the Royal Arch keystone are one and the same. He further asserted that "the head of the Sphinx" could be seen in "the inverted sacrum bone when it is turned upward," and also in "the inverted Masonic keystone." Then he elaborated even more:

> It is said that in ancient times the Sphinx was the gateway of the pyramid, and that there was an underground passage which led from the Sphinx to Cheops. This would make the symbolism even more perfect, for the gateway to the spirit is through the bodies according to the ancients.

These passages were accompanied by an illustration of the sacrum bone inside the Masonic keystone.

According to Egyptologist E. Wallis Budge, as I recalled, the sacrum bone was the root of the sacred *djed* pillar, the "spine of Osiris" which was thought to hold the different levels of existence apart. He also said:

> …There can be little doubt that the *djed* is a conventional representation of a part of the backbone of Osiris, namely the sacrum bone, which on account of its proximity to the sperm bag, was regarded as the most important member of his body….

Then I remembered that the ancient Mayans referred to the sacrum bone as a "portal to the underworld" (that being "the Place of the Seven Gods"). They compared going through it to going into the mouth of a serpent. Presumably this is because of the serpentine shape of tunnels of the intestines, considered analogous to the infernal caverns by many cultures, including the Greeks and the Hindus. In fact, going back to ancient Babylon, the spiral emblem found throughout the world has been used to represent these tunnels. This association is one of the reasons that intestines were so commonly used for divination—as maps, indicating the path that lies ahead.

I mused about the fact that alchemists have cryptically described their "red stone" (a product of the alchemical process) as being a "bezoar," a word for a clump of undigested food that has been caught inside a living creature's intestines. They called this stone the "red sun," and the "lesser stone," as compared to the ultimate alchemical product, the Philosopher's Stone, which was believed to be manufactured within, or otherwise utilizing, the brain human rather. According to the oldest Egyptian alchemists, I remembered, the red stone was formed in the human bowels the same way they thought of gold as being created within the bowels of the Earth.

This is the same thing as the stone that Rhea gave to Chronos to trick him, I thought as the understanding rushed down upon me. *And it's also how he was poisoned, through the anus, blocking his intestines and causing fecal vomiting.*

Recalling this brought me back in my mind to the Mayan beliefs regarding the sacrum bone, which they sometimes call a "second skull," or even "the inverted skull," because it sort of looks like one when you separate it from the rest of the skeleton. Then I thought about the Templar symbol of the skull and crossbones, and the fact that it basically shows a head in-between two thighs. I wondered if it might be connected to their alleged rite of induction involving the *Osculum Inflame* ("Obscene Kiss"). The same ritual was allegedly practiced by witches at sabbats, involving a kiss on the Devil's "second mouth" underneath his tail.

This brought to mind an articulated read somewhere stating that some Jews believed that this is where a deceased person's soul is stored, hibernating until the Resurrection at the End of Days. At that point, supposedly, all human bodies will regenerate from their sacrum bones, if they're lucky enough for that part of their bodies to still be intact, and then everyone will be presented for Final Judgment.

As I contemplated these things, I saw the pelvis of the creature, pregnant now with the diamond, fall downward as the recently and artificially-formed sinews connecting the tissue to the various legs began to melt. It slid slowly to the floor while the legs remained standing. The head fell off and into the surrounding goop.

The waterline in the pit started to rapidly rise as the flood of fluids from above flowed down the ramp and across the floor to join the pool below. But when it rose up high enough that the fluids reached the top of my feet, I saw them come alive. They began to twitch, and then to stomp.

"Come to me!" I shouted to them.

And they obeyed. They jumped up high, freeing themselves completely. Then, one at a time, they leap- frogged off the top of what was left of the monster's main body, which was now re-congealing around its remaining legs. They sailed through the air directly into my lap, slimy and bloody.

Like the flying feet of Mercury, I thought to myself.

As disgusting as they were, they were a part of me, and I was happy to see them. They seemed to feel the same way. I had to hold the feet down as they continued to hop around my lap in excitement for our reunion.

Then I heard something slopping around in the pile of coagulating flesh and blood at the bottom of the pit. I leaned over again for a look. I immediately regretted it.

Fresh sinews had just formed between the remaining three legs and the torso, which was now a triangle. Tentacles of bloody, rubbery meat reached out from the stumps to merge with it. Pindar's head fell backwards and dissolved into the mess. But his facial features, with his mouth curled in agony, now appeared within the triangle.

Within less than a minute, I was looking at a real, living trinacria, with a reddish-pink triangle in the center. The freakish creature was surrounded with the presently knee- deep and ever-growing puddle of sludge that was still pouring into it down the ramp from the floors above us. The eye caught my gaze as the grimace turned into a delighted smile that sent a shuddering chill through me.

Thank you, the voice of my informant said to me in my head. *Now Albion can rise again. Now I can come home to Jerusalem on the Thames.*

But then the face twisted in pain again, and its body convulsed once more, just as it had during the birth of each twin. Well as it turned out, it was not just a set of twins. They were triplets. A third sibling now began to emerge from the place where Pindar's head had been attached to the body.

It was covered in a pink membrane sac, but through it I could see two dark hooves. By the time half of it was out, I could tell that the "membrane sac" around it was actually a human stomach and attached esophagus, the latter with the front hooves stuck through it. The outline of a tiny horse head could be seen at the top of the stomach, twitching side to side.

But at this point, the birth seemed to stall. The baby horse was stuck. The face in the triangle howled. Its voice sounded so ... ancient, and loud. It reverberated through the whole room, perhaps the whole building, perhaps the whole world. I heard a rumbling sound all around us, along with a trembling sensation coming through the floors and walls.

Then in the corner of my eye I saw something stirring from behind the pit, amid the broken glass of the Gradalis. It was Leopold. He was getting up.

I couldn't tell how badly he was hurt because he was covered in filth. But he was able to get up onto his feet, take off his hood, press it against his leaking neck, then walk over to the pit and slide down into it, all without looking up at me. Next, he went over to where the little foal, about the size of a small cat, was still struggling to be born.

He grabbed its front legs and yanked it straight out, then caught the whole thing with both hands before it fell down. He walked up to the edge of the pit, sloshing through the sludge, and lifted the foal up over the side. He placed it down on the floor in front of me, still inside the stomach, where it continued to twitch. After letting go, he fell backwards onto his butt and sat silently in the pool of sewage.

Then the twins came out from hiding. They had been inside the emergency shower, and had apparently used it just now without me noticing, the noise drowned out by all the rest. The piebald one was now clean, and the blue one had washed the syrup off itself.

They were both quite beautiful. I was happy to see them looking relatively well. Silently, in my own mind, I uttered a prayer, to what god I could not say, asking that they should be allowed to somehow survive this ordeal. I knew the future of existence itself somehow depended on it.

Both children, who from birth had always known innately what they needed to do, now gathered around the membrane-covered foal and, using their claws, ripped open the stomach, freeing it. The horse, which looked like it was probably white, but was covered in goo, continued to twitch on the floor for a minute or so, while the piebald twin grabbed the tub of "Peepee-roni" from the refrigerator.

Then the toddler toddled back over to the foal and knelt down next to its head. The child took the cover off of the tub, revealing, as I had suspected, small preserved human penises. The foal smelled the meat and then sat up eagerly. The child fed it one, then another, with the child and its sibling helping themselves to a few as well.

The horse began to grow before my eyes, just like the two children had done, and did even more as they too ate the penises. Then the horse began stretching out its wings. Yes, it had wings.

Maybe it needs some water, I thought.

I wheeled myself over to the shelves over the fridge, which was no easy task now that the floor was flooded, and looked for an uncontaminated vessel to put water in. At first there was no luck. Every beaker, jar, and bottle was full of either biohazard material or harsh chemicals. Then I found a large beaker labeled "H20" on the bottom shelf. It was half- full. It was. I could reach it, just barely.

I grabbed it and brought it to the eyewash station, where I filled it up so that I had about a liter of water. I wheeled the beaker over to where the children were feeding the horse, and handed it to the blue one. The child looked up at me and smiled in gratitude. Each of the kids took a long draught. Then they gave the rest to the horse, who drank it greedily.

They were all a bit larger by the end of this. The foal stood up finally, and exercised its wings a bit more. I saw that it was male. Both children led the horse over to the shower, where they washed off the afterbirth. When the foal came out of the booth a minute later, he looked much better. I could see that his fur was definitely white.

The two children now walked the foal over to the dissection table, which they were both able to climb on top of. This enabled them to mount the back of the horse. The piebald one sat in front. The blue one turned around to wave at me and smile, as the piebald one leaned forward and patted the horse's neck. It neighed, whinnied, reared up, and then took off, up the ramp and through the exit door. I knew where it was headed next.

The ramp winds all around the building, I thought. *That will give it plenty of runway to build up speed so it can take off.*

About a minute later, a shockwave shook the room, like the one I had experienced during dinner at New Court, but louder, with a similar waterphone-like sound reverberating through the air. A clear glass container, shaped somewhat like a Kool-Aid pitcher, fell off the shelf towards my lap. I caught it with my hands before it landed. It was filled with a translucent pinkish liquid and labeled *Liquor Amnii + PROTEANS*. At the bottom of the vessel was a dead human fetus, about an inch in length, like a worm in a bottle of tequila. I shuddered at the sight of its beady eyes. Then I heard a thunderous crash from the floor above us.

I looked up. There was the body of Baron Carrickfergus, smashed against the bottom of the Vortex. I couldn't tell if this last blow had been the one to finally extinguish his life. As before, the eyes were still frozen open.

I turned around again, towards the pit, and surveyed the scene around me. Paris and Chesterfield were still praying. Rosenberg was slumped over on his knees, perhaps dead. As for Leopold and the trinacria in the pit, their present status was unknown to me. But then I heard Leopold's voice coming from the pit.

"You should look for the bottle marked *Liquor Amnii + PROTEANS* on the shelf, Pamela."

Yes, he said 'PROTEANS,' I thought to myself. *So it wasn't just a misspelling of 'proteins.'*

You can use it to put your feet back on your legs."

I immediately looked in his direction.

"How?" I asked. "I have it right here."

"Come on over here. I'll help you," he said.

I wheeled over to the pit through the sludge on the floor, past the unconscious body of Rosenberg and the kneeling figures of the two MI5 agents, who remained oblivious to all else but their mantras. As I approached, Leopold stood up from within the pit, so that he was now visible from about the waist up. He had tied his hood around his leaking neck. His fancy suit was covered in revolting filth, the stench of which I barely noticed anymore. He held out both of his mangled hands in a cupped position.

"Give me the feet and unwrap your stumps," he instructed. But I didn't trust him. He was the one who had cut them off in the first place. I just sat there and stared at him severely.

"Look, you're going to need my help. You need to regenerate the broken bone that was removed. No doctor can do that for you."

I looked at the feet in my lap. Then I unwrapped my stumps, which were hurting again, as the morphine had worn off. Also, I had felt the "phantom limb" sensation several times already, but now my ankles were crying out for the feet like a lover separated from her beloved. The wounds were looking gangrenous and infected.

"Hand over the feet, then pour the elixir on when I give you the signal," Leopold said.

Reluctantly, I gave them up. He placed both feet onto the stumps. I could feel the flesh on the end of my ankles eagerly embracing the contact with the estranged limbs. But he was right. A portion around the break point had been removed. The two ends didn't exactly match up anymore, and even if my body accepted them as-is, I'd now be shorter than I was before. Still, it was better than no feet at all. I waited to see what would happen. Leopold seemed to lift up on one side of his body, like he had just put his foot on top of something. Then he closed his eyes as if straining for something. He gave the signal.

"Pour!" he shouted.

I poured the "elixir" liberally on the ends of each piece. As soon as I had done so, I felt an electric current run from Leopold's body through the feet and into my legs. It riveted him in place, but did not seem to be harming him. He just looked directly into my eyes intensely for the next few seconds without moving.

Immediately I felt the feet beginning to adhere to my ankles. I witnessed the miracle of new flesh forming, just as it had when the creature that had borrowed my feet reformed itself into a trinacria. As it coagulated, the meat gelled into a spongey substance before solidifying. During these few seconds of plasticity, Leopold slowly and expertly pulled my feet down an inch, so that the missing segment was reformed, good as new, including, somehow, the bone and marrow within.

"Astounding," I said, involuntarily, with my mouth wide open in amazement.

Within a few moments, the electricity stopped. Leopold let go, and the feet stayed in place, continuing to meld with the leg. A few seconds after that, I found that I could feel them again. The sensation spread from my ankles down to my toes as my nerves came alive once more. I flexed my toes gleefully.

All these little piggies went to market, I thought. *And now they're all home. Wee wee wee!*

And not a moment too soon. Leopold had now climbed out of the pit, which I found threatening. I instinctively jumped on my newly-recovered feet to run away. But when I tried to take a step, they buckled under me. I found myself on my knees between Paris and Chesterfield, positioned the same way they were. I wretched at the smell of the gook that was pooling up around my legs.

Leopold walked over to a panel of switches on the wall and flipped one. Something happened inside the pit. The creature screamed, but his scream trailed off. He was falling down, along with everything else that had been pooling up in the recess. The bottom must have been a trap door. And Leopold had opened it! I heard a splash as everything hit water in the depths below.

The Walbrook, I thought. *He just threw the trinacria into the Walbrook.*

Then the ground beneath us began to quake, and a large crack formed in the floor of the room. I decided that begging God for mercy, whomever he or she might be, was a prudent thing to do at that point. I knelt and bowed my head, but not so far over that I couldn't keep an eye on what was happening.

Kyrie, eléison, Kyrie, eléison, Kyrie, eléison... I droned. As soon as I started, Paris, without looking up, switched from Arabic to Greek, and joined us. The sound of our chanting vibrated strangely through the air, as though we were speaking directly into the whirring blades of a fan. A breeze seemed to be blowing down the ramp from the floors above.

Then there was another rumble, louder than the others. The ceiling and walls were all cracking now. The Vortex and its contents came crashing down through the ceiling to the floor behind us. We were dusted by this, but because we had our heads pointed down, we managed to avoid being hit in the face by shards of glass, and everything seemed to magically bounce off our backs.

The body of Baron Carrickfergus fell down into the pit and hit the underground river below. The fragrant fluids and broken glass spread more broadly, contributing several more inches to the overall flooding of the room. But luckily for us, the fluids were falling into pit and other cracks in the floor now. This meant that it was draining away from our particular position.

Leopold then chose to come over and kneel in the middle of our triangle with us. There he uttered his own prayer.

"Mother Rock, have mercy. Stand firm beneath us, we implore you," he said. "Deliver us from the mire." Strangely, while addressing a pagan goddess, he quoted *Psalm 69*:14. Then he went on, mumbling in what sounded like … Gaelic? Elvish? I'm not sure.

Now "mother rock" is another way of saying "mother lode," and simply refers to the main vein among any collection of underground ore deposits. But I am pretty sure he was praying to the Magna Mater, the Rock Cybele. Yet I suppose it could be taken either way, considering what was subsequently revealed beneath the ground on which we were kneeling.

Then all at once, there was a sharp jolt from below, and the ground all around us collapsed. Everything was gone except for a small circle, about eight feet in circumference, around where we happened to be kneeling. But I didn't have time to appreciate the miracle of being so chosen for preservation, because the ceiling came down on top of us.

Yet here again, most of it seemed to somehow just fall away from us, into the immeasurable abyss surrounding us. Not all of it, however. The last thing I remember before I lost consciousness, just before a piece of masonry hit me in the head, was seeing three large yellow circles directly above me in the light blue morning sky, arranged in triangular formation. In an instant they coalesced into one yellow orb, which immediately started bleeding and fell out of the sky. This left a circle in the sky where it had been, appearing as an indigo field studded with white stars, which then immediately opened like a window, revealing a huge eye that stared back at me. It blinked, and I blacked out.

Chapter 25: Albion's Aeon

> The light of this star surpassed that of all the others; its brilliance was ineffable and its novelty was such that all those who looked at it were struck with astonishment.
>
> The sun, moon and the stars formed a choir round this star.
>
> –St. Ignatius, *Epistle to the Ephesians*

Okayness is not only a concept that is relative to the situation, but one which, quite often, when invoked, teeters dangerously on the verge of being meaningless, threatening to render impotent the dramatic import of anything which preceded it. Therefore, when Leopold Black/Thomas Weir, having pulled a stone away from the rubble that buried me, asked, with a disfigured hand extended, if I was "OK," I did not have an immediate response.

I opened my eyes, but as they began to adjust to the light and to focus on Leopold's face, I remembered once again how he had tricked me getting involved in this nightmare. I tried to move my feet to push off whatever was weighing on them, cutting off the circulation. Then I recalled that the man standing over me had actually sawed them off the previous night. So I decided just to close my eyes again, thinking that my feet were still gone.

It wasn't until I heard Paris and Chesterfield's voices amidst a cacophony of sirens and car alarms also that I opened my eyes again. Then it came back to me: how my feet had been restored, and how the small piece of land we stood on had somehow been spared from what seemed at the time like both the collapse of the earth and the collapse of the sky. Paris lifted a piece of the digital ceiling, with its hexagonal light grid, up off of my ankles. My feet were really there! What's more, I could move them! It was painful and the muscles were stiff, but they did respond to my mental commands. I sat up.

Then I heard the piece of ceiling that Paris had just thrown over his shoulder hit bottom, after an extended delay and with a splash.

A splash? I thought. *Why? And how far down did it fall?* At first my eyes focused on the three men directly before me, who were all staring back at me with concern. They all looked worse for the wear, dirty and badly beaten, but surprisingly unfazed considering the circumstances, especially the wounds I recalled them having on their necks, underneath the hoods that were still tied around their necks as tourniquets.

But then my eyes adjusted to take in the surrounding landscape. A few feet behind the men that stood in front of me, the earth dropped off into an abyss, all the way around. With help from Chesterfield, I stood up to get the full panoramic view. I tried to get closer to the edge of our island of safety, but the others insisted I "shouldn't look straight down right now," because it was scary. They also said it would be dangerous, since it was still quite difficult for me to stand without using Chesterfield as a crutch. So I looked around us, which was shocking enough.

We were surrounded by a vast chasm in the ground, which, from the sound of it, was at least partially filled with water now and quickly becoming fuller. The entire site had vanished—the whole of Bucklersbury, and everything around it, from Queen Street to Lothbury to Gracechurch, all the way down to the banks of the Thames, in a perfect circle. Rosenberg Plaza, the Walbrook Building, St. Stephen's, New Court, the Bank of England, the Bullion Association, Mansion House… they were all gone.

I turned to the south and saw the river unobstructed in front of me, with a waterfall pouring down from it into the depths beneath. There it joined up with the Walbrook, which was now open to the light of the Sun once again and rapidly forging a brand new mouth for itself. The collapse of the earth below had caused three bridges to fall there also: Southwark Bridge, the Cannon Street Rail Bridge, and London Bridge.

But of course you know about the sinkhole in London that formed suddenly on Easter morning 2018, creating a precisely round hole in the earth a half-mile in circumference right next to the Thames—except for the estimated nine-by- nine plot of land that we four stood upon. You surely know, then, that this anomalous spindle of soil disintegrated, while we watched from above in awe, as soon as the rescue helicopter lifted the last of us up off of its surface. I wondered, of course, if it was our prayers that prevented us from being subsumed by "the mire," *a la Psalm 69*:14, as referenced earlier by Leopold:

Deliver me out of the mire, and let me not sink….

Therefore, I gave thanks accordingly, silently, with *Psalm 40*:

> *He brought me up also out of an horrible pit, out of the miry clay....*

If you already knew about the sinkhole, then you undoubtedly know about the Herculean efforts that were made to rescue all the other casualties of this catastrophe. As I write this, they are still working to dam up the river, pump the water out of the hole, and fill it in with concrete. It's the largest construction project in London since the building of Rosenberg Plaza, which now, ironically, must take a step down in history to become the second-largest.

The Prime Minister, enthusiastically embracing the Broken Window Fallacy, has praised and taken credit for the economic stimulation this has caused. But the real stimulus has come, of course, from the unique new element that was discovered within the depths of the chasm, and from the worldwide sovereign debt jubilee that was negotiated, beginning the following Wednesday, during talks between G20 heads of state, the International Monetary Fund, and the Bank of International Settlements.

Experts in Karst Topography and water table science told the news reporters that this was a disaster waiting to happen. The land was already inherently unstable because of the network of underground rivers, which, they said, after lying dormant for over a century, had been partially-re-activated in recent years by state-sponsored environmental scientists as part of the London Rivers Action Plan, which Rosenberg had bragged to us about at dinner on Friday night. Thus the underground development that had taken place in the intervening centuries since these rivers were last active— everything from miles of subway and service tunnels to multi-level basements in massive buildings—contributed to the weakening of the foundation beneath many of the structures.

So it didn't help that Rosenberg, in collusion with some friends in the Corporation of London governing the City, decided to re-channel the underground waters on the sly, without permission, restoring the Walbrook to full capacity years ahead of schedule. Water had since been pooling up in caves that had been formed by the underground river over thousands of years. All it took was a seismic jolt to get the process going, though nobody's sure what caused that.

England is far away from the world's major fault lines. But the motion of the tectonic plates elsewhere can still cause regional compression that affects the island. There hadn't been another earthquake with its epicenter in London since 1750, and the one in 2018 was unrelated to tectonic movement.

However, many earthquakes have affected London throughout its history. Supposedly one in the fifth century leveled the Temple of Apollo that is rumored to have once sat beneath the present location of Westminster Abbey. Other earthquakes with their epicenters elsewhere have been felt especially in that place many times, often accompanied by strange lights seen near the cathedral. One such earthquake, which took place on April 6, 1580 during "Easter week," originated in the Dover Straights and inspired the following poem by James Yates:

> Oh sudden motion, and shaking of the earth,
> No blustering blastes, the weather calme and milde:
> Good Lord the sudden rarenesse of the thing
> A sudden feare did bring, to man and childe,
> They verely thought, as well in field as Towne,
> The earth should sinke, and the houses all fall downe.
> Well let vs print this present in our heartes,
> And call to God, for neuer neede we more:
> Crauing of him mercy for our misdeedes,
> Our sinfull liues from heart for to deplore,
> For let vs thinke this token doth portend,
> If scourge nere hand, if we do still offend.

Another earthquake, which originated in Canterbury on May 21, 1382, was associated in the popular mind with a synod called by the Archbishop of Canterbury that took in the Blackfriars area of the City of London. The purpose was to condemn the heretic John Wyclyffe for his doctrine on transubstantiation. Wyclyffe eventually died of a stroke, still amid controversy, but he was later excommunicated in 1415. His bones were eventually exhumed by Pope Martin V in 1428 to remove them from consecrated ground, then burnt to ashes and dumped into the River Swift.

With the London earthquake and "aftershocks" of 2018, it is thought by some that a chemical reaction took place right underneath the *mithraeum*, where the Rosenberg Plaza alembic system connected with the Walbrook. I believe this is accurate. This was the real reason why the London stretch of the Thames, all of London's underground rivers, and much of the local tap water "turned to blood" for a time. It wasn't because the red Moon had fallen into the river, although this is obviously connected on the mythopoeic level, one of the many meaningful coincidences that occur along with a supernatural event of this magnitude. Tests confirmed that the red stuff in the water really was largely blood, along with other human biofluids one would expect to find when sewage leaks into the water supply. But they also found many rare chemicals not normally found in traceable amounts.

Officials admitted to the public that Rosenberg restored the Walbrook to obtain the volume of water he needed for the "bizarre" and "illegal" scientific experiments taking place in the basement of Rosenberg Plaza. They claim that he was attempting to create "red mercury," a solid form of the element rumored to exist, and to be used in the creation of nuclear bombs, but which is quite possibly just fictional. However, several "real" (set up by intelligence agents) terrorist plots have been "foiled" that involved attempts by the criminals to purchase what they believed would be red mercury.

There are stories circulating which allege that red mercury can be used to create gold, to locate buried treasure (like a magic peepstone), or to invoke "jinn" (an Arabic word for demons). One popular urban legend states that Singer sewing machines contain red mercury, which the news media claims is the reason that Rosenberg's company purchased thousands of those machines over the previous year. But I think that the real "red Mercury," the real "red stone" of the alchemists, was made in that ritual when the "Superman diamond" became transmuted with the invisible pink light from the heavens. The "emerald stone" of the alchemists was then formed when it was hit with the Hyperuranian light. This green diamond was the real "kryptonite" that created the explosion.

Officials have never identified or even acknowledged the 736 victims of the two-year-long orgy of death that had taken place there. To this day I still don't know if they were mostly kidnap victims, adopted for the purpose, or given over as sacrifices by their parents (and raised in secret). But it seems to me that the answer could be any of these, or a combination of all three.

Of course, these are just some of the many details that I don't know. These are only known to the people who were involved in orchestrating the rituals. Of those people, the ones that I can identify have all either disappeared or died. I haven't seen any of them since that day. Leopold got on board the helicopter with us when it came to our rescue an hour later. But there were paramedics on board, not police. Nobody handcuffed or tied him down. When we got to the St. Bartholomew's Hospital, which was overwhelmed with victims of the sinkholes, he disappeared.

But, you'll be relieved to know, Chesterfield's cat Lenore was there at the hospital waiting for him. She had been left at the office of Nahid Paris, Parvin's sister, who ran the IT department from the basement of the hospital. I actually got to meet this woman, because I was sent down to her office to fetch the cat while the two agents engaged in a top-secret debriefing with their boss Miss Equitone.

I had assumed she would be a Muslim, like her brother seemed to be. So I was surprised to find a sign on Nahid's bulletin board showing a diamond shape, like the Superman logo, with crossed lines on it forming seven facets on the crown (just like the one on the QAPHQA sign). Inside of these facets were six eyes, with the one in the center filled with text from the Bible. It was *Zechariah* 3:9, describing a stone with not six, but *seven* eyes:

> For behold the stone that I have laid before Joshua; upon one stone shall be seven eyes: behold, I will engrave the graving thereof, saith the Lord of hosts, and I will remove the iniquity of that land in one day.

I assume the cosmic purpose for the poster being there was for me to see it, at the moment which I did, so that I would be reminded yet again how perfectly every little bit of reality has been arranged for us.

Lenore scratched Chesterfield as soon as she saw him, which was probably the worst injury he endured through this entire ordeal, strangely enough. There was no trace of the neck incisions, and no sign of spinal fluid loss, on either Chesterfield or Paris by the time doctors examined them. My ankles seemed as good as new. You could not tell, even on an x-ray, that they had ever been cut, or that the bones had been broken. These are among the many mysteries from this episode which remains unsolved.

There is still one mystery in particular that I often ponder, though: If Rosenberg had managed to escape to the hyperuranian realm, as he had planned, what would have happened to the rest of us? On the one hand, it seemed like we were in danger of existential collapse. At the same time, he seemed to speak of enslaving us, using us all as a source of sustenance for those on the other side, and as collateral for making deals with them.

Would that have been possible if the realm above had crashed down on us, after the mysterious "Pillars of Heaven" fell? You might think we'd all be dead, and our universe snuffed out. In one sense, yes, certainly. But now I realize that everything beneath our feet is a foundation provided by the past, keeping us from sinking into the depths of chaos.

Our ancestors from forgotten aeons provide a valuable service, holding us up on their shoulders, bearing the burden of the present. If the pillars fell, then we would become the new foundation for the future, holding up the new aeon on our backs, like slaves. Then just like the Titans before us, some of us would be fated to serve in the role of Atlas as the pillars of the new heaven. It might even be that most of those who populated the new realm wouldn't even realize that we were doing this for them, because they would think of us as dead, or even worse, as simply mythical. Maybe that has already happened to us, and neither we, nor those exploiting us from above, are aware of it.

A good parallel is the story of Atlantis, which is at once described by myth-tellers as a fallen "city," and also as a representation of an entire fallen aeon. Its name derives from that of its fabled foundational king, a guy named Atlas, said to be a son of Poseidon. Now, he just happens to have the same name as the Titan from the Golden Age who was enslaved by Zeus after the Olympian revolution, thereafter burdened with the obligation to eternally uphold the sky. This is a clue that the fallen aeon symbolized by Atlantis had its own Pillars of Heaven, represented in Plato's tale by the two pillars of the Temple of Poseidon said to be in the city's center.

When Atlantis fell, these pillars collapsed (and who knows if one caused the other, or if there was another cause common to both events). Everything was submerged into the waters of Chaos, becoming mire, which eventually solidified and was used as the foundation for the aeon that came afterwards. In my mind, the story really represents the fall of the Golden Age, when the Titans were imprisoned beneath the Earth, and made to serve as the foundation of the realm above them.

It's quite possible that Rosenberg himself is the only person who knew fully what he was up to. His minions didn't, and the self-appointed geniuses of esoteric statecraft—the Worshipful Society of Butchers—certainly didn't. Perhaps Consivia knew. Maybe she killed herself in front of her congregation during Easter Mass because the truth was too horrible, knowing that all of those murders and rapes were for nothing. I imagine that, after being kidnapped, castrated, and then raped repeatedly throughout her youth, she had to cling desperately to Rosenberg's vision of escape from the Earthly prison, and conquering the realm of the godhead above, in order to live with what she'd been through. It certainly wasn't depression from Gender Identity Disorder, as the press office of her parish claimed, that made her disembowel herself with an ancient ceremonial *harpe* just after raising the Eucharist host up to the light of the three suns shining through the crucifix on the stained glass window behind the altar.

While we were in the helicopter, just before he disappeared again, I asked Leopold if he had known Consivia before, since he had called himself the "Baron of Alphamstone," while she had been living and working there for years. He didn't really answer.

"She had an axe to grind against the Butchers and Barber - Surgeons," he replied. "The Stockholm Syndrome didn't prevent her from feeling resentment towards those who had helped the Comprachicos destroy her body." Then he closed his eyes, shook his head, and fell silent for the rest of the ride.

Comprachicos is a Spanish word, coined by Victor Hugo, for gangs that steal and mutilate children, then use them as freak performers or panhandlers, emphasizing their (deliberately-created) disabilities to elicit donations. I presume Leopold used this term to refer to those who had arranged for the boy to be kidnapped from Piccadilly Circus and castrated in 1956, turning him into the sad, frightened girl we saw in the Easter dress in the second half of *Easter Sunday April Fool*—the poor waif who grew up to be the Bishop of London.

I had a revelation regarding Consivia when I entered Nahid's office at the hospital. She was wearing large red headphones when I came in, which she took off immediately. I heard the song "Dear Prudence" bleeding faintly out of the headphones as they sat on her desk. I remembered that one of the interpretations of the name of the goddess Metis was "prudence" (along with "cunning" and "wisdom.")

This made me think again about my idea that Metis, Rhea and Gaia were all the same figure: a goddess who kept helping her son plot against their father, only to marry the son afterwards and start the process over again in the next generation. Then I thought about how Metis was prophesied to produce an heir that would overthrow Zeus. But the only child they are known to have made together was Athena, while the figure who seems to have actually taken over the role as king of the gods was Jesus, as I mentioned before. The ancient writings claiming that "Apollo" was his first-born son and therefore successor are hinting that the Greeks knew this was coming. The Romans, with their numerous solar cults popular at the decline of the empire, were the ones to usher it in, as I stated previously.

When I got the chance, I researched the word "Opiconsivia." A specific entry had been made for this term in Wikipedia sometime the previous year. It had not been there a few months earlier, when I was trying to help the man I hired to translate *Mysterium Baphometis Revelatum* figure out the meaning of the word *consivia*, which he did not at first know what to make of.

But now there was an entry for this word, where it was said to be the name of a pair of festivals for the goddess Ops (the Roman name for Rhea, the wife of Saturn), held on August 25 and also on December 19, two days after the commencement of Saturnalia. The first Opiconsivia took place right after the August 21 planting festival for Saturn, called "Consualia," which was named after the god's alternate title of "Consus." I noted mentally that August 21 had been the date of the solar eclipse the previous year, and wondered what role that had played in the symbolism of Rosenberg's Mithras cult.

They probably had a very special orgy in the mithraeum that day, I thought.

The name "Ops" means "plenty" and *consivia*, as I stated before, means "to sow." Mythology experts claim that she was first associated with planting and harvesting. This connected her to the earth in the minds of the ancients, and everything that was thought to be under it. This is how she became a symbol of the underworld and mineral wealth also, they say, just like Saturn, whose name is connected to *satur* ("full, rich") and *saturitas* ("abundance, satiety"). Thus, Saturn and Ops have a lot in common with the king and queen of Hell, Pluto (the Roman Hades) and Proserpina (the Roman Persephone). Interestingly, a minor character in the Roman Catholic canon is St. Satur, who I think is quite possibly an iconotropic cover for Saturn, and whose feast day is on March 26.

After learning about Opiconsivia, I understood that I was right about the goddess who had given birth to each new king of the gods in each aeon, and protected him from the wrath of his father.

Is he always the 'sun god,' I wondered, *or is that just the language we use for the concept now, because the Sun is the king of the gods now?*

I still don't know the answer. But meditating upon the meaning of the lyrics to "Dear Prudence" once again, I realized that it's a song about Metis emerging from the body of Zeus for the first time in at least an aeon, possibly two, at the dawning of a new one. It's about the old world order being subsumed by the birth of the next. I believe that's what I witnessed taking place, both in the rituals at Bucklersbury, and in the sky's firmament.

I also thought again about the words in the Sator Square. "Sator," as I stated before, is Saturn, "the sewer," "the begetter," "the father." "Arepo," it occurs to me now, might well stand for "Harpo," another name for Eros, a.k.a. Cupid, the child of Aphrodite. "Tenet, we know, means "to hold." "Rotas," like I said, means "wheels," and has always been combined with "Opera" ("work") when interpreting the formula. So it is commonly rendered "Saturn and Arepo hold and work the wheels," although my

"Eros" interpretation for "Arepo" could render it "the Sewer of Love works the wheels," or some combination of the various conjugations of those words.

But "opera" could also refer specifically to Saturn's partner, Ops, "the planter," and some kind of "work" that she did with him involving these wheels." I think there may be some connection with what William Blake referred to as the "Starry Wheels, Which revolve heavily in the mighty Void above the Furnaces" in his poem *Jerusalem*. This poem was obviously very important to Rosenberg when composing the rituals, for reasons that I will explain shortly. It was quoted repeatedly at the end of the New Court ritual, and I recall being inspired by the voice of Chronos in my head to mention "Starry Wheels" in regards to the carriage ride in the New Court ceremonies. I figure the "wheels" are the invisible controls that move the celestial bodies above us.

I know that not everyone in the world had the same experience of the signs in the heavens that Easter weekend. In fact, the only witnesses to these events appear to be the people who were in the square mile of the City of London at the time. There really weren't very many people in the business district on a holiday weekend. Even among those who *were* there, most of those who have survived claim not to have seen the events in the sky. This was because, for some reason, almost all of them spent an inordinate amount of time sleeping that weekend. They only woke up when the earthquakes and the sinkhole formation jolted them.

The few who were awake and watching the skies in the City of London during this time saw the Moon grow large on Friday night at sunset. If they kept watching, they then saw the six colored balls of light gather around the Moon from various directions, just as I saw out the window of the Sky Box at New Court. Shortly after this, witnesses experienced what seemed like a "shockwave" that went through the air, and "sonic boom" heard at the same time. But no recordings or measurements taken corroborate this.

These people generally report that at first the light balls looked like planets usually do when you catch a rare glimpse of one making itself visible to light-polluted London. But because of the way in which they appeared from out of nowhere, and because of their subsequent inexplicable behavior, they can only be categorized as UFOs. Besides, there was no conjunction of planets scheduled on any ephemeris that night.

Many things were witnessed next that I didn't get to see myself because I was inside the *mithraeum* at the time. Around 8 pm, about a half-hour after sunset, people saw the Moon emit a beam of blueish-white light directly into the Thames for a few seconds. Those who were on the waterfront on the north side of the river from Temple to the Tower of London, as well as those driving along the Blackfriars and London bridges, saw the beam drop down into the water between the Millennium and Southwark bridges.

The beam was wider at its source and got narrower towards the bottom. Some people say it almost looked like the Moon was being projected in the sky from a beam of light on Earth. This of course gave fodder to people who believe that everything in the sky is a holographic projection. They have videos on YouTube claiming that everything that was seen in the sky from London over the weekend was a "glitch in the Matrix."

This is fitting, for after his death, it was revealed that Rosenberg was the leader of secret syndicate of "tech billionaires" who had been the subject of news stories two years earlier, without being named at the time. The articles, published simultaneously by several news outlets, claimed the syndicate's members were convinced that our reality was just a computer simulation run from somewhere else. They were supposedly funding research projects to "find a way out of the Matrix." *The Atlantic's* headline at least properly stated that the businessmen's goal was to "Destroy the Universe." But they didn't mention that the methods would involve alchemy, rape, murder, and black magic, or that only a few members of Earth's population were slated to make it out safely to the other side.

At about 8:30, witnesses report that one of the spheres next to the Moon grew larger. It was the pinkish-white one, which, they say, initially looked like the Evening Star, but wasn't in Venus' proper location. People then describe a glowing stream of something pouring out of it like water into that same spot in the Thames, appearing pink like moonlight. They also saw a small red dot form in the center of the Moon at about 9 o'clock.

The next sphere to enlarge and pour forth its essence into the river, at about 9:15, was the orange-red star, which took on a fiery appearance as it grew. It shot forth what looked like a flame into the Thames. Approximately forty-five minutes after that, the pink orb plunged from the sky all of the sudden, landing at the same spot in the river, leaving ripples in its wake. Following that, the orange-red fireball also fell from the sky, smoking as it came down. Because this took place shortly after the war drama created by the torpedoing of the Russian submarine in the Straight of Dover — for which we still have no explanation — some observers thought it was a missile attack. Others thought it was a meteor. Luckily, tensions did not escalate further, and the incident was smoothed over in the coming days, as you know.

Next, around 11:00, about the time that our hastily - arranged ceremony on the rooftop terrace of New Court began, people saw the whole arrangement of Moon and stars eclipsed by dark clouds, just as we experienced. Then they saw the purple orb peaking through, now enormous in the sky and hovering directly above the City. It emitted a lightning bolt, which, people said, must have hit one of the office buildings.

A few minutes later, those present report, the purple orb let down a yellow rope of some sort, which hung for a moment between the orb and the River Thames, before detaching and dropping down into the same spot in the water that the other orbs and their emissions had dropped into.

At about 11:15, the Moon and one of the strange lights next to it reappeared from the clouds. The greatest detail about this part comes from a homeless man named "Slow Henry," interviewed in a popular YouTube video, who stood on Blackfriars Bridge for two days watching the show. Next, he says, one of lights seemed to grow to the exact same size as the Moon in seconds. It looked just like the Sun, except that it did not light up the Earth or the sky at all.

Slow Henry reports that the sun -like object pulsated for a while, and then merged halfway with the Moon for a few minutes. He specified that the Moon still had one large red dot in the middle of its face before this merger. According to Henry, the yellow orb actually changed the color of the portion of the Moon that it merged with during the union, including that of the red dot. Afterwards, when they separated, the Moon's original red dot had grown even larger, and a new, smaller one just like it had begun to form right beside it.

Shortly after that, the purple orb also merged with the Moon, just briefly. Afterwards, the larger red splotch in the middle had gotten bigger still. Then the purple orb drooped beneath the others, finally plummeting down moments later into the same area of the Thames as the others. This is estimated to have occurred at 11:30. According to other witnesses who were closer to the area of impact, the purple orb appeared much larger in size then the previous light balls, and made a more noticeable splash when it touched down.

About five minutes later, say observers, an indigo-colored laser beam came down from out of nowhere in the sky (or at least from no visible source). It shot down into the Thames, and a black sphere was seen descending upon it, becoming smaller along the way. Then at approximately 11:45, the Moon was half-eclipsed, very briefly. Afterwards, the largest red circle inside was noted to be even larger, and it grew bigger as people watched.

The Moon changed even more over the next quarter of an hour, witnesses say. It became dark red all over, fading to black at the edges, and the red spots that were there before now became distinguished by their bright glow. A third red glowing spot, smaller than the others, formed within it also. At about midnight, all of the dark clouds that had enveloped the City of London alone suddenly dissipated.

Next, a flying carriage with four horses was seen by some crossing the sky, which one might associate with Santa Claus had it been Christmas. But on this occasion, people who saw it thought only of the Four Horsemen of St. John's *Revelation*. Of course, each horse in that story is supposed to be ridden by an angel, and not tied with a team to a small scythed chariot. However, classical education has been absent from British schools for decades. Nobody knows Greek or Roman myths anymore. In fact, I'm surprised Britons even recognize anything from the Bible.

Only Slow Henry saw both the flying chariot and the movements of the Moon and sun-like object that mirrored it. Only he saw the yellow orb actually slip behind the Moon and become covered by it, invisible. Only he sat up and watched all night as it remained motionless in the sky, until dawn the next morning. Then, he says, the sun-like object came back and replaced it, covering the Moon with itself, while the thing Henry took to be the "real Sun" rose in the East as expected.

I told you that a sleepy comatose state came over the City's population from late Friday night until dawn Easter morning. This episode is now referred to by your prostitute news media with the cutesy nickname "the London Fog" to keep you from taking it seriously. Because of the Fog, there are only a handful of witnesses who observed the various states of the Moon over the weekend.

There are quite a few people who say they saw the strange lights next to the Moon at sunset on Friday night. But then, inexplicably, many of the people who had been watching this spectacular display in the sky decided to *go to bed* quite early. Those who had fallen into the trance of "the Fog" then dragged themselves groggily through the next day and night, not recalling the events of Friday until those of Sunday morning shook them out of their stupor.

Later, these people were kicking themselves for not looking up even once on Saturday. Those who were affected by the Fog can't even remember what they spent their time doing that day. It was only from the vigilant few who not only remained watchful at the time, but had the courage to testify in public afterwards, that some of the sleepers have learned about what they missed.

According to Slow Henry, the sun-like object remained at the sky's meridian, motionless, all day, while the "real Sun" rose and set. Then at nightfall, the bloody red Moon with the three bright red spots came back, covering the sun-like object again. It just came over it, "like a coin being turned over," he said. The Moon was suddenly there at the top of the sky, and remained motionless in place throughout the night. Then early on Sunday morning, while it was still dark, the Moon started turning bright violet throughout.

He didn't have proof, like I had seen, that it was acting as a filter for something inside that was putting out strong UV light. But he did instinctively compare the way it looked, the light that came from it, and the way it made things appear— so that "the whole City looked like a discotheque"—to the characteristics of a blacklight. Assholes on YouTube, trolling the video where Henry is interviewed, keep saying that the Moon doesn't put out its own light. They don't know what the Moon even is. Nobody does.

Attempts to come up with "scientific" explanations for the things that people saw that night are extremely insulting. Several commentators have mentioned that none less than Sir William Herschel himself, discoverer of the planet Uranus, witnessed three glowing red spots on the Moon on April 19, 1787. Around the same time, something described as an "aurora borealis" (in other words, a green light in the sky) was observed simultaneously by the people of Padua, Italy, quite far from where such phenomena are usually observed, in the Arctic Circle. Shortly afterwards, there was a huge spike in the number of sunspots recorded.

It seems to me that Herschel witnessed something similar to what we in the City of London saw on Easter weekend 2018. Nonetheless, the same lame explanation of lunar "outgassing" has been given for both events by the incredulous scientific community. As usual, they have no respect for the intelligence of the observer when it comes to things they cannot explain.

Most unexplainable of all from the morning of Easter 2018 was the hole that opened up in the sky later that morning, just before dawn. As Slow Henry describes it, sun-like object at the zenith of the firmament disappeared through a circular window that opened up behind it, revealing an indigo field studded with stars — a bizarre sight in full daylight. Then the entire window became a solid bright green color, which shined down on everything below. At that exact moment, the first earthquake took place.

The hole stayed open, and the green light continued to shine down, for another twenty minutes, illuminating things that witnesses wish they had never seen. It stayed open even as the Sun began to rise in the East, blurring out the ghastly visions somewhat. Then the window turned indigo and star-studded once again, and a few minutes later, a black sphere fell out of it, into the Thames.

This is according to both Slow Henry, and also "Phicus," a YouTube user who filmed much of Sunday morning's events from the viewing platform at an office building known as "the Shard." The video confirms a lot of what both men described, although much of it is also open to interpretation. Slow Henry didn't see the rest because he was on his knees praying. And when he got up again, after he was all over, he couldn't see anything anymore. The Hyperuranian light had blinded him.

Unlike me in Rosenberg's basement, Slow Henry didn't have a magical diamond keystone plugging up the hole in the sky, protecting him from the Hyperuranian rays whilst refracting the light and allowing him to see by them. So the horrible sights they showed him were the last things he ever got to see. But this is, in fact, what the Masonic keystone represents. It is a stone that does just this: acting simultaneously as a deck prism and as a protective light filter. It is because it provides protection that it was represented as a "buckler" or a shield in Rothschild heraldry.

This is why it's so often represented on Masonic tracing boards in the arch of the sky, between the Sun and the Moon, forming a third, and higher, source of light. It's a window that plugs up the hole, allowing the transcosmic God to see you, and perhaps for you to see him as well. This is why the Masons also represent the same concept with an eye in a triangle, sun-like rays often streaming out of it, like a prism refracting light. Also used interchangeably with these symbols, or in combination with them, is the letter G, the seventh letter of the alphabet—which I believe stands for the Gamma ray, as I mentioned before. These Masonic images amply demonstrate that my interpretation is correct.

The two aftershocks that followed the first earthquake, as Phicus documented, each coincided with the events in the sky that took place next. The first, was accompanied by another "shockwave" and "sonic boom," similar to that of Friday night at sundown, but louder. This happened right after two naked children riding a flying white horse through the air.

The second aftershock occurred at the same time as the solar polarity flip and the formation of the sinkhole. As the Phicus video shows, this coincided with the re-emergence of the sun-like object from the portal, followed by an egg-white globe of equal size that came out right behind it. This is what formed the triangle of circles—yellow, white and star-flecked indigo—that I saw in the sky when the ceiling collapsed, just before I blacked out.

As I witnessed myself, the all three circles then turned yellow for a few moments. Then they sort of "rolled together" into one yellow orb, which immediately started "bleeding" into the Thames. A few seconds later, the yellow orb itself fell straight down into the river, revealing the indigo star-flecked circle just behind it. Scariest of all was what happened right afterwards, when that indigo circle, which had previously seemed to be an open window—a portal— then rolled up to the top like an eyelid, revealing a gigantic eye behind it. This eye then eerily blinked twice before it closed for good an instant later.

I think that the yellow orb bled and descended when the body of Baron Carrickfergus finally died. As I shall explain shortly, I have surmised that his body was devoured by the trinacria as they both floated away down the Thames a few minutes after the sinkhole formed. But by then, the trinacria had already consumed another creature and taken on another transformation, which I will soon describe.

It is my belief that the trinacria was possessed by the spirit of Chronos/Saturn. Plutarch wrote that the former king of the Golden Age was buried somewhere beneath the British Isles, in a death-like sleep in a tomb that is also his prison. He was kept alive by birds, who brought his ambrosia to eat as he slept, and with his dreams he communicated to his followers on the surface of the Earth. I think Rosenberg was one such follower, and that those ravens in the Tower of London were the ones feeding Chronos, somehow. When Rosenberg had them killed, it released his spirit into the body of a waiting golem that Rosenberg had prepared.

Plutarch wrote that the tomb of Chronos is guarded by someone named "Briareus." This, we know from other sources, is the name of one of the Titans selected to serve as a guard all the others imprisoned in Tartarus. So Plutarch was saying that somewhere beneath the British Isles is the location of Hell, which is also the womb of the Earth goddess that Chronos had to chop his way out of so that he and his siblings could be born.

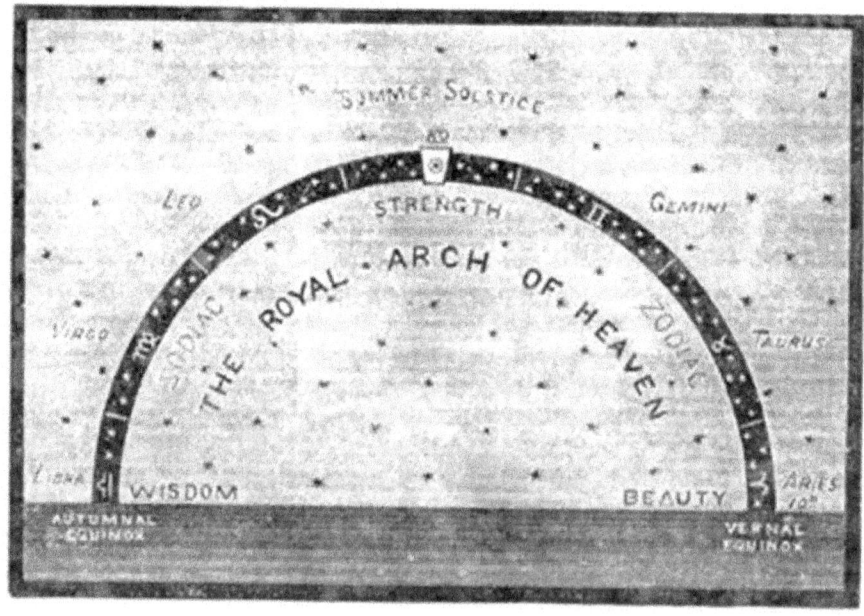

I recently discovered, while writing down these memories, that Man Ray-the surrealist artist whose cover illustration for Marquis de Sade's *120 Days of Sodom* was reproduced for Rosenberg's invocation of Venus in the mithraeum—was once commissioned to make a poster for the London Underground (the subway system) in which he made the system's logo appear to resemble the planet Saturn.

I wonder if he was aware of the myth of Chronos being buried underneath Britain, or if one of the people in charge of hiring him suggested it. In my mind, the symbolism of both Man Ray pieces can be connected. The *120 Days* illustration was an inverted Christian cross superimposed over the buttocks of a young man. Saturn is specifically associated with sodomy, as the root words connected to his name attest.

Satu means "sewing," referring to planting seeds in the earth, just as Saturn's title *sator* means *sower*. His epithet *Sterculius* comes from *stercus*, meaning "dung." The English word "sod," referring to earth covered with grass, may come from this connection in Latin between feces and agricultural fertilizer. It's also probably no coincidence that in Britain the word "sod" is a slang term for "sodomite," or that the inhabitants of Sodom were known to be haughty because of their vast mineral wealth, which the subterranean Saturn (imprisoned in Tartarus) was thought to be the ruler of. Vulgar words for feces are often used colloquially to refer to gold, money or treasure in cultures around the world, probably because of the traditional connection between these things and the underworld. The Etruscans called Saturn *Satre*, and said that he "hurls his lightning from his abode deep in the earth."

It seems pretty clear to me that the entrance to the infernal prison of Chronos was right there at Bucklersbury. But I don't think Chronos is there anymore. I think he safely floated away down the Thames, contained in the diamond inside of the trinacria.

The creature was actually spotted by witnesses who were standing on the waterfront next to the Traitor's Gate of the Tower of London. They were there to participate in a recreation of a historic April Fool's joke: "the Washing of the Lions." In centuries past, the joke was simply to invite people to attend this oddly-titled "annual event" at the Tower of London. The victim would then arrive at the Tower and find nothing going on.

So when something called "the Washing of the Lions" was announced in the "Festivals & Events" section of the *Sunday Telegraph* on Palm Sunday, slated to take place at dawn on Easter morning at the Tower of London, everyone knew it was going to be a joke. Most of those who were standing there that day were aware of the history of the prank and were waiting to see how it would be improved upon from previous performances.

Each one of them, when interviewed individually, reported being confused about the location of the Sun that morning while traveling to the event, but nobody spent much time analyzing it. Therefore, when these people felt the earthquake, and finally looked up to see the amazing sights in the sky, they at first tried to convince each other that it was somehow part of the show.

"I thought they were using holographic technology and sound effects," said one person to reporters. "You never think there's going to be an earthquake in London."

Therefore, when guards from the Tower, dressed in full regalia, came out with a lion on a leash, everyone present felt even more certain that they were merely watching an elaborate April Fool's hoax. I am surprised that the event was still scheduled to proceed, considering what had already happened to the ravens of the Tower. But that had already been completely covered up, as it continues to be, by the government.

Then the animal did something that could only, under these precise circumstances, be taken by the audience as part of the show. It hissed, growled, and lurched out of its handler's grasp. Then it dove head-first into the water like it was completely mad.

But it wasn't. It was defending itself against something that it felt threatened by. Those watching said they saw the lion attack a creature with "three human legs and a demonic glowing red face" that was floating in the water. As soon as the lion and the monster made contact with each other, the front end of the lion began to "dissolve into" the body of the hellish beast, until it was completely gone. Then, observers say, they noticed that the creature had taken on some of the features of the lion's face, including its large teeth, as well as its mane.

Next, floating down the river from behind the creature came another horrific site: a naked white male, seemingly deceased. As soon as the monster saw it, he lurched forward and devoured it. It was then that the bleeding sun fell into the river, right before the eyes of the people watching the monster's attack. After it had finished devouring the guts, the monster snarled at the people watching him from the shore, and swam away.

Officials admit that this was the body of Baron Carrickfergus, though they deny he was attacked by anything other than a lion. However, they don't even attempt to explain why a lion would jump into a river to attack a person who was reportedly either already dead, or almost dead.

I know that the trinacria made it all the way out to the Thames Estuary, where the river empties out into the North Sea. There, witnesses spotted a "ruby-colored crystal" rise out of water and into the sky, where it took the form of a red star with seven rays. From the tips of these rays then appeared seven stars of different colors. All of these objects seemed to come from the center of the ruby mother star except for one, which shined with a light that appeared to be constantly changing color. This one seemed to have come from the south, as if attracted to the end of one of the rays of light by an unseen force.

Once assembled, the entire arrangement of lights began spinning counterclockwise to the cheers of the crowds assembled on the shore. Then, all of the other stars lowered themselves beneath the one in the center. After that, the red star and its entourage shot off further out to sea, then took a turn southwest. They floated past the White Cliffs of Dover, the last place they were seen.

It wasn't until after this adventure was over that I learned about William Blake's mystical "prophetic" poetry on the topic of London. To him, writing during the Industrial Revolution, London was a sort of microcosm of the universe, and analogous, or even truly identical to "Jerusalem," which he likewise interpreted as a transcendental, non-local place. At the same time, it still *was* his own contemporary London, possessing all the same monuments and street names. His own pet name for this primordial London-Jerusalem city was "Golgonooza," a word unique to his vocabulary.

William Blake saw this city as the first created space, out from which creation radiated as it came into being at the beginning of time. This would make it analogous to the "Even Ha-Shitiyah," the "foundation stone" of creation in in the real, terrestrial Jerusalem that I mentioned earlier. This object is located in the Dome of the Rock, which the Knights Templar maintained as their official headquarters during their day. As I said, this stone was replicated for the altar of the St. Stephen Walbrook church, which Rosenberg "borrowed" for use in his *mithraeum* during his sick rituals.

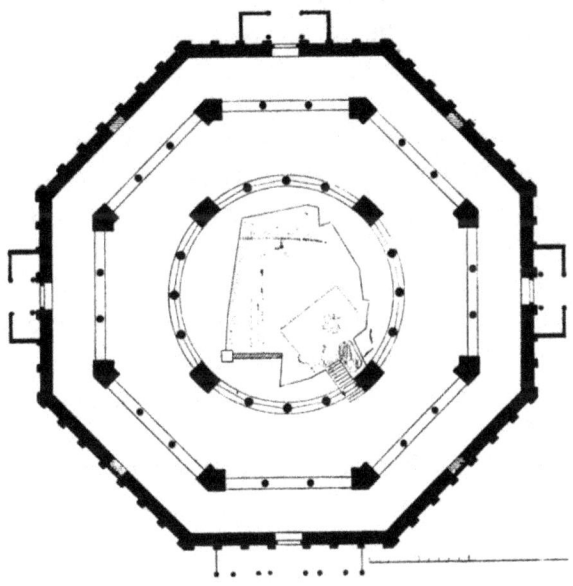

Even Ha -Shitiyah

If a "foundation stone" was the point of origin for everything, then it follows that all the dimensions of space should be measured from there. Thus it should be used in the same manner as the Roman *millarium* stones, which is what many think was the purpose of the London Stone. This would explain why Queen John Dee thought the artifact was magical, and moved his residence to Cannon Street to be near it.

In William Blake's poems, London/Jerusalem/Golgonooza was not just a city, but also a living being. It was at once the female sex partner and the "emanation" of a more all- encompassing being called "Albion," an ancient name applied to the British Isles. Blake's Albion has everything in common with Chronos, as even Wikipedia acknowledges.

Perhaps the diamond we found within it is the actual "foundation stone." Maybe it contained the damned and imprisoned soul of Albion/Chronos/Saturn. If so, I think he has been set free now, the consequences of which I cannot predict. It may be that the burden of holding up the worlds has now fallen on the shoulders of the ambitious Mr. Rosenberg. In that sense we can say that he achieved a bit of the universal importance he strove for.

Since the spectacular events of Easter morning, the people in the City of London have only seen one sun in the sky, and one moon at night, just like everyone else in the world. The stars have returned to normal as well — or at least, that's how people perceive it.

I tend to think that a new normal has been established, and we simply don't remember that things used to be different. We are under the order of a new Sun, but we don't realize it. We think it has always been this way.

It's no shock to me that almost no one has suggested the signs in the heavens seen in the City foretold the birth of a messiah. The rumor mill only manufactures paranoia and hate. Nobody ever tells you that anything good will happen, unless they're trying to sell you something.

According to the Royal Observatory in Greenwich, the only thing unusual that happened in space that day was an inordinate amount of sunspot activity which hadn't been predicted. They admit that the Sun's polarity flipped just before the earthquake and the sinkhole occurred. A few experts have been allowed to hint that there could be a connection between the two events, but always with the caveat that it was far too complex for anyone to ever understand and therefore not worth the effort. They also admit that the tides on the Thames Friday and Saturday night were "a bit wobbly," but can't say why.

The connection between the solar anomalies and the widespread sporadic interruption of electronic communications throughout the weekend has not been denied. Nor is it denied that this contributed to slowing the spread of information regarding the sudden shift that was occurring on the precious metal markets.

As you all know, when France pulled out of the Eurozone it caused a run on gold, starting late Friday night. That night at the party, Marcia Martina and her son Philip were quite satisfied with themselves. Of course, the Rothschilds had been among the world's largest gold-holders for centuries, despite a misleading headline published in *The Telegraph* in 2004:

"Rothschild to pull out of gold market after 200 years." More recently, they had been calling in huge quantities, and tightening their purses.

In the previous two months, the price of gold had gone up considerably because of this hoarding. It was all part of tightening the screws on the central banks, particularly in the West, as Ms. Martina had explained to us. This was payback, punishment, and reigning-in after decades of poor fiscal governance.

Because of this, it had become increasingly difficult for governments to sell bonds. It was also difficult to obtain gold as a back-up reserve. The states of the Western world were inarguably at the mercy of the moneylenders, and this one family in particular. This was because they controlled such a large share of the market, and they had decided to collude to bring about this crisis.

The night of the crash, we all assumed that a major shift in wealth had happened to dramatically concentrate it even more amongst the so-called "one percent." Rosenberg's own newspaper ran with the headline "Gold sky high, silver to the Moon." But nobody knew that Rosenberg's people had just suddenly dumped trillions of dollars worth of gold and silver on the market. As you know, gold went from being the 72nd most common element to the 65th, taking the place formerly held by silver. The simultaneous silver dump bumped that metal down to 50 on the list.

It wasn't until Monday morning EST, however, that people took full account of this in the financial news media. The market was already presented with the difficulty that both the place where the gold prices were fixed each day—the London Bullion Market—and the place where the pound was issued—the Bank of England—had both fallen into the sinkhole. Aggravating the delay of the reaction was the fact that this specialty of journalism had already been crippled by the destruction of the main offices of both Rosenberg network and the Financial Times. Then there was the issue of the Niptron Terminal hacks, involving the so called "CAPUT 58 virus," which caused every single one of the machines to freeze up on the traders at 10:30 AM GMT.

Simply put, a pop-up window opened on their screens demanding the solution to a riddle involving computer-generated three-dimensional image of a diamond shape with 58 facets (by inference, a "head" with 58 "faces") encoded with an 8-character set of symbols referred to by the virus program as "the OPERANTS" (the seven planetary sigils, plus John Dee's Monad symbol). Infected terminals were also presented with what purported to be a key: a five-by-five Latin square image cipher. By the time security experts figured out a way around the challenge, it was too late to save anybody's bets.

It was only after reading about the details of the virus that I figured out the meaning of the term "PROTEANS" that had been used on the bottle with the *Liquor Amnii* that saved my feet (an anagrams of OPERANTS). It is a reference to the Ogdoad of eight archons. These are the seven planets, plus a transcended twin of Mercury, who is also the goddess Sophia-Achamoth—Metis or Mete, the Great Mother, "Dear Prudence."

They are represented by the eight characters used in the Sator Square, with three different magnitudes of use, representing three different levels of divine power. T, R, E, O, and A are used four times each, representing the five wandering planets. P and S are only used two times each. They represent the higher powers of the Sun and Moon. N is the letter in the center of the square, and it is only used once. It represents a god-power transcending the others, but one which is mutable and open to interpretation, like Proteus of Greek mythology, and like quicksilver, corresponding to the Philosopher's Mercury, the Universal Solvent. By dissolving, separating, and re-coagulating the essences of the gods themselves, any imaginable change is possible, including chemical changes otherwise not allowed.

When it was discovered that the total global quantity of gold had suddenly increased drastically over the weekend, there were many theories introduced by the experts on the news. First, of course, was to suspect counterfeiting, and so all the vaults forced to assay their gold holdings, to the embarrassment of all the companies involved. As we all saw, none of them had the physical reserves they had claimed prior to the dump. All of them had been committing fraud, as had all of the world's governments, with the full knowledge and collusion of all of the world's banks. This, analysts say, is what really destroyed Barclays Bank when its stock price evaporated on April 2.

We all remember Rosenberg's crazy rant that Black Friday evening, during an interview on his own TV network, Skyped live from his office right there at Rosenberg Plaza. I didn't get to see it at the time, as I was walking with Chesterfield to New Court to meet Rosenberg and his friends for dinner. But of course I saw the highlights, endlessly replayed on the news for weeks.

There, to an interviewer who was utterly confused, he declared that the "the 'so-called' noble metals of the old plutocracy" would soon be "dethroned like the noble families of old Europe had been dethroned by money." He then announced his vision for a new system of wealth and power distribution based on the value of the human body: its parts, the fluids it produces, and its "perceived value" (to which he added finger quotes) as an "object of affection."

It was so bizarre, commentators on his own network said that they actually thought he was drunk. In a way, they were right. He was drunk on the blood and suffering of innocents.

The conspiracy crowd claimed the sinkholes were the result of a "false flag attack," a Jewish plot to consolidate their wealth. Furthermore, they said, the earthquakes, sinkhole, solar activity, and orbs in the sky were all caused by weather modification technology, they purported distracting investors from the coming changes in the gold and silver markets. Why? Because when the price of gold, the value of paper, and credibility of credit collapsed simultaneously overnight, the jig was up. Time to cover your tracks and run away to your private islands, right?

But the source of this crowd's real complaint had also been eliminated. The "anti-Zionist" movement against "Jewish banksters" lost its *raison d'être*. Because as it turns out, nobody really cares about Israel one way or the other, except for a few freaks, and most cannot tell a Jew apart from a gentile unless they are told what's what. The thing that really bothered these people the most was the vast amount of money, gold, and property — a large portion of the Earth's entire treasure — locked up in the hands of one family, who had then successfully managed to deflect attention away from themselves.

Many historians had falsely claimed that the Rothschilds had waned in wealth and influence, but the exact opposite is true. Those who knew this, or felt that they knew it, had been frothing at the mouth for decades, trying to "wake up the sheeple" to the truth. Now, although this truth had been covered up even more completely with the collapse of New Court into the Bucklersbury sinkhole, the problem was gone as well.

The Rothschild fortune has essentially been obliterated. The membership of their incestuous clan has been decimated, in the classical sense of the word (one out of ten gone, not nine, as the common modern misnomer implies). Moreover, it was the older, more corrupt ten percent that was killed, as many of the tribe elders were asleep in the New Court building at the time of the collapse, having gathered there Friday night for a week-long Passover celebration.

But that very night, they lost the value of all their money, though at the time they thought they had just made a killing. The properties they owned lost value as well, and, of course, their most important piece of real estate: their London headquarters, which fell down into its proper final resting place in the depths of Hell.

They even lost their pet project, the Bank of England. For it's not just the building that has disappeared, but the whole institution as well. At the present writing, it looks like it will soon be shut down in favor of the new solutions currently being proposed in the House of Commons. It's a humiliating defeat for a once all-powerful dynasty. Those Rothschilds who are left will probably change their names again within a generation, and be entirely forgotten by their descendants.

On a related note, it is interesting to consider that that the Superman character is broadly considered by media experts to be a representation of Jewish identity. As I learned in college from a Jewish film history professor who lived in New York City, the Superman character was literally created to represent Jewish immigrants from Europe who were hiding in plain sight in the entertainment industry by using Westernized names, just like Superman hides behind the persona of Clark Kent. Now here's another amazing coincidence to keep in mind: It is known that the character of Lois Lane, Clark Kent's girlfriend, is based on a girl that Superman's creator, Jerry Siegel, had a crush on in high school in Cleveland. Her name was Lois Rothschild.

None of the articles written on this subject say she's related to the banking family. But even if this is just a coincidence, I sense that it points to something significant, as coincidences often do.

As for the future of the "Hyperuranium," the new element that was discovered at the bottom of the sinkhole (along with considerable amounts of platinum), it could be the foundation stone of a new Golden Age. I think it was probably created naturally somehow when the sinkhole formed, transmuted from the gold, silver, and other precious metals and gems that were present in the underground vaults of the Bank of England. But I fear that it will be monopolized and controlled like gold has been. I also think it's very likely that new war technologies will result from the research and development with it that is to come. In other words, I think it will only serve to further enslave us.

The presence of a lump of it in my pocket, along with a note from Leopold, discovered when I got to the hospital, just after he disappeared, is another miracle that I cannot explain. The note came with a phone number, and instructed me to contact Harut Al-Hazrat, a broker, who, it said, could help me sell the piece of metal. I don't know if it was a blessing or a curse.

On the one hand, the sale did bring a tidy sum, which has eliminated my financial problems for the time being. On the other hand, just before I gave it over to the broker, I did an experiment with it in which I rubbed it across the skin between my eyes. Ever since, my clairvoyant powers have been dramatically increased, which is sometimes a problem now. Some things you just don't want to see.

It is mind-bending to try to grasp the reflexive, sympathetic relationships that must exist between the orders of the universe which make it possible for an action performed on the body of a "divine" child — anal penetration — to rip holes in both the Earth and the sky. But then again, what made it possible for such a divine child to be bred using the perverse means that I have described? Is the human conscience ready to accept the realities that this is based on?

You now know the truth about what happened to change the head of state in the UK, who is said to have died in Westminster at the exact moment that the sinkhole formed in the City. You also now know what happened to the other two waiting in line. They didn't just die in a sinkhole while visiting a friend during an experiment gone awry, as your media told you. I have given you the real reason why the British people now have a screwball for a Regent and a toddler waiting for the throne.

But you should take it as a positive sign that the screwball in question was not present at the ceremony that took the lives of the other three. There must be a reason why he wasn't invited. I am not saying you should trust him. I am only saying it's a possible sign of hope for the future. I took quite seriously the rumor I read on 4Chan about him, stating that he personally discovered a white horse grazing on the lawn of Kensington Palace, along with two naked children playing nearby in the grass. Word on the street is that they have been secretly adopted into the royal household.

It is a relief that certain people lost power, and were denied their ambitions to greater power, that weekend. But the ruling class still has the same perverse proclivities as always. They are still using the same tactics of violence and blackmail to maintain that power. You see that the exposure of the Lord Mayor's child abuse, caught on video, led to no further investigation of organized pedophilia among the elite. You see that the 729 murdered children of the year-long rite (not counting Philippine, I presume) were never identified, and nobody was ever arrested for that.

However, I think it's possible that forces were unleashed during this ritual, both for good and for evil, which will play an important role in events to come, possibly deciding whether or not this state of affairs shall continue. We shall see what comes of it. For a sign of prognosis, I will continue to watch the skies and the headlines, and wait.

> HERE ENDS THE WORK OF THE SUN. LONG LIVE *SOL NOVUS*.

Before the consummation of the age, the whole place will shake with great thundering. ... Then the sun will become dark, and the moon will cause its light to cease. The stars of the sky will cancel their circuits. And a great clap of thunder will come out of a great force that is above all the forces of chaos, where the firmament of the woman is situated. ... Then she will pursue the gods of chaos, whom she created along with the prime parent. She will cast them down into the abyss. They will be obliterated because of their wickedness. For they will come to be like volcanoes and consume one another until they perish at the hand of the prime parent. When he has destroyed them, he will turn against himself and destroy himself until he ceases to exist. And their heavens will fall one upon the next and their forces will be consumed by fire. Their eternal realms, too, will be overturned. And his heaven will fall and break in two... fall into the abyss, and the abyss will be overturned.

—*On the Origin of the World*

Translated by Hans-Gebhard Bethge
and Bentley Layton

www.ingramcontent.com/pod-product-compliance
Lightning Source LLC
LaVergne TN
LVHW060813010425
807422LV00006B/194